# Savage Champion

Carla Swafford

Ebook ISBN 978-1-956518-19-1

Paperback ISBN 978-1-956518-20-7

Hardcover ISBN 978-1-956518-21-4

*Many thanks to my copy editor, Betty Bolté.*
*You're wonderful!*

# Prologue

Tori

Taut ropes cut into my wrists and ankles as my body jerked and shuddered. Each time the blade ran along my skin another thin layer drifted to the floor. How did I know? The whipcord-lean man standing over me followed each piece with his gaze, his head swaying side to side as if watching a feather float on the air.

When he sliced again, my nearly silent screams lasted a lengthy time. The cloths stuck in my mouth and the leather muzzle over my lips muffled the sound, ensuring it wouldn't penetrate the walls, windows, or ceiling.

He paused and tilted his head to admire his work. After a long, weary sigh, he said, "I enjoy the way the blade glides through your lovely skin like butter."

The pain was unbearable, but I had no other option but to suffer through it. Every time I fainted, he placed a bottle of smelling salts beneath my nose. I jerked awake as overpowering spasms flitted down my limbs. Nausea churned in my stomach. I wanted to vomit so badly but with the gag in place, I'd drown in the filth.

If only I could die. If only I was stronger, smarter. If only I had been more careful, more observant.

If only, if only...regrets were no help.

If horses were wishes, as the old nursery rhyme goes.

The horror had started on my favorite shopping day of the year, the day after Thanksgiving. After hours of picking and choosing gifts for my family and friends with my little sister, Lizzie, I juggled the bags hanging on my arms as I walked to my car in the crowded parking lot of the newly built Eastwood Mall. Lizzie had one more present to pick up before meeting me at the car. My dark-blue Ford blended with the hundreds of other cars, and was hidden further by the larger trucks, station wagons, and vans.

It had been still daylight. What was there to be afraid of?

Head down, I walked between the parked cars, searching for my keys in the bottom of my purse. How was I to see the opened side door of the black van? The sides and back windows grimy with filth, large peace signs and childish flowers painted on its beat up panels. Black Sabbath blared from its depths.

With a swiftness that took my breath away, a man grabbed me by my arm, bags tumbling to the pavement. Before more than a squeak escaped my lips, sharp pain then darkness washed over me.

That evening, I woken to the nightmare I'd been living in for who knew how long. The passage of time was a mystery in the dark, dank basement where the madman kept me.

His meticulous routine included lining up his tools on a tray near the platform I lay on. Even the way he tied my wrists and ankles to the corners appeared precise. So many knots all facing in the same direction.

No mattress softened the surface. Blood would soak it through and through anyway.

Long after he stopped his work, my body jerked and shuddered throughout the hellish night. I was finally allowed to sleep though it was often a fitful one. Agony woke me if I moved even a pinkie.

With the skill of a surgeon, he'd skinned the right half of my body, starting at the ankle, skipping my breast, and stopping below my neck. He said he would do my left side next while saving his favorite parts for last.

Even if I was rescued by some miracle, I would be scarred for life. That was, if I survived the infections.

<<<>>>

The next day, I woke as he began working on me again. The dried blood coating his instruments thickened until he sloppily wiped it off with a dirty towel. From day one, they had been coated black with so many layers of blood. That told me there were prior victims he worked on. Why should he care about giving me a disease or infection?

"Your blood is getting sluggish. Time for water. I'll leave off your muzzle for the evening if you promise not to scream. You know and I know that if you make that horrendous noise once more, you'll make me discipline you again. You don't want that. Understood?"

I slowly nodded.

The man...no...monster was lanky to the point of thinness, and possibly six-foot or more. His hair combed to one side failed to hide the bald spot above his forehead. Fresh blood smeared his dirty butcher apron. The cloth's original color, white or cream, only appeared on the edges when he turned his back.

A wave of nausea broke a cold sweat across my forehead. Living through his brand of discipline was unthinkable the first time, but to live through the slashing of my palms and bottom of my feet again would be miraculous to say the least. Coward that I was, I held on to my life with both hands.

He tugged at the buckle of the muzzle and pulled the material out of my mouth. When the cool copper-tinged air hit my face, I swallowed several times to hold back the sickness and wet my gums and tongue. The last time I puked he'd become so angry...no, I refused to think about it.

The water he placed against my lips tasted bitter, a metallic flavor. Did it include some kind of drug or was it only being overpowered by the smell of blood?

Whatever he'd fused with the water, it numbed my senses enough to survive one more night. Then sadly I'd woke to the nightmare again.

A cool cloth floated around my body. Like an artist with a piece of unfinished art, he covered my body and face with a white sheet. I fought my panic. The whisper-thin sheet allowed me to breathe, but still I worried I'd inhale it and choke to death. He turned off the overhead light. With no light at all, and the sheet covering my eyes, I began to shake and cry. Not knowing what was happening around me was nearly as terrifying as the torture. Sounds magnified as hours passed.

On the floor above me, I heard his footsteps, and time crept by with each chime of the hour and half hour. My sanity was fragile, and held on by the thread of necessity, and if I let go, I'd never find a way to escape.

I drifted in my horror-filled slumber. My mother's voice

echoed through my brain, repeating how I was the strong one, and how I always kept my head on straight in the chaos around me.

A whimper escaped my lips. I wasn't so brave or strong now. If only I could turn back time and save—

What was that? A small shuffling sound brought the hairs on my left arm to attention. Mice made a noise that sounded like scratching, not the scrape of a shoe sliding on cement.

"Who's there?" My voice was stronger than I expected but croaked on the last word as my throat was ruined from the screams. Was the crazy man trying a new torment?

Another shuffle, that time closer, near my feet.

"Please help me." Could it be somebody else? Maybe they'd be willing to help. "Move the sheet from my face and let me see you," I whispered as hope filled my consciousness.

Maybe I was an idiot to be so optimistic. But as long as I was alive, I had to believe I would find a way to leave that hell. I was willing to do anything.

Someone walked around the platform and stopped near my head. As several moments passed without another sound, I began to wonder if I had hallucinated.

More tears began to flow down to my temples before soaking my hair. I squeezed my eyes shut. Stop. Crying. Wasted energy.

Coolness brushed my face. My eyes popped open.

Peering down at me was a handsome, pale man in dirty, torn clothes. The tattered lace on his shirt reminded me of a style from two centuries past. Had a street person found a way into the basement? Or was this a cosplay friend of the psycho upstairs?

With his long fingers, he gently settled the sheet over

my chest, politely keeping my breasts hidden. His blue eyes glowed eerily in the dim basement.

It had to be a dream.

"You wish to leave?"

His voice was low and soothing with a slight accent I couldn't place. A coldness swirled around me as if his body emitted the chill.

Dream or not, I wanted to shout at him and say he was as crazy as the man upstairs if he thought otherwise. Maybe he was deranged enough to help.

After a few shallow breaths to steady my voice, I whispered, "Yes. Please help me. Untie my hands and get me out of here."

"You smell of blood. The coppery scent fills the room, surrounds you in a halo of red. The sweet aroma drew me here. Many deaths have permeated these walls. A slaughter house. Your blood has made the fragrance too strong to ignore and has woken me," he said in his strange lyrical, old-fashioned way. An odd half-smile came to his thin lips.

He waved his hand over my body. The gesture seemed dramatic but an odd feeling of calmness came over me. His glowing eyes examined my cloth-covered body as if looking through the material. His scrutiny continued but slowed at wherever the whiteness was broken by dark splotches. Blood saturated the cloth above my right foot, knee, and breast.

"As you can see, the man has nearly filleted me." My voice came out so clear and even. Like I hadn't participated in this horror-filled scene. Had the pain made me insane, and maybe a little detached from what was happening?

An inner voice warned me not to scream or show terror at his abnormal glowing eyes or he'd take it as an invite to attack.

He leaned back and glanced up to the ceiling as if he heard something I couldn't. When his attention returned to me, he pursed his lips and nodded as if he had reached a decision.

"That one"—he pointed upward, the nail on his finger long and jagged—"plans to kill you soon."

I agreed with his assessment, but hearing someone confirm it brought a surge of energy shooting through my body, overriding the pain. Yanking on the ropes, I struggled and pleaded, "Don't let him kill me."

He placed a hand on my uninjured arm and heat ran along my skin and over my body. "I won't" His touch and soft words instantly calmed me. I stopped moving.

"Untie me. Please," I croaked out.

Pride had no place in my predicament.

"I will, but you must understand there is something I need from you."

I stared at the man. What could I trade? His penetrating bright gaze unnerved me. Lust was easily recognized. I gasped and shook my head. Surely he wasn't expecting to use my body in its current condition.

A grin spread across the handsome face.

"No, I have no wish for the use of your body, not in that way."

Had I said it out loud?

"Then how?" I asked.

He confused me as I waited for his answer. How much longer could I stay conscious?

His grin widened, sexy grooves near his mouth making him even more handsome. That was when I saw them. His canines lengthened, becoming sharper. I'd read how people obsessed with the vampire myth filed their canines to points. Yet they weren't naturally like that before. I was certain I saw them change. He was the real deal.

"Your sweet blood, of course." His meaning obvious in his reply.

Maybe I am hallucinating. That had to be the explanation for my calmness, my acceptance of his madness.

"I never believed in vampires before."

His hand cupped my face, tenderly rubbing his thumb over my cheek. "We work hard to keep our existence a secret. We want humans to believe we're only tales told to frighten misbehaving children."

"Will it make me a vampire?"

"The taking of your blood does not. You will experience only pleasure. Thus why we always have willing prey. Then you will drift off to eternal sleep."

"Eternal sleep?" I shook my head. "Please don't kill me."

He shrugged." No? You can escape the pain and feel immense pleasure if I take a little or all of it. Wouldn't you rather die in pleasure than by what the creature upstairs will do to you?"

"What if I want to be like you?"

"You wish to be of the colony?"

He tilted his head, studying me.

"If you mean a vampire, then yes."

Real or not, why not accept what I could become. If it was a dream, then I could escape for a few minutes. If real, I would escape for an eternity. I did know I wanted the power and strength to punish the one who planned to kill me piece by piece.

His grin faded as he stared into my eyes with curiosity. Whatever he read in them apparently convinced him I wanted to become like him.

"Very well." He ran a finger down my right side and

licked the blood off. "Yes. You are a good possibility. Only people with special blood can be reincarnated." He smacked his lips. "Be forewarned. It's a lonely existence and there are those who always track us."

"Is it true your strength is like ten men?"

"Yes. And though your wounds are deep, they will heal. But the scars will take decades to fade away." He shrugged again as his eyes examined my wounds. "Maybe never." He touched my arm.

A wave of pain caused me to gasp.

"It'll be a reminder," I whispered.

"The man will not see a new day," he muttered.

I knew he was right. This might be an illusion, and if not, I welcomed a chance to right the wrong done to me and others.

It was destiny that brought me to this moment. Once I was a vampire, I'd never be a victim again. If I could help others against the scum of the earth like the one upstairs, so much the better. No sacrifice was too great. A chance to be the people's champion.

"Are you ready?" The vampire smoothed my hair off my face.

For an answer, I turned my head, giving him free access to my jugular vein.

# Chapter 1

## *Ronan*

### Present Day

I hated this part of my job. Winter in the south sounded like a good time of the year to visit, but not when the high was thirty-six degrees Fahrenheit, and it was the third day of nonstop drizzle. From the weather report on my phone, there would be more of the same tomorrow.

Every piece of clothing clung to my body. Damp and cold. Fuck this.

Florida. That was the place to be as their cold warmed my blood and my Northern soul. But no, I tracked down a spoilt runaway from Nashville to a small town northeast of Birmingham. A mom-and-pop bar called Wilma's sat across from the entrance to the neighborhood the girl had entered hours earlier. If there wasn't a chance of missing her, I would be sitting in that warm bar drinking whiskey out of a Glencairn glass. My mouth watered with the thought.

If not for the big incentive fee, and lucrative rate agreed upon by the client when the job ended, I'd never contemplate taking the case so far from my home in Illinois. But the weird guy apparently possessed deep pockets.

So there I sat, staring out my cracked windshield at the house along the tree-lined street, bored out of my mind. I let my attention wander back to two weeks past.

"Mr. Brannon, if what you're telling me is true, the local and federal authorities would be very much interested in what you have to say. In fact, I strongly suggest you contact them."

I worked at keeping my tone friendly. Most people tended to resent being referred to the police after they decided to hire a private detective.

Edgar Brannon sat in front of my desk, no taller than five-eight with a receding hairline and washed-out blue eyes. His cold, empty gaze made my skin crawl. The man wasn't right in the head.

"I've already gone to the police, and they've said I don't have any real evidence. Besides they'd only be interested in tracking down the murderer, not protecting a potential victim. On top of that, they claim the murders aren't connected. Their contention is, it was only coincidence they were sorority sisters. They pointed out the women died in different states. Last thing I need is for them to foul it up. I need your help in finding my sister before she gets hurt. The killer is after her. So far, four of her sorority sisters are dead. From the note you're holding, he plans to kill them all. He blames the women for a simple college prank."

I looked at the strip of white paper. The red inked words were neat and to the point. *You are next. You cunts will never blue ball another boy again.*

"Blue ball?" I asked.

"The girls would hold a boy down, strip off his pants, and paint his balls blue. It's in retaliation for seducing one of their sorority sisters and then dumping her." One pale hand waved in the air, accenting his words.

The man's smirk irritated me. Did he think it was funny?

No matter how strange the people and their stories, nothing surprised me anymore. This was no exception.

Not too many years ago, a gang of women raped a young man. They claimed he'd asked for it. Rather double-edged when you think about it. Anyway, the man had the women arrested, having his revenge, but I heard he was never the same again. The humiliation became too great and he killed himself.

I pushed my chair back and rested an ankle on my knee.

"Do you know the boy's name?" I only hoped it was that simple.

"Yes and no," he said.

Of course, it wouldn't be simple.

"There's a rumor that they did it to six boys," the strange man added.

"Six? That's a lot of people being sexually assaulted for the girls to get away with it."

"It's a large campus." The man slid another sheet to me. "Protect my sister by bringing her back to me."

"Which college was this? Were the campus and local police involved?"

"That's not important. What's important is my sister. She dropped out and disappeared." The man fisted his hands on the top of my desk as he leaned forward. "Last I heard, she was partying with friends in Lexington."

"What about the killer?"

"Chances are he's following her. I've given you a list of her friends and the young men and their last known addresses."

"There has to be at least thirty names on this."

"Yes. Like I said, it was a large campus. No one will

admit they were a participant and only a couple reported it. We can only guess who all were really involved. If you track her down through the names, I believe one of the women is hiding her. Do hurry and find her. She's likely the next one he plans to murder."

"What about the killer? Any evidence I gather will need to be handed over to the police."

"No. The important person on that list is the one who is hiding my sister. Once she's safe, you can do anything you want. I just want you to bring her to me. No matter what it takes."

His frustration was evident. Being an ex-cop myself, I ignored his attitude.

"What it takes?"

I wanted him to clarify. I had no trouble manhandling women if they deserved it, but clients could be funny about that.

"She's rebellious and will even tell lies to keep from returning home. Our parents spoiled her terribly. She's so stubborn. It won't be easy to get her cooperation. Call me once you locate her, and I'll have one of my men to take her off your hands."

I stared at my new client.

"So you want me to force her to come with me or go with your men? From the information you provided, she's over twenty-one."

"Mr. Michaels, her life's in danger, and I'll pay you enough to force your own mother to come with me."

That was how I ended up in the middle of the winter in a suburban Alabama town watching a party-filled house with numerous cars lining the driveway including her black Maserati mere feet from large iron gates. I had tracked Brannon's sister from Lexington to Nashville to finally Birmingham the day before. A gas station cashier had overheard her talking on a cell phone, saying she planned to drop by a party before heading to her new home. Besides the addresses—majority were their former residences—her brother had also provided an undated picture—a shitty grainy one of a dark-haired, well-shaped girl—and the description of her car. About the time I'd caught up with her car, she'd turned down a street to a well-lit house...fuck, mansion. The gates were open but military-dressed men guarded every entrance. Was she visiting her drug dealer? What kind of people was she hanging out with? Did it belong to someone on the list? Most likely Brannon was full of shit and didn't know what he was talking about.

So I waited for her to leave. Per her brother, she was a party girl and loved the night life. That meant if she left at a decent hour, she'd probably hit some of the downtown nightclubs.

Anyway, I still hadn't seen the woman but from a distance, and in the dark. When she exited her car, she'd been wearing an ankle-length black coat with a hood.

The patter of rain on top of my car's roof muffled the music coming from the mansion. Would it ever stop? A shiver ran down my back. Fuck, I wished I'd brought my heavier jacket from the motel instead of a thin denim one. The temp was dropping like a stone. Every breath I took released a cloud of condensation.

It sucked big time. So there I sat, exhausted, watching the car through the damn gates, about to fall asleep while waiting for her to leave.

Up to my eyeballs in debt, I was in a spot where I needed to do whatever it took to make the customer happy. The fee would cover my bills and leave enough for a nice nest egg. Jobs were scarce in Mokena, Illinois, and clients had become scarce.

Telling Brannon to fuck himself would be a pleasure I couldn't afford. Poor judgment calls in the past had changed my circumstances. All because I trusted a damn woman. My fucking cheating ex. Before her, I'd never accepted such a shady job. But money was my master for now. It was a matter of life or death. My death.

I shivered again, wishing I could crank my car and turn up the heat. But the steam out of my exhaust pipes would reveal my presence. I hated waiting. Action solved mysteries, and I preferred to keep moving.

Time dragged by without a change, and when I was about to give up and try out the nearby bar, I heard the gates open. Then the luxury car pulled through and eased onto the road, the headlights spotlighting my blue Mustang—I ducked down—and then drove off. I hoped she hadn't seen me.

My plan was to follow her to wherever she lived and call my client with the address. Less fuss, less mess. I didn't need a stranger to jump in and save the *damsel in distress*, causing a ruckus. I was so thankful the gated mansion hadn't been her home.

I had no problem staying a couple of blocks behind the Maserati down Highway 11. The road changed to First Avenue as we moved into downtown Birmingham. The woman expertly maneuvered between the late Thursday night traffic. After about twenty minutes of green signal lights and a few turns, we were in the Southside portion of the city.

Nightclubs and restaurants of all types and sizes were at every corner. Her car stopped near a club lit up with a line of clubbers outside. On the front of the building, black lettering outlined in red lights proclaimed Bloodsucker's.

Hanging back, I eased my car to the curb and studied the couples waiting outside. Dressed mostly in black, some wore white makeup. Female and male. Many had long hair hanging between shoulder blades and farther; a few wore it short and sticking straight up. Tattoos and piercings covered every visible curve and crease on their bodies.

Damn, what a way to wrap up the night. A Goth nightclub. After days of following the woman, I decided it was time to change tactics. The best way to break from surveillance was to join in the fun. But how would I blend in with that crowd?

Tattoos weren't a problem. I had two ink sleeves and various ones under my shirt. My hair wasn't a big deal. I brushed the ends back off my collar. It was my clothes. Faded jeans and blue cotton shirt would stand out; even my jacket was denim. What a shame the woman hadn't stopped at a country and western joint.

At that moment, the Maserati door opened and one long leg stretched out followed by another. Damn. Black hosiery and stilettos covered shapely limbs and dainty feet. She'd dumped the ugly ass coat. With a subtle wiggle, she smoothed her short leather skirt and turned to close the door. A flash of pale skin under her open leather jacket caught my eye. Only a strip of some type of clingy material covered her full breasts.

She moved like a panther, smooth and seductive. I grabbed my phone and hit video record. No one would believe me. The woman was fine. When she strolled beneath a street light, I remembered the grainy picture her brother had given me. It hadn't done her justice. She'd cut her dark hair. Chin-length strands caressed her enchanting face with each toss of her head.

My stomach clenched, answered by an unwelcome swelling in my groin. Her hair was dark red, more of an auburn color. I was a sucker for redheads.

Damn. She was the sexiest woman I'd ever seen in my life, and she was my client's crazy sister. Fuck.

<<<>>>

Tori

Out of the corner of my eye, I noted the Mustang idling a block away. He was good. Certainly better than the others who'd tried to track me over the last few years. But if the truth were told, I really didn't care if he followed. What was there to worry about?

I'd checked in with the Alabama master vampire over an hour ago. He'd been happy to see I'd returned home. If he hadn't been my master—the vampire who created me—I would need his permission to stay in his domain. This would ensure they wouldn't send an enforcer or assassin to remove me.

My only concern, momentarily, was the man following me. If he'd been a vampire, I would merely ask him to state his business. But with his being human, there was a different protocol. For now, the questions were, what did he want? And was he part of the LVH?

The Legion of Vampire Hunters drove white cars and vans, and it was unlikely they owned a sporty blue car like his. Possibly a human private detective had decided to follow me. Didn't he know curiosity killed the cat? Or the nosey investigator?

I grinned, flashing my deadly canines. It didn't matter if

someone saw them. In and around the club, others would only think I was part of the crowd, pretending to be a child of the night. Little did they know the real thing was among them.

Waved in by the bouncer, I threaded my way through the thick, pulsating crowd inside. The smell of sexually excited bodies filled my senses. The music thumped through my body. Couples swayed on the dance floor, many grinding pelvises together more than dancing.

As a human, I had enjoyed the night life and the pounding music. As a vampire, I absolutely loved it. So many sensations to drink in. I closed my eyes for a second and inhaled the wonderful smell of humanity. Liquor had nothing over heated bodies and hot blood. The high was better than a manmade drug, legal or illegal.

Strategic black lights lit the large room, leaving several dark corners, ideal for feeding. And I regularly exploited them. Dim lighting wasn't a problem for me. Vampires' night vision was excellent.

Tonight, blood didn't drive me to the night club, but the need for human company. A frantic feeling saturated the air in the nightclub. A sensation in the air to live for the moment for tomorrow might never come. Like many, I believed in the fast-paced world—*live fast, die young, and leave a good-looking corpse.*

I sniggered at the ironic thought. I was a step above a corpse.

Coming to a stop at a corner booth, I stared at the young couple occupying the V-shaped bench seat. They completely ignored me. Their arms and legs entwined, clothes in disarray. I leaned over the table and lightly tugged at the man's sleeve and then fanned five one-hundred-dollar bills in front of his face.

"What's that for?" His eyes widened with interest.

"The booth?" With a hint of a smile, I waited for his decision.

He shrugged, snatched the cash out of my hand, and pulled the protesting girl out of the booth, heading toward the bar.

I slid in until my back was against the corner. A great place to see the majority of the room. With one leg tucked beneath me, I waited to see if my stalker had followed.

A little bit of time passed before he walked into the club. Though I'd seen him distinctly in the dark as he followed me in his Mustang, seeing him this close was a treat. So masculine and striking.

I studied him. He appeared to be six-foot, maybe six-one, late twenties. Looking at the lines around his eyes, I changed it to early thirties. His wind-tossed dark hair gave him the air of a poet or musician. Thick strands framed his lightly tanned, high-cheekboned face giving him an untamed look along with his five o'clock shadow. He had an aquiline nose above pouting lips. The type of lips that I would enjoy sucking and licking, and having the favor returned.

What would it be like to touch him, taste his blood? A shake of my head cleared my mind of that notion. Hunger for blood was always below the surface, but tonight my hunger was for what I sensed in the man.

Not since my reincarnation had a human interested or attracted me to such an extent I almost felt as if he spellbound me. But he wasn't a warlock. Otherwise, I would sense the magic surrounding him.

While I studied him, I sensed his discomfort with the nightclub. Was he wondering how many were actually vampires? Would he be disappointed to find I was the only one in the club tonight? Did he actually know there was such a creature?

He was good. Not once had he looked my way, but still he maneuvered through the gyrating crowd and stopped at the bar nearest to my booth. He motioned to the bartender and leaned over, probably so he could be heard. The bartender nodded and began to pull a draft.

Without glancing around, he sat on a stool and lifted his gaze, staring straight at me.

Such soulful hazel-green eyes. I sighed. Vampire vision was a blessing. Had he sensed me? Obviously, he knew where I sat. I was alone. Did he feel my interest? Was he psychically sensitive? Was that why my attraction for him was so strong?

Of course, the overwhelming question was, why was he following me? Well, I could wonder about him all night. Or with certainty, I could learn my answers the easy way. I gave him a big smile.

<<<>>>

Ronan

I grabbed the edge of the bar. Her smile...fuuuck. It was seductive, challenging, and pure femininity all rolled into one. I wanted so badly to be wrong about her. Why did she have to be my client's sister? I never mixed business and pleasure. That was what she would be, ultimate carnal pleasure.

Scenes of hot sex and rolling bodies flashed through my mind, the images so clear that I could believe they had happened moments ago. What the hell?

I jerked my gaze away and stared sightlessly at the tall glass the bartender placed near me. Uneasy with my reaction to her being in the same room, I forced myself to turn and look at her again. The booth was empty.

Dammit to hell.

I pushed from the bar and stood, turning my head one way and then the other, looking over the crowd, and searching the area near the front door. Had she exited through a back door or gone to the ladies' room? I turned to check the other side of the club.

She stood inches away with a crooked grin and heavy-lidded eyes. Several inches shorter, but still tall enough for me to look into her dark eyes while I fucked her.

I took a step back. The edge of the bar bit into my back. Normally, I had little use for overconfident females. I liked being the hunter, the one who did the chasing, but there was something about her self-assurance that turned me on.

"Hi," she simply said.

"Hi." I wanted to say more. Most of what came to mind wasn't something I should say to a woman I'd just met.

"Come here often?" White even teeth flashed in a teasing smile.

Her husky, smooth voice forced me to shift my weight to loosen suddenly tight denim. Standing near the partially backlit bar, her soft chocolate eyes twinkled in amusement. She was aware of her effect on me. Instead of being embarrassed, it only made me harder. Damn.

"I see women have the same problem as men," I taunted.

"What problem is that?" The corners of her lips fought another smile.

"Good pickup lines."

"True. I heard it in a movie and thought you would appreciate the irony. You were to say, 'All the time.'"

I had no idea of the movie reference. But her relaxed small talk was nice.

"Okay." I grinned. "All the time," I repeated the line and then added, "Do *you* come here often?"

"Actually, I do. The energy bounces off the walls. Don't you feel it?" When she leaned forward, her jacket fell open, drawing my eyes down to her barely contained breasts. Nice.

Reluctantly, I dragged my attention back to her face. "Would you like to dance?"

I should say her brother had sent me to find her, but I wanted one dance without an explanation.

"I'd like that. I've already told the band to play a slow one." She held out her hand.

Damn, the woman had balls. I wondered who would be leading whom. When my fingers wrapped around hers, heat spread up my arm, speeding across my chest. Her grip was strong, but the palm soft and feminine. I took a couple of steps and led her onto the dance floor.

Politely, I guided her hand to my waist. But she wasted no time and slipped her hands up and around my neck, swaying her body against mine to the music.

Every inch of my body swelled and tightened. I had never met a woman with such animal magnetism and boldness. My whole being focused on her. An overwhelming feeling to possess her, to take over her body and soul, engulfed me. Almost a caveman attitude so foreign to me. I wanted to take her by the hair, cover her mouth with mine, and devour her.

I nuzzled her hair, enjoying the smell of rain and blossoms, not too sweet, but the light, fresh fragrance of a single rose. She rested her lips to my throat and licked the pulse. I became so hard, I expected my cock to explode in my jeans.

Since my divorce, I preferred one-night stands. But my attraction to her was different. Never had a woman turned me on until it took all my power to behave properly in public.

She moved the collar of my shirt to the side and nipped the skin where my shoulder met my neck, the sting quickly forgotten as she sucked at the bite. A shot of need traveled down my torso; my knees were even shaky.

The room faded. I became lightheaded. My attention centered on the woman in my arms. Then brilliant colors swirled around me. Indescribable hedonistic sensations rippled through me and filled my brain.

My fingers splayed over her hips and rubbed over the swell of her buttocks. Her body was the softest I'd ever held. Uncaring about our audience, her bold fingers matched mine, caress for caress.

Somehow we continued to dance. Her body followed my lead. Each step in sync, brushing against each other. Fire ran through my veins with her touch. She pulled gently with her teeth at my earlobe. Then her laughter rang in my ears like bells on Christmas morning, sweet and clear.

Her lips and tongue travelled down my neck again. Lights burst in my head. Dancing with her was like floating on a cloud. Swirling and drifting, I felt masterful and enslaved all at once. She made me forget my job, where I was, what I was doing. She was a drug, and I knew it wouldn't take much to become addicted.

The night continued in a sensual blur. Her whispers in my ear made little sense, but I wanted her to say more. Her Southern accent stoked a fire as hot as her roaming hands and mouth. Her kisses on my ear and down my throat were intoxicating.

Once again, I felt a sharp prick on my throat, but the

heaviness of lust instantly clutched my body before I even thought to question it.

The room became darker and I floated near the ceiling. I reached out to pull her closer and she wasn't there any longer. Cold darkness fell over me and then nothing.

# Chapter 2

## *Ronan*

The pounding pain and my moans woke me first. The lamp on my nightstand pummeled shards of brightness into my skull. I pulled a pillow over my head. Dammit, I'd forgotten to turn off the fucking thing last night. Not helping my pounding head at all.

"Open up, Mr. Michaels!"

That explained the continued hammering. It better be important.

With a grimace, I bellowed through the hotel room door, "Wait a minute."

Fuck.

My neck ached like a son of a bitch. I stretched and rubbed the sore area. Two small scratches near the nape told me I needed to cut my fingernails.

In slow degrees, I moved and sat on the edge of the bed. What the hell happened last night? I remembered following Tori, going into the club and dancing with her, but nothing after that. Nothing but the dream. And, man, what a dream. It felt so real.

With the scent of Tori still in my nose, my adrenaline

shot sky-high and my dick stood to attention remembering how she felt in my arms. I was hornier than I'd been for years, but to fuck her in my sleep? Not since I first became interested in girls had a dream been so vivid.

Damn, I wanted her. To have those long legs wrapped around my waist. To press into her warm pus—

"Mr. Michaels, I'm waiting." The man started beating on my door again.

"Okay, okay. Keep your shirt on." I grabbed my jeans off the nearby chair and eased into them a leg at a time, cussing my rock-hard cock for picking a wrong time.

As I reached the door and opened it, I'd regained control of my body somewhat and had worked the zipper closed, proud not to hurt anything vital. After a quick snap, I finally looked up.

A police detective stood in the hallway, staring at me with eyebrows raised. Even without the military-style haircut, cheap suit, and tie, I could recognize one from a block away. They always had a cynical tell-me-another-one look to them. I know it. I had the same expression on my face for years before I left the force. Fuck, I probably still did.

He held up his hand with his identification opened, confirming what I already guessed.

"Mr. Michaels, I'm Detective Jameson and I have a few questions." He waited for me to invite him in.

How did he know my name? What the hell did he want? Uneasy with the detective's presence, I figured the only way to find out the answers was to let him in.

"Sure. Come in."

I waved him into the small sitting room. My hotel bed was easily seen from where we stood and looked as if I'd wrestled with the sheets or better yet a woman. I hesitated with that thought. Something told me I hadn't. It'd only been a dream.

Right?

I walked to the small refrigerator and grabbed a Coke, silently offering the man one.

With a shake of his head, the detective turned his back and walked around the room. He picked up a book from the nightstand, looked closely at the cover, then placed it back. Not a sci-fi fan. Hmm.

After giving the rumpled bed a quick once-over, the detective stared at the open suitcase on the luggage rack. What did he expect to see?

"Is there something I can help you with, detective?" I asked, tired of waiting for my unexpected visitor to explain his presence.

"Have you been in Alabama long, Mr. Michaels?"

"Came in yesterday. May I ask what's this about?"

"In due time, sir. What is it that you do for a living?"

I sensed that Detective Jameson already knew the answer, but I was willing to play along. "I'm a private investigator."

"Who are you investigating?"

"A runaway. A sister of my client." Simple was best.

"What's her name?"

"I contacted your department and gave them a rundown on my reasons for being in and around the city. That's why you know who I am." I said the last with certainty, ignoring his unnecessary question.

No need to give the detective any more information. Besides, Tori wasn't a minor or in trouble with the law.

The detective nodded his head as he took another turn around the room. Coming to the partially closed bathroom door, he shoved it open with one finger, before turning to look me in the eye.

"Where were you between the hours of nine and ten last night?" The detective's attention never wavered as he continued his questioning.

My irritation grew. I knew the method, keep asking until the other person lost their temper and said too much. Only I had nothing to confess.

"Has something happened?" I asked.

"Please answer the question."

"On a stakeout," I simply said.

Asshole. I always tried to get along with the locals, but he was pushing it.

The detective's eyebrows rose. "Where?"

Enough was enough. I crossed my arms and narrowed my eyes. I hadn't broken a law and really didn't owe him any more explanations.

"It's time for you to tell me what's this all about?"

My refusal to answer didn't faze Jameson.

"What would you say if I told you a concerned citizen reported you spent two hours and twenty minutes watching 3049 Imperial Drive?" he said in a low voice.

The address I'd watched. The one my client's sister had visited. Obviously, the concerned citizen got my car tag.

Determined to show only indifference, I flopped onto an overstuffed chair near the couch and took another sip of my Coke.

"That's what a person does on a stakeout. So?" I worked on looking bored. It would be nice if the detective would tell me something useful.

"Robert Moore lived one street over on Superior Way for eight years. The housekeeping service that cleans his home twice a week entered the residence this morning and found his body." Jameson waited for my reaction to the news.

I remained calm and continued to act unconcerned. The detective was suspicious enough without me showing interest.

"There were several cars parked on the street, why would anyone complain about one more?" I pointed out.

The detective shrugged.

His attitude was pushing me to the edge. Robert Moore had been on Brannon's list. Though I hadn't killed the guy, there were a good many men in prison for crimes they hadn't perpetrated.

What about Tori? She'd left the house after ten. Walking over one street while her car stayed parked at Imperial wouldn't be a problem to someone wanting to kill. Just because I was attracted to her didn't mean she was innocent.

"How did he die?" I asked.

Anger rolled through my gut. Had her pretty face thrown off my instinctive self-preservation?

"You should know I can't reveal that. I can tell you, it was a death I wouldn't wish on my worst enemy. How do you know Robert Moore?" The peeved look on Jameson's face wasn't a good sign.

I was looking over the edge at big trouble. Being accused of murder was not a good career move and wouldn't encourage future clients' confidence.

"I've never met the man."

"It would be easy to walk the short distance."

"I never left my car."

If I told the detective about Tori, I wouldn't have a chance to...do what? Return her to her brother? Or turn her over to the police? No. I needed time to find her again and ferret out her side of the story. Or figure out what the hell she did to me? I had a feeling it wasn't a dream.

"I was told to watch for my client's sister. That she might arrive at that house."

"Did she show up?"

"Not that I saw." I made sure I looked the detective straight in the eye. Tori had already been there by the time I parked down the street. So technically she hadn't *shown up*.

Jameson didn't believe me, and it was obvious he'd watch me for the next few days.

"Where did you go after that?"

"To a club on the south side of Birmingham. Bloodsucker's."

No harm in giving him the name. I would have to provide it sooner or later, if they didn't already have it.

The surprised look on the detective's face was almost worth the hassle of being investigated for murder.

"You don't look the type."

I understood what he meant. If it hadn't been for Tori, I'd never have entered the place. I shrugged like he did earlier. Two could play at that game.

"What time did you get back to the hotel?" The detective glared at me.

Damn. This was where it'd become hairy. If I told Jameson I couldn't remember, my spot on that list of suspects would rise considerably. Nevertheless, if I made up a time and someone in the hotel told him differently, everything I said would become suspect. There was no way around it. I had to lie.

"I got a little drunk last night and really don't remember." I took another sip of my soda, watching the detective. If he suspected I lied, he could blow up my career.

"The clerk said you stumbled in, appearing drunk."

It was a strain to keep the look of relief off my face. I needed to buy the early morning clerk a big steak dinner.

"How long are you going to be in Birmingham, Mr. Michaels?"

"Really not certain. Probably another week or two."

Detective Jameson handed over a small, white card.

"Be sure to contact me if you decide to leave. I may need to ask you some more questions."

"Will do."

No way was I getting off so lightly. The detective probably already had my home address and had pulled a credit report. Standard procedure for a murder suspect in most states. And I had no doubt I was a suspect, probably on Jameson's top five.

Impatient for the detective to leave, I nevertheless remained seated until my visitor closed the door.

*What in the hell have you gotten me into, Tori Amherst?*

# Chapter 3

## *Tori*

Before sunset, I woke up in my underground bedroom, staring at the ceiling, thinking of soft green eyes and long fingers and big hands. I savored my memories of the tall stranger. Sexy, strong, and oh, so tasty as I remembered the flavor of his electric blood, the feel and flavor of his warm skin against my lips, the cool strands of hair slipping between my fingers, his intoxicating scent. A delightful mixture of masculinity and potency.

There was something special about him, something had me reminiscing over and over again about our time together instead of preparing for tonight. His eyes drew me, and every nerve ending tingled for the feel of his body sliding along mine.

Maybe after I finished my business, I'd visit Bloodsucker's. Would he show up looking for me again?

Last night, I was tempted to suggest it to him, but my ego interfered. More importantly, I wanted him to come looking for me on his own. Those few stolen moments in the dark corner of the club had been magical, despite my notorious willpower failing me.

It'd been years since I allowed my baser vampire instincts to take over. Without a thought of the consequences, I'd sunk my canines into his neck, and as the blood —sweeter than wine, infused with more energy than I had ever experienced—flowed into my system, I'd teetered on the line of forgetting myself. Fierce erotic sensations had flooded my senses. I'd been a step away from exposing his cock and fucking him in the club. To restrain my appetite, I'd *suggested* he leave the club and remember nothing after our dance. One of the advantages of taking a human's blood, they become susceptible to suggestions.

Had he awakened this morning believing he had one too many drinks? Weak and wobbly from loss of blood, chances were he'd believed he drank more than one glass of Jack Daniels. Whenever a vampire took blood, the stoutest drinker or teetotaler felt aroused beyond measure and drunk afterwards. People always explained away the unexplainable by claiming it was alcohol or a prescription.

Without taking their blood, I had to touch the person's skin with my fingers to read their emotions or past actions. Most of my fellow Americans were so protective of their personal space, they often made it difficult. Though in the South it was a little easier. Southerners enjoyed shaking hands, slapping backs, and hugging.

Besides, I enjoyed the power to plant false memories or decisions into people's heads after taking blood or read their emotions and past memories from those I hadn't partaken of yet. As all things, it had a couple of drawbacks.

One, other vampires I'd shared blood with were immune to my *suggestions*. Even if they allowed me to place my hands on their skin, reading their memories would be forbidden. Any attempt could lead to my death. Vampires considered those actions as a move of dominance. Dealing with angry vampires was not a pretty thing. If I killed a vampire, who did not belong to me—which would be another story entirely—I would be punished by death.

And two, after the experience of the first one, I never read the memories of the humans I kill. It was amazing how perverted and grotesque their thoughts were at the moment of death.

I'd rather think of the human I enjoyed last night.

Ronan.

He'd told me it was a family name. With a touch on his firm forearm, he divulged so much, about his client, tracking me, the hotel he resided in, and why he needed the money. It became obvious he had no idea I was a vampire and his memories confirmed it.

On waking, he probably imagined he'd scratched his neck. A common explanation used by past donors.

One concerning note was Ronan's client. Who in the world was Edgar Brannon? Why was he lying about being my brother? I only had a sister and my parents didn't have any more children. What did he hope to gain?

A chime tinkled nearby. Time to push the stranger and his client out of my mind and get dressed. I had much to do once it was completely dark.

I stretched and slipped out of my bed. The room decorated in subdued colors of light gray and blue soothed me. The few pieces of furniture sprinkled throughout the spacious room kept the area from being cluttered. I pressed the button on a remote and soft lighting and music gradually increased to a respectable level.

When I built the house, I had my bedroom built underground with a hidden door and stairwell. A staged master bedroom was above it. I told the builders the *secret* area was a panic room and tornado shelter. With six-foot-thick, cinder block walls lined with steel then oak, they believed me.

My favorite part of the chamber was the closet. It was as large as the bedroom. Not only did it hold an immense selection of clothes, but a large array of weapons, from Renaissance epees to AK-47s. I was prepared for every type of killer imaginable.

Often my vampire strength and fangs stopped my prey, but at times I needed more. I could only fight off maybe five humans at a time or a couple young vampires. Older vampires were different. If they were close to my age—in vampire years—or weak from lack of blood, I could possibility fight more than one, but I hoped to never test that theory.

Tonight, my prey wouldn't be hard to subdue and terminate. A wiry fellow a little taller than my own five-six. He enjoyed young boys, by terrorizing and hurting them. He wouldn't anymore. Not after tonight.

After a quick shower, I walked into my closet. Unlike humans' homes, there was not a mirror anywhere. Despite what movies show, most vampires had a reflection. But their images were faint, translucent—like we were slowly disappearing. The sight could be most disturbing. I had heard the ancient vampires' reflections were no more than a blur or ripple in the background.

I looked down at my body. Thin scars marred my skin on my right side. In the beginning, they embarrassed me but no more. Badges of honor. Marks of my courage. They proved I survived no matter the means.

Besides, in the shadows they were rarely noticeable, and most mortal men have their attention elsewhere on my body.

Like Ronan last night, once I bit him, his lust blinded him.

What would he say of my outfit tonight? The skin-tight black leather jumpsuit was supple, perfect to hide blood stains with no loose material to get in my way while fighting. The zipper stopped to reveal plenty of cleavage in the sleeveless portion of the top. I enjoyed being a woman and used every weapon available. The titillating view of my full breasts often distracted men to the point they would forget to fight back before it was too late. Finishing off the classic cat-suit were flat sole, soft leather boots and gloves to match.

A dainty gold cross with deep-red rubies hung from a chain around my neck. My only jewelry.

It was rather ironic. For centuries, humans thought the cross frightened vampires. It wasn't the cross, but what it represented in their own lives. Their fall from grace. Their damnation. Taking and drinking of human blood was sinful, but I needed it to live. Forgiveness would not be in the hand I was dealt.

Nevertheless, I was damned not for just being a blood-drinking vampire but for being a murderer. No matter how much the men deserved their death, I wasn't God. It wasn't my right to kill them. But I swore while stretched out on a cold stone in that psycho's basement, I would never let another woman or child suffer without hope. Rather a champion to avenge them.

Who else was better equipped than a vampire? If I could prevent psychopaths and pedophiles from practicing their perversions, I would. My damnation would be worth it. The best weapon to stop monsters was with a stronger and more dangerous monster like myself.

I looked at my hands. Too many times to count, blood had covered them. Clenching my fists, I pressed them against my skull in frustration. I'd done it for the horror I went through. A horror I could prevent for many others.

A monster was what I'd become and no one was allowed to get in my way, to interfere with my crusade.

What was it then about Ronan that made me rethink my decision from long ago? My lone crusade to find and kill those who prey on women and children.

It would not do to have my attention split between what I need to do and what I crave. Was he the one I'd been waiting for? I felt the pull, the connection last night. Strange. I never knew I was waiting for someone, but when I looked into his eyes...I felt as if I was home again, safe and loved.

A shuffling of feet drew my attention outward to the room.

"Byron, have we heard from Connor yet?" I turned and waited for the handsome man standing in the doorway to answer.

Three inches taller than me, with a lean build and long, wavy chestnut hair, he silently stepped into the room. Technically, he was older than I, but with the help from sips of vampire blood over many years, he looked to be in his late teens. I was uncertain of his true age as he always played coy with his birth year, but I guessed he was in his eighties.

He'd been orphaned by his previous master when hunters had attacked their home, staking his master in bed. No one knew how the location had been uncovered, but I'd felt sorry for the frightened man. It was standard procedure to slice the servants' throats when an attack was questionable. Over the years, I had visited the home several times and knew he'd been treated well by his master and unlikely to betray him. So I had pleaded his case and provided him with a new home. In the ten years he'd been with me, except for the occasional squabble with Connor, he'd been well-mannered and trustworthy.

He stopped a few steps away with one hip thrust out and thumbs hooked in the back pockets of his low-riding jeans. His heated gaze ran up and down my body. From the swell beneath his zipper, he liked how I looked in black leather.

"Yes. Here's the address you wanted," he said, his voice deep and thick with sultry nuance.

He sauntered over and brushed the folded paper across my collarbone and slipped it into my bulging cleavage.

"Behave yourself," I chastised, lifting one eyebrow.

I had neglected him lately. So much on my mind. Normally, I wouldn't have a problem with his touching without permission. Vampires were *blessed*—such a funny word considering my earlier thoughts—with a strong libido. So servants were helpful when we were in death sleep, but even more so as sexual outlets, and I was no different. My two male blood servants were quite enjoyable, and in the past we had even played with an extra human or two.

Memories flashed through my mind of strong forearms with ropes of blood vessels sitting beneath tanned skin, muscular biceps bulging, moss green eyes darkening with desire—

I quickly blocked the image of Ronan from my mind.

"I wish to please you." His fingers trailed over my scarred arm as he walked around me.

I ignored him as I read the note. Not until his hands slipped over my breasts with his chest pressed tightly against my back did I pull his hands away. Excitement shot through me, but regretfully, time was short.

"I have things to do." I kissed his fingers, and then stepped away and strolled toward the front door.

"Tori."

A hand grabbed my scarred arm.

I spun around. Before Byron could blink, my hand clasped his neck and shoved him to the wall. Canines bared, long and menacing, my mouth an inch from his.

"I told you I have things to do." I spoke each word evenly and precisely.

His gurgling warned me that I was becoming carried away. Crushing his windpipe would be too easy. I released my hold, shaking my head. Caressing his cheek with the back of my hand, I kissed his neck in apology.

"Baby, you know better than to grab me by that arm."

His action had surprised me. He loved to caress and touch my breasts and scars but never grasp me without warning, I didn't care for surprises.

"Please forgive me," he rasped. Taking advantage of my being so near, he rubbed his groin against my hip.

Tenderly, I skimmed my thumb over the red marks I'd made on his neck and kissed him on each cheek. It wasn't his fault I was tortured by regrets and self-pity. When he tried to press his body once again to mine and bent down to cover my mouth with his, I stepped away and headed for the door.

As I pressed the button to open the hidden entrance, I turned.

"There's nothing to forgive. Just remember, no surprises. Now it's time I take care of this scum. I need you to concentrate on protecting my home while I'm away. Make sure the security equipment is on if you leave. Connor is doing recon on another asshole and will not return until tomorrow before nightfall."

Relieved when he nodded, I took a minute to really look at him. He was handsome almost to the point of being pretty. His unexpected aggression was an additional distraction I didn't need. After my uncharacteristic wanton behavior last night with the stranger, I was ready to return to my mission.

I needed to do some thinking too.

<<<>>>

Tree limbs swayed eerily in the windy night. The frantic rustling of leaves drowned the roar of traffic on the nearby interstate.

I strolled across a moonlit backyard, easily springing over a four-foot fence without hesitation. A Doberman charged from beneath a porch and lunged at me, barking nonstop. I grabbed him by the scruff and stared into his eyes. Trembling, he whimpered, and his back legs curled up as he dangled above the ground. Once I released my hold, he yipped all the way back, crawling under the structure to hide. A corner of my lips lifted, and I shook my head. Funny how animals sensed how dangerous I was without the need to hurt them.

After so many years, I'm still amazed by my powers and abilities. Reading emotions and past events helped in tracking my prey. A light touch on a passerby's arm and I could picture each pedestrians' direction he'd seen moments earlier. But it was also a danger in itself to me, for people's cruel thoughts were often near the surface. The monsters would often replay the worst of their crimes when faced with death. The scenes stayed in my mind for months, years, nearly driving me crazy. Blocking them was best for my sanity. The easiest way to do so was to wear gloves, soft leather did the trick.

I reached the address after jumping a couple more

fences. The house was like so many others in the poor section of larger cities, with long strips of peeling paint floating off in the light breeze, black bars on the windows giving a menacing appearance, and a corner section of the rusty metal fencing on the ground. The backyard was rock and red clay with patches of knee-high weeds. The lack of grass was concerning. How many bodies had he buried?

A kitchen light shone like a small square on the backyard. I gingerly walked around it. Being spotted from a neighbor's house was the last thing I needed.

There was no sound from inside, not even a TV or electronic device to betray the inhabitants. Two large overgrown bushes hid the back door from the neighbors and the cars passing on the secondary street a block away. The door was locked, not a surprise considering the vicinity and time of night.

With my preternatural strength, it was easy to slowly push the knob until the latch bolt or other parts broke with little sound, allowing me to open the door.

The malodor slapped me in the face. The hint of blood teased my fangs to drop despite the ammonia stink. There were drawbacks to having a heightened sense of smell. I squeezed my eyes shut for a couple of seconds, shaking my head to regain control.

He was already at work.

I stepped inside. I had no problem crossing the threshold without his permission. Thank goodness most humans were ignorant of spells that prevented a vampire from entering a private residence. Of course, most were unaware of the more dangerous creatures.

Thick vinyl muffled my well-placed footsteps across the kitchen floor. I stopped at a doorway that led to a short staircase. Next to it was a long hallway. Uncertain of the direction to take, a soft cry in the depths of the house helped me make the decision.

With blurring speed, I ran down the hallway and burst open a thin door. If I had been human, my stomach would have emptied. A young boy, naked, bleeding from numerous cuts and bruises, lay curled in a fetal position at the feet of a well-dressed man.

That was always surprising, no matter how many of these deviants I punished. They always appeared so damn normal. Yet, while working on their perversions, they had the same look in their eyes. Manic excitement. Their version of lust.

"Who in the hell are you?" The man wiped the back of his hand across his lips as if in anticipation of performing his sadistic art on me next.

"I'm the angel of death," I answered coldly. My sneer big enough to reveal sharp canines.

"Well, little girl, you've played Halloween at the wrong house." He reached for me and missed.

In a fluid movement, my leg came up and flattened his nose with the side of my foot. Blood sprayed over his mouth and chest. The kick, aimed to hurt and not kill, was followed by two more on various parts of the man's body.

There was something to say about getting intense satisfaction from hitting a pervert. On the last kick, the man fell against the wall, crushing the sheet rock with the force. He bounced back and shook off the white powder. In an unexpected move, he crouched in a fighting stance I recognized.

It seemed I was in for a fight.

Finally, competition.

Each thrust and parry was like a dance, a macabre dance of death. I had no doubt that we were both fighting for a life. He worked on saving his own, and for me, the boy's.

Determined to draw the man away from his victim, I placed my strikes and kicks so he stumbled out of the back room and then down the hallway into the living room. Tables, chairs and lamps overturned, broken in the fight, sprinkling glass over and around us.

A scream echoed through the house.

I turned my head toward the back room. Was there a second person in the house I missed? If so, I would have to deal with them after I finished this asshole.

The scream came again. Then I realized it was the young boy crying for help.

The man took advantage of my distraction and grabbed a fire hook from beneath the mantel. He swung and hit my side. The loud crack echoed in the room. One or more ribs were crushed.

Staggering back with pain, I braced myself and charged at him, ramming him in the gut with my head. There was something to be said about vampire tolerance of pain.

I seized his arm and squeezed until a bone cracked. He shrieked and dropped the hook.

Tired of playing, I straightened and brought my foot up, connecting the point of my steel-toed boot to his chin. His head snapped back as he flipped backwards in the air, landing stunned and stretched out at my feet.

At that same moment, the front door crashed in. Ronan stood, chest heaving, taking in the shattered room.

"Need some help?" Ronan's eyebrows lifted as he waited for my answer.

I turned my face away to give my fangs time to withdraw.

"Yes, I do. The boy's in the back room." The screaming

continued from the hallway. "He needs an ambulance. I'll take care of this bastard."

I picked up my foot and pressed hard on the man's neck. A human's neck with several important bones was so fragile, so easily broken.

"Tori, you can't kill him."

"What?" I imagined blood streamed down my face from the successful impacts, the pervert's blood mixed with mine. I likely looked grotesque. At this point, my fangs probably looked like slightly overlong eyeteeth and not fangs. What he said finally registered. "Why not?"

I kept my gaze on the floor in case my eyes had transmogrified into glowing orbs. Every time I breathed, my ribs ached. I needed blood quickly to help my wounds regenerate bone and tissue.

The ordeal of seeing a traumatized child and then fighting his attacker was always draining. I was tired of the inhumane way people treated those weaker. They deserved a strong dosage of their own medicine, and I was the perfect monster for that.

"We have to turn him in. Let the police and the justice system handle it." His green eyes filled with concern as he waited for my decision.

"It was the justice system that put him back out on the streets to harm more children. They released him because of a technicality. How long do you believe he'd stay in jail this time? Ten years, twenty? He'll be back on the streets before the police can finish the paperwork."

I pressed a little harder on his neck. A whimper escaped the man's lips.

"Come on, man, get her off me. I swear she's crazy," the creep started pleading with Ronan. He probably believed in "bros before hoes."

I moved my foot and with a sharp movement of my hand to his neck, I knocked him out. A piercing ache shot through my side. Though I struggled to hold it back, I finally gave in and my wretched moan caught Ronan's attention.

"You're hurt." He reached for me, but I sidestepped his touch.

After the energy I'd expelled, my skin would be dead cold to a human's touch. I needed blood desperately. If he touched me, I was uncertain I could stop from taking his.

"I'm okay. Only a cracked rib."

"What if it's broken? It could puncture a lung."

I leaned toward him for a moment. I wanted his gentle touch. Even his arms around me, but I had a more pressing situation to take care of. In my present condition, I was a danger to him.

"You win this time. Call the police for the deviant and an ambulance for the kid." Distant sirens filtered into the room. "It appears one of his neighbors took care of the first call for you." I took a few wobbly steps toward the door. Why was the door so far away?

"Where're you going?" he asked.

Out of a large pocket in his cloth overcoat, Ronan pulled a pair of handcuffs and fastened the man's wrists behind his back.

Chuckling, I nodded toward his efficiency of coming prepared.

"Were you a Boy Scout?"

He ignored my attempt at humor. "Aren't you going to stay and explain to the police what happened?" From the expression on his face, my answer wouldn't surprise him. His gaze drifted down my outfit, hesitating for a couple seconds on my heaving breasts. "Then again, maybe it would be best if you left."

I nodded, giving a small chuckle.

"Take care. I have a feeling I'll see you again soon." While holding my side tight, I loped out the back door and toward my car parked several houses away.

Sirens echoed nearer.

# Chapter 4

## *Ronan*

I no longer felt comfortable in police stations. Too many bad memories. After staying there for nearly three hours, I was beginning to hate this one.

Only luck and another nosy neighbor—they could be helpful at times—saved me from being charged for breaking and entering along with assault and battery, not counting several other lesser crimes.

Joe Carson wasn't talking from his guarded hospital bed and refused to discuss who had attacked him. Only after entering the police station had I found out the man's name. Shocker—yeah, sarcasm implied—Joe's name was on the list my client had provided.

Sitting in Detective Jameson's cluttered cubical, I stretched my neck, checking out the stacks of files for any familiar names. No one. I stood, hands on the small of my back, and twisted as if getting the kinks out. Was Tori somewhere nearby? Had she gotten away? I didn't see any other names I knew. My patience was coming to an end, waiting for the detective to bring some paperwork for me to sign. With no fanciful illusions, I was quite aware they suspected me of being a crazy vigilante, and probably their number one suspect after the fiasco tonight despite the witness.

Throughout my childhood and my twenties, I spent a lot of time in police stations. Most people would assume I was the troublemaker. The fact was my dad had been a police officer, and when I grew up, I tried out the profession until my life had imploded, and I resigned.

I scanned the room. No Tori. I had mixed feelings about her no-show. I wanted her to do the right thing and bring in the psychos she was tracking. But I was aware if she did, she would be arrested too. A dilemma of grand proportions.

Dammit, I was ready to go searching for the woman again. She was certainly more than she appeared. And oh, man, that outfit she had on...my cock had sat up and waved. Good thing she hadn't noticed my body's appreciation. Where was she? Who was she really? One thing for certain, no way was she that asshole's sister. My gut told me he lied.

Tons of questions swirled in my head. It was time to hunt her down and force some answers out of her.

Her actions last night had stunned the hell out of me. When I'd followed her to Carson's house, I never expected to find her beating the shit out of the man. Most women didn't have the strength or the know-how. But she handled the situation like a pro and showed no fear even with a busted rib. From what she said and did, she was a vigilante with a mission.

Had she killed Robert Moore by accident? Or did she play with her victims before eliminating them? I didn't like the possibilities. That would mean she was a cold-blooded killer and a serial one.

A gut feeling told me there was more to her story. She was a fascinating woman.

"Ahem. Here you are, Mr. Michaels." After getting my

attention, the detective handed over what appeared to be a ream of papers, pointing out several places to sign. "Don't forget my warning. Contact me before you leave the area or you'll be enjoying our city's finest hospitality."

It didn't take a genius to figure out he was threatening jail time. I sat down and began signing and initialing.

Yep, that settled it. I hated police stations.

"One more thing, Mr. Michaels, the list you had in your possession was from a protected database of released suspected pedophiles. How did you come about having that list?"

He towered over me in a weak attempt to threaten physical action to obtain an answer.

As I did when the detective originally found the list in my pocket, I stared at him without a word.

A copy was hidden away at the hotel and rested in a file on my phone. So if I didn't get it back, no problem.

Frustrated, the detective sighed and sat down behind his desk.

"If you continue to show up outside or inside their houses, we may get the idea you're involved in taking justice into your own hands. I can tell you, we won't put up with it. Do you understand?"

I merely lifted an eyebrow. I hadn't broken a law yet and nothing could be used against me.

It was true more than one man had spent time in prison for something he hadn't committed, but I was careful. Besides, the detective made a grave error, he'd given me the men's real connection. Not the bullshit Brannon had given me. What I suspected was true. It was all a lie.

The danger wasn't of Tori being murdered by any of the men on the list, but in fact, she was a danger to them. And from what I'd seen and heard, that confirmed Edgar Brannon wasn't Tori's brother.

Who was Brannon and what did he want with her? Had she harmed someone the strange man knew?

The door couldn't hit my backside fast enough. I had only a couple of hours left before the nightclub closed. With only a small chance I would find Tori, I still had to try.

<<<>>>

Tori

I sunk lower in the large tub, wantonly soaking in the oily water. The soothing heat and a small cup of warm blood helped to heal my ribs. Within seconds of drinking the blood, the scratches on my face disappeared and by tomorrow my ribs would mend enough for another hunt. The soft glow of candles in the bathroom further relieved the pounding headache I had after returning to my house. A concussion was a son of a bitch even for a vampire. But in my case, no sooner than I'd walked in after midnight, Byron and Connor began arguing over whose turn it was to prepare my nightly bath.

Where Byron was handsome in a young, decadent, hippy-rock-star way, Connor had the sensual pull of a dangerous street punk. The rows of small thin hoops in his ears matched the rings he had in his nipples. With one black eyebrow pierced, a stud in the side of his nose and a colorful tattooed snake running from the side of his neck down under his clothes, he was a walking billboard of what parents warned their daughters against.

Two weeks after becoming part of my household, he'd proudly dropped his pants and shown his Prince Albert piercing. Slyly, he had said that women loved the feel of it.

I was suitably impressed by his tolerance to pain along with his size. Lifting my head, I'd politely ordered him to my bed to try it out. As if I had to order him. He practically ran. That was when I learned where the snake's tail ended.

His thick black hair with dyed red streaks hung down his back to his waist, usually kept in a long braid. Definitely a man who enjoyed walking to the beat of a different drummer. And he was the best at sniffing out information.

With his wild looks and shy act, women of all ages wanted to reform him. While they babied him, he picked their brains for information about former or present lovers or jobs and anything else he thought useful. He had a memory like a steel trap.

Despite having an I.Q. higher than most Mensa members, he had a bad habit of picking on those meaner and bigger. When I'd first met him, I found him covered with blood and fighting off a gang. They were pounding him into the pavement. After I threw a couple of the members over a six-foot fence, the others backed off and high-tailed it down the street, leaving Connor nursing several nasty bruises and a couple of knife wounds.

Fighting so many humans had drained my strength. So I'd struggled with my urges as his fresh blood filled my senses. My fangs lengthened enough to be menacing, but not to their full length. I'd pretended to ignore them in the hope he wouldn't notice.

Connor's curious gaze hadn't wavered as I cleaned him up and sewed his flesh back together.

Instead of being frightened, he'd asked questions. Lots. I admitted to being a creature of the night. He then offered to help and protect me during the day. That was almost fifteen years ago when he was sixteen. Now at the age of thirty-one, he'd seen things he never imagined existed. I trusted him with my life. Unlike Byron, in the beginning, he didn't sip on my blood as often, in turn, his body had matured and reached a height of six-two. I was thankful for it all.

"Tori!" The bathroom door burst open and Connor walked into the steamy room. "Sorry, but Byron's being a prick again. It was my turn and he knows it."

Byron and Connor normally got along, but on occasion, Byron would get jealous of some attention Connor received from me, or Connor would decide to tease Byron, then all hell would break loose. Byron was easily riled.

The two servants not only protected and maintained my household during daylight hours, but they supplied the fresh blood I needed. I was too active for just one, two barely sustained me. Some of the older vampires had large households that included twenty or more blood servants, despite not needing as much blood. Connor had offered to find another servant, but I preferred to handle it myself.

Unlike many vampires, mine were free-will servants. No coercion or dark powers used. The blood they sipped helped slow or stop aging and caused a mellow feeling, but didn't control them. Connor compared it to smoking pot. I personally refused to force a person into providing nourishment or sex. One of the benefits for humans and vampires was how feeding enhanced sexual pleasure for both. And doubly so for vampire on vampire.

Yet I avoided other vampires except when I was required to visit the local master vampire. Thankfully, that wasn't often. Master vampires were a possessive and territorial bunch, so I learned to keep a low profile.

As a person could imagine, master vampires were often ancients. Living for hundreds of years, they were hard to entertain and often were big assholes. Rarely, a younger vampire would come into dominant powers that challenged their master's supremacy. Luckily, there were only a handful of masters in the U.S. The one who made me had been one. He'd been in hiding for a lengthy time before my blood woke him.

One thing I learned about vampires. There were rules to changing a human. Number one was, a vampire must be a master or have permission from their master. Not all vampires were able to make fledglings. Only humans with a rare gene could be reincarnated. I'd been lucky to be one.

"Tori, are you listening to me?"

Eyelids barely open, I cut my gaze over to Connor in time to see Byron shuffling in. I sank further into the tub. I wasn't shy, but they fought enough without adding fuel to the fire.

Byron sighed. "I only filled your tub since he's been so busy today."

"He knows that it's my turn." Connor lifted his hand and gestured one finger at Byron. "Fuck you!" Looking back at me, he said, "I looked forward to it all day. He gets to do it the rest of the time. Isn't this his night off? Why's he still here?"

"Go on, Byron. I'll talk to you later."

"But—"

"Now."

Shooting a glare at Connor, Byron, with a pouting bottom lip, slunk out of the room and softly closed the door.

Shirtless, Connor wore fatigue-style pants hanging low on his hips that showed off his toned abs and the vee of his torso and upper edge of his hip bones. The view was most alluring, but I wasn't in the mood. Thoughts of a tall, hazel-eyed investigator filled my mind.

"Connor, what do you want?" As soon as I said it, I knew what he would say.

"To crawl into the tub with you and lick you all over. To taste your sweet cunt and suck hard on your clit until you scream my name." His dirty words and heated look almost brought my arms around his neck to pull him into the water with me.

Unable to hold back a smile, I shook my head to clear my mind. He tempted me to spread my legs and let him go for it. He possessed a wicked tongue in more than one way.

How often would I need to remind him I was boss? Maybe I'd been too kind with both of them. One day, Byron's antics would backfire. Connor wouldn't put up with his tricks for long and his reaction would guarantee a severe punishment.

"No. I have too much on my mind." I couldn't get the human out of my mind. It wouldn't be fair to Connor.

He kneeled next to the tub, crossed his arms on the edge, and leaned his cheek on top, blinking his eyes in all innocence. "Byron told me that you let the perv go."

He was such a compassionate person but believed in my campaign.

The end of his braid slipped into the water and floated toward me. I wrapped the thick plait around a wet hand before flipping it over his shoulder.

"It was for the best." I knew Connor well enough to know he was working up to something else.

"The investigator...P.I. Are you going to make him like us or like you? Have you fucked him?"

I turned and glared at the door. Byron had such a big mouth.

Connor had asked many times to be made into a vampire. I hadn't explained the dangers in changing him as I was uncertain he had the gene. I was told the blood would taste like the sweetest wine. Connor's was sweet, but did it mean his was the correct type? Besides, my master would have to okay the transition. The men in my household wanted to be vampires and live with me forever, sharing my bed and providing their blood. If I went any length without fucking them, one or both, they felt I no longer cared. They'd made it clear many times. I blocked their feelings, out of respect, but occasionally their impassioned desires would filter through. Really, it would be silly to wear gloves to bed.

"No. I don't *plan* to reincarnate him." Why lie to him? It wasn't his business, but I'd always been honest with them. Well, as much as I could. I swiped at my eyes in my tiredness. "If I take him, it'll be for only one night. Nothing more."

His face quickly masked his relief.

"Well, I guess that's something," he said with an ambiguous shrug of his broad shoulders. Instantly, his normal teasing returned. "You're certain I can't get in the tub with you and help you bathe."

I smiled, happy to see he took my rejection so well.

"I'm certain. Now go before I lose my patience with you."

He blew me a kiss and then sauntered out of the bathroom.

Funny. I hadn't planned to sleep with Ronan, but after turning down two available and willing—Byron would have joined in—sexy men in my house, all I could think about was making love to the human.

If I hurried, I could make it to the club before it closed.

Ronan

I parked my Mustang and sat staring out of the cracked windshield at the wet parking lot. No black Maserati. Maybe she wasn't coming or had another car. I slammed shut the driver's door behind me and walked toward the nightclub.

As I prowled through the crowd, I noted how at twelve-thirty on a Thursday night, correct that, Friday morning, the place was packed, though no line outside as I heard there was on weekend evenings. The sporadic rain hadn't thinned out the weeknight patrons. In a way it looked like the same horde from before. Then again, with all the strange clothes, makeup, and piercings, how could I really tell?

As soon as I stepped into the cavernous room, I sensed her vibrant presence. Fuck, my cock even wanted to salute her. As if in slow motion, I turned. There she was, holding court in the corner booth.

Looking so sensual and mysterious, she entertained two men—two fuckboys—both with dishwater blond hair. Twins? Her face beamed with laughter. They pressed her body between theirs, competing for her attention by kissing her hands and whispering in her ears.

A rush of anger had me visualizing grasping the boys' heads and banging them together and then breaking their wrists. How dare they touch what was mine? As insane as it sounded, the feeling was there and bordered on overpowering any reasoning I possessed. She belonged to me.

In long strides, I came to a stop in front of her table. Unable to voice my rage, I glared at the pretty men. They wouldn't be so pretty when I got finished with them.

"Well, hello, Ronan." Tori's smooth-as-chocolate voice flowed over me.

My body relaxed a little on hearing my name on her lips.

Turning my attention toward her smile, my heart warmed. Audible sighs of relief came from the boys next to her.

Why was she with such wimps? My jealousy disturbed the hell out of me. Almost as much as the fawning boys sitting next to her. Why was she putting up with them? I wanted them gone and preferably never around her again.

What the fuck was wrong with me? When my ex-wife left, I'd sworn off women and the games they played. But this woman had me all tied up and willing to play her games.

Dammit. Those two motherfuckers just sat there, not leaving. Obviously not a bit of sense between the two. Unable to hold back any longer, I placed my knuckles on the table and leaned over, making sure they understood the distance wasn't enough to protect them.

"Get lost, little boys," I said coldly enough to send a spasm of icy fear running down their spines.

When I glanced at Tori, her eyes twinkled with delight. Normally, it should piss me off, but instead I liked how she took pleasure in my jealousy. I wanted her complete attention. My rage grew to the point it was ready to explode. I fought the need to grab her by the hair and drag her off, letting everyone know she belonged to me and no one else.

Obviously deaf or not too smart, the twins stared, mouths open. Out of patience, I reached for the larger of the two and pulled him over the table, glasses and bottles crashing to the floor.

The music stopped and the club became unnaturally quiet.

Holding the front of the man's shirt, I turned to the other one.

"Scat." I actually growled.

Out of the corner of my eye, I noted a burly fellow charging toward me. *Bring it on.* I was ready to fight them all.

<<<>>>
Tori

I raised my hand, stopping the bouncer.

"Everything's okay. It's all a mistake. He's going to release my friend now and I'll pay for the glassware."

The big guy drew to a halt. "Okay, Ms. Amherst, but he better behave."

"I understand. He will, after I talk to him." I smiled at the bouncer and turned to Ronan.

Leaning back in my booth, I raised my eyebrows. Ronan finally let go of the twin. The blond stumbled away and was followed by his brother through the exit. Then my gaze rested on Ronan again. He looked at me as if he wanted to eat me whole.

My smirk gradually changed to a bright smile. What could I say? I loved the idea of his dark head bobbing between my thighs.

Maybe he was thinking the same. His broad chest rapidly rose and fell from his exertions. His masculine beauty had intensified with his fury by showing flashing hazel-green eyes and pouting sexy lips. A grown, well-formed man with pouty lips? Who would have ever guessed?

Once the crowd realized there wasn't going to be a fight, they started talking all at once, and as if on cue, the music resumed its pounding.

No matter how hard I tried to stop grinning, I couldn't. It had been a long time since someone had shown such single-minded interest in me without drinking my blood beforehand.

Maybe he was more caveman than my normal taste, but he was so beautiful in his anger. I usually became bored with dominating men, but I couldn't imagine doing so with him. If I'd been human, I might've been a little leery of him and his strong emotions, but I could handle anything he dished out.

"Have a seat." I waved to the space next to me. "You got what you wanted. I'm all yours."

He slid in the booth, pressing a muscular thigh to mine. He sure was confident. I liked it. For now.

Then he turned to face me, one arm along the seat's edge near my shoulders, the other in front of me on the table. His hovering was meant to intimidate and prove ownership. His heat, his smell surrounded me in a good way.

"Mine?" His deep and husky voice insinuated he agreed but wanted to be sure I felt the same way.

"Was there something you wanted to ask?" I chuckled when his gaze drifted to the vee of my leather top. "Ronan?"

"What?" With a slow appreciative grin, he raised his warm gaze.

"You have questions." If only I could avoid the lies, the subterfuge, but he'd never understand why I did what I did, or what I was. Most humans were not ready for the reality of vampires.

In a low, deep voice, full of concern, he asked, "Did we fuck last night?"

Wow! Of all the questions he could ask, that was not what I expected. It had been a long time since someone had surprised me in such a good way. I squeezed my thighs together.

"I hope not, especially as I'd want to remember."

He continued to stare at me. I almost lifted my hand to check my hair. Had something changed about me? Had I given myself away? Had he figured I was more than a human?

I was so tempted to touch his skin and read his emotions, but I hesitated. Possibly a little afraid to find that he was insane. What was it about this man that pulled at me? One deep look from those gold-sprinkled green eyes and my blood heated until I was sure my body would ignite. Flames would overtake me if I touched him, caressed his body, tasted his skin, inhaled his scent.

His hand rested on top of mine. It was so large and warm. Before I gave in to battled temptation, I did my best to block his memories from being revealed.

Time was running out for me and this sexy investigator.

He was a complication I didn't need. I may regret it later, but first, I wanted one night with him. I couldn't resist his sensual pull.

It was a shame really to not reincarnate him. He would make a potent vampire; the aura of danger and sex hovered around him. When I tasted him last night, his blood had been better than any wine. Maybe he was one of the chosen.

I shook my head. No way was I going to reincarnate him. He was too beautiful to corrupt, too perfect. I would be lower than the men I killed if I changed him.

"You dreamed about us making love, didn't you?" I leaned toward him, caressing his cheek, blocking his memories. My lips so close to his, I gave into the temptation and slid my tongue over his full lower lip. Oh, yes. I adored those pouty lips. "There is no reason for you to dream about it any longer."

His sharp intake of breath was all the encouragement I

needed. My fingers trembled as I threaded them through his cool dark hair. I floated in a sensual haze. My mouth, traveling behind his ear, stopped long enough to nip his earlobe before laving the skin over the throbbing artery running down his neck. I wanted another sip of that rich flavor.

His bold hand slipped up my thigh and cupped my pussy, drawing a gasp from me as a thank you.

He whispered into my ear, "Your place or mine?"

After blinking a few times, my eyes focused on the delicious man hovering over me. I never had a human affect me in such a way. Like I was blood drunk. Even when I feed on my bondsmen, I never lost my wits. I took a handful of seconds to register his question.

"Yours. I believe it's nearer," I answered, slurring a couple of words.

A question flared in his eyes, but I ignored it. No need to admit that I'd made it a point to find out where he was staying.

# Chapter 5

## *Tori*

The drive to his hotel had a surreality to it.

High on his seductive masculinity, everything made me laugh. In a basic way, he reminded me of Wolfric. Ronan's allure was similar to my master's way of captivating everyone by merely walking into a room.

It had been too long since I felt this way. Happy and maybe a little enamored. I'd worry over my vulnerability later. Tomorrow could certainly take care of itself. Here and now were more important.

I reminded myself over and over again, Ronan had no idea I was a vampire.

Within moments of arriving, we stumbled into his hotel room, kissing and caressing each other. The door slammed shut. With my arms wrapped around his strong, muscled neck, I played with his silky hair. He slipped his hands down to cup my ass and thrust his stiff cock against my mons. I almost came from the wonderful rhythmic pressure.

He walked me backwards until the back of my knees hit the edge of the bed. Heat flowed off him in waves. I reveled in sliding my hands down over his biceps, across his pecs, and lower to his warm, taut abdomen. He started unbuttoning his shirt and my hands worked on the snap and zipper of his jeans. In no time, we stripped every piece of clothing from his body. Roped muscles lined his arms and legs, revealing he was a man of exercise, maybe a long-distance runner. Abs and pecs defined enough for my fingers to tingle with need to feel the dips and swells to his groin.

The erotic picture he portrayed would be burned into my memory for many centuries to come.

I moved around him. He turned with me, keeping his eyes on mine. Then I pushed his shoulders. He fell backwards onto the bed. I stepped away again to admire his toned body. He stretched over the white bedspread, his hands almost touching the headboard while slender feet remained planted on the floor. Every muscle tightened and then relaxed on display to captivate. My gaze stopped at his most gorgeous thick cock—oh, I did enjoy that particular view—hard and stretched across his flat belly.

I lifted my gaze to his face. Half-closed eyes glittered between thick eyelashes, revealing every bit of his lust-filled thoughts.

Unable to resist, I firmly gripped his cock and lowered my mouth, deep-throating him until his moan ended on a sigh. So many decades of practice helped me satisfy him. As I sucked and tongued, my fingers played with the tight sac beneath. My concentration almost got away from me, when my fangs started to drop as he gripped my head and sped up my ministrations.

Not wanting to hurt him or be cheated of my own satisfaction, I tugged at his hands and pulled away.

Lust had grabbed me by the throat—what a play of words—and without another thought for foreplay, I slipped out of my clothes and bra. I bit my bottom lip staring down at the wet dream of a man. With my gaze concentrating on his cock, I pushed down my panties, gave them a careless toss over my shoulder, and promptly straddled him.

"Love a woman who doesn't waste time," he said with a wide grin.

I trailed one hand down his chest to stomach to his erection. I was growing rather fond of his cock. My fingertips traced the pulsating vein.

"I believe in seizing the moment," I said in a whisper. My fingers wrapped around him.

Once again, my fangs tried to drop. One of the drawbacks of letting myself become overexcited. I was so used to biting my bondsmen when we fucked. Maybe later in our liaison—what a fancy word for fucking, I'd been hanging around Wolfric too much, he loved the word—when I was more in control of my impulses.

Holding his thick shaft, I eased down, arching my back, moaning with pleasure as every inch filled me. The fullness felt so good. Touching his virile body engulfed all of my senses. Each firm muscle pushed me to explore him from angles that made his breath catch.

Ronan was unlike any of the human males I'd previously taken. In fact, more male than I'd ever experienced, he gave as much as I had to give. His fingers were so naughty as they delved into creases and forbidden passages.

His whispers of "harder, sweetheart" assured me my unnatural strength wasn't harming him.

Throughout the night we wrestled, twisted, and turned, savoring every position and technique imagined. I finally found a male who could match me in staying power and imagination.

One I must give up before the sun rose.

<<<>>>
Ronan

I pounded into her hot pussy from behind, driving us to a climax I was sure would kill me. Never in my life had I possessed such stamina. It was like I was on a high I hadn't experienced before.

The woman beneath me was the reason. From the moment I met her, the most intense emotions overloaded my system. All I could think about was her touch. Her smell. Her taste. I was a man obsessed.

With her, I felt powerful, a sexual animal staking a claim on his female.

One final thrust and then I dropped to the side, pulling her into my arms. My energy had been sapped by the all-night marathon of sex. My bones ached, especially my neck. Hell, I was getting old.

Tightening my hold, I maneuvered her across my torso. I couldn't stop touching her soft skin. Had any other woman in my life felt so silky?

When my fingers skimmed one side, I noticed something odd about the skin on her arm and hip, but when I leaned over to examine the anomaly, a strange prickling swept over me. She faced me and I looked into her eyes. They glowed with an eerie gold flame.

"Are you okay?" Her voice sounded so far away.

I swiped my damp forehead with the back of my hand.

"I feel odd." That was an understatement.

She smoothed my hair from my face.

"Rest. All will be fine," she reassured.

The world was twirling and fading in and out. My hand caressed her side, a large bruise showed where the asshole had hit her that evening.

"No broken bones?" I asked with each word becoming more slurred.

A sad grin broke across Tori's face.

I wanted to say, *be happy.* That I would take care of her, protect her. The hell with the money, I would find a way to pay it back. I'd fallen for her. I never experienced such overwhelming emotions before.

The room began to spin. What was happening? She was the most intoxicating woman I'd ever known, but this was more than a fantasy. She was a flesh-and-blood woman that made my body throb with only a touch. Hell, a look.

Frustrated with my tingling, numb lips, I opened my mouth but only garbled sounds emerged.

Her grin widened until she bared her teeth and that was when I saw them. Two unusually long, pointy canines. It was so unreal that I began to chuckle.

When had she picked up some *play* vampire teeth from one of her buddies at Bloodsucker's?

As if from a distance, I watched my hand reach out to cup her cheek. Instead, my arm became too heavy. My hand dropped weakly next to the pillow, palm up.

Her fingers pressed the side of my chin, turning my face the other way until I saw our reflection in a long mirror on the wall. Something was wrong. I saw my supine, naked body clearly, but Tori's reflection was faded, almost like an illusion.

Was I asleep? What a crazy dream. I waited for my imagination to conjure up more.

She leaned over me and ran her tongue behind my ear. Yes. I wanted more. What a hell of a dream.

Chill bumps shot down my arms and lust heated my blood. My cock and balls tightened until I was sure I would burst. Her mouth slipped to the nape of my neck and I felt her teeth scrape tender skin. The sensation was unlike anything I'd experienced before. Not like a human biting another in a moment of passion, but something more.

Then I heard a pop echo in my ears. The pain of canines sinking into my neck instantly melted into a hot surge of pure sexual pleasure, flowing through every muscle, tendon, blood vessel, artery, and hair follicle. I licked my lips, wanting to suck, taste the same gratification she partook.

My body began to drift from side-to-side like a leaf falling from a tree. When I landed back on the soft bed, Tori continued to caress my body as if I was her favorite pet. Of course, I acted like one for I panted and whimpered from need for more.

I tried to reach out for her, but my arms and hands refused to cooperate. Again her teeth sunk into my body, piercing the skin of one pec, beside a small, brown male nipple. My body bowed in immense waves of an orgasm. I was on fire but rejoiced the sensation.

Weak, but begging for more, minutes or possibly hours later, I sensed her teeth sinking into my inner right thigh, her nose pressed against one tight ball. Was she inhaling my scent? Her rhythmic sucking brought my body to another climax. How could my body produce more fluid?

My nerve endings prickled with tiny shots of electricity, causing me to writhe and shake. Intoxicated and exhausted by her expertise, I closed my eyes and dreamed of beautiful gold eyes and skin of hot silk.

<<<>>>

Tori

I stared at his limp, blood-smeared body on the bed.

Shit. I almost drained him dry. Carelessness had no place in my world. It could get me killed and those I cared about.

A vampire and a human. Humans were nothing but bondservants as caregivers or blood slaves, nothing more.

Who was I kidding? I'd worked so hard not to feel true emotions, but this inconsequential male waltzed into my life and turned all of my plans upside down. I refused to let him have my heart. I surely had thrown that useless organ away years ago.

It was merely sexual attraction. Connor had said I needed more bondsmen to keep me satisfied.

I took one last look at the man sleeping on his back with artist hands flung above his head. Sinfully dark hair hid part of his face, bringing a softness to such strong masculine features.

A steady rise and fall of his chest assured me he slept peacefully. Tomorrow, he'd remember our lovemaking, but the bite marks would be gone. He'd believe what happened at the end was only his imagination. A wild night of fucking.

Time for me to leave.

Still, my gaze kept straying to his cock. Such a beautiful instrument of delight. His soft phallus rested on dark, tight curls. I leaned over and licked, kissed, sucked at the tip. He groaned as it stretched and hardened. In pleasure or pain from being sorely used, I wasn't sure for I had enjoyed him immensely.

Never would I get enough of him. Never would I allow myself to try. Like they said, never was a long time and, in my case, an eternity.

Only with strong willpower I forced my feet to move away from the seductive man.

Throwing on my clothes, I eased out of the room,

slipped through the deserted lobby, and jumped into the waiting tinted-window Lexus before the sun rose completely.

<<<>>>

I was being stupid.

It was my own stubbornness that brought me there. Though I claimed I came to Bloodsucker's only to see if Ronan was okay, true that I could've sent Byron or Connor to his hotel. But I couldn't resist one more time.

Two days had passed since that night of hot passion and heated blood. Two nights since I'd tasted every inch of his delectable body. I could no longer hold out.

Several regular customers murmured their surprise at seeing me show up so early. Normally the earliest I'd arrived was eleven. This evening, I'd slunk in at ten.

I avoided his hotel. Too many beds to tempt me to take him again.

I had to remember taking too much blood in a short span would kill him. Already I regretted the number of bites I gave him. Thank goodness I hadn't let him taste my blood. It wouldn't make him a vampire, but a devoted bondsman to my every desire.

The only way to reincarnate one into a vampire was to drink them near to death, leaving only one breath separating them from this life and the next. Then the person would need to drink from my body and not just a sip.

In the past, when I was less trusting and more cynical, I would sprinkle my blood into the drinks I shared with Byron and Connor. The aftereffect was better than a drug. Just like my bite, it brought a euphoria and sexual need. It also slowed their aging. Not to the point of stopping it, but nearly doubled their life span. After a few years, I realized the two men had grown to care for me and I began to allow them to lick drops from my flesh.

Or had they felt that way all along? This growing feeling I had for Ronan was muddying my relationship with everyone.

Love was a new concept. I loved my family when I was human, but never a man, and certainly not to the point of wanting to spend my life with him. And the life I now offered was everlasting.

I'd decided Ronan was merely a craving I should do without. I needed to remember he was a dangerous and deadly distraction to my well-being. There was a reason the man showed up at the nightclub and my target's home at the same time I did.

Throughout the evening, several young and gorgeous men attempted to draw my attention. With a wave of a hand, I sent them sulking to other tables.

I didn't have time to fool with them. Once I saw with my own eyes Ronan had survived without any ill effects, I'd go on to my next target.

When my cell phone reached eleven o'clock, I almost left, afraid I was acting like a fool, and he wouldn't show up.

Me? Afraid?

I'm the champion of the underdog. The defender of the weak and helpless. Known for bitch-slapping a three-hundred-pound wife beater and laughing when he cried for his mother; the mother he had admitted to killing six years before with one blow and then had blamed a homeless man for the crime.

After another hour, I'd given in to self-pity and allowed several brave men to join me in my booth. But sadly, their macho antics and flowery compliments failed to bring me out of my melancholy mood.

Finally at twelve sharp, tension shot through my body when I spotted the tall, rangy figure of Ronan enter the club.

I snapped my attention back to the men in my booth. I remained sitting sideways on the bench seat with a leg stretched across one man's lap and my back pressed against another's bare hard chest, his shirt having been unbuttoned by me.

The man massaging my thigh and testing my limits slipped his hand too close to the heat between my legs. Handsome, though he gave off an eighties rock vibe. His dark eyes lined in black matched his leather clothes of the same color. Numerous sliver chains wrapped his waist signaling his love of Dominant/submissive play. I absent-mindedly tugged on his thick purple-dyed hair, twirling a lock on my finger, pretending to admire the color against my red fingernail polish.

I slowly turned my head back toward the entrance. The half-naked man I rested against lifted my hair and kissed my nape.

My heartbeat picked up speed. Yes. Vampires' hearts function like humans. Thus why stakes killed them when struck there. The rapid beating of my heart was due to the man standing across the club floor, not the one slobbering on me.

Ronan stood in the same spot as the other night, barely inside the club. He wore a white shirt, unbuttoned to show a little chest hair and sleeves shoved up his forearms. The shirt barely tucked into his black jeans gave him the air of a billionaire ready to play. His dark hair framed his masculine face, a five o'clock shadow emphasized his machismo even more. He watched me with the sleepy, sexy look I knew so well from the night before. But in this instance, his anger radiated from a wound-tight body.

My canines dropped instantly. Only my appetite to taste Ronan again could cause that. I hadn't reacted so carelessly without a lick of control since I was a fledgling. My core clenched with the remembered feeling of Ronan slamming into me. I needed him again.

"Leave me," I ordered.

They hesitated, obviously wanting to protest, but quickly changed their minds when I growled, flashing my fangs.

As if the crowd knew better than to stay in his way, they parted as he walked straight toward me. His steps sure and smooth, his eyes never strayed from mine. I loved how he did that.

That walk with broad shoulders and small hips moving as if he were a gunslinger took my breath away. Gunslinger or billionaire, the man was welcome to place his hands on me again. It mattered little if he wished to strangle me or fold me in his arms.

By the time Ronan made his way to my booth, I had salvaged my control and solemnly waited for his tirade.

"Playing slutty vampire again?" Before I could take offense, he slid in next to me and covered my hands with his. "From now on, play with me and no one else. Understood?"

Would he ever stop surprising me?

"Pardon?"

"Are you okay?"

His clean scent of soap and heated skin had my brain spinning. "What?"

"Dammit, I was worried about you. Blood was all over

me when I woke up and you were nowhere to be found. You scared the shit out of me. I should turn you over my knee." He lifted my hands up as he scrutinized me from head to toe. "You look fine. In fact you look wonderful."

I laughed, soaking in his concern and regard. Like most women in the world, I enjoyed a handsome man's attention.

Perversely, the idea of my torso draped over his lap and his broad hand smacking my bare ass turned me on. My body's uncustomary electrifying reaction to him never ceased to amaze me.

"I'm fine. The blood was from you."

"You're like a wild cat in bed and a few scratches from these"—he kissed my palms and then sucked in the tip of a forefinger before finishing—"sexy long fingers drive me stark raving mad with desire for you."

He leaned toward me, looking deep into my eyes while smoothing my hair away from my face and then his gaze dropped to my mouth.

What sane woman could resist his invitation?

My passion took over as I clasped his head and brought his lips to mine. My need for this man was so great it was frightening.

I trembled. I had to stop. I was losing control. If I didn't stop now, in a matter of seconds I would have him stretched across the table and my teeth piercing his neck while I rode him like a bucking stallion. I needed space from this man.

Furious at my lack of willpower, I jerked away and scooted out of the booth. Restraining my vampire speed down to a human pace, I still made it to the door and outside before Ronan caught up with me in the parking lot.

"What the hell happened back there?" He grabbed my scarred arm and placed his body in front of me, stopping my forward movement. "You're going to another name on the list," he accused.

"The list. What are you talking about?"

"My client gave it to me to find you. It was a list of men you and your sorority sisters hazed."

"Sorority sisters? I have no idea what you're talking about."

"So who was Robert Moore to you?" he asked.

"Listen. It's best that you forget about whatever list your client gave you. Someone is playing a trick on you. Now get out of my way." A flick of my wrist could send him flying through the air, but I balked at harming him more than I had already by taking so much of his blood the other night.

"Try me. How can I understand if you won't explain?" He took a couple of steps back, releasing my arm. "Whatever crusade you think you're on, it's wrong. You need to let the police handle those fellows. You're a suspect in Moore's murder and who knows how many more."

*Hundreds across the nation over the many years.* The thought was frightening. What would Ronan think if he knew? But I was a little surprised Joe Carson had told the police a woman beat him up. Or had Ronan reported her to the authorities?

"You don't know anything about it," I said, frustrated with the whole useless argument.

"True. So tell me. I can help."

No, he wouldn't.

"It's best that you keep out of it. The police already believe you're involved too."

"I'll be fine. They can help," he said.

Why wouldn't he listen? "It's only the ex-cop in you that makes you believe that."

He stiffened and said under his breath, "Fuck." His eyes narrowed.

I knew I had gone too far to stop now.

"How did you know I was on the force?" he asked in a soft voice. "You had me investigated," he stated before I could think of an answer.

No way was I telling him I could read his emotions, his past. Though I worked at blocking our connection every time he was near. Self preservation and all that. Feeling someone's pain was an experience I avoided at all cost. From his dark expression alone, he was feeling betrayed. Maybe it was for the best.

Time was wasting and I had work to do. Making him mad would guarantee he wouldn't interfere. I wanted Ronan elsewhere and safe. I had gotten what I came for, assurance that he was okay.

"Your full name is Ronan Caleb Michaels. Your father died last year from lung cancer and you owe money to nearly every relation you have in the state of Illinois, along with your cousin. During your father's illness, your wife divorced you. You lost your job in the Chicago Police Department because your superior found out that you had borrowed money from Gino, who, in turn, has mob connections." I watched for his reaction. Nothing showed. No anger. No grief. He looked more dead than I was. In an indifferent tone, I asked, "Did I miss anything?"

Of course, I had Connor do some snooping around.

"No. You got the gist of it. It would appear your investigator does a better job than I do. I don't know anything about you. Not really."

The flash of hurt in his eyes almost made me cave-in and—do what? I couldn't reincarnate him or have him in my life as a bondservant. Ronan wasn't bondservant material.

Scanning him in the white shirt and black jeans, his olive skin and dark hair, I realized he would make a dangerous vampire in so many ways. Looks, knowledge, physically able to do big damage, and an attitude that revealed he may not think twice about killing a person.

And hazardous to my heart. With thoughts of that sort I definitely knew it was time to end it.

"He doesn't sleep with those he investigates. He just does his job." Not quite true, but blinded by anger, I let the lie spill out.

His head jerked as if I hit him.

"It's time we parted company." My heart ached. The pain compared to the time the psycho filleted me. No. Correct that. It was worse. I had let him get too close to me.

"Yeah. You're right. I need to concentrate on my job."

I turned to walk away and stopped. Looking back, I said, "You know that I don't have a brother."

"Yeah. I guessed as much."

I watched his jaw clench and eyes harden.

"It's for the best." Every inch of my being screamed that it was wrong, but I had to believe Ronan would be safer this way.

He stared at me for a few tortuous seconds, then turned on his booted heel and left.

# Chapter 6

## *Edgar Brannon*

I enjoyed the show they put on for me in the parking lot.

Hidden in the dark shadows of my black limousine's back seat, I spied on all types of iniquitous activities.

She was a delightful sight. All woman. I looked down at the grainy picture in my hand. I never imagined she was so tall and well-formed. If I hadn't had definite plans for her, I might be tempted to keep her for a while to play with her.

That type of indulgence wouldn't give me what I really wanted. Power. The power she possessed. For a nearly ninety-year-old woman, she was in perfect condition. She didn't look a day over twenty-three. Soon I would find out the secret to her eternal youth.

I watched as she slid into her Maserati and cranked it up. Red tail lights streaked by the limo as she drove down the street, headed for the interstate.

Every day, I ordered my driver to cruise by the large house she'd recently built. I had tracked down the contractor, and found him to be very generous with the plans. That was, once he received a substantial pile of cash.

From the outside, it looked like so many others in the upscale neighborhood, but the brick house had a large, hidden underground room. Lined in thick steel, the room was protected by a high-tech fingerprint lock and a concealed entryway. I knew where the entrance was.

Obviously, Victoria Amherst was cautious and had built a panic room. Or was it to hide her secret? Her formula or her fountain of youth or some far-fetched time capsule?

I relaxed into the leather seat, gazing out the side window.

Decades ago, in my childish innocence, I had no idea my brother would be dead a month before Christmas. Sure, he'd been a sick son of a bitch, but he'd been the best big brother any five-year-old could ask for.

As a child, it had been a yearly tradition for me to search for my Christmas presents after the big shopping day for the season. One fateful night, I tiptoed down to the basement to see if they were hidden there.

Only once had I dared to look under the numerous blood-soaked white sheets, though the shapes told me enough. I'd been fascinated by the carved bodies. Under one sheet, a woman's bare chest faintly rose and fell. She'd been alive, either asleep or passed out. That woman had been Tori. I'd believed my brother to be a skillful artist for the living and dead. Talented, sensitive, and thoughtful, Tim had been misunderstood.

I hadn't found my presents that year, but I became fascinated by his work. He would often let me watch as he worked as long I'd promised not to tell others.

Then my life changed one morning and was never the same. Usually Tim had breakfast waiting for me when I woke. I'd searched his bedroom, master bath, and the back-yard. After a lengthy time for a five-year-old, I became hungry and started to cry. My brother had never left me alone before. Then I remembered his artwork in the basement. I'd been certain he'd forgotten the time as he worked.

When I'd found his body, I threw up.

I took a deep breath, seeing my reflection in the limo's side window. Tears streamed down my face. I hadn't realized. Using a linen handkerchief from the inside pocket of my suit coat, I wipe my face. I wanted to forget, but it was important to remember. My hatred for the woman recharged my revenge and energized my ambition to discover her secrets.

The horrifying scenes flashed behind my eyes. Ligaments and muscles glistened eerily in the fluorescent light. His neck and chest split open. His heart had been missing. The head almost faced backwards, broken ribs stuck out of his torso like white sticks with strings of meat spilling onto the floor. Blood sprinkled all of the walls, but not as much— I would later learn—as there should have been.

I'd stumbled upstairs and found his cell phone next to his bed and then ran to the kitchen. A daisy magnet held the police department's number on the refrigerator. My brother had made sure I would know how to call in case of an emergency. Tim had always understood how weak a child could be in times of peril. Seeing someone you love in pieces was certainly one of those times.

After dialing the local police force, I'd waited for them while sitting next to my big brother, holding his head in my lap. I had wailed as I turned his head until his sightless blue eyes stared at me. The police officers were nice to me but I didn't like them. They said horrible things about Tim, especially after they found his art projects. They never understood. I didn't like how they looked at me as if I was weird or something to pity.

No one pitied me now.

By the time I entered my sixth foster home, I'd found I could manipulate those around me, and they would gladly give me whatever I wanted. When I turned to lonely older women, they loved giving me money for my attention. Later, I moved to the next logical step. I used the funds I saved to buy old houses and then rent them, or buy businesses and lease the spaces. By the time I reached thirty, I was a multimillionaire and ready to find my brother's killer.

A few years ago, I bought the house my brother died in. It was a shambles as no one wanted to buy the "Hell House" where so many women had died. Luck was with me. As I started the remodeling, in his bedroom I found what my brother had hidden under a loose floor board. Inside was a long box filled with a small book and photos my brother had taken of his women. Their names written on most of the backs.

Two grainy pictures were of the woman I saw beneath the sheet and on one of the pictures was her name, Victoria Amherst. That woman wasn't listed in the papers among the bodies. She had to be connected to my brother's murderer.

Yes, Lady Luck was fickle, but not to Edgar Brannon. The woman in the picture had returned to Birmingham. She returned on the day I found the picture. Coincidence? No. My brother was telling me something from the grave.

I tapped on the glass between the backseat and the driver. Wordlessly, my driver took me back to the hotel. The same hotel where I reserved a room for the investigator.

I chuckled. It'd been too easy. A year ago, I had just happened to be on a business trip in Chicago and saw the scandal. *A Local Medal-Winning Police Officer Fired For Receiving a Loan From a Notorious Mob Shylock.* I'd heard money had poured in to help the ex-police officer but he refused it. "Pride goeth before destruction," and Ronan Michaels was full of pride.

It was pure genius. Distract the woman until I arranged her downfall into my clutches. After I learned her secret, she would understand that what my brother had done to her was nothing compared with what I planned.

# Chapter 7

## *Ronan*

I threw my keys onto the bed and stripped off my jacket, throwing it on top. Pissed? I was more than pissed. I was furious.

The woman was a total nut case.

One moment, she was all over me, and then the next, she was telling me to get lost. My body hummed with the memories of our night together. I craved her so much. During our time together, I forgot all of my obligations.

For days, I searched for her, always ending each night at the club. No sign. No one had seen her. No unexplained murders during that time. That didn't say much as she could be hiding the bodies now.

My obsession with her was pushing me to act as bonkers as she was. I had a job, and allowing my dick to lead me around wasn't getting it done. I owed a ton of money.

Though a first cousin to Gino through my mother, for years I had avoided contact with that branch of the family. When my father fell ill and our savings and insurance money ran out, I'd tapped out the few close relatives I had. My last recourse had been Gino.

Gino worked for ATR Industries in Chicago. Everyone in law enforcement knew import-export business was a front for Arturo Salvatore Renata, a New Jersey mobster. But desperate times brought desperate measures.

When I went to my cousin for the loan, I'd been beyond desperate. My wife had walked out after the bank foreclosed on our house. My last hope of saving Dad was a new treatment that cost more than I earned in a year, but I had to try.

After I got the money and Dad started the treatments, the doctors informed us the cancer had spread into every vital organ. All that was left was to make him comfortable. How could someone be comfortable when every part of their body was in pain?

I wiped my face as if it could remove the memories of those horrible weeks leading up to my dad's death. The funeral had been small and tasteful. No more extraordinary than the man who'd died.

He'd been a good dad, fiercely proud of his law enforcement son. He died never knowing the insurance had run out and I was in debt up to my ears.

The investigation money Brannon had paid up-front had already been sent to Gino and covered me for the next few months. It had only taken care of half of what I owed him, and the interest was piling up while I fucked a gorgeous, unpredictable woman who was possibly a man-killer. Supposedly, she was being chased by another murderer. If I believed what Edgar Brannon relayed to me. No matter what the truth was, time was running out fast, and I needed to find that woman and decide what to do next.

I couldn't turn Tori over to Brannon, not until I knew the man's true motives. But I badly needed money or I might disappear into the dark depths of Smith Lake with cement shoes.

I'd seen Gino's man sitting in the lobby of the hotel. He'd grinned when I walked by this evening. My cousin wasn't taking a chance I'd skip out on him without paying.

After a quick shower, I stepped out of the bathroom and my phone rang.

Could it be Tori?

I shook my head. How sad was it to keep thinking of a woman who didn't want anything to do with me? Frustrated with the situation, I forgot to check the screen when I answered.

"What?"

"Is that any way to talk to your generous cousin?" Gino's greasy voice shot a chill down my back.

His massive ego constantly required stroking and I refused to play the game. No matter how much I owed the asshole. Considering the amount of interest accumulated on the loan, Gino wasn't doing me any favors.

"Sorry." I almost heaved. "I was busy. What can I do for you?"

"I wanted to thank you for that big chunk of change. So glad one of my own flesh and blood hadn't shirked on a deal. I expect the balance in a reasonable length of time."

"You'll get your money." I gritted my teeth, holding back what I wanted to say, but knew it wouldn't pay to provoke Gino.

"That's my boy. Lacy was wrong about you. She told me that you would disappear and I wouldn't see a red cent. Don't you love it when women are wrong?" Not expecting an answer from me, he added, "You know, you should've taken better care of her. Ladies like her need a lot of attention. She can't get enough—"

"Is there anything else you need to tell me?" I interrupted, not wanting to hear any more of my ex-wife's opinions. Gino was only trying to see how far he could push me until I exploded and looked like an idiot. Lacy had left me for Gino...more like, for Gino's money.

"I'll let you get back to work." He chuckled in his greasy way. "Time's money. *Ciao*."

"Asshole," I said to the silent phone. Every successful criminal I ever met was a self-serving, egotistic sadist. He loved being part of what brought me low, and the icing on the cake for Gino was marrying my ex-wife. Good riddance. He could have the gold-digging shrew.

When the chips were down and funds in short supply, she couldn't take being married to a lowly cop any longer. I had no idea she'd been seeing Gino on the side, but the day after our divorce was final, she and Gino flew to Las Vegas and got married.

But Gino was right. Time *was* money and I had a woman to track down. Again.

<<<>>>

Tori

I checked the number on the mailbox. Yep. It was the right one.

Normally, I would have driven by the address days in advance, ensuring oversights to be at a minimum. Connor had watched the pervert and noted his routine, passing on the info to me, but with Ronan's constant surveillance and his use of that damn list, we had to restrict our movements. Though it hadn't stopped me from my campaign. I had become cautious and less boastful by having Connor handle the clean up of the bodies instead of letting the authorities find them. I preferred for everyone to know what happened to the people who misused children or women. I was certain it would frighten those contemplating that sick path, but the police become insanely focused on multiple cases with an obvious link, all perverts. I couldn't take a chance, especially in town.

So the two perverts I took care of a few days ago, Connor had cleaned up and dumped the bodies in a marshy area in the next county.

The residence at the end of a neat asphalt drive was the nicest home on the block, regardless it was a double-wide. Flowers and well-trimmed shrubs framed the front yard and a brightly painted swing set swayed in the light breeze.

Over the years, I'd tracked down serial killers, pedophiles, and wife-beaters. Some lived in fine mansions and others in the seediest dumps, but all had something in common. A sterility to them that even defies trash-strewn yards. They didn't look lived in and loved. The mobile home in front of me had a different look. Loved and well-cared-for, but not sterile.

Connor's report had no mention of pets, but I still used caution walking toward the back. No need to alert anyone. The Doberman the other night wasn't really anything I wanted to repeat. An oversized window with curtains open provided the best view inside. Was the man still inside?

A worn, green couch sat beneath the window and two recliners to the right, all facing a large-screen television. The room was clean except for a few magazines scattered on the floor near one recliner. It all looked so normal. Staying perfectly still for a few seconds, I listened for any sound coming from the back of the mobile home. No one was home.

I walked around to the front and squeezed the doorknob. Metal crunched and pieces fell to the small wooden platform. The door didn't budge. Deadbolt. I stooped down and looked inside the opening left behind from the destroyed doorknob. The wood was thin. I slammed my fist into the hole. Dammit. I cut my hand. Blood streamed down my arm. Placing the side of my hand in my mouth, I sucked the wound until it started to close. Then I carefully reached through the space and flipped the latch. The door drifted open with a creak.

Without a light, I checked the bedrooms. The little girl's room was filled with white-and-pink gingham curtains, bedspread, and a small cloth-covered table near the bed, giving the room a fairy princess look. Everything looked so new. Was the bastard feeling bad about what he'd done?

It was horrible enough when pedophiles preyed on small children, but when it was their own child...incest made it horrendous. I left the sad little room and decided to wait for him in his bedroom.

The room I walked into had bare walls, no pictures and no nick-knacks. This was more what I'd expected. Sterile.

A double bed and a dresser filled the room. In the closet, his clothes hung to one side and a large box on the other side. Inside were miscellaneous tools and a couple of badminton rackets.

The front door rattled. I rushed across the room and stood behind the bedroom door.

"Oh, no. Someone has broken in. Bastards." A few more words were mumbled.

I watched through the crack made by the hinges on the half-closed door.

He carried a bundled blanket and clothes in his arms and walked into the little girl's room, Then he came out empty-handed.

I waited until he entered his bedroom and jumped him. Probably six-two and two-hundred-thirty pounds, he didn't go down easily. Even with my vampire strength, he took my hit like a linebacker.

"What the hell?" He staggered a couple of steps before falling to his butt.

"I'm your judge, jury, and executioner." They needed to hear why they were dying.

"I haven't done anything." He struggled to his knees and with a twist of his body, his arm swung out, flinging me off balance.

Smashing into the thin wall, creating a shoulder-sized indention, I took a step toward him.

"Your kind doesn't deserve to live. Preying on those weaker and smaller."

I'd forgotten to wear my gloves. I blamed how my mind had become cloudy with need for Ronan. How had he become so important to me in such a short time?

I could tell by the man's face something wasn't right. His face crumpled in tears and soul-sucking sadness.

"Did Maxine send you? When did she get out of prison?" he asked as he whimpered between the questions.

I had no idea what he was talking about, and I wanted it over with.

"Sam Kerry, you're charged with child molestation, sodomy, pornography, and death of your daughter. As your executioner, I will show you mercy in your death. More mercy than you did your own daughter."

"You're crazy, lady. How are your eyes glowing like that? What drug are you on? If you don't leave, I'll call the cops." He took a step back toward the cell phone sitting on the floor near the bed.

In a blink of an eye, I stood next to him, my hands grabbing his neck. He gurgled when I lightly pressed my thumb against his windpipe.

"It's my personal mission to see that creatures like you never enjoy another breath." The menacing face from many years ago replaced the man's face in front of me. A red haze of hate and anger threatened to take over my reason. Fighting the hallucination, I released my grip and stepped back. With a shake of my head, I rubbed my eyes and reached out for the man again.

"Daddy?"

The tiny voice sent a chill down my back. He had another daughter? Another victim?

"Heather! Run, baby! Go! Now! Run to Jennifer's!" The man edged along the wall toward the phone again.

The little girl stood in the bedroom doorway with a rag doll clutched in one hand and a blanket in the other. Her long, brown hair reached her waist and her toes poked out from under a long, pink gown.

"Why are the woman's eyes funny looking?"

I ducked my head, not wanting to scare the little girl.

"You better do as your father said," I ordered in a deeper voice caused by long canines. Anger boiled inside me. Anger at the man inflicting his perversion on another helpless being and sadness in knowing this child would be alone tomorrow.

"Don't hurt my daddy." Then the little girl did the oddest thing. She ran to me and grabbed my arm. Unprepared to block her hold or the result from her touch, I was engulfed by terrifying images and raw emotions.

In the shadowy world of visions, I saw a woman slap the little girl.

*"You'll tell the man in the black robe whatever I tell you. Your no-good father will never get custody of you and your*

sister, even if I have to lie to the President himself," the woman shouted, spittle spraying the little girl's face. Sadness poured through my body and I shook from head to toe, experiencing the child's feelings.

Another vision from the girl flashed and I began to realize something was terribly wrong.

*Sam Kerry on his knees crying as he pleaded with the woman, "Don't take them away from me. You never wanted the girls. Why are you doing this?"*

*The woman laughed and then said, "You, son of a bitch. I've hated you ever since you turned down that promotion. We could be living in a real house with nice cars and lots of money by now. Since you kept me from what I wanted, you can't have what you want either. Poetic justice, I say. They'll fire your ass when I tell them you molested the girls and the judge will make certain you never get your precious princesses."*

*"I've never touched them like that." His words became muffled as he covered his face with trembling hands.*

*"It only takes doubt." Her face red and twisted with hatred, the woman sneered and turned to the little girls. "Both of you. Get your butts in the car now."*

Then the vision faded. But I knew the truth. The mother had killed the older sister. She had hit the child once too often. She'd accused her husband of being the abuser. The dad would have protected them if he'd realized they were being mistreated while he was away at work. His sixty hours a week job paid the bills the woman had created in her need to outdo their neighbors. In his ignorance, he never imagined the mother would harm them.

I stumbled back, and shook my head, trying to wipe away the horrifying images. Momentarily blind to my surroundings, I blinked several times in an effort to regain my vision.

The man had finally snatched his little girl away from me. Eyes wide in terror, they huddled together across the room, staring at me.

I almost killed an innocent man.

Backing out of the room, I watched as the man picked up his phone and started punching numbers. On reaching the hallway, I turned and ran for the front door.

The night air was cool and moist against my face, and newly mown grass gave off a sweet scent. Tree frogs trilled in unison in the nearby woods, bringing back bittersweet memories of my childhood.

By the time I reached the Maserati, I felt like a rag doll, limp and weary. I drove aimlessly through the countryside. Hours later, I looked with tired eyes at the sky. Time for me to return home or I would be caught in the morning sunlight. With only seconds to spare before sunbeams burst over the trees, I pressed the button for the garage door to close.

Byron knocked on the driver's window. I still sat in my car. It wasn't safe there. Though heavy material covered the windows, it was never intended for me to be in the garage during the day. Besides the death sleep would be taking over my body soon. I hadn't fed as I had planned while on my mission. I needed blood.

My world was falling apart. First, my infatuation with a human and, second, I almost killed an innocent person. Had I killed innocent people before and never known it? I always wore gloves to block any wayward visions from the perps I killed. Before that, I would try to block the memories, but during unexpected touches be bombarded by their foul deeds, almost being destroyed by their past. It was only a fluke the little girl touched me, and I hadn't blocked her memories. She saved her daddy tonight.

I never had to worry about someone interfering with my mission. The victims were usually grateful and certainly not crying for the criminal's safety.

Byron helped me out of the car and without a word led me to the bathroom. I allowed him to undress and help me into the filled tub topped off with bubbles.

The world appeared gray and heavy. Dazed, I sat in the water until it turned tepid and the bubbles disappeared.

From a distance, I felt Byron's hands massage my back and scrub my body without crossing the line between cleanliness and sexual play. After about fifteen minutes of his tender attention, I remembered why keeping him was the best decision I ever made. More often than not, he knew how far he could push without getting killed.

"Byron."

After pulling me out of the tub and securing a towel around my torso, he looked into my eyes. "Yes, mistress?"

"Thank you for not asking questions."

"You know I would do anything for you, mistress."

With another towel he knelt at my feet and began to dry my ankles and behind my knees. He stopped when I stepped away. I turned to slip on my silk pajamas before crawling into the nearest bed. I was too tired to dismiss Byron and go into my underground chamber.

After the week I had, it felt good to stretch out and look at a desirable man who expected little from me. A man I could control without question. Was that really what I wanted?

"Mistress?"

I chuckled. He rarely called me mistress except to be

sarcastic or if he was worried about me. So far I counted three. He must be terribly worried.

"Yes, Byron?" I closed my eyes, but smiled when he added another one to the count.

"Mistress, your skin is cold and the water didn't warm you. You haven't fed tonight." His voice held no question. When I didn't answer, he asked, "Can I serve you?"

My canines dropped with the thought of sinking them into his strong, delectable neck. Pleasure prickled over my torso but at the same time I wished Ronan was there.

A sigh escaped my lips. It was time to move on and forget about him. Time to think about my uncertain future and what I planned to do.

Byron took the sigh as acquiescence and climbed into the bed beside me. He'd stripped off his shirt and tight leather pants. He pressed his lips to my cheek. Then he lifted his head, holding his hair to one side and exposing his neck.

The long throbbing vein was luscious looking. His whole body had the sensuality of a young rock star. The tattoo on the back of his neck proclaimed him to be a vampire's blood slave, a bondsman. A red heart with black drops of blood dripping from two holes. Those had been there before he came to my house. His previous master had it done. I didn't require markings for my servants.

The heat from his skin drew me. I clasped his thick hair and before I could reconsider, my teeth sank into his flesh. Sheer bliss flowed through me. My hands caressed his taut body and grasped his hard and full cock.

Within a few minutes of caressing, and squeezing, and pulling, he came in my hand and began to whimper his shame. I stopped long enough to assure him I wasn't angry.

Wanting another taste of his blood and to calm him, I lifted his arm and clamped my teeth near his elbow.

His blood was so clean. No drugs allowed to sully the purity of his blood. It irritated Byron but I knew he craved my touch, craved my bite more than any drug, and resisted the possibility of losing an opportunity to be chosen as my bedmate for the day.

# Chapter 8

## *Ronan*

That woman drove like a bat out of hell when she hit the long, winding Old Springville Road. She had apparently let me follow her that first night, but not this evening. I lost her as I reached Chalkville Road.

I sat at the crossroads between Chalkville Mountain Road and Sweeney Hollow Road. There were two possibilities on the list. One was in Heflin, almost at the Alabama–Georgia border going toward Atlanta, and another in Center Point, northeast of Birmingham.

It made sense to drive to the nearest one. Only the woman was unpredictable. After waiting for a time with no sight of Tori, I headed for the interstate.

Over an hour later, it was confirmed, I had picked the wrong one. It wasn't the one near Georgia. So I had turned around and driven to the double-wide. The horizon was painted a grayish-pink while the blue lights from seven police cars flashed on the surrounding pine trees.

I slowed my Mustang and watched the uniforms and civilians mill around the mobile home. Obviously, Tori had been there and left, but I didn't see an ambulance. When an elderly couple walked by my car, I rolled down my window.

"What's going on?"

The heavyset woman looked at me with suspicion, but the equally heavyset man perked up. His obvious pleasure in recounting exciting news to someone outweighed any qualms of gossiping with a stranger.

"Well, it appears that Sam Kerry has bad luck when it comes to women. A crazy female broke into his home and tried to kill him and his daughter. My wife and I believe it was a friend of his ex-wife, Maxine." He jerked his bald head toward the woman standing next to him. "Probably her friend escaped prison and decided to punish them for Maxine. His ex-wife was pure evil. She surely had the devil in her."

One thing I knew for certain, Tori would never harm a child. People like the man in front of me blew stories out of proportion and ruined innocent people's lives in the process.

The man started rambling about some niece of his in Kansas, so I interrupted him. "The man and child are okay?"

"Yeah. Sam got a little bruising on the side of his face, and a scraped elbow. His girl was babbling on about a strange woman with glowing eyes and big teeth." The gossipy man chuckled. "Children do have imaginations."

When I looked at the double-wide again, I spotted a deputy walking toward me. It was best if I left.

"Thanks. Well, I better get going. Thanks again, folks."

I turned my car toward Birmingham, my hotel, and a change of clothes before heading for Bloodsucker's.

Tori hadn't killed the man. Was the child's presence the reason? Compassion was obviously not a foreign concept to her and maybe the reason she pushed me away was some misguided notion of protection. From her? Or the police?

There was hope for her yet.

The memory of our night together was enough to stiffen more than my resolve. Lifting my hips, I straightened my jeans and adjusted my cock. I had never had gotten so hard from a mere thought until I met Tori. At least, not since I was a teenager.

I had no business wanting her. Despite the beautiful package, something wasn't quite right. Every time I was around her, something happened to my libido, and all thought of learning more about her flew out the window.

What facts I knew were from the unreliable source of Edgar Brannon and his crazy accusations.

Chances were, she'd gone to college and participated in a revenge prank that went too far. Possibly, she'd murdered pedophiles. And certainly, she was deadly with her hands and feet.

I'd seen her skill when I'd walked through the open door and saw Carson flying through the air. Sam Kerry was the second man on the list I knew of who Tori hadn't killed. What else did I know?

When I made love with her, it was like exploring a new world. Energizing. Mind blowing. Never knowing what to expect. Having her long legs wrapped around my waist made my heart nearly pound out of my chest. The way she looked at me as if I was the sun and stars. Her big brown eyes glowing with anticipation whenever I entered her warmth.

With a slight shake of my head, I quickly realized my car was headed straight for a ditch. With a smooth maneuver, I returned it to the road. That was a close call. It was time to keep my head out of the clouds and my car between the lines. Later, I'd decide what to do about the enigmatic woman called Tori.

When I arrived at the hotel and walked across the lobby, I was greeted by Detective Jameson. *What a terrific way to end a shitty night.*

Out of the corner of my eyes, I noted Gino's man stand from his seat and walk down a side hallway. He didn't want the man's attention either.

"Hello, Detective." I waited for the detective to reach me. If I was going to be arrested, I saw no reason to go up six floors.

"Mr. Michaels."

The detective's face was an unemotional mask, except his cynical eyes glittered with pleasure.

My butt was sunk.

"Is there something I can help you with?" Why should I make it any easier on the detective than I had already?

"Mr. Michaels," he formally said. A corner of my mouth lifted. So it was going to be like that. By the book. "You're under arrest for suspicion of the murders of Robert Moore and Billy Spencer."

I recognized the names. Robert had died the first night I'd met Tori. Billy Spencer's home was where I had gone before arriving late at Sam Kerry's. There was no way Tori could've been at two places at once.

Then I spotted a uniformed officer standing between me and the front door. Another one grabbed my arm, ordering me to put my hands behind my back. As the detective recited the Miranda warning, a crowd began to form.

Most of the people were dressed in business causal, but one young man stood out. Dressed in skin-tight, black leather pants and a black silk shirt opened to his navel, he watched me with a smug grin. His wavy, shoulder-length brown hair and flashy clothes gave him a Jim Morrison vibe. Who was he?

<<<>>>

I rubbed my wrists, then stretched to ease the kinks in my back. After sitting in a metal chair for over four and half hours, I'd actually looked forward to reclining on the thin mattress of a cell's bunk.

The noise of metal clanging in the distance and the snores of a nearby inmate assaulted my ears. Body odors fought with the smell of vomit mixed with sanitation cleanser, which almost overpowered my senses. The last time I had experienced such a mixture, I'd been a young rookie touring lock-up.

Never would I have imagined being suspected of murder, no less arrested. For ten years, I'd been the one who put the murderers away.

Tomorrow, I would have to start looking for a lawyer. For now I needed some rest. Staring at the spotted ceiling overhead, my over-stressed body began to loosen. My eyelids became heavy.

After staying up for over twenty-four hours, it didn't take much to fall asleep.

The hand shaking my arm brought me sitting up on the mattress, banging my head against the top bunk.

"Fuck." I rubbed the bump already forming beneath my hair.

"Michaels. Your lawyer's here for you." The guard backed out of the cell and stood to the side. "You're a lucky son of a bitch. Somehow after getting a judge out of bed, he got him to agree to set your bail."

I couldn't make heads or tails about what the guard was telling me, but I was all for leaving.

After they returned my personal items, I looked at the man waiting in front of the sergeant's desk. There were only two people I knew in Birmingham and I doubted Tori even knew I'd been arrested.

"Mr. Michaels, I'm Richard Hanson, legal counsel for Mr. Edgar Brannon. Would you please follow me?" The curly haired and squinty-eyed man handed me a business card before heading out of the building.

So it was Brannon who posted bail. Without a good reason not to, I followed the man into the early morning air. I shielded my eyes and looked away from the sun peeking between the buildings. I felt like a freaking night owl. For one reason or another, it had been days since I'd seen more than thirty minutes of daylight. The fresh air cleared the last cobwebs from my mind.

Hanson stopped beside a black stretch limousine. The back passenger's door opened and Brannon's voice came from inside. "Come, Mr. Michaels, I'll give you a ride back to your hotel."

I hesitated. Edgar Brannon had lied. Brannon wasn't Tori's brother but he wanted the woman for something. One thing was for sure, I wanted to know the answer and the only way to find out was to go with him.

What did I have to lose? I was now a suspected murderer. What could be worse?

"Sure. Does this rig have a bar?" I ducked into the limo and closed the door.

<<<>>>

Tori

After changing my clothes for the evening, I exited my chamber and Byron was waiting for me, stretched out on what I thought of as the community bed. Bare-chested, with his black leather pants unsnapped and riding low on his hips, he oozed sex and rock and roll.

"Can I assume you've seen him?" I asked.

He moved to his knees and began crawling slowly toward the end of the bed. The catlike movements showed every refined muscle in his arms and down his back. His pants slipped down enough for me to see he wore no underwear.

I raised an eyebrow, amused by his display. He worked tirelessly every day to get between my legs, wanting me to take more blood, to play with his body, anything. He was shameless.

It was rather endearing but presently irritating as hell. I needed answers.

"Come to bed and I'll massage your back," he offered. He ran his hand down my scarred arm. "You've never told me how you came by them. It must've been horrible when they did not disappear. I had always thought vampires' bodies could heal any wound except those through the heart."

He liked touching the scars, commenting on them and asking questions. He had a fetish for any sign of trauma on a person's body. I wasn't sure why it fascinated him, but I refused to play. Giving or receiving pain was never one of my favorite pastimes.

And what I did to deviants was a mission, not a passion.

"It was done while I was human. The scars are slowly fading." Becoming tired of his cocky attitude, I commanded, "Now tell me about Ronan."

"He was released on bond." With a huff, he flopped on his back and crossed his arms, staring at the ceiling.

"Who posted bail?" I couldn't imagine he had the money to hire a lawyer.

"Some lawyer." Byron turned his head away.

From his expression, I decided he was hiding something. He hoped I would play his game and pet him and so much more.

"Byron?" My voice sounded stern in warning, as I was coming to the end of my patience.

Face stiff, he looked at me and gave in. "Richard Hanson, a lawyer for Brannon. Edgar Brannon."

Was he Ronan's client? Probably. Why was he interested in me? What did he hope to gain? Over the years, more than one man had escaped my justice or fate had intervened and they survived.

While I was thinking of the possibilities, Byron had taken my distraction as an opening to trail kisses over my scars. With his head turned to the side to kiss my arm, his hair fell away from his neck.

I loved the taste of his skin and the feel of the muscle beneath my lips. He won with his distraction. My canines dropped and without another thought, I sunk into his flesh. So fresh and sweet. My hand traveled to his groin. Yes. His cock was hard and pressed to his leather pants. I rubbed up and down the length. I leaned back and enjoyed the view. Long and beautiful beneath the soft leather. I should take a picture.

I licked a path down the covered cock. Even through the material, he smelled of man and sex. He felt wonderful to touch.

Byron and Connor had satisfied me for several years. Maybe I was wrong in trying to keep Ronan separate. I never thought I would want to add another. In fact, Ronan would be perfect to bring into the mix. They would help me forget, to forget that I was a monster. To immerse myself in the world of flesh and blood.

Byron nuzzled the top of my breasts. With a little pressure, my nipple would be exposed in the low-cut blouse. The mental image of him sucking on my nipple while I sucked on his neck brought a rush of heat to my pussy, but also unintentionally released my hold on blocking his thoughts.

I gasped. "What did you do?"

The color drained from Byron's face. He knew he was pushing it. With a twist of my wrist, I could snap his neck.

"Ronan was distracting you. I had to do something. It was simple to break into the perverts' homes and separate their heads from their bodies." His voice cracked in his uncertainty.

"Do you have any idea of what you've done?"

The angry glow in my eyes was reflected in his fear-filled ones. I had left Robert Moore alive, for he swore to turn himself in, and I planned to visit Billy Spencer another night.

"I did what you would eventually do. The old men were easy. Practicing with you has improved my martial skills," he said as he regained his confidence. "It wasn't my fault some neighbor called the police and reported a strange Mustang parked across the street from Spencer's house."

He slipped out of bed, his hard cock beneath leather pressing against one thigh until he adjusted it. His shaking hands revealed he truly understood the danger he invited. He struggled to zip up his pants. I grabbed Byron by the throat and slammed him into the wall.

"Leave the killing to me. You're never to do that again,"

I said, nose to nose. "It was sloppy and allowed Ronan to be connected to the murders." I stared at him a moment longer. A guilty expression crossed his face.

A gurgle escaped his throat, yet his dilated pupils gave away his exaltation. For a fraction of a minute, I'd forgotten he was a masochist. With a jerk of my hand, he flew across the room and landed on the bed.

"You did it purposely." Restraining my anger, canines bared, I walked toward the door. The need to hurt him mounting by each second convinced me I needed fresh air.

"Mistress, please forgive me." He followed across the room.

Though his hand hadn't touched me, I felt the heat from his body.

"Don't...touch...me," I said as fury punctuated each word.

Suddenly, I felt so tired. Controlling the monster inside of me caused my shoulders to ache with the weight. The big question was, how much of a monster was I? It was my fault Byron had felt it okay to kill the men.

"Mistress, please let me explain." He fell to his knees, his arms clutching his waist.

I turned my back and with one hand on the door knob, I stopped. Not wanting to look at him again, I stared at the polished oak door.

"Explain?"

"I did it for you. He was changing you. He doesn't deserve to be of the night. I had to do it because I love you."

I flinched. The horrible things done in the name of love were endless.

"What else did you do?" Weary with the game, I'd used my sternest voice.

"That Brannon guy. He's been asking questions." He

began to weep silently.

I steeled my heart, turned back to him, and placed my hands around his head and squeezed. His dark eyes widened. He knew I planned to have all his secrets. Extracting information by such a way was very intrusive and painful. Not like a casual touch on the arm or thigh. I had a feeling time was running short.

After a couple of minutes, I understood why Byron had been afraid to tell me. I should kill him. His betrayal was monstrous. I wasn't sure if I was being merciful by not killing him. Living with what he'd done would be pure hell for us both.

I left his unconscious body on the floor and walked out.

<<<>>>
Ronan

I struggled with the ropes that tied my wrists and feet to the steel chair. Fuck. What was it with people and pain-in-the-ass steel chairs? Police and crazy people. Nope. I wouldn't go there. I was a cop in another lifetime.

The thin rope and heavy metal wouldn't budge, even when I rocked it back and forth. All it got me was a lot of noise, a painful fall to the side, and a right arm going numb.

Brannon was insane. Not a fucking original thought.

Earlier, I had started to enter the limo, and Brannon surprised me with a gun pointed straight at me. With the pistol inches from my forehead and in the close quarters, there was no way the man could miss.

So I'd raised my arms and waited to see his next move. My only warning was the sound of shuffling feet behind me, and before I turned, pain came crashing down on my head with what felt like a tire iron.

When I became aware of my surroundings, I was tied to the chair with a pounding head and a stiff neck. The thick, white cement blocks and metal poles screamed basement.

"Well, Mr. Michaels, it appears that you're in a bind." Brannon's snickering at his sense of humor was as warped as the man.

"Why? What do you hope to gain?" Fuck, I ached all over. I wasn't as young as I used to be.

"I thought you were smarter than that." Brannon's snide grin didn't reach his dead eyes. "You're the bait."

"Bait for what? Tori? Your pretend sister?" I kept my cool, trying for an even, calm voice.

"Yes. Tori. Victoria Margaret Amherst. Such an old-fashioned name for a remarkable woman. Those long legs and big eyes, and of course..." Brannon cupped his hands in front of his chest.

I renewed my struggle with the restraints. Furious, I wanted to tear him limb from limb. He better not touch her.

Brannon leaned down, hands on bent knees, and asked, "Do you have any idea how old she is?"

"No. And what the fuck does it matter?" I asked between gritted teeth. The cold cement floor sent a chill through my body.

"I was curious after I came across some interesting—how should I say it—physical data. It made me want to know more." Brannon straightened and momentarily looked down his nose. "In the beginning, I needed her to be distracted while I study her a bit longer. So I hired you." The man walked across the room and dragged over another steel chair. The squealing caused me to cringe. My head pounded so hard I was sure I would pass out. Brannon sat with his feet near my chest and stared at me lying on the floor. "She's quite a woman, wouldn't you say? You knew she was dangerous, but you still slept with her and I find that most interesting."

I wanted to deny it, but damn his beady little eyes, Brannon was on to something. Every inch of my body had known there was something not quite right about Tori. Despite it, I wanted her.

"If she's so dangerous, why set all this up? Aren't you worried you'll be next? That she'll come after you?"

"I'm counting on it." He leaned back and tilted his head. "You never answered me on how old you think she is?" That snide little grin appeared again.

What would I give to knock it off his face?

Brannon had the look of a cat spotting a mouse. Anticipation mixed with his deadly stare.

"At this time, I don't give a shit." I moved my arms, instantly regretting it. Biting back a moan, I fought the excruciating fire shooting across my shoulders. No matter how I moved the pressure off my right arm, the cement floor was cutting off the circulation.

With a snap of Brannon's fingers, a mountain-sized man stepped over and lifted me in the chair as if the combined weight was no more than the tire iron he'd wielded against my skull. Immediately, my arm began to burn from the blood flowing back through the veins. I closed my eyes for a moment to work through the pain.

"There. Isn't that better?" Brannon said in an excited voice. "You can now listen without distraction to what I have to tell you. Her age hasn't mattered because you have no idea what she is."

I opened my eyes and stared at the madman. High-voltage energy was coming off Brannon in waves. The lunatic really was excited about whatever he had to say.

Brannon squinted his eyes in concentration.

"Let's see, her hometown is Birmingham, and investigating her isn't so easy. You must understand, she's been gone for over thirty years. Ah, I see that confused look on your face. Your dear ladylove is over eighty years old."

"You're full of shit!" I shook my head. Each time the man opened his mouth, he proved how crazy he was. Sure, the advancement of cosmetic surgery had been remarkable. Even some doctors worked miracles, but no way was she a day over twenty-six.

I wanted to tell Brannon he was a wackadoodle, but one of the first rules of dealing with someone mentally ill was to never tell them they're stark raving mad. In their minds, they are the ones with their heads screwed on right.

"But it's true." Brannon was enjoying this. His snide grin had grown to a full-blown smile. "It was quite simple to put two and two together. Only in her case, it came up to six. Especially, after I found her photograph in my brother's things." His cold, beady eyes stared straight through me, causing goosebumps to skitter down my back. "Oh, that's right. I forgot to tell you my brother was Tim Gordon. We had different fathers. You don't recognize his name? That's no surprise. He killed only six women. Not the twenty-eight or more that Ted Bundy had. It would have been seven, but the last one killed him. She slaughtered him. She slit his throat, jerked out his heart and crushed it like a rotten peach, and then tore him apart, limb by limb."

"Any police detective can tell you women who kill rarely do anything that gruesome." I watched Brannon's face turn red as I tried to reason with him. "They're too frightened to stick around and mutilate a body."

I wouldn't go into what some wives did to their husbands, besides I figured it was irrelevant at this point.

Spittle collected near the corners of Brannon's mouth.

"She has the power to do things you and I could never imagine. I thought at first she had some elixir that kept her young. When I scrutinized the evidence I came across with an open mind, her trail of murder and mayhem became clear." Brannon leaned back in his chair, puffing out his chest. "At first, I thought my brother had converted her into some kind of superhuman machine. After I hired you and my plan began to come to fruition, I had a visitor. The visitor said if I promised to get rid of you, I could have a sample of her blood. Of course, I promised. The sample he brought was remarkable. No matter what was done with it in the lab, they couldn't destroy it. That is until they put it in the sunlight." He lifted his hands and flipped his fingers out like a magician. "Poof. It disappeared and only a smidgen of ash and dirt remained. Imagine, ash and dirt." He spit out the final T.

What was the man saying? Was it someone's sick idea of a joke? I had to get out of there. Every time I wriggled my tied wrists, Brannon's guard placed his hand on my shoulder in warning.

"So?" Without a choice, I played along.

"You disappoint me. Don't you have any imagination?" Brannon stood and began to pace. The man waved his hands, punctuating the air with his fists. I watched, keeping my lips pressed together. I refused to feed the madman's drama.

Brannon stopped with head bowed, annoyance revealed in every inch of his body.

"She's a vampire." He said the last word with all of the drama of a diva.

How could anyone fault me for what I did next?

"That's fucking stupid." I howled with laughter. His words proved it. The man was totally off his rocker. With tears in my eyes, I almost missed Brannon's signal to the guard. The hit to the side of my head jarred my teeth. Warmth trickled from the corner of my lips down my chin. The taste of blood in my mouth didn't surprise me.

"Never call me stupid." Brannon's voice was even and mild, detached from the violence he ordered. His cold stare studied me for a second before he returned to his chair.

Pissed and frustrated by the whole situation I'd gotten into, I looked up at Brannon.

"Would you rather be called a lunatic?" I taunted.

All I saw for the next few minutes were fists, stars, and the ceiling above me. When the guard returned my body with the chair to their upright position, I spat blood onto the floor. My left eye was swollen shut. I figured the stinging above my eye and the warm sensation running down my face meant I had a cut on my forehead. Damn, I hurt all over.

A gleam in Brannon's eyes exposed the pleasure he received from watching his man beat me. In the interest of self-preservation, I decided to keep my mouth shut. There had to be a reason for Brannon to keep me alive. From what he said, someone close to Tori had worked out a deal. Get rid of me and he'd get Tori's blood. Brannon had the blood. So why was I still alive?

That snide grin I hated so much was back on Brannon's face.

"Mr. Michaels, it would be in your best interest to keep your opinions to yourself. It would disappoint me to have to kill you before your usefulness is played out."

So the final card hadn't been played. My gut told me it was Tori they waited for. I closed my good eye and prayed like never before.

*Tori, whatever you do, don't come here. Stay away.*

# Chapter 9

## *Tori*

Hidden behind bushes set in the woods, I watched the ranch-style house settle down for the night. Guards checked windows, shining flashlights at gates and doors.

Part of the information I'd pulled from Byron's mind included the time he'd followed Brannon's limo to this house. The huge home sat in the older section of Vestavia, a rich suburb of Birmingham, at the end of a long drive that snaked up a mountain. On one side of the building was a large plate-glass window overlooking the bright lights of downtown Vestavia.

Keeping to the shadows, I edged closer to the house and watched for movement through the windows. Though no lights shone through the glass, I knew people were inside. Too many cars and trucks were parked outside while men walked around with M4 assault rifles.

I ducked when two guards patrolled a few yards from the house and motion sensor lights flashed on as they moved along a path to the back.

After I settled behind some small bushes and thick

pampas grass to watch the house, a couple questions came to mind. Why was I risking exposure by attempting to rescue Ronan? Being a big boy, he could take care of himself. Was it simple curiosity that made Brannon want a sample of my blood? What a shame Ronan had to be caught in the middle.

My attraction to Ronan wasn't just physical, though he was hot and well-defined, and his raspy, deep voice made my legs weak and toes curl. And when he looked at me with those warm hazel eyes, half-closed in desire, and smiled that sensual half-grin, I would almost promise him the world. But I'd seen his past, the hurt he'd endured growing up without his mother, the pain of watching his father die from such a debilitating disease like cancer, and of having a wife walk out on him when he needed her most. He expected people to abandon him.

Stunned, I flopped on my back across the cool fescue grass and stared up between the tree branches at the stars. I was falling in love with him. Closing my eyes in horror of my stupidity, I shook my head. After decades of seeing how humans reacted to vampires, I knew better. But Ronan had changed me. He'd made me softer. Caring about him would likely come with a steep price. A broken heart.

Sure, the realization I could kill an innocent, if I hadn't already, had opened my eyes to past actions. But it was the ex-cop with soulful eyes and sinfully dark hair that brought the tenderness out of me. That gave me some of my humanity back.

The little voice in the back of my mind whispered, *you're still a monster.*

After I saved him tonight, I would leave town. Maybe go to Seattle. I missed the town. Or maybe Chicago. No. Too close to Mokena and Ronan. Being in the same state would be too tempting. There was New York City or Los Angeles or Atlanta. The night life was never-ending.

At first, it would hurt like hell. But my heart would mend. Connor would help. Byron could no longer be trusted.

Leaving Ronan behind...though I must be practical and realize a hole would exist in the middle of my soul. How many times in the last eight hours had I thought to myself he'd be better without me? Safer? He must never find out I was a vampire. A freak. A monster.

Rolling over onto my stomach I waited for the late evening to creep by, for everyone to become negligent in their duties.

After midnight, activity near the house began to ease off and I moved closer. Lax guards stood behind a tree, smoking pot from the smell of it, and whispered about whatever was on the screen of a phone.

With little trouble, I crept up and knocked them out. All it took was a well-placed chop to the neck of one and a jump kick in the back of the head for the other. Large and burly, they supplied me with a quick boost of nourishment, though the last one I regretted. Drugs in the system didn't bother me, but gave the blood a bitter taste. The guards were still alive but would sleep until morning, waking with a morning-after ache and tiredness due to lack of blood.

At a side door, I pressed my ear to the wood and listened. A television blared in the background. I heard dishes clinking and the sound of running water. Someone was washing dishes.

Before I came to the door, I had seen a small window around the corner. Likely the sink's location was beneath the window and the person's back would be to me when I opened the door.

Testing the knob, I found it locked. With deep concentration, I slowly turned the knob until I heard the click of tiny broken metal pieces. Holding my breath, I waited to see if the person heard. The sounds of glasses and plates continued to come from the room. Exhaling, I eased the door open.

Luckily, well-greased hinges allowed me to slip in. A man with rolled-up sleeves stood over the sink, his back to me as I predicted. As I took a step toward him, he turned.

"Where did you come from?" he asked, pulling his head back in confusion.

His wide face and red cheeks gave him a merry expression, but the eyes always gave predators away. Lifeless, deadly dark eyes narrowed before he charged.

I remained still until the last second. As he dove to knock me down, I stepped to the side and grabbed his arm, twisting it behind him. He gasped in surprise. He'd obviously never been manhandled by a woman. With his wrist between his shoulder blades and the side of his face pressed to the wall, I started asking questions.

"Where is Brannon? What has he done with Ronan?"

"Listen, lady. I don't know who you're talking about." He grunted when I jerked his hand higher. "Shit, lady. You're killing me."

"I want answers now. What does he want with Ronan? Why has he been following me?" Before I sensed the other man, it was too late. A half-empty wine bottle crashed down on the back of my head. That hurt like hell. Keeping my hands on the first man, I whipped my head around to look over my shoulder. Wine and glass in my hair sprayed the second man in the face, but the momentum of swinging a rolling pin in his other hand unerringly met my temple. Excruciating pain slammed through my skull.

Damnit. I fought the engulfing blackness, but was pulled under.

<<<>>>

I woke chained to a brick wall. It was so pathetic. With my vampire strength, a simple snap of my wrist would pull the anchors from the brick.

Grinning, barely holding back a laugh, I turned to see Ronan tied to a chair with a gag tied across his jaw. The sick humor left the situation. With one eye swollen shut and blood covering part of his face, he apparently wasn't cooperating with Brannon. Other than the bloody mess, he didn't look worse for wear. Though the distrustful look from his good eye sent my stomach churning.

Did he know? Had Brannon discovered my secret? For now, I'd remain chained, play it by ear and see what happened.

"Good evening, Miss Amherst. Glad you could join our little group." Brannon, with his swept-over hair and greasy smile, stood to the side between Ronan and myself.

"Hello, Mr. Brannon." I received immense pleasure in seeing his consternation. He hadn't expected me to know his name.

Connor wasn't successful in turning up any dirt on Edgar Brannon, but I read the dry facts on the printouts he provided. Brannon was rich. The only logical reason I could think of for the man to follow me was he wanted to be a vampire. Why? Was he dying from an incurable disease? Nothing in the reports showed an unusual number of doctor visits, so sickness of the body wasn't the problem. Or had one of the deviants I'd killed been a friend or relative? Was this revenge?

Looking at Ronan's bruised face again, I decided Brannon needed to die. No one touched my man and lived.

"It appears our Mr. Michaels has been talking about me."

"Actually, not really. I was interested in the man who claimed to be my brother, and I simply had you investigated. You know, you lead a rather boring life. It makes me wonder what you're hiding."

That wiped the snide grin off his face.

"Well then, let's talk about why I wanted you here."

"I'm hanging on your every word," I said, shaking my chains.

"Miss Amherst, I'll ignore your misplaced humor for now." Brannon walked behind Ronan and placed his hands on the battered man's shoulders. "I have an offer to make you."

I gave Ronan a quick look. All the color had drained from his face, making the bruises stand out. I wanted to get him away, to care for his wounds, bathe his bruised and battered body and never let anyone hurt him ever again.

Frustrated with Brannon's game, I returned my attention to the asshole.

"Spit it out."

"Impatient, aren't you?" Brannon released Ronan and stepped between us, blocking my view. "First, I thought you might be interested to know, the man you slaughtered so many years ago was my brother. Tim Gordon. He was an artist, a dreamer, the best of men."

"That deranged serial killer? No wonder you're insane." I wanted to throw up. Brannon needed to die. He sounded so proud of his psycho brother.

"You owe me. I want you to make me a vampire and I'll let Ronan go. See how reasonable I can be?"

"What makes you think I can do that?" My heart dropped. "How can I trust you to let him go?"

What was Ronan thinking about this weird conversation? If he thought it to be true, the next time he looked at me, it'd be with revulsion. Another roil of my stomach had me swallowing hard. I was having a hard time handling the news Brannon revealed along with his idiotic request.

Brannon moved to the side and leaned against the wall. "You should keep closer tabs on your blood slaves than you do. Byron was most helpful. In exchange for killing Ronan, he provided me with a vial of your blood."

I saw Ronan stiffen. Was he seeing who the bigger monster was in this room? Only problem was, I was unsure it was Brannon.

"Ronan looks rather healthy for a dead person." I wanted to know the whole story. I had been certain Brannon had connected me to the criminals' punishments but unaware I was a vampire. That was, not until Byron made his mistake.

Ronan glared at me. It probably sounded as if I was rushing Brannon to honor his agreement with Byron.

"That's rather humorous, because that's what I thought the first time I saw you." He walked behind Ronan, grabbed a handful of hair, and jerked his head back. Ronan's words were muddled by the gag, but it was easy to guess Brannon was being called some imaginative names. "I believe it's time that you took me seriously."

Out of nowhere, a long switchblade appeared in his hand and he pressed it to Ronan's throat.

Brannon's remark baffled me, but I had to keep my mind on protecting Ronan. Dark anger washed over me. Though a big boy, this was way out of Ronan's league.

I narrowed my eyes.

"Oh, Mr. Brannon, I take you more serious than you ever can imagine. It's *you* that's not taking me seriously."

A flash of confusion crossed his face. He'd expected me to give up by his threats alone? Then he pulled the blade across Ronan's throat, leaving a thin red line.

I shook my chains. Luckily for Brannon, I had enough sense to know he wouldn't kill Ronan so soon. Or maybe I was overconfident he wanted my cooperation more.

"Look at that delicious blood. For the benefit of Ronan's skeptical mind, show him your fangs. Or do you need me to make the cut deeper?" Brannon's warped smile revealed how the man was a brick short of a full load.

Ronan swallowed, pain mixed with relief clear on his face. Assured it was a mere scratch, I said, "He's seen them."

Brannon's eyebrows lifted. He turned to Ronan. "Is this true?" When Ronan didn't answer, he loosened the gag. "Answer me."

"Go fuck yourself," Ronan said in a hoarse voice.

With a nod from Brannon, the huge bodyguard back-handed Ronan across the face. There was no way I would stand back and let Ronan be hurt further. Time to act. I tugged and then struggled with the chains, twisting and jerking them, trying every means to break the anchors. I would use the chains to kill them. But they held firm. What the hell? Was it magic?

Brannon turned toward Ronan, while keeping an eye on me.

"Mr. Michaels, you must be a poor lover. No imagination. I can only assume you saw her fangs and had no idea what they really meant." On returning his attention to me, he said, "You need to stop before you hurt yourself. The manacles and chains are made from titanium and built to withstand the strongest in the world." Nervousness made his voice sound edgy. "Implanted in the wall are titanium rods that go at least ten feet into the ground. You didn't think I would attach the chains to plain brick, did you?" Shaking his head. "Tsk, tsk. You underestimated me. Time for you to cooperate or would you rather have your lover boy suffer for it?"

"Don't listen to him, Tori. He plans to kill us both," Ronan warned me. Then spat blood onto the cement floor. The thin line on his neck appeared to be slowing.

"There's where you're wrong. I plan to keep you alive." He pointed to Ronan. "As long as you're useful. While I plan to keep Tori alive for quite some time."

The malicious gleam in his eyes did little to comfort me.

"If Ronan dies, you're a dead man," I said through clenched teeth.

"Now you get it. I wish to be one of the walking dead, a creature of the night, vampire, and I know you can do this. But first you need to show Ronan the real Victoria Amherst."

"The only thing you've shown him is that you're off your rocker." I fought to stay in control of my temper. As long as I remained amused by Brannon's arrogance, my fangs wouldn't drop and my eyes wouldn't glow. Why was it so important for Ronan to see my fangs?

"Why must people continue to call me such names?" He muttered a few more words and shook his head. "If you insist on being that way." Brannon opened a side door and commanded someone in the next room, "Come in."

A man, no taller than four-foot, strode up to me, and thrust a needle through my leather pants into my thigh. Immediately, I felt the drug burning a path up my torso and slammed into my heart. I had to fight it. *Ignore the stinging pain.* Though I fought the emotions twirling through my brain, consuming anger and terror overrode them all.

"No," I screamed. The horrible knowledge Ronan watched as I turned into a feared and hated creature, made me even more furious.

*Fight the anger. I must fight the need to taste blood. Oh, my God. Please help me.*

I felt my canines drop and at the same time I knew my eyes glowed in their unholy brilliance.

All was lost. Ronan would know me for the monster I was.

"Ah, now we see the true Tori. A killing-machine that drinks human blood." Brannon stood farther back in the room, eyeing me with excitement and a little wariness. "Isn't she magnificent? Look at her. I must know, how many men have you killed? Three, ten, forty? A hundred?"

I shook my head, trying to clear it from the drug and the images of those I'd killed. All killed in the name of justice. But was it really justice or my own brand of insanity? Last night had placed those doubts in my head.

"You shouldn't have done that. You don't know anything." I nearly growled out the words.

The drugs had freed my aggression and fury. Unable to control my body, I jerked and shook the chains. Visions of pulling Brannon apart limb by limb danced before my eyes with the dark need to drink his blood, bathe in it. Intense heat flashed across my body. I howled.

After I caught my breath, I looked into the eyes of the man that meant so much to me.

"Ronan, oh, God! Please forgive me!" Tears streamed down my face and another flash of pain rolled through my torso and limbs. My body bowed and twisted, while the anchors in the brick wall held. Grotesque images swirled through my mind. "Ronan. The drug—agh! I can't control it. Run! Hide before it's too late," I pleaded and shook, afraid for his life.

Groaning, I flung my head back, smashing it into the wall.


<<<>>>
Ronan


"Damn it, Brannon! It's killing her!" I rocked the chair back and forth, not caring if the guard hit me again. Later I would come to terms with the truth, but for now Tori needed my help. No matter she was some kind of freak. A demon.

Brannon watched her with amazement lighting his face, his attention never leaving her. "Only a wooden stake through the heart or sunlight can kill her. She'll have a headache for a few hours, but she'll survive. Isn't she glorious?"

Frustrated and helpless, I wanted to smash the asshole's head in. Delirious with fear for her, I almost didn't hear the voice.

"Please." She sounded like a little girl. "Please don't believe Brannon. It wasn't pleasure to kill them. Please don't believe Brannon. I didn't kill all of them, only those that weren't repentant, but I know I was wrong to do it that way now. It was because of you and Sam Kerry. That night I realized how wrong I was. Oh, God. Please help me. Forgive me. I've changed."

Then she started tugging and twisting in the chains. Blood dripped from her wrists and ankles. Cold metal cut into her flesh. Her eyes turned golden. When she opened her mouth to scream, her eye teeth were longer, sharper than the others.

She was a vampire.

"See. What did I tell you?" Brannon laughed maniacally.

Helpless, I could only watch as her limbs twitched from the pain. Her eyes rolled up into her skull, followed by another fury of spasms.

"Help her," I roared. "The drugs are tearing her apart!"

"Don't worry. She'll calm down in a moment. If she was human, she'd certainly be dead by now. I just wanted you to witness the true Tori. A creature of the night. The monster that you fucked, allowed to take your blood, to love you."

"No!" I pulled at the ropes at my wrists and ankles, wanting to stop Brannon's insanity. "You're a fucking psycho!"

Out of the corner of my eye I saw the big guard move, but I couldn't do anything to stop what happened next. Pain and a bright light was followed by sudden darkness and unawareness.

<<<>>>

I opened sand-filled eyes. At least I thought I had. The room was black. I struggled to push up to a sitting position against what felt like a brick wall.

The foulest taste was in my mouth. I pressed my tongue against the roof of my mouth, grimacing as I remembered the moments before everything went dark again.

I had woken earlier to Tori passed out and hanging on the wall. Brannon had disappeared from my view, then returned wearing a long, black robe with red symbols sewn over the chest and down the sleeves. Brannon had ordered the guard to hold me as he forced a foul thick brew into my mouth and down my throat. Nearly choking to death, I swallowed the substance and the guard finally released me.

Then Brannon had started chanting something I couldn't understand. It sounded like Latin mixed with a few English words. As the room rocked and swayed, I knew the brew was causing me to hallucinate. My eyelids had become heavy and then nothing. I was out.

No chains or ropes encircled any part of my body. I rubbed my wrists and ankles and stopped when they stung. They were raw.

What kind of game was Brannon playing now?

The total empty feeling in the room brought a heavy sensation across my chest and confirmed I was still in the underground chamber. Or was the sensation something else? Fear from the creature hanging from the chains nearby?

Damn. Tori was a vampire. There were really vampires in the world. What little I remembered from the horror flicks my dad enjoyed watching, vampires couldn't go out into the daylight and they sucked blood out of their victims' necks. Occasionally, Tori would be a little pale but the rest of the time she appeared normal.

I remembered another trait of a vampire. Their allure. Bewitching their victims. That would explain my unnatural attraction for Tori. I couldn't remember feeling for anyone as I did for Tori. Not even my ex-wife.

Was there some way I could break the spell she cast over me? Did I want to?

I closed my eyes. One thing at a time. First, I needed to get out of there.

Keep it simple. Light. I needed light. Recalling how the room looked, arms stretched out, I took a few steps toward the wall I believed had the light switch. With a sigh of relief, I pressed my swollen face against the cool block. I took a second to catch my breath—the beatings had every inch aching and it was hard to walk with one eye closed—I found the switch and flipped it.

When I got out of there, I was going to make sure to pay back the guard and Brannon for their hospitality.

When. Not if.

I chuckled. My dad said optimism was one of my finer points, but keeping my feet planted firmly on the ground was better. I missed the old man. No regrets. At the time, I did what was needed and my dad lived the last year in dignity. Exactly. There were no regrets.

The groan behind me brought to mind one recent decision I might regret.

I turned to the woman hanging from the chains on the far wall. Another groan had me across the room and checking her pulse. None. Her skin was cold and dry, and wherever my fingers touched, the area remained white.

If it wasn't for the groans, I would swear Tori was dead. I'd seen with my own eyes the changes that came over her. Sharp fangs and glowing pupils. Was there a logical explanation? There had to be one. They could have shot me up with some type of drug before I woke the first time. That would explain the hallucinations.

Determined to find a way to release her from the manacles, I reached above her head to where the chain was connected to the wall.

With my face next to hers, I didn't feel her move until the sharp sting of her teeth grazed my neck. I jumped back and stared at the creature. She was still human-like and gorgeous, but her brown eyes glowed gold and her top two canines narrowed to razor-sharp points.

Two long scratches on my neck stung, irritating the thin cut. The scratches reminded me of the morning after we had met and I had woken to identical ones. The conclusion was simple. She'd bitten me the first night. It must take more than a few bites to make me a vampire. Or had she changed me—

Before I could finish the thought, she stiffened and then went limp. She looked for all intents and purposes dead.

"Tori?" I wasn't sure if I wanted her to answer or not. Everything pointed to a truth I could no longer deny.

The woman I was obsessed with was a vampire. A bloodsucking demon. Damned to walk the earth and feed on human blood. She'd killed Robert Moore and Billy Spencer. Brannon said she probably killed many more. A soulless creature using me, playing me for a fool.

No way would a creature like that have feelings for me. It would know only hunger and destruction.

I studied her hanging on the wall. With two fingers, I checked her pulse. Nothing. Her body wasn't the first dead one I'd seen and she was certainly dead. If she woke in the evening, I would know I wasn't losing my mind.

If she was a vampire, my decision would be made. There was no way I could allow Brannon to become like her. More lives would be lost. There was no way around it. I would have to stop her. But could I bring myself to destroy her?

# Chapter 10

## *Tori*

I waited for my eyes to clear. How many hours had gone by? I felt the softness of night, so it was at least the next evening. My chin remained against my chest and my weight pulled the manacles at my wrists above me. I gradually straightened my knees and lifted my head. Immediate relief followed by searing pain shot through my arms. I bit back a whimper. My head felt two sizes too large. Blurred vision and aching joints would quickly disappear once I started moving around and fed. The ache in my heart would take longer.

Memories from the night before washed over me. Before passing out, I heard Ronan shouting no. Denying his desire for me hurt more than being called a monster, a demon. It shouldn't hurt. It was what I expected, but his denial didn't stop my desire for him.

Squeezing my eyes shut for a moment, I regained control of my emotions. I opened them to a clearer view of the room and turned my head toward the chair.

Empty. I stared, unable to focus on what it could mean.

Had Brannon killed him? A movement in the corner caught my attention.

The angriest eyes framed by multi-colored flesh watched me without a word. With his back pressed to the wall, Ronan sat as far away as possible from where I hung.

His face was cleaned of fresh blood, and the swelling in one eye had lessened.

How had he reacted when I fell into my death sleep? Cold to the touch and dead in every sense of the word, most humans reacted in horror by the change.

"Hey there," I said as neutrally as possible.

The metal biting into my wrists reminded me to stand straight. Damn, my shoulders were stiff with pain from hanging for hours.

Hazel eyes flickered beneath his lowered eyebrows. Concern and skepticism pulled at his features. He remained quiet as he continued to scowl my way.

"Are you okay? He didn't hurt you anymore, did he?" I asked, keeping my tone nonchalant to comfort him. Had Brannon done more to Ronan while I *slept*?

Ronan turned his head away and shoved a shaking hand through his hair. No new bruises or cuts were visible. Was his anger keeping him from talking? He then broke the silence.

"Do you like being a vampire?" His voice was hoarse, most likely from the beating he'd endured.

How could I answer that? How could I explain the need for revenge? So many years. So many deaths. I had my revenge that night decades ago, and hadn't allowed it to be enough. All the years after, I held a grudge against the world, calling myself a champion of the people, a crusader for justice and a woman who didn't need anyone. But I was wrong. When had it got all twisted and perverted? From the beginning?

"It has its advantages." That wasn't an answer. Not compared to the turmoil roiling in my gut. I closed my eyes. Chills racked my body as the pain around my heart took away my breath.

"Are you going to do what he asked?" he asked in a threatening tone. "Are you going to...change him?"

The way he kept his face turned away bothered me. What had I expected? He'd been through a lot and any normal human being needed time to digest the possibility vampires existed.

"No. I've never reincar . . . made someone a vampire and I certainly don't plan to start with him."

His grunt told me he wasn't convinced. There wasn't much I could do about that, but I needed to get him away from Brannon, and quickly.

I eyed Ronan. Except for the bruises on his face, and the long cut on his neck, and his expected weakness betrayed by his shaking, he appeared to be in one piece. With my super-human strength, it would be a breeze to carry him, but with his male pride, he'd only hurt himself by fighting me, and I didn't have time for that or arguing with him.

Tired of hanging around—thank goodness, my sense of humor hadn't left—it was time to show Ronan one of my vampire skills.

I smiled. My purpose in allowing Brannon to chain me was no longer needed. He'd revealed his purpose in kidnapping us. I would love to wait for his return, but my worry for Ronan's health, mental and physical, overrode my need for revenge. He wouldn't survive another beating. Gambling with my life was one thing, but gambling with Ronan's was quite another. The manacles, chains, and titanium rods were ingenious but I had other ways to escape. I couldn't do it while the asshole was nearby.

"Are there cameras or listening devices in here?" I asked in a whisper.

"I've checked. Nothing," he answered as he rubbed his temples.

"He appears the type to be overconfident." I grimaced when I tried to straighten my spine. "Do you feel well enough to walk out of here?"

The look he gave me was easy to read. He was sure I'd lost my mind. With eyebrows raised, he stared pointedly at the manacles around my wrists.

I shook my head.

"Oh, ye of little faith."

Believing was seeing. So I turned and stared at the manacle on my left wrist. A surge of power flowed down my arm. My thumb popped and folded in an odd angle. The pain blossomed and I took in several breaths.

"What the hell?" Ronan took a step toward me.

"Shh. I need to concentrate." Then I did it to my other thumb. Crap. It never was easy. Breathing in and out for a few seconds, I then beckoned with a nod. "Come over and slide off the manacles. Be careful going over my thumbs." I didn't enjoy pain.

He hesitated for a couple of seconds but then rushed over and carefully pulled the manacles off. When they dangled against the wall and I stepped away, he backed up and glared.

"Why?" His frown deepened. "Why didn't you escape before he shot you full of that drug?"

Stretching and twisting to relieve the kinks from my joints and popping my thumbs back in place—goodness, the pain disappeared, leaving only a manageable throb—I kept my gaze on him. I only hoped the look he was giving me was for my miraculous recovery. More than likely, he feared I was the demon he called me. Or a total nutcase like Brannon. So I had to show him he had nothing to worry about.

"Think, Ronan. If I had burst out of the chains while Brannon and his bodyguard were here, they would've killed you before I could get to them." I sauntered up to him. He pressed his back to the wall, his action speaking to his uncertainty of my truth.

The wall of ice around my heart hardened, freezing shut the cracks made by Ronan. I'd known better than to feel anything for a human, other than lust for his blood or body.

Nevertheless, getting him to safety was my priority. Time to leave and part ways. Once I made sure he was safe, I would be back to track down the psycho.

With a sigh, I stood, towering over him.

"I know you don't trust me and would rather not touch me ever again"—I offered my hand—"but we need to get out of here before they come back and finish what they started."

He hesitated only for a second longer, looking at the bruising around my thumbs, then he gently clasped my hand, and I gripped his, helping him to his feet. Once I was sure he was steady and would follow, I released his hand, and we walked to the door. I pressed my ear against the wood.

No noise from the other side.

Though I feared someone might be waiting to ambush us as we made our escape, I was willing to take the chance. Otherwise, we would meet our death in the room we were leaving.

I squeezed the doorknob and the whole thing fell to pieces. So glad it wasn't made of titanium.

"That's some trick you do." His grudging admiration brought a heated flush to my face. Amazing, considering my lack of blood lately.

Easing the door open enough to peek around the edge, I saw a short hallway and stairs disappearing into darkness.

"Come on. No one's guarding the door." I looked back to watch Ronan leave the last of the light behind. By pressing his hands on the wall, he followed, limping and grimacing with each step. The stairwell ahead was pitch black, but I could sense the depth. We were around twelve feet beneath the ground. We had a lot of steep steps before coming to another door.

At the landing, I put my hand out to stop Ronan. Unable to see my signal, he walked into my outstretched fingers. My nails jabbed his chest.

"Shit!" He bit off his exclamation as I covered his mouth.

I stood still for a few seconds, listening for anyone coming after us. Nothing. Only the smell of his blood. The delicious scent had me contemplating taking a nip. I sighed in frustration. Time was too short.

"Sorry," I whispered, shaking my head. Then I remembered he couldn't see me. So I softly added, "I should've warned you." I pressed an ear to the door. "I can't believe how arrogant Brannon is, but I'm grateful he didn't leave guards or use video surveillance. He underestimated us." I carefully stepped back, giving Ronan a little space. "I don't hear anyone on the other side, but we need to move quickly and quietly."

The escape was too easy, but I didn't have time to examine our good fortune.

The door was unlocked. Easing it open, I peered around the edge and found a hallway running crosswise from the stairwell. We were on the ground floor. Across from the door was a tall window overlooking the woods beyond.

I slipped into the hallway and checked the window. The latch slid to the side without any trouble and I lifted the pane. After checking both ends of the hallway, I waved for Ronan to come and climb out the open window.

He stopped beside me. What the hell was he doing?

"We don't have time to waste, Michaels, get your butt out the window. Go." The hairs on the back of my neck were standing up. Time was running out.

His voice weak and body trembling, he shook his head. "You first."

"Listen. We don't have time for your male ego. Think of it this way, it's as dangerous to be first one out as it is to be the last one in. Okay?"

Why did women put up with men? I rolled my eyes. *Of course, hard bodies and other hard parts that go bump in the night.*

"Then you go first." Pain pulled at his battered face, but he stood firm. He wasn't budging.

Damn, we didn't have time to argue.

"Okay, okay." I jumped out the window and gingerly landed behind a bush, then immediately moved to the side in a crouched position.

Relief eased my tension when Ronan landed a couple of feet away. His exit wasn't as graceful or as quiet as mine, but his body couldn't heal as quickly either. Only a small *humph* escaped his lips.

I remembered the window from my search of the grounds the night before and felt, if we ran a straight line toward the woods, a motion sensor light shouldn't be triggered. Keeping low to the ground, I rushed across the yard. I was right. No light yet. If our luck held out a little longer, we would reach the woods without mishap. Ronan moved slower, but wasn't too far behind when I heard the shout.

"Stop! Or I'll shoot!"

A guard rushed toward us with another rounding the corner of the house, their M4s pointed straight at us.

"Hurry, Ronan," I hissed.

I kicked into vampire speed and soon reached the woods. Peering around a large oak tree, I watched Ronan limp across the final few yards. I should've said the hell with his ego and carried him.

At that moment, the guards swept the ground with bullets near Ronan, sending rocks and dirt flying through the air. Ronan landed face first on the ground.

He wasn't moving.

"Ronan!" Had they hit him? I couldn't stand back and let him die.

One guard stopped next to Ronan, checked his pulse.

"Get the woman," he shouted at his comrade and two more guards coming from the house.

Holding the gun out from his body, the nearest guard cautiously trotted around the tree. What an amateur. I kicked the gun out of his hands, but not before shots went wild, hitting the two new guards. With a couple more well-placed kicks, I knocked him out.

As I ran back to Ronan, I slammed into the last guard, knocking him down. He landed in a weird way. Carefully, I rolled the guard onto his back, his head almost sat on his shoulder. Sightless eyes stared into the sky. His neck had broken in the fall. He was dead.

I squeezed my eyes shut for a second before checking on Ronan. Forcing my feet to move faster, I reached him in seconds. Encouraged by the absence of blood on his back, my hands shook as I tenderly rolled him over and gasped. One small black hole beneath his breast pumped out blood with each beat of his heart.

"No, Ronan," I exclaimed. "Don't you dare die on me. Stay with me." Determined to save him, I ripped his shirt off and pressed the cloth to the wounds. "You've got to stay around to make sure I don't kill any innocents." Afraid if I stopped talking he would die, I babbled about anything that came to mind. "You don't know how much I admire your guts. Remember, when you stood up to me in Joe Carson's house? It's true that you had no idea how dangerous I could be, but you still saved the deviant. You knew it was wrong for me to kill him. You're a good man and there are so few in this world. The first time I saw you, I knew you were special, and I need you. This world needs you. Oh, please don't leave me alone."

Without thinking, I lifted him like a child and briskly walked through the woods. Who knew, despite my strength, how hard it was to carry a tall man, even though I wasn't a shorty? The distance to my car never felt so far. All my strength was needed to hold him steady and not let his feet drag the ground. His warm body was limp like a rag doll, reminding me of the little girl from the other night. A young daughter defending her innocent father. Was Ronan's death my punishment? Was I to lose the only man I could love because of my sins?

I stumbled, but kept my footing. Ronan groaned.

"Hold on a little longer, my darling. Everything will be okay," I whispered in his ear. How could I promise him that? It was because of me he was in this predicament. A monster never deserved happiness.

Wishing I'd brought my SUV, I opened my Maserati

passenger door with one hand and arranged Ronan in the seat with the upmost care, sliding the seat back as far as it would go. He groaned and coughed. Blood and air bubbles poured out of his nose and from the corner of his mouth.

No, no, no, no…

The bullet must have bounced off a rib and nicked a lung too. He was drowning in his own blood, and I was helpless to stop it. I could try to take him to the nearest emergency care center, but this kind of wound, and my jostling him had done him no good. Gut-wrenching sorrow welled up inside of me.

I looked up and shook my fist at the sky.

"Agh! No. You can't have him. I'll not be alone. He's mine!" I screamed in frustration to whatever powers were in control of this mad world. I examined his handsome pale face. He was minutes from taking in his last breath. Time was about to run out. "Ronan, there is only one way to stop this. We're too far from a hospital or emergency center. You have only seconds left. Please forgive me, but I refuse to let you die, no matter what."

I knew what I had to do.

Whenever I imagined reincarnating someone, I expected it to be a mutually satisfying exchange, not an act of selfishness. Desperation had chosen the path for me and once again desperation was coming into play, but for Ronan. The same path I recently regretted, but I couldn't regret keeping Ronan part of my world.

If I follow through—and I would—the questions would be, would he take revenge against Brannon? Or me? Was his blood the type to accept the reincarnation? I suspected it was. Deep inside I'd known.

Feeling weak and unsure I knew all of the steps, I kissed Ronan hard on the mouth. Savoring his unique taste and his sweet blood. My hands trembled while smoothing his hair. My fingertips caressed the cool dark strands, brushing them from his face.

"Ronan, I'm sorry." Afraid to think of what he'd say if he knew my plans, I repeated to myself I was doing what was best. I ignored the pressure in my chest. It was as if I was dying a little inside with him. "No matter what you believe later, I did this because I'm falling in love with you and losing you is an option I refuse to accept."

It was true. Death wouldn't separate us.

Straddling his lap, one knee on the console and the other out the open door, I sank my fangs into his neck, drinking only a little before I felt his heartbeat slow to a near stop. I reached beneath the driver's seat and pulled out a leather case with a jewel-encrusted dagger inside.

Sharp, shiny, and deadly, the dagger was given to me by Wolfric. He'd said he used it to kill the woman he loved two hundred years ago. When I asked him why he was giving it me, he refused to answer as such profound sadness pulled at his face, and I never asked him again.

Wanting Ronan as my equal, I ran the razor-sharp edge across the side of my neck. The position mattered. If I had wanted him as a slave or servant, I would've given him my wrist. Blood flowed in a thin line over my collarbone and down my chest. Without hesitation, I lifted his head and pressed his lips to my neck.

At first, he didn't respond. I pressed his lips to my neck harder. Then I felt the tip of his tongue lightly touch the cut. Rocking side-to-side with my hands cupping the back of his head, I closed my eyes and waited for him to live or die. The next moment, he clutched my arms, his fingers digging into my flesh. His chest pressed to mine was warm and his heartbeat pounded harder with each second he drank.

I knew the reaction to my blood was immediate, but the sensation of his feeding on me was beyond imagination. The bulge beneath his pants' zipper pressing against my lower stomach revealed his enjoyment was as great as my own.

His sucking at my neck grew in strength until I became lightheaded. With a jerk, I pulled away.

Pale, yet bruised in so many places, he still looked dead, except for the rapid rise and fall of his chest. His eyes flickered open, hooded with desire, but glowing with vampire life. Their green glow indicated he would survive the clumsy reincarnation.

The next few hours would be hard for both of us. His body would try to reject the unnatural blood and I'd suffer from the guilt of making him like me.

I hoped he would allow me to show him a new life beyond his dreams.

Or was that beyond his nightmares?

# Chapter 11

## *Ronan*

I rolled to my back on the soft bed, stretching my arms above my head. Hotels were providing better mattresses. Basking in the clean-smelling sheets, I let my arms fall straight out on each side. One hand landed on warm flesh. What the hell?

I turned my head and looked into two beautiful brown eyes.

Tori.

Her lips lifted slightly at the corners. Such a sad smile. Lying on her side next to me, she picked up my hand and began to kiss each finger, while her gaze remained on mine. The sensation of her tongue caressing my scarred knuckles brought heat to my groin, a hardening and lengthening of my dick.

Beneath the silky sheets, I realized I was bare. Where the hell were my clothes? My gaze drifted down Tori's body. She was covered by the sheet too, though her torso and long legs were clearly outlined. She was also naked.

"About time you woke up. How do you feel?" Her husky voice filled my head with images of limbs entwined, breaths caressing sensitive skin while torsos strained to each touch.

I wanted to stay in bed and indulge in all my fantasies with her body, but something bothered me. A niggling in the back of my mind told me something was wrong. For some reason, I shouldn't feel this good.

Over her shoulder, I noticed walls covered with brown-and-gold material and gilt-framed pictures with castles and couples dressed in clothes from centuries before. Curtains in the same material as the walls hung from each post of the huge bed. The room was from another time, another century.

"Where am I?"

"We're at...a friend's home. We're safe." Tori leaned over and felt my forehead, concern clearly written on her face. "How do you feel?"

"Strange. Not bad actually. More like my gut telling me something isn't right." I rubbed my chest, soothing the small ache near my heart, and my fingers touched a small circular scar.

Then the memories slammed into me.

That was it. The basement. Escaping out a window. The pain of a bullet ripping into my chest.

After the ordeal I'd been through, I should be nearly comatose from pain, but I felt as if I could run twenty miles without breaking a sweat. I shoved the covers back and looked at my chest. Only one dark red spot remained of what should be a fatal wound.

"Ronan?" Tori's voice was filled with concern.

"How long have I been out?" I asked, without looking up.

"About sixteen hours."

"No. I mean how long ago was it since I was shot?"

"About sixteen hours," she repeated in a flat voice.

What the hell? Curious, I lifted my gaze to hers.

"It wasn't a dream, was it?" I needed to hear her say it.

"No." Despair shaded that single word.

Was she lying? But what would she gain? Maybe it was the cop in me. Never trusting others. Never letting others close enough to use me.

The last time I'd allowed someone in my life, the woman had left me high and dry, without a job or house and with a broken heart.

"Explain." Time for her to admit what the hell was going on.

She turned her head away, refusing to answer or look at me.

I struggled to hold my temper as her refusal sent something dark swirling through me. An uncontrollable urge clawed to be free. Anger and another strange sensation overtook my restraint. A need to tear her apart with my bare hands, to clamp my teeth into her flesh, to feel her hot blood flow into my mouth, over my tongue and down my throat. The thought sickened a part of me, yet another part became excited, thrilled by the thought of taking Tori's blood.

I watched the pulse in her throat. Pulsating and begging to be taken. My mouth opened and a tingling in my gums had me running my tongue over my top teeth. Two sharp canines lengthened as my cravings deepened.

With the need engulfing me, it brought a rush of heat soaring through my body. Thick desire flooded my senses, bringing thoughts of feeding and fucking her at the same time. Suddenly I found my fingers entwined in her hair as I pulled her neck to my mouth.

"Stop, Ronan," she croaked.

My first hunger was too great to control. I wanted to

dominate her, brand her with my bite, make her crave me as much as I did her.

As soon as my canines sank into her neck, she stilled and moaned. The sound wasn't one of pain but immense pleasure. When her body undulated against mine, I continued to feed while I adjusted our bodies, shoving the sheets away, pulling her body beneath me.

She cupped my face. I forced myself to let go and look into her eyes.

"Baby, you need to be careful," she pleaded, her gaze soft and filled with sadness. "Drinking too much from another vampire can cause a connection you might regret."

I only half-listened to her as my mouth dropped down to her beautiful breasts. While sucking and licking her stiff little nipples, I spread her legs and settled my dick against her hot pussy and rubbed her slick folds. I was hard, throbbing like a son of a bitch, ready to drill her into the mattress. So with a forceful thrust I was inside, pumping to the accelerated beat of our hearts.

Her hands smoothed over my shoulders and down my chest, nails scraping a trail, heading to my groin.

I clasped her wrists and jerked them above her head, stopping her caresses and controlling my mounting response. My other hand pushed against the small of her back while I pounded into her. Driving my body to lengths I never imagined. I continued lunging into her. Feeling as if my heart would burst, I slowed, rotating my hips for her pleasure and slamming back into her heat.

Swept up in lust, I felt her body pulse and shake at the same time my body jerked and shuddered. After a few more thrusts, spent and weak, I rolled to my back.

I pulled her over to rest on top of me, wanting her body touching every inch of mine. Panting from our exertions, I held her, enjoying the sensual feel of her breasts rubbing along my chest with each labored breath.

I chuckled. Could I survive another round? Then hunger slammed into me. I opened my eyes, staring at the ceiling with true realization.

Fuck. She'd made me a vampire.

<<<>>>

Tori

I nuzzled his neck, scraping my fangs across his skin and laving drops of blood.

"Ahhh." His heated groan encouraged me to become bolder with my caresses. "Stop it, Tori. It's time for us to talk." He gently moved my hands from his groin.

He turned on his side to face me. His gruff tone held little hope I could keep him absorbed in fleshly activities as my master would say.

Looking him over, lust pulled at my senses, and I struggled with my craving to feast on him again. Muscular, but not too muscle bound, his chest and arms tempted me with their hard curves and ridges. The sheets barely covered his lap, providing a lickable view of the twin lines between hip and groin. The Adonis belt was well-pronounced and beautiful on this man. With a mere tug of the sheet, I could also admire his thick and long phallus.

I already knew so much about him, yet again so little. I knew he enjoyed the small of his back kissed and the rim of his ears licked. I could distinguish between his moans, one telling me he was at the point of no return and the other that he wanted me to move faster. But when it came to important aspects of his life, details of his past and his beliefs in the Ever After, I knew nothing.

With a finger, I traced one of the lines that had fascinated me so much. He grabbed my wayward finger and held my hand on the mattress, looking pointedly at me.

I sighed in exasperation. "You were on the brink of death. The bullets punctured a lung and possibly nicked an artery."

His face didn't reveal his thoughts and I could no longer read his emotions. Now that he was a vampire, my powers were useless against him. Only while he was human had it been possible.

Being a vampire suited him. Vitality shone from his eyes and skin. Self-assurance showed in the way he held his shoulders, even in his speech.

"Tell me what the paramedics told you," he demanded.

"There was no time to wait for them. You were bleeding internally. Blood was pouring from your wounds, your mouth, and nose. If I had waited until the paramedics got there or I got you to a hospital, it would've been too late."

I watched him move and sit on the edge of the bed with his head bowed and a sheet spread over his lap. Sitting behind him, my gaze savored the dimples above his firm butt cheeks.

"You should have let me die." His voice emerged flat with finality.

My heart stopped. Surely he didn't really want that?

"I couldn't."

I moved and rested my chest against his bare back and slipped my arms around his chest, kissing his shoulder. With a shrug, he rejected my offer of comfort and moved from the bed, dropping the sheet behind him. He stopped near the dresser where a large ceramic lamp lit the room.

With his back to me, he placed his hands on the dresser and dropped his head. I renewed my admiration of his taut cheeks and added my regard for his muscled thighs and calves. So damn hot.

I closed my eyes for a second, the sight too much to take in. He was all-male, and deep inside, I'd do anything to keep him.

"You're a selfish woman." He glared at me over a hunched shoulder. Anger filled each word.

"Me? How was it being selfish to want you to live?"

"Sometimes love is not enough to save a person."

"I didn't say that I love..." I stared at him for a few moments. "You're talking about your dad, aren't you?" Not for the first time I wished I could read a vampire's emotions too. I had become too dependent on my gift.

"That's beside the point. No matter how hungry I get, I'll not kill—"

"Feed," I inserted.

"—feed on people," he scoffed. "I'll not take their blood."

Anger darkened his face, giving him a devilish edge that suited him. He turned to face me, standing with his arms crossed, naked in all his glory.

It was difficult, but I kept my gaze on his. Though in my peripheral sight, I could still admire his beautiful body. I wanted to stretch him out on the bed and lick and kiss every square inch, especially his lovely cock.

"You took my blood without harming me," I reminded him. Though he did come close to taking too much. Seeing he wasn't convinced, I continued. "You don't have to kill a person to take their blood. I took blood from you two different times, but you had no idea. You only remember the dreams, filled with sex and colors. Pleasure was your reward for giving me your blood."

His eyes widened for a flash when the truth struck him.

"So you bit me and we didn't have sex, I only thought I did?"

I nodded.

"You bit me and those times didn't that make me a vampire?"

I nodded again and explained. "Only when a human's at the brink of death and his blood nearly drained from his body can he become a vampire. Once I replaced your blood with my own, the change takes place. Your body regenerates the new blood and the First Hunger comes over you."

It was important for him to understand. Later, I should tell him we were in danger from my master. I took a big chance in changing Ronan. I had illegally reincarnated him. Vampires required the local master's or mistress' permission before creating fledglings from their humans. Yes. Vampires are territorial about the humans living in their territory. They are protective of their food source.

"What if I had taken all of your blood?"

So the thought finally came to him. I was delighted with his concern.

"Some say, it would place me in a comatose state. Others say, I would come under your control, become your slave. No matter, it didn't happen. Why worry?"

"Slave?"

"Servant. Slave. It's one and the same in the vampire world."

"So you're saying, vampires have slaves?" His voice held a mixture of disgust and fascination.

I was intrigued by his reaction.

"We need human servants to serve and protect us during the day. Even during this modern age. Though the big cities remain open twenty-four hours, seven days a week, we still need someone to deal with the power company and other essentials that are maintained during the daylight hours." I wasn't sure how he would react to Connor. "To ensure their loyalty and cooperation without turning them. It takes only a few drops of vampire blood in their water or beverage and they're willing to do your bidding."

"And they don't mind?"

Though pleased with his curiosity, I was uncertain of where he was going with his questions. But he was obviously struggling with his hunger as it took a couple of days for a fledgling to gain self-control. Sweat beaded on his forehead and his gaze continued to stray to my neck. The desire to feed could be confused with lust, and often when denied, could turn into rage.

Seeing his cock harden more and stretch before my eyes, thrusting out for my touch, was a sight I enjoyed immensely. I couldn't stop from grinning.

"They don't know or care. When a human drinks a vampire's blood in small quantities, it's like a drug. A very potent and addictive drug. They'll do anything for another boost." Sadly, that was part of why Byron and Connor had fought over me. Chances were their affection had grown to something more after all of this time. I treated them well. They had more freedom than most vampire servants. I cringed inside. Was that why Byron had found it so easy to betray me? Would Connor be next? How would Connor react to Ronan joining my household? It would be different. Though I would be mistress to both, Ronan would be a vampire.

I tilted my head and licked my lips. Ronan's cock moved.

Yes, the First Hunger wasn't over. I'd forgotten how thrilling it was to be around a fledgling. My master had often let me train his. Only by satisfying all Ronan's blood lust throughout the night would it stop him from killing a human.

I'd seen a few cruel master vampires change a human and leave them to fend for themselves. Such cruelty would often result in the creatures going insane and getting killed. The Hunters was always on the outlook for fledglings. Dangerous but so new that they were easily eliminated.

I looked forward to teaching Ronan all I knew and living with him for decades to come. If he allowed it. If he didn't resent my part in his reincarnation.

"Anything?" His eyes narrowed.

"Huh?" Then I came back to our conversation. In a low voice, I answered, "Yes. Anything."

"Is that why I can't think of anything but fucking your brains out?"

With a gentle laugh, I opened my arms. "Come. It's your First Hunger that's making you so horny. It's either blood or sex. It appears this round will be mostly sex."

"You don't know shit about me," he murmured as he crawled into the bed and covered me with his firm, big body.

Two hours later, I rested across Ronan's chest, staring off in amazement. He was magnificent.

"Maybe you know more about me than I thought," he said in a satisfied deep voice.

I grinned.

The room was quiet with only the hum from the air vents and our breathing. So peaceful, such a wonderful evening.

"Tori, why didn't you kill Sam Kerry?"

"He was innocent." Why couldn't he leave it alone?

"How do you know?"

"I'd rather talk of something else." Still emotional about my discovery that I was truly a monster and not a champion of the people, tears welled in my eyes. The horror of almost killing an innocent man and wondering how many were innocent in the past haunted my thoughts and dreams. Only monsters killed innocent people.

"No. We need to talk about it." He sat up beside me, unaware of how his nude body made it difficult to concentrate on anything besides fucking him again. When would I get enough?

"Fine." I rolled my eyes. "I have the ability to read emotions. Sorta. If I touch their skin, I can't read what they're thinking, but I get a sense of how they are feeling. And I can see a person's past."

"Are you reading mine?" His dark look said he wasn't happy about the possibility.

"No. I can only read a human's. But I read your feelings the first night. When I'd realized I was becoming too attracted to you, I blocked out your emotions and your past memories at our second meeting and from then on. I couldn't take the chance you would become more important than what I was doing. You have to understand, I had to end it. You were becoming a danger to me and my purpose, my crusade."

Female vampires' feelings were more volatile than their male counterparts. But if the female was stable enough and had a strong enough will, she learned to control her emotions. So many females killed themselves or were killed by male vampires within the first year of reincarnation.

I guessed that my preoccupation with my crusade channeled my passions into revenge. Until I met Ronan.

"You'll tell me about the others then."

Confident of my cooperation, was he?

I couldn't help smiling like an idiot when his gaze moved to my breasts, but I quickly stopped smiling when his observant look dropped to the right side of my body. The side I tried to keep tucked beneath the sheet or his body. When he was human, it had been so easy to keep his attention elsewhere.

"Now tell me about the scars and how you got them, and why I've never noticed before," he said with a voice firm but filled with concern.

Nosey asshole. That was what I deserved for making such an alpha male a vampire. I couldn't keep him in a daze of lust, hiding my scars. So he wanted to know the facts? Well, why not? I did nothing wrong.

"They're thanks to a madman when I was human. No more than that." A numb feeling came over me as I remembered the reason for killing the psycho. I recited the events leading up to my reincarnation, then looked into his face. Nothing. No emotion was revealed. Did I disgust him?

"You're leaving something out. It's the oddest thing. Something tells me that you're not telling me everything." He rubbed his face with one broad hand.

Obviously, he was uncomfortable with sensing people's feelings. In the nightclub, I suspected he might possess psychic abilities. The signs were there. In particular, his finding me in the night club without really trying and guessing correctly on three of the four deviants I was tracking down at the time. Whatever capability a human had, if they're aware of it or not, would be magnified after becoming a vampire.

Would his powers become greater than mine? If they did, in a few short years, he would truly be a might to be reckoned with. If his power increased to the point he was more powerful than my master, there would be trouble. Worry and dread filled me. I needed to be held.

His strong arms closed around me, pulling my body on top of his. Resting my cheek on his shoulder, my eyes drifted shut in contentment.

Yes. His power of intuition was strong.

# Chapter 12

## *Ronan*

"Ah, I see that our fledgling has decided to wake and discover the new, bold world he's joined."

I turned toward the intruder with the odd accented voice. The man leaning against the doorframe looked to be nothing more than a junior executive. Caucasian, maybe six-foot or just under, short black hair, a lean build with no noticeable scars or tattoos. He wore a pullover sweater and dress slacks, rather harmless looking.

Until I looked into his penetrating eyes. They studied me like a panther anticipating the movements of a rabbit. With a push from the doorframe, the man moved toward the bed I'd slept in and still lolled on with Tori, his graceful strides proclaiming him vampire.

Sprawled across my chest, I felt Tori stiffen. She slid off and pressed her back to the pillows. With a jerk, she covered us with the top sheet.

Never having seen Tori worried or rattled by another person's presence, even hanging from chains in Brannon's basement, made me wary of the stranger. Waves of power came off the creature and surrounded me.

I moved and crouched in front of Tori, shielding her with my body. Her breath tickled my ear.

Tori placed a hand on my shoulder. "Ronan, may I introduce our host, my master and the local master of this territory, Wolfric Jarmann. Wolfric, Ronan Michaels."

The vampire lowered his head in acknowledgment, keeping his eyes on me.

Danger permeated the room, old power covered me with a suffocating feeling held in check. Understanding the master vampire's warning, I nodded and lowered my eyes for a second. Wolfric recognized it as acknowledgment of not only the introduction but his restrained power.

The master's gaze moved to Tori. "Is all well and to your liking?"

"Yes. Edwin has been...most efficient," she said.

Her sarcasm was not lost to the room. Edwin must've been Wolfric's servant who had tended to them earlier. The man had resented their presence, but had provided the towels and linens needed.

The master vampire chuckled. "Ah, Edwin. He is fussy. Let me know if we can do more. We haven't had this much excitement in years."

Wolfric came closer to the bed and moved to Tori's side. He lifted her hand and kissed the back with irritating slowness.

I growled, a fucking growl left my lips. Surprised by my reaction, I swallowed the next one. Reining in my temper, I reached for Tori's arm and pulled her hand away from the master vampire. I didn't care for the way he looked at her.

Wolfric chuckled again. "Shani will bring you one of her brews. It'll clean the drug out of your system for good, and you should be more yourself. I merely wanted to see how you were doing and see if your fledgling was surviving the night." The vampire looked at me with a challenging sneer. "You better be kind to Victoria and understand that not only do you owe her your life, but your un-death too. She's a rare pearl in a sea of faux jewels." His attention returned to Tori. "When you're well rested and recovered from your ordeal, we'll speak of your penalty."

Tori simply dipped her head. "Of course."

Penalty? I didn't like the sound of that. What had Wolfric meant by that?

When the master vampire left the room, I turned to ask her, but was struck by how tired she looked. Dark circles sunk her eyes and hollowed her cheeks, sure signs of exhaustion.

Self-absorbed with my change, I neglected to think that Tori needed to recover. Between the drug shot into her and my insatiable need for her body and blood, it was no wonder she was exhausted.

"Damn it. Lay down before you pass out or something." I shoved her shoulders onto the mattress, leaning over her.

Laughing, she nestled into the pillows and sheets as I arranged them around her. Her eyes glowed in pleasure. "I'm worn out, but I did enjoy the way you make my body sing." Her crooked grin had my heart doing flips.

"Make your body sing, huh?" Unconsciously, I picked up her hand and kissed the back in the same place Wolfric had, erasing his touch. "Once you've rested, maybe we can do a duet?"

She giggled. That was surprising. I never thought of her as a giggly little girl, but at one time she had a mother and father and maybe siblings, a whole life before she became a vampire.

"I've been around Wolfric so much, I catch myself talking like him."

Unable to hold back, I asked, "Do you have any brothers or sisters? Is your mother and father still alive?"

I regretted the questions no sooner than they came out. Her smile vanished like a wall falling between us. She shut down.

"Where is that witch?" she asked, looking around as if expecting someone to pop out of the furniture. She turned onto her stomach.

"Witch?"

"Shani works for Wolfric. She's his in-house witch."

Witches? In-house witch? A few days ago, I didn't know there were vampires. So of course, there were witches.

I wasn't pissed about her shutting down or changing the subject, not with the waves of sorrow coming off her. For some reason, she was remembering something painful. What had happened in her past with her family that tormented her?

"Tori, what happened to your family?"

Her eyes were so sad. Were they all dead? Had she killed them for some fathomless reason? No. I couldn't imagine her harming the ones she loved.

"Please. Can we talk of other things?"

With one finger against her cheek, I turned her face and waited for her gaze to meet mine. "Okay. When you're ready to tell me, I'll be here. I know how important family is."

"Thank you."

Sharp grief flowed from her. Maybe our connection had me feeling her sorrow or it was all part of being a vampire.

A need to comfort had me pulling her into my arms, resting my cheek on the top of her head. Pain and deep sorrow broadcasted from her body in waves. I squeezed a little tighter, hoping I wasn't hurting her and began to run a hand down her hair over and over again. I wasn't sure if it would help.

After a few minutes passed without a word being spoken, I no longer could hold back the questions. "What did Wolfric mean by penalty? And what would you two speak of later?"

"It's nothing."

"Penalty means you did something wrong. What right does he have to punish you?"

Her arms came around my waist and held me tight in return. At first, I was certain she merely wanted me closer, but once her words sunk into my slow mind—her body felt so good against mine—I realized her concern was I would break loose to kill Wolfric.

"Wolfric is my master and I've broken a covenant with him. It's his right to punish me." She began kissing my chest, probably in the hope to calm me.

"Over my dead body." I grabbed her shoulders and held her away. "What covenant have you broken?"

"Only the local master can give permission to reincarnate a human into a vampire. I hadn't planned on you." She pulled away and crawled out of the bed.

My gaze followed her well-formed ass as she bent to pick up her clothes on the nearby chair. Keeping my attention on her movements, I slipped on the shirt and slacks brought earlier by Edwin with the towels. Relieved to hear her say she hadn't planned to make me a vampire all along, I watched her dress, enjoying the view. At the same time, I wrestled with regaining control of my body. Determined to concentrate on something besides fucking her again I exhaled and straightened my shoulders.

"Wolfric? Was he the vampire who transformed...reincarnated you?" I asked when I stepped in front of her.

She cut her eyes toward him. "Yes. He was the savior of my sanity and benefactor of my crusade. Why?"

"What kind of control does he have over you?" Bothered by the thought of Wolfric being her master anything, my tone was harsher than intended.

Laughing, she smiled and leaned her head back to gaze into my eyes.

"Don't be worried. He's only responsible for me if I go rogue or break a code." Her expression became solemn for a moment. "Only exposure of the colony brings true death."

"True death? I thought we were immortal?"

"Obviously your knowledge of vampire lore is lacking." Her grin widened. I was glad to see her expression lighten again. "No one on this earth is immortal. We can die by a stake through the heart, and fire or daylight can burn us to a crisp."

"What will his punishment involve?" Concerned for her safety, I couldn't let the subject be dropped.

She walked away and ran slender fingers through her hair in an effort to tame the wild curls, and ignored me. I grabbed her arms and turned her.

"What?" Her innocent look wasn't lost on me.

"You're not going to tell me, are you?" I watched her struggle with whatever internal demons she possessed while keeping her mouth shut. "Then you understand this. I'll not let him harm one hair on your head. Do you understand me? You're mine."

Tears welled in her eyes.

Dammit. I hadn't meant for her to cry.

My temper and feelings were ricocheting all over the place, and in the back of my mind I sensed something wanting to come out. Something dark and terrifying. All of my efforts to control and shut off that part of myself was becoming harder as the evening progressed. While we made love and fed off each other, the beast—

That was it.

It felt like a beast inside, waiting to be released, to bathe in blood. The blood of anyone or anything that harmed what I claimed was mine. And as I had told her, she was mine.

<<<>>>
Tori

I was ashamed of how his possessiveness brought heat to my pussy. And like a silly little girl, tears came to my eyes with each sweet word he uttered in his manly arrogance, expecting my total obedience.

I loved him. More every night. It had been too many years to count since someone truly cared for my well-being without expecting something in return. This evening was a time I would always cherish. Afraid of confessing how I felt, I pulled away and walked over to an overnight case sitting in a chair.

Normally, I kept it in the trunk of my car. Besides makeup, the mid-sized black case held shampoo, a change of underwear, and clothes, all to bring relief from my blood-stained appearance whenever I went on a hunt.

A knock on the door was a welcome buffer from his hot gaze and my chaotic feelings.

The witch wasn't what I expected the first time I'd met her. I had thought they were all dark little creatures with moles on their faces and hook-shaped noses. Shani was none of these with her long, sun-kissed blond hair and clear blue eyes. She looked to be a mischievous elf.

Jealously swamped my senses when I noticed how

Ronan watched the witch move into the room. Was he interested? I didn't like it one bit. Sure, I understood why he reacted the way he did. As a newly made vampire, his emotions and senses were going in every direction, even his skin was ultra sensitive.

He stood. His black jeans and long-sleeved black shirt suited the new Ronan, hanging and molding in the right places. With his longish, dark hair and five-o'clock shadow, he stalked around the room, casting a spell of carnal danger in the room. My jealousy could easily cause me to go crazy and contemplate chaining him to my bed and never letting him loose.

"Shani, how long have you known the master?" I was determined to break away from the green-eyed monster.

The blond witch grinned. "Since I was a kid, though he wouldn't let me visit until I got out of college. He said that a vampire's house was no place for a young lady."

It was unheard of for a vampire and witch to get along. They were mortal enemies, at least that was how I understood it.

After setting down the tray in her hands, Shani shook a small envelope of brown powder into a cup and poured in tea. After stirring the brew, she handed the cup to me, but my hands trembled and I shook my head.

A weakness had enveloped me. I stretched out on a nearby low divan. With a dip of my chin, I indicated the tiny tea table within reach. She set the cup down and nudged it a little closer to me. Still feeling shaky, I ignored it.

The adrenaline from our escape, giving blood to Ronan, and the sex-a-thon had drained me of all my energy. I was lucky the divan had been nearby, saving me from further embarrassment by falling to the floor.

Shani stood by and waited for me to pick up the cup.

Staring at the tea as if it contained acid, I wasn't sure if I trusted the witch. "What is it?"

"Nothing more than a strong vitamin-and-mineral mix that will strengthen your blood."

Something in Shani's face told me I could trust her. If she'd been merely human, I could touch her hand and check her truthfulness, but vampires never touched a witch without permission. Witches normally had a spell protecting their person that could cause pain to a vampire.

I lifted it and took small sips. My eyes widened. Nice. It tasted like the orange-flavored tea that my mother made at Christmastime. "I expected it to taste bitter."

"Why should medicine taste like crap? I've learned people are better at finishing their medication if it tastes good." The witch gathered the tray, smiling once again at Ronan on the way out.

"She's a witch?" he asked, a look of curiosity on his face.

Even though I had the same thought the first time meeting her, his interest in the witch irritated me.

"Yes and she belongs to the master."

Ronan turned his glowing eyes to me. "What's Wolfric to you?"

I liked that jealousy was a two-headed monster. "Besides being my creator, he's the local master vampire for Birmingham and the surrounding county plus three more. I had to get his permission to carry out my crusade in his area, and he helped me obtain permission from other masters to hunt down perverts in different parts of the U.S."

"So he gave you permission to kill the men in his territory."

"Yes and no. He asked me to use discretion. He understands the danger of drawing the local authorities attention. So, I've only killed one and beaten others in this area."

"Only one?"

"One."

"I've been told others are dead. What will he do about you killing more than one?"

"Nothing. Don't you remember? You stopped me."

"What about Robert Moore and Billy Spencer?

"I don't know what you mean."

I hated lying to him. I'd rather not mention how a servant of mine had gone on a rampage beheading two. That would make me appear to be losing control of my servants. Wolfric would have a lot to say about that.

"Robert Moore and Billy Spencer are dead."

"Robert Moore? How?" I cringed inside at the lie. I turned away and looked out the window.

"Moore was found with his head cut off. The same as Spencer."

"When I left Moore, he was alive. He'd promised to turn himself in to the police. Besides, I hadn't planned to kill him. He was nothing more than a chicken-hearted asshole."

Besides, I couldn't tell him my normal method for killing humans was by snapping their necks without leaving finger-shaped bruises. Fewer questions about their deaths that way. They appeared to the authorities as no more than a bad fall. I worked at keeping my voice even. "Besides, decapitation is too messy."

I looked back at Ronan. Stretched out on his side across the end of the bed, he made me think of a lion lazily sunning but ready to attack at the first sign of weakness. One palm pressed to his cheek as he leaned on his elbow and waited.

For what? For me to confess I was a monster? He would find out soon enough.

"That's Moore. But you never said anything about Spencer."

Why was I reluctant to tell him about Byron's fatal error of judgment? Too many years protecting my own? But why hide it from him? Ronan was going to be a permanent fixture in my household and Byron would be dealt with by vampire colony laws. Ironic, right?

Because I was a vampire and good at hiding the deaths or bodies, I would get away with it, but a human would be punished for the murders he committed.

"I might know who killed Spencer and I'll deal with it."

"Okay."

I closed my eyes for a second. Relief loosened my shoulders. I was glad the questioning was over. When I opened them again, the heavy-eyed look he gave me brought my legs together in a tight squeeze. How could he make my center pulse without touching me?

All of my self-control was needed not to jump his bones. First things first, I needed to tell Wolfric about Byron killing Spencer and Moore before police somehow traced them back to him. If Wolfric believed I had killed those guys—in such a gruesome, sloppy way—my butt would be in a sling for sure.

Creaking springs brought my attention to Ronan. He'd rolled over on his stomach, resting his chin on his arm. Concern for me obvious on his face. But my gaze kept drifting to his tight ass. His pants cupped his rear beautifully. Oh, yes, he was so delicious.

Energy zinged through my body. The brew was doing the trick. Though I wanted to jump back in bed and do nothing but lick him all over, I had to enlighten Ronan on the nuances of existing in a vampire colony. Not knowing the rules would get him killed. The eternal death kind.

The rules would be strange to him, stricter and harsher than those he had to enforce as a police officer. How would he react to vampires' centuries-old rules? Then again, some had been corrupted by loopholes, like those of death of humans. If the death didn't draw the local human authorities, then a vampire could get away with it.

"Ronan, you must understand how the colony works. The purpose of every rule and law is to protect our existence from humans."

"You mean humans from vampires."

"No." Feeling better, I felt the need to move around. "Think. The few humans aware of our existence hunt us. Once the world knows that vampires are real, a panic would spread and humans would kill anyone or anything that resembled what they believed to be a vampire. There may be a few who are fans." I shook my head. "Some are not mentally capable to handle the powers, but they would beg...needless to say, it would be chaos."

"So you're protecting the colony. What about Wolfric? Did he control you when you had lived elsewhere?"

I grinned. He was still worried about Wolfric. Jealousy looked good on him. Maybe he wouldn't hate me in the end. I stared into the empty fireplace.

"He's my sire, no matter where I go. But each region has its own mistress or master, and I must acknowledge their authority."

"Mistress?" He stopped behind me. Heat rolled off his body in waves. My sigh vibrated through my body as I leaned back, shoulders against his chest.

"Though several of the colonies in the southern region are controlled by male vampires, the majority of the colonies are ruled by females." In an effort to control my raging desire, I said, "Ratio wise, the male vampires outnumber the female by ten to one."

I couldn't help but smile at the thought. I always liked those odds.

"Does that mean the female vampire is stronger than the male?" he asked.

I could feel him playing with my hair, stroking, threading his fingers through the strands.

"Not in the way you're thinking. The females rule, not because they're the oldest or strongest, but because most males are susceptible to the females' greatest power. Her sex."

Ronan's hands dropped to my waist and came around to hold me. "I can imagine the males are unable to get enough."

Ignoring his teasing, I continued. "Rarely is sexual intercourse required to keep male vampires in line. A powerful vampire can do it easily with the appeal of her sexuality and femininity. Male vampires are sensual creatures and rarely follow rulers with their intellect alone."

"Why does Wolfric lead this colony?" He said Wolfric's name like a curse.

His hands came up and covered my breasts. I groaned, enjoying the feel of his masculine hands squeezing and stroking the sensitive skin through my blouse.

"Only the colonies with military purposes have male vampires leading them. Wolfric's colony is a training ground for enforcers," I said, breathless at the end.

Before he could ask questions about enforcers, I turned and began returning the caresses he started. I loved this fledgling and hoped I could protect him.

<<<>>>

"What's happening? My legs and arms feel so heavy." Ronan's puzzled tone was expected. I'd felt the same way when the first death sleep came over me.

He stumbled toward the bed, an angry look coming over his face. "What have you done to me?"

"Shh. Do you not feel it? The sun is just moments away from peeking between the trees. When you're first reincarnated, a fledgling has difficulty staying awake beyond sunrise."

I helped him into bed, and he stretched on his back across the mattress.

His unwarranted anger was so typical of a male vampire. Aggressive and territorial, the young vampire was unpredictable, but I hopefully waylaid the worst by providing an outlet for his aggression.

"Isn't it bothering you?"

"The longer you're a vampire, the longer you can withstand the lure of the death sleep. Rarely can a new vampire stay awake through dawn, and never to high noon."

I watched him fight the sleep like a child, though nothing about the way he looked was childish. The black, cotton shirt, unbuttoned to mid-chest, and black jeans combined with his dark hair and olive skin, gave him a dangerous air. Heated desire taunted me. Temptation to touch him while he slept almost overtook me. He'd resent that. It would be too much like taking advantage of him during a weakness.

His eyelids fluttered to half-mast. Their beautiful depth glistened in the bedroom's lights as he tried to keep me in his sight. He slowly closed them and snapped them back open, then they closed again.

I lifted his large, rough hand to my lips and pressed a kiss to the back.

"Relax. I'll watch over you until it's time for me to join you. Guards surround the place and the house is secure. Wolfric wouldn't have reached the ripe old age of a millennium if he was careless."

Immediately, his hand fell limp and his body sank further into the mattress. His chest no longer rose and fell with his breathing, and I knew his heartbeat would be near to nonexistent. I brushed the back of my fingers against his cheek, his skin cold to the touch. Like death.

Wolfric was too wary to have vampires sleep in his bed when death sleep overtook him, if he did. I really had no idea. Only once had I been near another vampire during death sleep. It had been when I traveled to Atlanta on Wolfric's orders.

There, the large vampire colony had consisted of artists and musicians. Though during that period, I'd spent most of my time recuperating from my wounds and controlling my urge to kill every deviant in a twenty-mile area, I'd allowed a tall, blond male vampire to slip under my guard.

The slightly older vampire had never met an instrument he couldn't play and my body had been no exception. He'd been the only vampire I ever made love to or slept with before Ronan. After the Atlanta experience, I spent my sexual desires on my servants. Less of a distraction and I didn't have to pretend softer feelings to achieve satisfaction.

Looking down at the man beside me, a softening around my heart eased the ache I endured for so long. I loved him, but how long would it take before he decided I was wrong to change him?

Tired and no longer feeling the brew, I pressed my body to his and kissed him on the cheek. His shoulder was perfect for my head to rest on.

<<<>>>

Decades may go by, but the dreams were so vivid and always the same and always before I woke to a new night. I watched helpless and weak as the madman sharpened his blades, preparing to work on my body once again. Pain washed over me with each swipe.

The muzzle tasted of old and fresh blood, and smelled of sweat. Another wave of pain pulled me under and I turned my head as if watching the reflection in a mirror. But the image revealed my body totally filleted as my brown eyes stared sightless back. Lifeless. Dead. I was truly dead.

It was too late. I was too late.

"Tori, Victoria. Wake up. It's just a dream."

Ronan's husky voice pulled me back to the present.

Opening my eyes and seeing his concerned face above mine was what I needed to forget the nightmare. Would he wake me every night for centuries from the horror of my past or would he leave once he truly understood what I'd made him?

"Ronan. Make love to me. Please." I hated begging. But his touch, his hard body, and cock would help me forget why I became a monster.

# Chapter 13

## *Tori*

"Tori, have a seat. Do you understand why you must be punished?" Wolfric sat in the shadows, giving him the advantage of seeing my face, while not seeing his. "Ronan, your presence wasn't requested," he said before I answered.

I turned and looked at the newest vampire in Birmingham. I hoped he didn't say something that would get him killed by Wolfric. I'd explained the protocol after we woke this evening, but there were too many rules to cover them all. That was one of the many drawbacks of living so long, a mixture of too many customs and unwritten rules becoming part of a vampire's life.

His dark hair was brushed back from his face, ragged ends hanging to his shoulders. A sensual heat filled the room with his unexpected presence. It was hard for me to concentrate. My fingers tingled with a need to touch eyebrows, lips, chin, and so much more.

"Ronan, I'm okay," I said softly, worry behind each word. "Go and call Connor. Tell him to have the house ready for our return on Friday." I glanced at Wolfric, hoping his patience wasn't stretched too thin. "They'll send for you if you're needed," I added to Ronan.

"Why Friday, not before?" he said in a gruff voice. Obviously becoming angry by the tension in the room.

Had I really thought he would be easily maneuvered?

"Please. I'll explain everything later. Wolfric has graciously extended his invitation until I...you regain your strength." I hated the slip and closed my eyes for a second. "We need the time to ourselves anyway and Wolfric's compound will ensure that."

"I'm not going anywhere," Ronan said in a firm voice.

Before I could leave my chair, two burly vampires walked up behind Ronan and grabbed his arms. Ronan roared. With a back thrust of his elbows, the two vampires released him and clutched their bellies. Ronan turned, jabbed one with an upper cut, and before the other could recover, two more vampires came into the room and jumped Ronan.

"Stop!" I pulled one vampire off Ronan by kicking his legs out from under him, then I reached for the other one. "Leave! Don't hurt him."

"Halt!" Wolfric's commanding tone brought everyone to a standstill. Only in extreme anger was his German accent significant. "Take him to his chamber and make sure that he doesn't leave."

I reached for Ronan, but was stopped by Wolfric's hand on my arm.

"Let me talk with him," I pleaded.

I wanted Ronan to understand our survival depended on Wolfric's tolerance. Being the master of the area, Wolfric could easily kill us without blinking an eye.

"They'll not harm him, unless he fights." Wolfric jerked his head and the four vampires took Ronan from the room.

"If you harm her, I'll kill you," Ronan warned Wolfric as he was pulled away.

I inhaled in horror. The dangerous words hung between Wolfric and I. As soon as I recovered, I would need to find a way to keep Ronan out of Wolfric's way until the stubborn fledgling learned his manners.

Upset and worried, I faced the master vampire. "Okay, let's get to it."

"You do understand the gravity of the situation." Plainly, he felt a need to reiterate. "If I allowed every vampire under my command to reincarnate every human they lusted after, our colony would soon be opened to exposure. Our kind has lived for thousands of years, and each time we were exposed, they hunted and killed us to near extinction."

I worked at hiding my impatience. Last thing I needed was to piss off Wolfric with an angry face. So I crossed my ankles and clasped my hands in my lap, as if resigned to wait for his chastisement.

He grimaced at my poor playacting.

"On your knees before me," he commanded. "Show me your respect for my authority. Never make me punish you for this again." In a whisper, his next words sent a chill down my back. "Death is the next punishment, and you and your lover only live because I have a soft spot for you. Don't make me regret my leniency."

How could I argue with him? As if. But he was right. The dangers were too great for me to allow my emotions to rule my head. I owed Wolfric too much. Over the years, I had heard of the cruel pettiness other vampires inflicted on their colonies. Wolfric was not petty.

"I hadn't planned to reincarnate Ronan or anyone for that matter." Even to my ears, my voice sounded harsh and not the least bit repentant. I kneeled in front of Wolfric and bowed my head. "Of course, I never expected to fall in love with a human."

"Beware." Such sadness filled that word. I had always known a woman had hurt him badly centuries ago. Now I added to my guess it had been a human woman. He cleared his throat, then said, "Most are weak creatures and their weakness becomes greater weaknesses after being turned." I heard him walk to the doorway, then stop behind me. The clink of glassware resounded above me. "You've been betrayed by one already."

Byron's betrayal still hurt, but I couldn't worry about him. Wolfric knew of Byron helping Edgar Brannon, but nothing about his part in the beheadings. I wished Wolfric would finish my punishment, so I could relieve Ronan's fears.

No matter the chastisement Wolfric decided, I would survive.

"I'm yours to command." The punishment he inflicted could range from disfigurement that would take years to heal to long-term imprisonment in a coffin. I preferred the former over the latter.

"Drink this."

In his hand was a delicate china cup and saucer with tiny roses painted on the side. The cup held what smelled like the orange-spice tea I loved so much.

Why was he offering me another vitamin drink before the punishment? Was it in preparation? Was it poisoned?

I looked up into Wolfric's face. Nothing showed. Like all old vampires, he was good at hiding his emotions. Even I was aware I could do the same with practice, but never had the need until recently. Nevertheless, Wolfric wouldn't hide the fact this was an execution. He would give me a chance to make my peace, even say my goodbyes. Besides, he'd already promised I would survive. My certainty in his fairness had me taking the cup and saucer out of his hand. They rattled. To cover my nervousness, I used both hands to lift the cup to my lips and sip. The flavor was rich but a little sweeter than I liked.

I looked at Wolfric over the cup's rim as I finished the brew. Handing the cup and saucer back to him, I waited to see what would happen. Except for a relaxing of my tense muscles, I felt the same.

"Go. Comfort your fledgling, and it would be best you not leave the compound until the brew is out of your system." His voice was filled with regret and almost apologetic.

"What have you done to me?" Was part of the punishment to be in the dark about my fate?

"The brew is a formula Shani worked up at my request," he firmly said. "It will not allow you to feed, and the pain and weakness will be great until it leaves your system. Three days will feel like an eternity and help you remember why you must obey me."

I stood but my knees buckled. Wolfric caught me before I fell face-first onto the Persian rug, holding me to his chest. My vision blurred and my head spun.

"Come, take her to her man," he ordered a servant.

I felt strong hands lift me beneath my arms.

Blinking rapidly, my head still spun, but my vision came back enough to distinguish shadows and furniture. Determined not to scare Ronan, I struggled until I was on my feet again. When I began to sway, the burly vampire reached out to me.

"No," I bit off and then I calmly added, "I'll make my way back to the chamber on my own two feet, thank you."

As I walked slowly down the hall, I heard Wolfric's orders. "Follow close behind and make sure she doesn't harm herself."

I ignored my dark, hulking shadow and shuffled to my chamber. With a few feet to go, I stumbled and the burly vampire grasped my arm. I jerked away.

"Do not to touch me," I said, almost with a growl.

Finally reaching my chamber door, I straightened my shoulders and took a deep breath. That was a mistake. Nausea almost had me bent over and crying. After a moment of waiting for my stomach to calm down, I reached for the doorknob.

Before I touched it, the door opened. Ronan stood in front of me. His soft, hazel-green eyes were anxious with worry. He was unable to hide his emotions so far, and I was so glad. I wanted a little sympathy, to be held and protected.

The brew was making me droll. A pitiful creature indeed. I knew there was no one I could really rely on. Byron proved that and Connor would eventually. Humans. I snorted.

No matter how much I loved him, most likely Ronan would turn on me one day.

Oh, I needed to lie down. Self-pity wasn't keeping my stomach from roiling and actually made it worse.

"What did that son of a bitch do to you?" He scooped me up in his arms and carried me to the canopy bed. "I knew I should have stayed."

That tickled me. Like he had a choice? I chuckled and kept my unfocused gaze on him. He was so beautiful, even if a little blurry, so alive. I couldn't regret turning him.

Cold, sweaty fear coated my whole body.

What if I had screwed up and hadn't been quick enough? He would have died before I reincarnated him. To reincarnate a corpse, made only a zombie. A foul, rotting zombie who ate human flesh. In the years of being a vampire, I'd only seen one and I hoped never to see another.

"Would blood help?" he asked.

My gaze dropped to his arm, held out for my hunger and instantly my fangs dropped. My nausea felt like it was fading. Was Wolfric wrong? Could I feed?

The smell of blood beneath his skin brought a craving I couldn't resist. I bit down on the bend of his arm and began to feed.

Ronan's shaky moan was music to my ears. Then a wave of nausea hit me. It was so strong I jerked away and rolled from him. I stumbled to the bathroom and barely reached the commode before throwing up the blood.

"Dammit, Tori, what did he do to you?" He knelt beside me, moved my hair out of my eyes, and tucked it behind an ear. "Are you dying?"

"No. I just feel that way," I whispered and shook my head. On seeing his concern, I added, "I can't feed for three days. That is how long the potion will stay in my system before it runs its course."

"That shouldn't be too bad." He lifted me from the cold tile floor and helped me back to the bed. Unable to hold my head up, I sank into the pillows and soft comforter.

"You hadn't realized yet, we need blood whenever the craving hits, otherwise the gnawing of hunger is painful, with the more energy we use, the more blood we need."

He nodded his head, but he didn't really understand and the next few days would open his eyes.

Throughout the night, Ronan sat by my side, bathing my forehead while I was sick and holding me when the nausea subsided. Several times my body racked with cramps that brought my knees to my chest. I faded in and out of consciousness, barely aware of Ronan's soft spoken words of sympathy.

About an hour before dawn, the pains began to ease, and I felt Ronan lean over and kiss my cheek. Weak and exhausted, I gave into the pull of death sleep.


<<<>>>

Ronan


I stood, looking down at the woman lying so still on the pillows. Her cheeks were as pale as the white sheets, and the dark half-circles underneath her eyes were the only color on her face. No movement. Not even the rising and falling of her chest.

Death sleep.

This time, she succumbed before me. Her earlier warnings kept me from panicking, plus I remembered the time spent in the basement and her hanging from the chains. I reassured myself with the thought each time she slipped into the sleep, her body worked on the potion and she improved.

That was, I hoped Tori was telling the complete story, but in case she kept the worst to herself, I would confront the one that caused it.

Wolfric wasn't hard to find. Reclining on a long, brown-and-gold lounger, he sipped brandy from a tumbler in one hand while reading from a small book in the other.

The room was lit by a floor lamp shaped like a large tulip, casting shadows and giving an otherworldly appearance to the vampire watching me over the top of the poetry book. If he blew smoke in circles from a water pipe, it wouldn't have shocked me.

Silence and tension filled the air between us until Wolfric spoke. "How's Tori?"

"How can you ask me that? It was you that poisoned her." I wanted to pummeled him. Take a pound of flesh for the pain the master had put Tori through.

"I don't take pleasure from it. If I had refused to punish her, the human race would be in danger from becoming eliminated. Every vampire with a desire to create a slave or mate for the evening would destroy society as we know it and expose us to danger from those that know how to kill us."

Wolfric took the last swallow of brandy and placed the glass on a small table, folding the book closed beside it.

"She explained the circumstances." Controlling my anger became harder with each moment that passed. The cool look I received from the vampire pushed me closer to the edge. "I want the antidote."

"There isn't one."

"What do you mean?"

"You think I'm harsh with Tori, but I actually have a soft spot for her and was kind to her." He looked away. "Maybe too kind."

"Kind, huh? To poison her. To make her body tremble until she's too sore to be held. To be racked with spasms so bad that she can't stand. To make her stomach reject nourishment until she dies from starvation."

"Vampires can't die from starvation."

"What are you saying? That she'll be a living skeleton? The pain's enough to drive her insane."

"You and Tori must believe me that it will end after three..."—glancing at his watch—"Two more nights." He looked up and asked, "It's dawn now. I can't help but wonder how a simple fledgling can stay up after the sun has risen?"

Ronan studied the thick curtains covering the window. Around the edging was a thin peach tint of light. The vampire lore also said we could burst into flames from direct sunlight.

"Do you feel the weight of the sun? Though you can never again see it through bare eyes, you can feel the pull. Pushing and shoving you to sleep." Wolfric stood, taking a step my way, lightly brushing his fingers across my hand. The master's tone was soft and even.

My eyelids became heavy. With a shake of my head, I said between gritted teeth, "Stop. I must watch over Tori and make sure you don't try any other tricks."

Images of Tori sleeping peacefully in our bed, waiting for me to join her, flashed in my mind. I remembered backing out of the room and returning to Tori's chamber.

"Tori was right. You're very powerful, but not more than I," Wolfric's whisper echoed in my head.

Then I lost consciousness.

# Chapter 14

## *Tori*

I was a little nervous. Though Ronan sat beside me in the limo, he stared out the window at the passing scenery. Not one word was spoken as we sped down the interstate to the northeast side of Birmingham.

Home.

It had been ages since I was there. That was, it felt that way.

My large ranch-style house was lit up. Ronan had done as I'd asked and called ahead. Connor's instructions were to have everything ready when we arrived.

We walked up the pathway together, not touching or giving anyone watching a clue of our relationship.

The front door opened and Connor greeted us in all of his pierced glory. For the occasion, his hair was pulled back in a braid. Shirtless, his low-riding jeans appeared to be held up only by his jutting groin. Two more rings pierced his navel, making it an even six that could be seen.

"Welcome back home, mistress." His grin showed he planned to put on a show for Ronan's sake and punish me for not letting him help.

"Mistress?" Ronan asked under his breath.

"He's a troublemaker and will regret his little act of defiance." I shook my head.

Connor smirked.

I fought an answering grin. It wouldn't do to encourage such behavior. Besides, I wasn't sure how Ronan would react.

When we walked into the foyer, I was delighted with Ronan's response.

"Nice. I like the openness of windows and bringing the outside indoors. Very nice indeed." He nodded as he sauntered around checking the glass doors and the twelve-foot ceilings.

The house had glass-paned French doors facing the inner courtyard. A rock and fern-covered waterfall provided the setting of a tropical paradise. Each room opened into the garden, extending the living area into nature.

"Never to exist in daylight didn't mean I can't enjoy the outdoors at night."

Mosquitoes and temperature were no longer a problem in my vampire state. So I took advantage of landscape lighting and used different colors for different areas of the garden and different seasons.

"Mistress?" The timid voice came from my left.

My growl was Byron's only warning. I grabbed him by the throat and lifted him above my head. His hands scrambled to wrestle with my hold, trying to loosen the grip. Betrayal and lies, the two hated traits I refused to put up with from my servants.

"You're either stupid or the bravest idiot I've ever met. I should drain you dry and feed you to the crows." I hissed my words in anger. My canines were long, ready to tear out his throat.

"Tori. Please put him down." Ronan's tone was more of an exasperated parent speaking to his child.

His hand pressed on my shoulder, no more than a gentle reminder to pause. A feeling of calm drained my anger and I lowered Byron to his feet and released my deathly grip.

Odd. Could it be one of Ronan's vampire gifts? This soon?

"Thank you. Thank you, Master Ronan." Byron leaned against the wall, rubbing the red marks on his throat.

"That remains to be seen. My years of being a cop taught me one lesson, things are never as they appear. But in your case, I believe you're guilty of all the crimes you've been accused of." Ronan turned to me. "I assume this is the Byron, the servant of yours, Brannon got the blood from."

I nodded my confirmation, disgusted with the younger man. Without Ronan's touch, my anger reawakened with each second. Self-control was my best trait, but I never expected Byron to be a traitor. I inhaled and exhaled in an effort to remain in control and see what Ronan had planned.

"Tori, why don't you go out into the garden and sit by the waterfall? You once told me the sound of water soothes you."

"I'm not a child to be sent out of the room while the adults discuss serious business." This new macho Ronan was beginning to irritate me. "I had sent him away, but he decided on his own to return. Byron is my servant and he's mine to punish."

Byron's face paled.

Connor stood to the side watching our drama. His forehead wrinkled, a usual sign he was disturbed by what was happening, and he stepped toward Byron. I wasn't sure if he planned to attack or protect him.

Before I could order Connor away, Ronan commanded, "Step away from Byron. Nothing you can say or do will save him now. His alleged betrayal will be thoroughly examined before any punishment is dealt out."

Connor looked to me with confusion written on his face. I understood. In all the years he'd been with me, I'd been the only one to decide their fate.

Time for Ronan to understand he was moving into my territory and I refused to be led by him. I cared for him deeply, but I refused to play second fiddle.

"Connor, take Byron with you into the kitchen and wait for me." I glared at Ronan as I waited for the younger men to leave. "You and I are going to come to an agreement. I'll not allow you to order my people around. I'll not allow you to punish them. When and if I decide to punish Byron, I'll be the one to administer it. Do you understand me?"

His crooked grin threw me off.

"What?" I narrowed my eyes at him. Why was he grinning?

"You're so beautiful when you're angry." The back of his hand caressed my cheek. He puckered his lips in concentration and tilted his head, and in a low voice he taunted, "Do you like your men on their knees?"

I fought the pull of his glowing eyes, pulling me under some kind of spell to deny it and tempting me to forget my anger. Normally, fledglings couldn't do that. Only powerful masters could. I caught the hand caressing my face and held it. The man was dangerous. Every inch of him was luring me to do his will.

With a shake of my head to clear my mind, I dropped his hand and stepped back.

"Quit that," I snapped.

"Quit what?" His too-innocent look wasn't lost on me.

"I know what you're doing. Your senses tell you when you're using your vampire gifts. Usually it takes a few weeks to sense your first one, but like I said, you're powerful for a fledgling. I feel you trying to get me to forget about Byron and to give in to you. How did you learn that so fast?"

I should be proud, but he was becoming too powerful, too quickly. Master vampires were protective of their territory. If a newly-formed vampire exhibited powers that could challenge the local master vampire, the fledgling would either be exiled or killed. Wolfric would exile only if he was the creator. That meant, Ronan's existence was in danger.

"Sweetheart, you need me to help you." His grin grew crooked, almost a smirk. "Don't look at me that way." He wrapped an arm around me, pulling me into his warmth. "When I say I want to help, that's what I mean. I want to help. And nothing more."

I wanted to give in. Closing my eyes, I inhaled deeply and rested my forehead on his chest. He smelled of woodsy body wash and the underlying man-smell that was Ronan. It would be wonderful to give him all my worries and responsibilities, but I couldn't give him such burdens. I was the monster. He still had hope.

"I'll keep your offer in mind." I sighed. Opening my eyes, I stepped away and pulled my shoulders back. "Byron must pay for his betrayal. You may come along, but remain quiet."

Ronan chuckled, nodded, and followed me. His presence filled the small space with heat and carnality. My constant fight to keep my lust under control was becoming a losing battle and, with him hovering nearby, it was becoming impossible, but I must tend to my betrayer first.

"I don't understand why you want to come with me," I muttered as I headed into the kitchen.

"I was curious about how you handle such situations," Ronan stated.

"To be truthful, I've never had a servant betray me before. He endangered my life and yours in his selfishness."

"The boy loves you."

"He's obsessed. He knows the rules and dangers, and he became selfish."

Ronan stopped me with a touch on my arm. When I turned, his look was one of seriousness, head tilted to the side and dark hair dangling to his shoulders. My heart ached just looking at him.

"How old were you the first time you fell in love?" he asked.

I walked away. How could I answer him? Would he believe too old and with a thirty-two-year-old private investigator from Illinois?

Connor sat on a stool at the kitchen counter, munching on an apple, while Byron was sprawled out in a chair. I couldn't help but wonder, how in the world did he do that? Byron made whatever position he assumed an act of indulgent boredom. Normally, his attitude was charming, but tonight it was in his best interest to be afraid. And I needed him to show it.

"Sit up." My temper flared when he took his time. "Now," I ordered, canines flashing.

His face paled—finally showing fear—moving quickly, he straightened his back, and spaced both feet on the floor.

"Yes, mistress."

"I don't care to hear your reasons for betraying me.

There's no excuse good enough for it to be acceptable." I strolled up behind him and rested my hand on his shoulder. He jerked as if I had struck him. "Did you have any idea he was the brother to the man who gave me my scars?" I fingered his hair. My usual sleeveless leather top flashed the many thin white lines crisscrossing my arm. The lines were the deeper cuts the blade made in its journey over my skin.

"I swear I didn't know. Do you really think I would give the creep the time of day if I had known?" He held still while my hand brushed his hair to one side.

"I believe you're still holding something back from me."

"No. I'm not." His body started shaking. "You got everything out of me the other night. Please don't, I can't take you raping my brain again."

"Yes. It's a lot like me raping you. The pain and invasion are horrible. What you don't know, is that I can turn your brain into mush, then you'd be nothing more than a zombie, a drooling creature to do my bidding." I couldn't do it. Only once had I made the error and it had been horrendous, but he had no idea.

I continued to play with his hair until I cupped his head. Byron started screaming.

From out of the corner of my eye, I noticed Ronan standing beside Connor and accepting the apple my servant offered. Before I could turn and warn him, he bit into the crisp fruit, swallowing a chunk. Immediately, he clutched his stomach and bent over, throwing up blood and apple.

I released Byron and rushed to Ronan's side.

"It will be years before you hold down a little food." A paper towel was shoved in front of me. "Thanks, Connor. Clean up the mess."

"Fuck." Connor raised his arms, staring at the puke. "Gross. He's the one who threw it up."

"He's vampire. Now pull more sheets."

"How was I to know you'd reincarnated him?" The hurt look on his face reminded me Connor had hoped I would reincarnate him.

Human men were such assholes at times. "Enough. Do what I said."

I checked on Ronan. Pain twisted his face as he clutched his stomach. His suffering tore at my conscience. I'm such a terrible teacher.

"Your body's rejecting what it now considers to be foreign." I grabbed a cloth towel near the sink and ran it beneath cold water. "Here. Wipe your face and place this on the back of your neck."

Within minutes, the color of his face appeared closer to its normal shade though around his mouth a white line revealed he hadn't recovered completely. An inner light glimmered in his pupils, signaling his need for blood.

The thought of him taking blood from me again brought a rush of heat through my body. Many times through the evening before, he'd fed from me, and I had taken from him, but vampires do not regenerate their own blood. Taking from each other would then cause us to feed deeply from another creature, human preferably. Too many problems existed for vampires to immerse in the ritual every night.

Human blood possessed the most nutrients required to heal a vampire, and humans enjoyed the attention. I made sure to leave them with the most erotic dreams and weak from satisfaction.

"Tori, Tori!" Connor's panic pulled me out of my thoughts and I looked up.

"What?" When I saw Connor and Ronan's look of anger as they stared over my shoulder, I knew. Byron had escaped.

Wrapped up in concern for Ronan, I'd ignored the honeysuckle breeze caressing my hair and face. The kitchen door stood wide open, showing the empty, lit walkway leading straight to the driveway.

"Let's go after him." Ronan rose to his feet, swayed, and sat back down, his hands shaking.

"You're in no shape to go anywhere. Besides he won't get that far," I said.

"Why?" Ronan asked weakly.

His face had washed free of all color. Maybe I should keep my explanation short.

"He has no money and nowhere to go. The colony in Birmingham is small and they know Byron belongs to me. Once I put out the word that he's run away, they'll return him to me."

"You make it sound like he's a missing dog." Ronan's eyes narrowed. "Or a slave."

What could I say? Back a couple hundred years ago or in some countries nowadays, he would be considered a slave. Goodness, some of the old vampires still called them blood slaves and considered them to be their possessions.

"How long do you believe he'll live, if he doesn't return?" I asked. "The colony knows of his betrayal and we must be careful with our existence. Punishment for betrayal is death. And the method is not pretty."

"You don't plan to kill him," Ronan said without a doubt. "What's the punishment?"

I wasn't sure why he would want to know, and I preferred not telling him. Explaining the brutality of my world would be better left for another time. My adopted culture was older than any present civilization and often was hard for me to accept, even with my savage crusade. The unwritten rules and rigid caste system were hard to fathom at times. Even after so many years, I was still learning what I was allowed within the structure and what was taboo.

"Connor, in twenty minutes come and bring a bottle of my favorite champagne. We'll take care of Ronan. Afterwards, you better get some sleep. You're on guard duty tomorrow. I can't take a chance of Byron or Brannon trying anything while I'm at rest with Ronan."

Connor flinched when I said he would participate in healing Ronan. His jealousy would have to be addressed. He never complained when I had company and offered his blood to another male.

Why did I feel like I was losing control of my household? For that matter, my life?

<<<>>>

Edgar Brannon

I gazed out the limo's tinted window at the well-lit house nestled in the cul-de-sac.

My spies reported Tori and Ronan had arrived only a couple of hours ago. Pleased by the way their escape had gone, I wasn't too pleased when my men lost their trail.

The news of her reincarnating the private investigator was most welcome, though I wished I'd been there to watch. When they disappeared for a week, I wanted to tear down Birmingham looking for their hidey-hole, but patience would reign. The whole week had been a seesaw of emotions.

Where had they gone? Was some ritual cave or magic voodoo required for the conversion? I looked over at the man tied like a Christmas turkey in the facing limo seat.

Having the woman's slave fall into my hands was a sign the time neared for my decision.

Tears of anger streamed down my captive's face. Thank goodness the gag was holding, his constant screaming had begun to get on my nerves.

"I'll take the gag out of your mouth, but you must answer my questions and no shouting. Do you understand?"

On seeing the nod, I loosened the gag and pulled it away. Hair came with it. He had plenty of curls.

"Hey, that hurt. Was it really necessary to treat me this way? Remember, I helped you and you still owe me."

"I owe you nothing."

"Ronan's still alive."

"He's dead."

"Undead, you mean. He's now a fucking vampire. And fucking the woman I love." Angry, Byron struggled with his bonds, shouting curses.

"You've told me vampire all this time, and I believe you. But if you don't shut up your ranting, I may have to teach you restraint." I picked up a knife and released the catch, showing the six-inch blade in warning. "That would be a shame for I have more questions. Tell me, how's Ronan taken to being a vampire?"

Byron sniffed and scooted his rear until he was sitting upright. "Okay, I guess."

Frustrated with the man's insolence, leaning over, I grabbed his hair and pressed the thin switchblade to his throat.

"Let's try this again." My knee landed on Byron's lap, evicting a whimper before easing up. "It won't take much to ensure your cooperation." I pressed harder and a squeak indicated Byron understood. "Tell me, does Ronan look healthy?"

"Yeah," he said after taking a deep swallow. "He looks like he normally did. Only there's something different about his presence, and it isn't from being a vampire. I don't know how to describe it exactly, but it's like the house got darker when he walked in. Like cold chills go down my back when I drew his attention. His eyes glowed liked Tori's, but he watched me as a cat watches a tasty mouse before pouncing."

Fascinated by the description, I released him, staring at the young man for a moment. "Is he the first male vampire you've seen?" Surely this aura that Ronan possessed was typical of male vampires.

"A few have visited. One in particular gives me the creeps. He talked kinda bossy to Tori. And she let him. The only male I ever knew, until Ronan, who could without being told she'd tear out his throat. I believe he's the local master, though I didn't hear her call him that. I did get the same feeling with him."

Wasn't he full of information? The way he was running his mouth, it assured me I would be doing the right thing in killing this man. I couldn't have Tori finding out what I now knew. So there were male vampires in the area. Who knew how many of those creatures existed? Many philosophies believe for every evil, there was good. The yin and yang.

So that means somewhere in the world was the opposite of vampires. The Van Helsings of the world? Vampire hunters?

I had a lot to think about. Which side did I want to join? My favorite side was on top and if what I believed was true, that was where I would land very soon.

<<<>>>

Tori

I half-carried and half-led Ronan into my hidden chamber. Without a second thought, I revealed the entrance and the high-tech fingerprint scanner.

"Don't tell me that you're actually a top secret project gone awry, you know, like bit by a spider," he said weakly in a teasing tone.

I grinned.

"No. The government had nothing to do with me being a vampire. You know that." At least his sense of humor hadn't left him.

"You can't blame a fellow for using his imagination."

In the stairwell, the lighting was dim as every other step was spotlighted. The shadows hid his features and his hair hung loose, swaying with each step, hiding his face so I couldn't see his expression. Was there more to his teasing?

"I like fellows with imaginations," I purred.

Luckily, we reached the small hallway leading into the side of the mountain behind my house. The level footing saved us when he looked up from my teasing.

"I'll gladly show you how far my imagination can go. In so many directions." His gaze searched my face.

My heart flipped. Even weak after the bout of sickness, he was so sexy, and with the cloak of power wrapped around him, he was even more desirable.

"I believe you need nourishment before you try imagining anything. We have an eternity. Don't get in a rush," I said with all gentleness.

I helped him onto the bed, pulled off his shoes and socks, and stood back. It suited him. Large and decadent-looking with old-fashioned bed curtains and several large, tasseled pillows, the bed had been a welcome home gift from Wolfric.

Stretched out and obviously aroused, Ronan had the

look of a pasha among his harem. Wearing his black shirt opened to his waist with his arms spread out over the bed, he patted the pillow next to him, inviting me to join him. His half-closed eyes watched my every movement.

"Where're you going?" His voice was low and mesmerizing.

"I'll be back in a few moments. You need nourishment."

"Come," he held out his arms, "and we'll feed from each other."

His allure was breathtaking and I almost gave in to him.

"No. That's not always possible. We must receive most of our blood from humans," I said. "I'll be right back." My gaze remained on him until I was near the stairs. Seeing him on my bed in his charming pose was stuff sex dreams were made of.

Connor stood leaning against the door that led to the cooler with a bottle of champagne in one hand and the other hand pushed into his jeans' pocket. The lighter material between the apex of his legs looked full.

"So is it a marathon of sex for the newly made vampire?" Jealously infused his every word.

What had I expected? Connor had begged me many times to be made a vampire. I had refused. Even when he made it clear how spending an eternity with me would be the ultimate high. That he loved me.

I sensed his feelings for me were mixed with the mysterious aura of being a vampire and the blood I gave him on occasion. Certainly, I loved him. Love in the vampire sense for humans who cared and fed a vampire's every need. I'm not sure what becoming a vampire did to a human's emotions, but from what I experienced my feelings were normally basic.

A servant receiving vampire blood would obviously

become attached to their master, in my case, mistress, as they remained young, healthy, and well cared for in return. Connor's respect and affection, I believed, were real.

Though before today, I would have added loyalty, but Byron proved that could easily change when another goal came into play.

"Ah, Connor, don't make me worry about you too. Come to bed."

I took the bottle from him, resisting the urge to touch him and read his emotions. My heart couldn't take another betrayal so close to Byron's. Maybe that was where I had gone wrong. Neglecting them in the recent weeks, they were able to develop resentments I had not corrected.

He stared at me for a few seconds and grinned.

"I can't help but wish it was me going to be between your thighs, but what the hell. I'm glad you have Ronan. You deserve someone stronger and more stubborn than you, and you need to cement your bond. I'll give my blood, but I'm not ready for fucking with him."

We stared at each other. Connor preferred women, but when being fed on, like vampires, he would become carried away and would fuck or be fucked by either sex.

"I will miss your cock. Your piercings are energizing to say the least." Smiling back, I leaned over and kissed him on the mouth. Instantly his tongue thrust into my mouth, and he wrapped his arms around me.

I pulled away and touched his face, resisting again the urge to read his mind.

"Thanks. I appreciate your loyalty and your love. You do understand why I cannot reincarnate you at this time?"

A sad look crossed his face, then he cleared his throat. "Hey, I've always appreciated your honesty. You've never lied to me. You would give your life to protect me and that is more than I can say of my family. No matter what you think of your bad self, you're a good person, Victoria Amherst, and I'm proud to be your servant."

He bowed and then walked into the bedroom, unbuttoning his shirt.

# Chapter 15

## *Ronan*

I looked into the large broken mirror. My image barely reflected in the glass. Chills sped down my back. What was wrong with it? Was it some type of trick mirror? I carefully lifted the largest piece and looked behind it. Nothing but a wall.

"Don't worry, you haven't lost your mind." Tori stood in the closet's doorway with a large bottle in one hand. "You're a vampire. Our reflection looks faded. Some say it's because we no longer have a soul. Others say a virus has warped our atoms and some of the light doesn't reflect off us anymore, or something like that. Bunch of crap if you ask me."

"What do you think makes us the way we are?" Part of my nature wanted to solve the mystery. That was why I became a cop. Watching too much television as a kid had me believing cops only unraveled mysteries. The reality had been paperwork took up most of my time, and when I'd finished with that day's, I had more paperwork waiting.

The job was nothing like TV and movies. Even private investigation work had been more paperwork and searching the internet than anything else. Most of the fieldwork had been nothing more than tailing cheating spouses.

"I have no idea and really don't dwell on it. You'll have centuries to figure it out. Are you thirsty? Liquids do not bother us as solid food can."

Just the thought of wine turned my stomach. "I'll pass."

"This brand is quite light." She popped the cork and poured the sparkling, pale wine into a crystal glass and then handed it to me before pouring one for herself. "Plus it will help loosen you up for what will happen next."

Then I spotted her servant stretched out in the middle of the bed.

"Hell no. I'm not fucking him." I shook my head and glared at the man and then Tori.

"No fucking Connor. Tonight." She actually grinned. "For now he's agreed to provide your nourishment. Vampires can feed off each other, but need more. Humans have all the nutrients required to keep us healthy. Animal blood is a substitute, but the taste is gamey and nothing can make it better."

"What about bags of blood like they show in the movies?"

"I can promise you wouldn't like the taste. They put sodium citrate inside to stop clotting. It's nasty stuff." She sighed. "Wolfric had someone create a nonclotting formula for blood, and he keeps it in store for emergencies. It's not for long-term use, but on occasion. I'll have him send one over for you to try out."

Another wave of hunger clenched my gut. I lifted my hands, they shook.

"Fine. But I need relief now." My words sounded garbled, but Tori understood.

She hooked her arm around mine and guided me to the bed. The shirtless man looked up at me.

"Then you must do it the most common way," she said and stepped back.

The man's light-gray eyes appeared eerie in the dim, curtained-off bed. His piercings and tattoos shouted how he was a risk-taker and a little unhappy with his body and thought it made him look like a badass. During my years as a cop, I had met many angry, confused young men like him. They meant trouble. The punk probably used her to cover up his nefarious activities. I couldn't see why Tori kept him around.

Damn, except to feed on. And probably fuck.

My gaze travelled over his broad and well-formed chest, the jeans that rode low on his trim hips. His cock pressed at his zipper. Was Tori's servant excited by the prospect of being used as meal supplement?

Hunger overtook my resistance. I kneeled on the bed, leaned over, and cupped his chin, pushing it to the side, stretching the muscles and tendons. Then I sank my teeth into his neck. Blood poured into my mouth.

Moments or hours passed, when Tori grabbed a hunk of my hair at the back of my head and pulled.

"Stop, baby. Don't drain him."

I finally stopped feeding. Fuck. My body was resting on the man's. We were chest to chest. My cock as hard as his. I looked down at him again. Those eerie eyes blinked at me as if he was drunk or high.

Then I remembered something Tori told me the other night. Raising my arm, I scraped my teeth over my wrist and held it out. The man latched on and sucked. His eyes rolled back in his head.

"Just a little," Tori whispered in my ear.

When I moved my wrist away, the man...Connor curled up on his side, a hand cupping his cock, and fell asleep with a grin.

I looked over at Tori.

She crawled into the bed, resting her shoulders against the headboard, sitting in the middle. She held the bottle from earlier and two wine glasses and nodded at the empty side. Tori waited for me to circle the bed and climb in.

"Here. Try this champagne." Tori handed me a glass filled with the light-gold liquid. Bubbles floated from the bottom to burst at the top.

We finished the bottle as we talked through the evening about so many things, life as a vampire, favorite foods she missed and I would miss, benefits to being extra strong and having great night vision. The wine was enjoyable, but blood was more potent. Better than anything alcoholic or chemical. When I finally fed on Tori, I felt a flow of energy so strong that every hair and pore on my body came alive. I couldn't care less that another man was in bed with us. I felt more animated than I ever had in my thirty-two years of life. Being a vampire didn't suck. So far. If life had taught me anything, I should never take anything for granted.

Eyelids heavy, I watched Tori sip the remaining drops from her glass. She was more beautiful to me, if that was possible. A rosiness to her skin urged me to run my tongue over every inch of her body.

As I caressed her cheek with one knuckle, she smiled at me and my breath caught on a sweep of desire. Her sweet floral scent brought to mind visions of a delicate lady from another century.

"Soft and silky. You're so fuckable." I nearly groaned the last word.

Damn, not romantic at all. I wanted her to know how I

felt about her. Fucking her was only one of the many ways I could show her how I felt.

She left the bed and walked across the room, setting the bottle on a tray. When she turned, heat flared down my torso to my groin. Earlier, my mind had been on the mirror and feeding on her servant. But now my attention drifted down to cleavage spilling out of a luxurious gown. The red material so thin I could see the small, brown circles of her nipples. When she slipped in beside me, her long legs stretched alongside mine. My stare refused to look away from the juncture of her thighs. How would she react if I parted her knees, pressed my face into her heat?

I wanted her now.

Before I was aware of moving, I pushed her back, barely registering her gasp of surprise. I ignored her laughter when I fisted the material and tore it from her body. Without checking to see where it landed, I threw the nearly nonexistent scrap over my shoulder. Her musky scent and the soft flesh brought a primal need to hear her scream my name. Her beautiful breasts jiggled as she thrust them toward me, desperately asking to be touched. They would wait their turn. I had a sweeter target in mind.

"Let's see how many times I can get you to say my name," I said with a growl beneath my words.

I pushed her legs open and licked her from perineum to clit and then sucked on the tight little knot.

"Oh, yes, Ronan."

I lifted my head and raised an eyebrow.

"One," I said with a wide grin.

She smiled back with eyelids heavy with need.

Returning to her lovely pussy, I rotated my thumb on her sweet, hard clit as my tongue lapped at her inner lips. I continued to tease her nub after each swipe. With my other hand, I dragged a finger through her wetness before I inserted a tip into the tight, little dark hole. She moaned with pleasure.

She clutched my hair as her hips lifted, silently begging for more. My sucking and licking brought my own desires to the brink of coming on the sheets. Her shout of "Ronan," the pulsing beneath my tongue, and the sweetness dripping from my chin demonstrated her satisfaction.

I grabbed her thighs and shoved her knees to her chin and thrust my rock-hard cock into her hot pussy. A sigh escaped my lips. This was where I belonged. I began thrusting. The musical beat of skin slapping skin filled the room.

Looking down into her lovely face, I smirked. "Two."

Her eyes widened and then she laughed, shaking those lovely breasts at me.

I bent down and began to treat the hard tips as I had her clit as I continued to pump into her.

"Ronan," she moaned.

"Three."

<<<>>>

I stretched, more out of habit than need, and my hand slid over the cool sheets. Where was Tori? The last time we made love was the hour before dawn. I discovered my extraordinary strength made new positions possible, and Tori's strength made it even more arousing.

Thank fuck, Connor had woken and crawled his ass out of the bed around midnight, complaining, "A man can't get any sleep around here."

Smiling to myself, I mused that had been moments after Tori had chanted my name for the twelfth time.

Feeling better than I could ever remember, I searched

the chamber for my clothes before thinking to look in the spacious closet. The closet was the size of my bedroom in Mokena.

My clothes hung on wooden hangers or were folded neatly on cedar shelves, along with several shirts, pants, and shoes that still had the tags on them, but were my size. Tori or her people had been busy.

While pulling on jeans and a button-down shirt, I noticed for the first time a flimsy curtain covering a glass door. Behind the door was a white-tiled bathroom with a sink, sunken tub, and a shower large enough for four.

Lights spotlighted each area, including a commode. I shook my head. It was strange to wake up without the need to pee or with a hard-on. The former I guessed was because of something to do with being a vampire and the latter because of Tori. Her appetite was as great as mine and I doubt I could get hard again for a week.

Thinking about her talented hands and the way she crawled over me, my body quickly responded. Nope. No waiting needed. Without another thought, I stripped, and started the shower. Less than fifteen minutes later I was dressed and walked up the stairs to the main part of the house. The dark stairwell wasn't as long as I had remembered and thankfully her fingerprints weren't needed to open the door from the inside.

I entered the pseudo bedroom and stopped. Connor stood, leaning against the wall, as if he'd been waiting. He wore baggy blue jeans, a T-shirt with some obscure rock band on the front, and a diamond flashed on the side of his nose. His red-streaked hair was tied back at the neck.

"What are you doing in here?" Something about Connor hanging around the entrance to Tori's private quarters bothered me.

"Waiting for you. Tori said that I should expect you to wake up around this time." His careless attitude irritated the shit out of me.

"And?"

"I'm to see if you need any blood."

"What do you mean?" The thought of holding the muscular body while I sucked on his neck brought an awareness I didn't like at all. Last night I'd been starving and a little crazed.

"Don't worry, big boy." He lifted his hand, the one he'd hidden behind his back. It held a wine bottle like the one Tori and I had drank from the night before. "You can get your nourishment from this. She had it sent over from Master Wolfric's. She said that fledglings need blood pretty soon after they wake up, and you would resent drinking from me." Then he added, "Again so soon."

Tori's assessment was correct.

"What do you do for her?" Though I wasn't sure if I would like the answer, I still wanted to know.

"Many things," Connor answered with a smirk on his face.

I tightened my hands into fists at my sides. If I slugged Tori's servant in the face, I imagined she'd be quite unhappy with me.

"What kind of things?" I asked between gritted teeth. It was damn hard restraining myself.

When I saw a flicker of amusement cross the punk's face, my temper burned hotter. After finding him in her bed yesterday, it was easy to guess.

"Just things," he said, the smirk growing to a full-blown smile.

Visions of grabbing the punk by the throat and shaking him flashed in my mind.

"What's your specialty?" Why was I insisting on a specific answer?

"Anything she wants." The asshole enjoyed pushing my buttons.

I didn't remember moving, but I clutched the front of Connor's shirt and pressed the punk against the wall.

My fangs had lengthened and his gaze narrowed. So the bastard finally realized the danger he was in. Had he thought I couldn't kill him because I had taken his blood and, I admitted to myself, caressed his body while in the throes of blood lust?

A particular fragrance drifted off the man. Tori. Sex wasn't mixed in the scent.

"You're pushing me," I growled. "She hadn't fucked you recently."

"Not for at least a couple weeks. I can tell you, it's not from me trying."

I shook him, but before the punk's neck snapped, I stopped.

"Damn it. Don't you realize I could snap you like a twig?"

"You wouldn't kill me."

Connor's calm tone brought out a measure of respect from me. If a vampire had gotten in my face while I was human and threatened to break me in half, I wasn't sure how calm I would remain.

"What makes you so certain?" I asked.

"Because it would make Tori unhappy, and we all try to keep her happy. Anyway, she loves me and—"

Without thought, I leaned over and scraped my fangs along the side of Connor's neck in warning—a shiver of need shot to my groin—and shoved my fist, still filled with his shirt, under Connor's chin.

"Finish it. And what?"

"Byron. Fuck! One cannot satisfy her. She loved him too. That was why his betrayal hurt so badly." His eyes widened when he realized how it sounded. "Man, don't worry. I imagine between vampires, it's different. I swear. It's common for vampires to use their servants as a blood supply and a sexual outlet. She's powerful and has needs."

A flash of emotion crossed Connor's face. Something that scared him and probably something I didn't want to hear.

"What was it? What did you remember?"

Connor turned his face away. As I stood holding the punk against the wall, Connor's hands remained limp at his side, submissively. Most people would tug at the hands holding them, trying to loosen their grip. But that would mean Connor would have to touch me. Had Connor expected me to have the same power as Tori? Only one way to find out.

I brought my other hand to cup Connor's cheek. Nothing. I didn't have the same power, but the punk didn't know. The panic-stricken look on his face ensured the power wouldn't be needed.

"Shit, man, I'll tell anything you want, just don't fuck with my mind. Byron told me when Tori did it to him, it felt like she was crawling around in his brain and later it burned and ached." Connor pulled his head as far away as my grip would allow.

"When you said, 'sexual outlet,' what did you remember?"

"It's not that exactly. It's the blood supply part. A week ago, Tori was all upset and Byron helped her through it."

"What do you mean, helped her through it?"

When he wasn't quick in answering, I raised his hand.

Connor said in a rush, "Byron offered her his body. Shit! Let go of me. You're choking me."

Unsure if I could stop myself from killing Connor if I stayed too close, I released my grip and stepped back.

"So she used one of her servants," I prompted. The thought of her touching another man infuriated me. Unreasonable, as we only met not long ago and considering what happened in bed last night.

"Tori never treated us like that. We willingly serve her. I love her. I thought Byron did too. Fuck, who knows what happened between them. Come on, man, you got to understand that Byron and I've lived with her for over ten years. She takes care of us, provides food, clothes, and money. She's more than a boss. For both of us, she treats us better than anyone in our lives ever had."

"Tell me. How did she take Byron up on his offer?" I wasn't sure how long Byron would live the next time I saw him.

Connor swallowed deeply.

"They didn't fuck, while she was sucking on his neck, she...you know, helped him with her hand on his cock and that's all," Connor answered.

"That's all?" The thought of her touching someone else should infuriate me, not make me hard. Fuck, what was wrong with me? My emotions were going all over the place. What was Connor leaving out? I wanted the details from Tori. Yep. Unreasonable, but I couldn't control it. She'd warned me my emotions would be over the top at times.

"Where is she?"

"Out hunting."

"Hunting for blood or deviants?" I had hoped she would let the authorities take care of them. Had I really expected her to be reasonable when I wasn't? Damn. All of these feelings swirling in me was about to drive me insane.

"Where can I find her?" I asked before he answered the first question.

Would I ever get her to stop her crazy crusade?

"Hunting for Brannon."

"Fucking hell!"

I had to find her quickly. Remembering Brannon's washed-out blue eyes, dead and unfeeling, a cold chill ran down my spine. The thought of the lunatic getting his hands on Tori again terrified the fuck out of me. Only by Brannon underestimating Tori were they able to escape last time.

I was certain the psycho would take better precautions to ensure she wouldn't escape again. Eternal life, super-human strength, and psychic abilities would enable Brannon to be a killing machine of the most dangerous kind.

Where would she start?

"The house," I muttered.

I walked through the well-lit hallway, jerking open every closed door and peering inside each room before going to the next.

"She's not here, man. I told you, she's out hunting," Connor said as he followed my every step.

"I'm not looking for her, Einstein. I'm looking for the door leading to the garage and the keys to one of her cars."

"She left in the BMW. Her Maserati's still here or you can use her Harley."

"Why are you being so helpful?"

"Remember? I care about Tori too. From what Byron's told me, Brannon's crazy and as long as I'm human, I can't help but you can. You have the power to protect her. She'd never brought anyone into her protected bedroom. That was the first time for me too. So it means you mean something to her. Maybe she'll listen to you and stop this craziness."

How could I disagree with that? I looked, really looked at the punk. Maybe I had underestimated him. There was a lot of that going on.

I nodded. Time for Tori to stop her solo crusade. Then we could plan how to take out Brannon.

"The Maserati will do," I said.

"I'm coming with you," Connor said firmly.

"Fine. But you stay in the car."

Tori

I wasn't sure of what I expected to find.

My footsteps echoed in the dark stairwell. So far, the empty rooms gave little away about the previous occupant.

The For Sale sign at the end of the drive told me what to expect, but I had to see it with my own eyes. I would have Connor call the real estate agent in the morning, but it was unlikely Brannon would make it easy for me to track him down.

A flip of the switch, then light flooded the room. The white walls shone brightly with a fresh coat of paint, hiding all evidence of holes, bars, and chains. Only a metal table and two chairs remained. In the middle of the table was a red envelope. The type that a birthday card would arrive in.

Unsure of why it was there, I looked around the table for wires or timers. Nothing. All was clear. I leaned over, without touching, and looked closer at the envelope.

*Tori* was scrawled across the front.

Cautiously, I picked it up and opened the envelope. On

the front of the card was a cartoon cat with a yellow balloon tied to its tail, and across the top read, *Thinking of you.* I opened the card and a picture fell onto the table. Inside the card was handwritten, *How many will die before you will give me what I want?* And it was signed with a large *B.*

Twice I inhaled deeply to calm my nerves. Then I reached for the picture lying upside down on the table. My fingers shook as I held it.

"No, no, no! The bastard's going to pay."

Tears streamed down my face, blurring the picture of soft ringlets framing a pale face frozen in horror and brown eyes staring sightless at the photographer.

There was no doubt that Byron was dead. Beneath his chin a dark-red line carved a grotesque grin across his neck. The same neck not long ago I had enjoyed sinking my teeth into. Several memories flashed through my mind.

His teasing puppy-dog ways of showing me how much he'd desired me. Posing and strutting to draw my attention. Byron lying on the community bed with his leather pants unsnapped and begging me to make him a vampire. His beautiful face in mid-orgasmic release. His whispered words of "I love you."

I pressed the photo to my chest, crying so hard no sound emerged from my throat. I dropped to my knees on the concrete floor. The pain barely registered as regret filled my chest.

I'd failed to protect Byron. As I'd failed everyone that I ever loved. Though my intellect reminded me the circumstances were beyond my control. That it was fate. My heart also told me they died because of my carelessness and selfishness.

So many had died. In a basement many years ago and so many more. If only I hadn't gone shopping that day. If only

I hadn't let my obsession with Ronan get in my way, Byron wouldn't have left. If only I'd stopped Brannon before he'd gotten to Byron.

Time for me to stop thinking of the *if-onlys* and get to work.

"Tori."

I closed my eyes for a few seconds in exasperation.

Why had he followed me again? Hadn't he learned anything?

I lifted my head and stared in his direction.

Ronan was leaning against the doorframe, watching me, nothing showing on his face. When had he started guarding his emotions? Dark power emanated from him. The air around me became heavy with restrained danger. A little over a week and his powers had magnified to the extent I wasn't sure how to handle him.

Oddly, he possessed the same height of power I felt around Wolfric. Not all male vampires radiated such a strength as a thousand-year-old or a fledgling. His power radiated in massive waves, it proclaimed him to be a master of his destiny. A master of his kind. A master vampire.

So I worried he'd...what?

That he would receive undue attention from the psychic community. The hunters used psychics to track newly-made vampires with such strong powers like Ronan's. He hadn't learned how to hide the magic flowing off him in waves. Would he be safer with Wolfric? Would Wolfric be willing to teach him how to control it? Or would he kill him?

So many questions for another time.

"What are you doing here?" I asked.

He pushed away from the frame with his shoulder and strode across the room. Dressed all in black, his movements brought visions of a panther stalking its prey or a shadow of death sliding in to snatch a life.

Though I had nothing to worry about from him, my heart picked up speed. All the hairs on my arms felt as if they were standing to attention, craving his touch. A tight feeling in my chest was promptly followed by a clenching in my lower belly.

After the marathon of sex from the night before, I couldn't understand why I craved him again. My desire overrode all good sense.

"Hunting you." He stopped in front of me and offered a hand. I ignored it and stood. "What were you thinking, coming here without someone to back you up?"

"I've survived many years without backup and certainly don't need you to tell me how to manage my business. There's no need to worry anyway. I checked the surrounding grounds before entering the house." I slipped the picture into the waistband of my pants. No need for Ronan to know about Byron. Besides, it was between me and Brannon.

"What are you not telling me?" He acted relaxed and unconcerned about whether or not I answered.

Yet I sensed anger boiling beneath his words.

"Why do you think I'm hiding something?" Chills ran up my spine. Had he seen the picture before I hid it? I wanted to get him out of there.

"When I walked in, you were on your knees crying your eyes out." His fingers slid into my hair and he pressed me toward him. "I couldn't believe you went through the torture Brannon inflicted on you without it haunting you in someway." I gave in to his gentle pressure and rested my cheek on his shoulder. "You have nothing to fear," he whispered. "I'll kill the bastard when I find him."

Even to me, my chuckle sounded sad.

"You're determined to play the hero and make me the helpless heroine." Did he think he was in some romance novel?

"Yeah, the helpless heroine with fangs and a mean kick." I felt his body relax. His anger was easing. "I've noticed you haven't left my side until tonight. Why can't you stop your vendetta?"

"This doesn't concern you." I moved out of his arms and started to the door. "Let's get out of here." I couldn't talk to him about it. How could anyone understand?

He grabbed my arm, pulling me back. Without thinking, I swung my leg around to kick his out from under him. But he smoothly blocked the kick, then jerked me off my feet. We landed on the floor with him on top, one large hand cupping the back of my head, protecting it from harm.

"Now. Tell me, why do you insist on continuing your crazy crusade?" His forehead creased as if he wanted to delve into my brain and pull out the reasons.

The feel of his long, solid body against mine was distracting. I had things to do before sunrise. I shoved at his chest. He wasn't budging.

"Get off of me."

"No. Not until you promise to wait for me each evening before you go hunting."

"What?" I tucked my chin in and looked at him.

The man never stopped surprising me. His eyes glowed with the inner light that revealed a vampire's heightened emotions. What was going through his mind?

Then his hips thrust against mine, and a growing hardness pressed against my groin.

"Let's get out of here." I pushed at his chest again.

"Where do you want to go?"

His suggestive tone made it obvious he wanted to return to bed. Though I was tempted, I needed to find Brannon. "Do you have any idea where Brannon could be hiding?"

"No idea. I didn't know he was in Alabama until the night he bailed me out of jail and brought me here." His hand smoothed my hair away from my face, and he looked in my eyes. "Forget about him for now. Let's go home."

He stood and held out a hand. This time I took it.

For some reason, I was tempted to give in to his suggestion. Then a ringing sound from his pants pocket disrupted the thought.

"You have a cell phone?" I quirked one eyebrow.

Strange, but I'd forgotten he owned one. I refused to use them for many years. Their intrusiveness proved too irritating. Now was a prime example. But I learned they were a necessary evil. I stepped out of his arms and eyed him.

His gaze remained on me as he placed the phone to his ear and snapped, "What?" A man spoke on the other end, but even with vampire hearing, I couldn't make out the caller's words. "Hunters? There's no game in this area. Connor, have you lost your mind?" He turned his back to me and stepped away.

"Ronan?" I tapped his shoulder, and he turned, glaring. "He's talking about vampire hunters." That got his attention. "We need to get out of here before they surround the place."

"Vampire hunters?" Disbelief widened his eyes. He spoke again into the cell phone. "Okay, okay. We're coming. Yes, you can drive the BMW. What? I don't care if Tori doesn't let you drive her vehicles. I don't give a fuck. Do what I say." With a touch on the screen, he cut off the call and Connor's shouting. "You need to talk with that boy. He gets a little excited in times of crises."

I couldn't help but grin at that. Connor was Mr. Cool, but hunters pissed him off. He never explained to me his intense hatred of them, but anytime he came across one, he was all for me beating the crap out of them. I normally knocked them out, and then spent the next few hours calming Connor down.

"Call Connor back and tell him to return to the house in the Maserati after he loses them. I had parked the BMW in the garage. They won't expect us to be here in two cars."

Sure enough, when we burst through the garage door, two men in night fatigues and blackened faces jumped out of the way before the BMW hit them. Ronan used all his cop defensive-driving lessons in getting away from the black SUV that followed. Next to him, I sat fuming from his manhandling. I had wanted to drive my own damn car, but he'd been as determined.

"If we're going to work together, I might as well show you what Brannon left me." I pulled out the picture and we discussed the Hunters and what we were going to do about Brannon.

<<<>>>
Ronan

I was smiling the last few miles. She wasn't used to having a man tell her what she could and couldn't do. From what I had heard and seen, Wolfric had mostly let her do whatever she pleased. Though I wanted her to do what I say, I wasn't interested in breaking her spirit. Her spark and determination were what made me fall in love with her.

Fuck. I love her.

"Tell me more about the hunters," I demanded, wanting to keep my mind off the revelation.

"What do you want to know?" The hardness in her voice warned she was angry, but she still was willing to answer my questions.

That was something else I liked about her. She almost had a male attitude about arguments and handled herself with a calm and logical manner I felt comfortable with. I wasn't saying she was unfeminine. She certainly was all-woman and could be gentle and prissy like the best of them.

It was more that she didn't waste time arguing, but was willing to listen. She understood where I was going with a conversation and could be reasoned with. Most times. I glanced at her. She looked unconcerned by our narrow escape.

"Are they part of the government?"

"No. Dr. Garry Morris created the Legion of Vampire Hunters in 1882. With donated funds from victims and religious fanatics, they were able to prove our existence to a choice few. Since then they've amassed a fortune donated by idiots who use the funds to track us down."

I nodded and grinned. She sounded like a history teacher, actually a riled one.

"So they won't kill us?" I asked.

"Oh, yeah. They will certainly kill us and won't be gentle or quick by doing so."

About an hour later, I entered her driveway. Tori reached over to press a small button on the dash. One of the four garage doors opened and I parked her BMW in the wide space. It would need to be replaced or repaired. I noted the Maserati sat in a slot two over. Connor had made it back without a problem.

Upstairs, the rooms were well lit and welcoming. Connor stood in the kitchen with two mugs and handed one to each of us. I looked at the contents and sniffed. Heated blood. Animal blood. My canines lengthened, craving the taste while my mind was repulsed by the thought. Guess it would take time for my brain to catch up with my body's needs in accepting my new diet.

I quickly downed the warm substance. It had a bitter, metallic taste. When I looked toward Tori with a grimace on my face, she was grinning.

"What?"

"Nothing." She turned away and took a few sips from her mug while she struggled out of her jacket.

I noticed again the thin scars on her arm. They were identical to the ones all along the right side of her body. Her calmness in talking about them didn't hide the fact they were from an experience few people survived physically or mentally intact. Instead, from what I've seen the ordeal probably made her stronger. More self-assured.

I helped her out of the jacket and hung it on the back of a kitchen chair when her phone rang. The musical notes were so unexpected, we froze. It was the first time I'd seen her with one.

Tori stared at her phone. "Who in the world? Only a few have this number and all are in my contacts. It shows to be an out-of-state number."

"Probably a telemarketer," Connor offered in an attempt at humor.

"The best way to find out is to answer." I plucked the phone from her hand, tapped the call button, and placed it against my ear.

"Yeah?"

"Well, hello, Mr. Michaels."

I darted a look at Tori before saying, "You'll be glad to know she saw your latest artwork."

"Brannon?" she mouthed. By the way she was moving

her fingers, she itched to yank the phone from my hand and scream at the monster. Instead she watched as I listened.

<<<>>>
Tori

Stone cold. That was the only way to describe his expression as he listened. Obviously, Brannon wanted to gloat over his sick deed.

"Enough. Give it to me." A coward, I wasn't. I reached for the phone.

Without looking my way, Ronan pressed the disconnect button. Head down, shoulders slumped, he took a shuddering breath. Dread chilled the back of my neck.

What had Brannon said that would cause Ronan to become pale and shaken?

"What did he say?" I barely got the words out.

He straightened and stepped away.

"You know, I'm not sure which is the worse monster. The kind like us." He looked pointedly at me. "Or those like Brannon." Irritation sharpened each word.

Something was wrong. Ronan had acted okay in the car, maybe a little quiet but nothing unusual as he weaved through the traffic, losing our tail and listening to what I had to say. I'd chalked it up as nothing more than concern about my plans and what needed to be done to stop Brannon.

What had caused the cold mask he wore?

"Hey, man. You need to change your tone when you speak to Tori." Connor stepped in front of Ronan. They were nearly the same height. Strange. I could've sworn Ronan was much taller. Maybe it was because of the power flowing off of him.

"Leave the room," I ordered Connor. If I didn't, he'd

receive the brunt of Ronan's growing anger. "Go. No arguments," I firmly said when he hesitated.

Connor glared at Ronan in warning and left, slamming the door behind him.

Returning my attention to Ronan, not wanting to jump to conclusions, I asked, "What do you mean by that?"

The glow in his eyes flared when he looked at me.

"What's the real reason for making me a vampire? Were your playmates, Connor and Byron, not enough for you? Couldn't they fuck you enough with their feeble, human bodies?"

I jerked my chin up as if he had slapped me. Was his anger only part of the stages in transitioning from human to vampire? When I'd changed, my anger had been directed at human predators, while Ronan didn't have a goal, a crusade to direct his anger. He did have me, the one who reincarnated him. Who knew during the brief phone conversation with Brannon what he could have said to Ronan?

It was the psycho's orders that caused Ronan to be shot. Sure, his humanity as he knew it was dead. That part I had caused, but I never had gotten angry at Wolfric for turning me. Of course the circumstances were different. Oh, hell.

I really didn't have time to deal with Ronan's growing pains.

"Tell me now, what did Brannon say?"

"What Brannon said has nothing to do with it. This is sick. Drinking blood, killing for revenge, lurking in shadows, never living—this is fucking crazy." He flung out his arms, "Living? This isn't living. To exist only at night, never seeing the light of day, never to feel the sun caress my face."

His body began to shake. Closing his eyes, he took a deep breath. Before I could react from the shock of his tirade, his eyes snapped open, the fire in their depths penetrating my soul.

He said with a cold even tone, "I'm outta here. You and Brannon can play your crazy cat-and-mouse games. You can keep your hunters, witches, and master vampires, and whatever fuck you haven't told me. I'm going back to Chicago where the ordinary, underpaid, understaffed police take care of ordinary fucked-up crimes."

I stood in front of Ronan, unmoving, giving him stare for stare. Who was this man? As I looked into his eyes, the fire died and only coldness remained. A coldness that chilled me to the bone.

Where did the hate and disgust he professed come from? What was happening? Where were all the tender emotions he'd shown the last few days? One phone call and it was as if something had overtaken Ronan's body and left no one at home. What happened to the tender and passionate man I fell in love with? What had Brannon said?

"Why the sudden change?" Were we playing a game and I didn't know the rules? Talk about confusing as hell.

"I've come to my senses. When Brannon came to my office that first time, I should have followed my first instinct and thrown him out."

"Maybe so, but we wouldn't have met." His words wounded me. I wanted to shut him up or kick him out or both, but deep inside I sensed something wasn't right. Again, the question was, what had Brannon said on the phone that made him change so suddenly?

"Exactly," he said in a soft voice as he leaned toward me.

The word sliced through my heart. I wanted to make the pain go away. Lashing out in response would feel good for only a moment. So I fought the urge and stepped away.

My pride reined in my temper. Showing him how much his words hurt would give him massive power over me.

I lifted my chin and smiled.

"But you would've missed the best fuck you ever had."

He blinked. Was he at war with himself? Did his words match his true feelings?

A few seconds ticked by. Then he grabbed the nape of my neck and covered my mouth with his. Smoldering desire heated to an inferno with each thrust of his tongue. Nothing chilly about his actions. Any idea of resisting flew out of my head when he crushed my body to his.

I rotated my hips against his cock, savoring the feel of his hardness. My height certainly had its advantages. Without thinking about his unreasonable anger, I reached for the buttons on his shirt, but strong hands pushed mine away.

"Enough. I've got to get away from you and this nightmare you've pulled me into." A wild look crossed his face. He was being torn in two by something and I was helpless against it.

I fought the need to reach out to him. The need to comfort and protect him was actually ludicrous, considering in our short time together how powerful Ronan was becoming. But it was second nature to take care of those I loved.

Only one thing kept me from ignoring his words. That was, he was right. He hadn't asked to be reincarnated. I had taken his right to choose away.

Now he had to deal with the consequences and come to terms with being a monster. Like me.

I pulled my shoulders back.

"Go, then. Nothing's holding you here. No matter what you think, the colony's a free society and we can come and go as we please within our rules. But don't think you can escape what you are." I watched his eyes fill with suspicion. "No strings. Just remember when you arrive in Chicago to introduce yourself to the master vampire there. I'll have Connor text you his name and information."

He looked as if he'd protest, so I continued. "It's common courtesy, nothing more than to let him know who's feeding in his territory. I assume you'll go back there until you can arrange for another job out of town." I sounded cold, but I was anything but.

I was crumbling inside. Pride held back my tears. For whatever reason he decided to hate me, I refused to force my presence on him. He was alive. Well, as alive as a vampire could be.

He didn't move or blink for several seconds. Was he changing his mind? Coming to his senses? Was he still fighting with himself?

Stiffening my spine, I planned to examine his words and actions later. For now, I had to protect my heart.

"I'm taking the BMW to the hotel. Connor can pick it up tomorrow. I'll leave the keys at the front desk," he finally said.

Without another word, he took the keys from the hook and closed the door behind him.

I stood staring at the door, not seeing anything. My chest hurt. I never knew a heart could be torn out of a body and the person still function, especially a vampire's heart. I gave a small grin at my sorry attempt at humor. I'd been hanging around Connor too much.

When I had pulled the heart out of the lunatic who had given me the scars, he had died instantly. Tonight, I felt like a vampire for the first time. Old and dead.

"Mistress, he'll be back." Connor took my hand and

placed it against his cheek. "Come on. I'll prepare your bath. You know it always makes you feel better."

For a hardened gangster, Connor was always attentive to my feelings. Unlike Byron, Connor had been aware of my need to touch and be touched when I was depressed. Normally, I would take him and Byron to bed, either to fuck or just lie next to each other. Skin-to-skin contact helped in so many ways. Baths helped too.

Minutes later I sank into the scented, warm water. I sighed.

The heat felt good against my chilled skin. Connor walked in and handed me a large mug, with steam rising from the contents. I stared into the red liquid Wolfric's people concocted and wondered if Ronan had reached the hotel yet.

"If you prefer something fresher, I'll gladly join you in the tub."

His half-tease was appreciated. It made me think of good times. The time before I made the mistake of falling in love with an ex-cop turned private investigator turned vampire.

"Thank you. Not tonight. It's fine. Go on and follow Ronan. Make sure he's gotten to the hotel okay and report back to me."

I downed the drink in seconds, grimacing from the above ninety-eight-point-six-degrees temperature of human blood I usually enjoyed.

Resting my head on the cushion hanging over the tub's deep edge, I closed my eyes and began planning how I was going to kill Brannon.

# Chapter 16

## *Edgar Brannon*

I turned off the cell phone, chuckling with the knowledge I was a genius. To cast a trigger spell on Ronan the night before their escape was pure perfection.

The trigger was easy. I simply repeated the words, "Red rum." And then poof! The protective Ronan was gone, and in his place, a hate-driven, resentful vampire descending into madness if he stayed near the woman.

How appropriate to use the words from my favorite author's book as the trigger to activate the potion I made him drink. Knowing Ronan now hated the woman he had loved, it was almost poetic.

It had been worth the cool million I had to spend to get the book of spells. The old witch didn't need it anyway.

I rubbed my hands together in anticipation. Give Ronan a little time and he'd kill the bitch.

She wasn't needed anyway. Ronan could give me what I wanted: An eternity to enjoy what the world had to offer.

Leaning back in my chair, I watched the news on the massive television screen that covered one long wall in my new living room. The solemn newscaster reported another body had been found with designs cut into the flesh, then added that the authorities were stepping up their investigation.

I shook my head in disgust. The public didn't appreciate art.

# Chapter 17

## *Tori*

Confused was an understatement for how I felt watching Ronan as he stepped into a black limo. I no longer hurt when I remembered how we parted, but a strong yearning squeezed my chest now that I saw him. It had taken weeks before I could function like my old self. From what I see, he continued on as if I nothing changed in his life.

First, he was still in the South, and second, I knew the owner of the limo wasn't Brannon, but instead belonged to Gino Renata, of all people, one of the higher ups in the Renata mafia. Connor spotted Ronan entering it only recently, months after he'd left, and followed it to a large mansion in the middle of Mountain Brook, a ritzy suburb of Birmingham.

With the mere thought Ronan had been only a few, short miles away all this time infuriated me. Despite our connections and Connor's talent, we were unable to learn why he hung around someone like Renata.

Not the gates, but the armed guards kept Connor off the grounds, and what little information he could get from neighbors and the internet told more than I really wanted to know. Gino was bad news and had landed in Birmingham about the time Ronan had left me. Ronan now worked for the bad guys.

Had Ronan revealed his reincarnation? Probably not. If he had, his death would be assured for Wolfric would likely know by now too. Why hadn't he returned to Chicago?

At least, Ronan was safe from Brannon for now, but what could the mafia want with him?

I sat in my new Porsche sports car, and watched the limo's tail lights merge with the traffic before I turned on the overhead light to stare at the pictures laying across my briefcase in the seat next to me.

Worrying about Ronan wasn't helping me catch Brannon. The psycho had disappeared, but his calling cards were stacking up. So far, four bodies had been found. All had different patterns and shapes etched into their skin and all were dark-haired women. The pictures brought back too many memories burned in my brain.

A flashback of familiar eyes, wide with terror, staring at me across the room. The smell of blood, urine, and sweat mingled with the musky scent of dirt and mold. Mounds of sheets spattered with reddish-brown spots. Pain and terror that made me the monster I am today.

Wolfric had only given me the means to an end, but it was my choice to use the powers I possessed to destroy. It would take twice as many years to make up for what I had done in the name of justice.

To clear my head, I took a deep breath and looked around. The neighborhood lights flickered off, signaling dawn was less than an hour away. Time to return home. Tomorrow, I'd start to work on tracking Brannon in earnest.

<<<>>>
Ronan

I stared out the limo's window, wondering what mischief Tori was up to minutes before dawn. I felt her presence and spotted the little Porsche she'd purchased recently. Then I knew I was right.

She was spying on me. What did she make of my alliance? I refused to have anyone, especially Tori, pay my debts. I would be no better than Connor. So I called the last person I ever believed I would ask for a favor, my asshole of a cousin, the same man my wife had an affair with when we were married. The same man she was married to now.

Fuck. I fought the bitterness. I reminded myself the cheating had been years ago, and I needed to move on. I had greater problems.

Unlike Tori, I hadn't worked the stock market for the last thirty years. From what she told me, Master Wolfric was a genius at picking stock. I suspected one of his special powers had something to do with it. So with no personal wealth—I sure as hell was not going to Tori or her master and ask for help—I had to make a living somehow. Damn, being a fucking vampire was expensive, unless I was willing to live in a cave. I needed a protected—from nosey humans and sunlight—place to sleep. Normal P.I. work wouldn't provide enough consistent funds to keep me safe and pay off the loan.

"See something of interest?"

Gino sat across from me, smoking a cigar and looking proud of himself. At five-nine, he was taller than most of my mom's side of the family and though he was arrogant, crass, and had the bad habit of smoking cigars, women flocked around him. His lean build, slicked-back black hair, and dangerous, dimpled grin made it easy to seduce women, including my wife...ex-wife.

"Thought I recognized someone." I turned my attention to Gino. "What's this fancy party about that we're attending tonight?"

"I've been asked to invest in a research lab. They claim they're on the cutting edge of genetic technology."

"Why would that interest you? Weapons and explosives are more your style." Did I sound bored? Probably.

I didn't really care and preferred to return to the apartment I rented and hibernate. If it wasn't for the money, I would do just that. My shortage of funds and the loan I owed him were the only reasons I worked for him.

How did that saying go...money makes the world go around? Yeah, that was it.

Watching my cousin as he continued his self-important opinion on what to invest in, I was aware of what he expected of me at the party. Gino referred to my job as ATR's new security chief. It was nothing but a fancy title for enforcer.

"Hey, you never told me the chick's name that you were laid up with for a while. Why don't you invite her tomorrow?"

"It's better that I keep my attention on what you hired me for," I said, refusing to give Gino Tori's name.

Besides I didn't need the distraction. Getting over my obsession was a night-by-night process and inviting the seductive vampire to a swanky party wasn't the way to do it.

The driver stopped the limo on a side street in downtown Birmingham. Several warehouses in the area had been converted to lofts, and I rented one of the smaller ones. Featuring almost bare rooms and walls, the loft looked unlived-in and empty. I liked it that way. Uncluttered and uncomplicated.

The way I preferred my life...un-life.

I gazed out the passenger window, ignoring my blurred reflection. So far, I'd managed to avoid explaining to my cousin why I preferred working and meeting at night. Gino had merely said it suited him as he did most of his work at that time.

"This should take only a few minutes." Gino exited the limo first and stood on the sidewalk. "Come on." He waved me out.

I hesitated. So far I hadn't killed anyone for the little asshole, but I had a feeling tonight might be different. He insisted I go with him and Lacy, my ex-wife, to some big to-do. He was providing me with a tux. Fuck. I'd rather kill someone, especially if I could drink their blood before they died.

I exited the limo and entered the tux shop behind him.

<<<>>>

Tugging at my fucking bow tie, I firmly believed someone with a sick sense of humor had designed the evil sons of bitches. My gaze drifted over my companions.

Gino and Lacy huddled together, facing me, my back to the driver in the stretch limo. Gino had insisted we ride together to the party. From Lacy's reaction when I climbed in, she hadn't been aware I would be going with them.

Funny how I could smell the fear floating off her. Why was she afraid? Unless she thought I still cared for her. Sure, it'd hurt when I found out she'd cheated on me. For the first few weeks, I had stayed drunk until I learned it'd been with Gino. After I stopped laughing my ass off, I decided it hadn't been love but ego keeping me in that marriage. Anyway, she was an idiot to hook up with my cousin.

After a few months, she made a point to come by my apartment and leave a note. I suspected she'd not liked me recovering from our divorce so quickly. The note claimed I wasn't a real man. That a real man took care of his wife and provided her with the best. The real man she wanted was Gino. A real man? What a joke.

If she believed such bullshit, she was in for a rude awakening. And from the looks of her, she didn't lack money, but the strain at the corner of her eyes spoke volumes of how the "real" man hadn't made her as happy as she expected. Probably had a little dick.

Gino cleared his throat to draw my attention. "Charles Winslow is filthy rich and our host. His family owns several coal mines and dabbles in medical research and finance. You should be able to enjoy yourself tonight," he said with smarmy grin.

Gino then traced a pattern on his wife's bare arm. Lacy's gaze darted to me and then away. Her discomfort obvious. She hadn't figured out I didn't give a damn.

When Gino leaned over and kissed her ear, the man glanced my way.

What was wrong with these people? Was he hoping for a reaction out of me? Gino would be disappointed.

"It's a shame you didn't bring that tall redhead you were banging," he said, obviously trying a different tactic. "Charles is known to have some wild parties with a few recreation drugs thrown in. So I expect tonight will be no different."

Gino smirked as he slipped his hand into the front

bodice of Lacy's dress. Her face flushed, but once again she didn't stop him. She sat stiffly, staring out the side window.

I never treated Lacy like a whore. Maybe this was what she liked. No. Her eyes were shiny with unshed tears. The asshole needed to stop.

"Gino, my job is to protect you. Not party."

That got Gino's attention. He sat up straight and pulled his hand away from Lacy, narrowing his eyes at me. I glanced at Lacy. Gratitude flickered across her features.

Lacy deserved a lot of things, including not to be embarrassed by the man she claimed to love.

"What do you mean by that?" Gino asked.

"If someone had a grudge against you, this party would be the perfect cover. An overdose would be one of many ways to get rid of you. Who would say you hadn't gotten careless?"

I watched my cousin's eyes darken in speculation.

"You're not trying to warn me against any grudge you have, are you?"

A blunt question deserved a blunt answer.

"Eight months...hell...six months ago, you would've needed to worry. But a lot has changed, including me, more than you can ever imagine."

Boy, that was an understatement.

"Yeah. I've noticed. You've grown some brass balls for sure." Gino laughed and continued laughing until he noticed no one else thought it was funny. "Who do you think would want me dead in Birmingham?"

"There are factions who believe you're trying to take over territory belonging to the Whitfield boys. That you're taking over their black-market alcohol distribution. You're an unknown little twat. Despite all the power your family has in the Midwest, it doesn't mean jack shit here. You need to take it slow and ease your way in."

Gino stared at me for a long moment.

"You've become a smart ass since you came to Birmingham," he said in a deadly voice. "Don't worry. I know just because Southerners talk slow, they're not stupid. Maybe sneaky, but not stupid. They'll smile to your face and steal you blind. And they have that in common with where we come from, right? Family means everything. That's why I loaned you the money and gave you extra time to pay it back. Hell, that's why I hired you and the only reason you're still alive."

I kept my emotions locked inside and returned his cold look. No matter what bullshit Gino spread, I would be dead meat if I disappeared, family be damned.

The limo driver pulled up to a large, wrought-iron gate and presented the guard with their invitations. Waved on, the limo followed a curvy drive to the front of a large mansion. All the lights were on and several additional lights hung in what looked to be silk-encased Chinese lamps.

A valet opened the door and Lacy stepped out first.

"You don't worry about me tonight," Gino said to me before following Lacy. "Charles will have the place well guarded. I plan to have a good time and don't want you looking over my shoulder every second."

I nodded and walked slowly up the brick steps, following him a few feet back. The crème de la crème of Birmingham was in attendance.

Each room was filled with people in various stages of dress or undress according to their amount of alcohol or drug intake. In every dark corner, large, deep-cushioned couches beckoned lovers to forget where they were and entertain the nearby guests with their erotic activities. The bittersweet smell of pot and cocaine mixed with every kind of liquor stirred in the air.

Only a couple of years ago, I was busting people at parties like this one. My life may have taken an unexpected turn, but I refused to immerse myself in a lifestyle that was more abhorrent to me than drinking blood. I chuckled. When had I decided taking drugs was worse than being a vampire? Not the opposite? Especially when the option had been taken from me?

Followed immediately on that insanity was the sensation of another vampire in the room, and it wasn't just any vampire. Tori.

Where was she? Why was she here?

The large room I stood in had two billiard tables in the center, a long bar near one end, and a wall of French doors at the other. I searched the room by slowly turning and surveying the occupants until I spotted her in the shadows near the French doors leading into a small garden. Seeing her again so close felt like walking into a brick wall. I was surprised, yet shattered.

Unable to resist, I sauntered over to her.

"Hi," I simply said.

Her dark eyes, wide and oh-so-innocent, stared up at me. "Hi."

"Come here often?" I wanted to snatch her up in my arms.

"All the time." She tilted her head, waiting for me to say more.

Then she smiled as she glanced away for a moment. Was she trying to hide her pleasure that I remembered our first meeting?

"I'm not sure what to say next. You never told me which movie you were quoting."

The billowy white shirt and black leather pants she wore gave her the look of a female pirate. I bet she'd have given Anne Bonny a run for her money.

"No, I didn't." She paused and then said, "*Queen of the Damned*. I guess I'm the only one who remembers the scene in the bar with the human girl and the vampires. The next line is 'I don't see any marks.'" With a crooked grin, she added, "Kinda ironic, huh?"

On hearing her husky voice, I realized how much I missed her. At the same time, deep down a knot of anger and sadness filled me. My gaze dropped to her lips. If I kissed and touched her, would I then crush her windpipe in my fury?

"You better leave," I warned in a deep voice almost unrecognizable to my own hearing.

"Why?" She blinked and pressed a hand to her throat.

My words and tone had hurt her. She tried to hide it by looking past me into the room beyond. It wasn't too long ago she could hide her feelings. Of course, that was when I was still human. Being a vampire, I was aware of people's emotions, human or vampire. Like in the limo with Lacy. I wasn't sure I liked this ability.

"Were you not the one who said too many vampires in a small area provided a greater risk for exposure?" I asked, reminding her of the many rules and warnings she provided.

Though I wanted her desperately, I felt the rage building again. It wouldn't be satisfied until I...what? Killed her? She needed to leave.

"You're feeding here?" Her words and raised brows proved I needed to work harder on making her leave.

"I don't want you here," I said as coldly as I could.

"My, that was terribly blunt." Her eyes looked over my

shoulder again as if she searched the room for someone. "Don't worry. I don't plan to feed on anyone. So you're safe."

"Who are you looking for?" When she didn't answer, I knew. "Brannon isn't here."

An inner glow in her eyes flashed for a moment then dulled. "My sources say differently."

I sat my drink down on a nearby table and moved closer. As I had expected, she stood her ground and glared at my attempted intimidation.

"How is good old Connor by the way? Is he keeping your bed warm now Byron is dead and I refuse to service you." I was proud of how I kept jealousy out of my voice. "Or have you replaced Byron with a new blood slave?"

"I thought you were better than that." She tilted head.

Why was I baiting her? Something inside of me clawed at my chest, wanting me to be cruel.

"Oh, I see, you had expected me to be your next slave. Maybe I'll switch the tables on you."

I stepped in even closer to tower over her. When she started to inch away, I grabbed her arm and tugged her against my body. My other hand grasped the back of her head and crushed those soft lips with mine. She didn't resist but dug her nails into my back and pressed her breasts to my torso. Hungry for each other, as one we stepped deeper into the shadows.

My body pressed her back into the nearest wall so hard a nearby picture rattled on its hook. I could feel her shape underneath her silk blouse, but it barred me from her skin. I yanked the material up and slipped my hand beneath her blouse, shoving the bra out of the way, and cupped a breast. My canines lengthened and I nicked her tongue with one sharp point. The tiny taste of blood sent me almost over the edge.

Angry, I pushed away and took several gulps of air. Before she could open her mouth and protest my erratic behavior, a large object came crashing through the French doors. Shattered glass sprayed us, stinging our faces and arms.

Without thinking, I shoved Tori behind me and faced the attacker. The rotten smell of flesh was the first clue. Spots of wavy brown hair were missing, and his blue eyes had glazed over and now only solid gray balls looked out of his skull. Skin hung in patches on his arms and face. It was what was left of Byron. A zombie. He was a zombie.

The partiers screamed and charged toward the opposite side of the room, flooding into the foyer and out the front door.

"Byron!" Tori shouted.

What had she done to transform Byron into such a monster? Why had she? Would she do the same to me?

I stepped forward and slammed a fist into the zombie's chin. The creature swayed and took one step back and then roared. Arms reaching out like in an old horror movie, he stiffly walked toward Tori.

"How do we kill it?" I asked as I grabbed Tori's hand and backed away from the zombie. This creature was no longer Byron or even human.

I knew how to kill vampires and humans, but not zombies. Though we discussed many things after my reincarnation, the how-to-kill-zombies part was not included.

"Well, not by punching it in the face. That only makes him angrier."

From her tone, she sounded as if she was enjoying herself. I glanced her way. There was a gleam in her eyes, not joy exactly, but more like anticipation in the challenge of killing the creature.

What the hell? Was this part of some scheme of hers?

The guests were now screaming and running in every direction. It was total mayhem in the huge house. I darted through an opening next to the bar, dragging Tori along the way. It was nice to finally be stronger than her. Part of the wall in the long hallway turned to glass and what looked to be an exercise room on the other side. Then I spotted another door. I reached for the knob.

"Let go of me. I need to stop him."

"Did you have something to do with this?" I glared at Tori, releasing her.

Before she answered, the door opened. Two women came running so fast the opposite way, screaming, their shoes flew off their feet.

I shut the door and leaned against it. There wasn't a lock.

Tori grabbed my jacket sleeve.

"How could you ask me that? No one deserves to be brought back as a zombie, even a traitor like Byron. Brannon did this, I would stake my life on it."

Her choice of words was rather humorous. Stake. Life. For a vampire to use such words meant she was certain. Was having a warped sense of humor a component to becoming a vampire?

Should I believe her?

First things first, I still had a zombie to kill.

"How do we kill it?" I asked.

"Though zombies are simpleminded and slow moving, they're the devil to kill and as strong as any vampire. We need holy water and a sword."

"What the fuck? Where are we going to find that? I

doubt Charles keeps stuff like that lying around." I had no idea where the nearest Catholic church was located.

"I've got it in my car."

"Of course. Just your usual survival kit." A vampire with holy water, who knew?

"Apparently so." Her crooked grin almost took my mind off the emergency.

"Where's your car?"

"Keep his attention on you and I'll be back in two shakes of a lamb's tail."

I watched her sprint across what appeared to be a living room.

Lamb's tail? What was it about hearing her say that that threw me? Was it because it made me remember at one time she'd been human?

Another roar from what had been Byron vibrated through the door I leaned against. I shook my head. Time to return my attention to the problem at hand.

The door shook with the force of the zombie's hits. I was thankful Charles had spent the extra bucks and installed solid doors inside his house. If only he had included a couple of extra locks.

At that moment, a hand crashed through the wood near my left ear.

Okay. Locks not necessary.

"Damn it, Tori, hurry up," I muttered and moved my head back from the grasping fingers.

# Chapter 18

## *Tori*

Running back across the spacious and now empty living room toward where Ronan pushed on the partially splintered door, I waved the sword in my hand.

"Move out of the way and let him through," I shouted.

I took a fighter's stance with the saber clasped in both hands and waited for the zombie.

Ronan stepped to the side.

"Where's the holy water?"

Before I could answer, the door came crashing to the floor. The zombie released a long groan and walked stiff-legged into the room. I couldn't call him Byron. My friend and lover was no longer in that body.

Thankfully, zombies were slow and not too bright. I swung the sword. One arm dropped to the ground, dark goop slid out of the opening, and he tottered then began walking toward me again.

"Tori, the arm," Ronan warned.

I glanced down and saw it moving. Its fingers crawled

across the floor like a crab on the beach. Bringing my attention back to the larger, remaining zombie, I stepped back.

"The holy water is stuck in the waist of my pants, in the back," I said. Not wasting time, Ronan reached behind me and removed the flask. "Sprinkle a little on his arm, then sprinkle it quickly on each body part I cut off. Be careful and don't get it on you."

The next hour was the worst I could remember since being tied down in that basement so many years ago. Wherever the holy water hit the zombie, it bubbled, and sick, smelly clouds of poisoned blood and burnt flesh filled the air. By the time we were finished, only a mass of melted body parts remained on the floor with a gooey substance that probably used to be blood.

"I don't understand." Ronan stood beside me, looking down at what was once Byron.

"What's that?" I glanced at Ronan, his face had become paler with each grisly chore.

"How is it that crosses don't bother us, but holy water does?"

He slowly raised his tortured gaze, waiting for me to answer. I suspected there was more to the question than just asking about the religious ramifications.

"We call it holy water, but it's really acid." At his surprised look, I grinned. "It won't kill us, unless we fell in a vat, but it would hurt like hell and take years to heal."

He let me take the flask, but watched my movements with a worried expression while I replaced the cap. When I started to return the flask to the waist of my pants, he snatched it back.

"I'll carry that. Get the saber and let's get out of here." Ronan took my hand and began walking toward the front door, then stopped. Looking back at the mess, he asked,

"Shouldn't we do something about what's left of the body?"

Before I could explain, there was a loud pop then sizzle and the blob of goo and gloop began to melt and disappear in a cloud of steam before our eyes.

"What the hell?"

I shook my head and shuddered.

"His heart must have stopped beating finally. It's the strangest thing. Once you melt every major body part and organ, the body will instantly disappear. Don't ask me why. I have no idea. It's like asking why we exist like we do. Only the ancient ones know that answer, and they won't part with their secrets. Maybe they believe it's not important for us to know."

The cool air felt good against my face after the grisly work was done for the night. I stopped beside my car and turned to face Ronan. "Are you coming with me?"

His eyes glowed beneath the moonlight. What was he feeling? Lust? Love? Hatred? Probably it was all those things and more.

When would I ever understand what he was going through? To be alone and have no purpose in his existence. I always had my revenge. Then again, it could be said the same for me now. Revenge was important but not the obsession it had been at one time. I was more cautious.

"No."

The answer was expected, but I was still disappointed. Determined I wouldn't show how much his continued indifference hurt, I looked away, staring at the swaying Chinese lanterns. A few people stood around watching us, but kept their distance. I didn't spot the couple who came with Ronan. Cars streamed out of the driveway, escaping the craziness they'd experienced in the mansion.

I turned back to Ronan. The wind lifted his hair, his eyes glowed slightly as he remained in the shadows. Why was he still standing there? Why hadn't he returned to my home? Had he expected me to beg for him to go with me?

I opened my car door and flipped the sun visor down. The keys fell into my open hand.

"Well, I guess I'll see you around."

He moved behind me, his body's warmth quickly heating my skin through the thin silk blouse. Unable to move, I waited to see what he planned. His knuckle grazed my cheek. Where had the wetness come from?

Oh. Tears were flowing down my face. The moisture felt strange.

"Why are you crying?" His lips were next to my ear. He held my shoulders, pulling me to him.

Pitch-hot desire melted my bones, and I leaned back against his chest. His breath tickled my neck. I missed his touch, the feel of his teeth sinking into my flesh, his slim hips thrusting between my legs. I missed him in my bed. Connor would console me if I let him, but I wanted only Ronan. I wanted his taste on my tongue. I wanted his broad chest covering mine. I wanted.... His hands dropped from my shoulders. Coldness seeped into my body as his footsteps crunched on the leaves.

"Ronan, when will you ever forgive me?" I whispered to the night air as he returned to the mansion and his new life.

<<<>>>

Ronan

In the middle of undressing for bed, I hesitated. I felt a certain vampire's presence. There was a shift in the atmosphere. Then a knock on the front door echoed through my loft.

Tori? I had enough of her for one evening. How does she do it? It had to be at least seven in the morning and no sun-fearing vampire handled being out in broad daylight, daring the hot rays to touch sensitive skin. As it was, it had taken me drinking extra blood to stay awake long enough to do a couple of searches online.

"Damn it, Tori!" I opened the door and a familiar face smirked at me, but not the one I expected.

"You're a hard man to get a hold of, Mr. Michaels." Detective Jameson stood in his rumpled overcoat, with the required badge hanging around his neck.

"Last I heard, all charges had been dropped. That you had a suspect in custody, and he admitted committing the murders." I had Tori's master to thank for that. Not that I liked it. Not one bit. Owing favors to someone like Wolfric would be very dangerous for my health in the future.

"That's true. Very convenient for you, wouldn't you say?" Jameson's sarcasm wasn't lost on me.

"So what can I do for you, Detective?"

I wanted him gone and wasn't in the mood for pleasantries.

"May I come in?" The detective's tone said he didn't expect to be allowed in. I was tempted, but knew he would make it harder on me later if I objected.

"Sure. Why not?"

I didn't keep pints of blood sitting around, so it wasn't a problem for the detective to come in. That was, if I stayed awake long enough. It wouldn't do for me to fall over into the death sleep in front of the man. That would surely shock the detective. He would think I had died on seeing his face.

Waving him in, I grinned. The detective glanced at me and then did it again. Nervous, huh? I'd seen how humans became twitchy around me. It was as if they sensed I was a natural predator.

Jameson walked into the spacious living-and-dining-room combination. Walls of glass looked over the valley below with Birmingham lights blinking through the early morning rain. The view was the reason I had bought the loft and the privacy it afforded. In a hidden notch on the wall, I pressed a button to close the curtains covering the heavily-tinted glass, ready to protect me from any deadly rays that may break through the clouds.

"You're related to Gino Renata." It was more of a statement than question.

So that was why he came knocking on my door. Certain that the detective knew the answer, but willing to play along, I answered, "He's a cousin."

Keeping my head down, I rebuttoned my shirt, leaving it untucked. No need to make myself pretty for the likes of Jameson. He would only think I was dressing for the morning, instead of preparing for bed.

"What does he have planned in Birmingham?"

"You'll have to ask Gino that. I keep out of his business."

I really wanted to end the conversation. Though my cousin was a son of a bitch, he was my boss now.

"You work for him. I believe you know a lot more about his business than you're willing to admit."

"Listen. I do what Gino tells me and none of it's been illegal." So far. The two words lingered unsaid between us. "If you want to get Gino, you need to find a different way."

"You borrowed a large sum of money from Renata."

"Yeah. So? He's family." It was taking everything I had to keep from decking this asshole. I knew what was coming next, but there was no way I was going down for assaulting an officer.

"Word on the street is that you paid off half with interest, and the interest for his kind is very steep. Where did you get the money?"

The detective's right hand was in his coat and probably holding the stock of his gun resting in a shoulder holster.

Did the man really expect me to attack?

"A friend decided to help me out." No way was I about to explain Brannon and the partial fee I had received before tracking down Tori. I'd just go along with the story the detective started unknowingly.

"I wish I had friends like that. What's your friend's name?" Jameson walked to the window and pushed the curtain back, then pressed his nose against the glass.

I admired how the detective appeared not to care one way or another for the answer.

"My friend wouldn't appreciate me answering that."

"Your cousin must pay good for you to afford a place like this," Jameson said, without looking my way. He pushed the curtains farther back.

The clouds were breaking up and the sun shone bright. Not taking a chance the specially-tinted windows would fail in protecting me, I stepped to the side into the shadows of the large room.

"He treats his employees decent," I commented.

"And his family." Jameson turned around. Surprise at my retreat clearly crossed his face as the detective came nearer.

What was the detective digging for? Of course, the mob is known for taking care of family, but it still didn't have anything to do with the murders. I wanted the man out of my home now.

"Is that all, Detective?" The curtain fell into place and I headed for the door, giving him a clue he needed to leave.

"Just one more question. Where were you at eleven last night?"

*Fighting Byron and helping Tori hack the zombie to pieces.*

The detective would be taking me in for sure if I repeated that out loud. Had someone reported the zombie? Did some of the body parts survive the acid? Would anyone believe all of that?

"I was with Gino and Lacy at Charles Winslow's party." I wanted the detective to hurry and leave.

"What time did you leave?"

"The party broke up around one-thirty in the morning."

"You're being very cooperative."

"I have nothing to hide." The look I received said the detective thought that was a bunch of bullshit.

I placed my hand on the door knob. "If there is anything else you would like to ask, you better have a warrant for my arrest next time."

With a step back, I opened the door and waited for the detective to leave. Thank goodness the door led into a wide hallway with no windows.

That ruffled the detective's feathers. Jameson straightened his jacket and stomped to the door, but stopped, glaring at me.

"I have a friend in Chicago who worked with you. He said you were a hell of a cop and it was a shame what had happened. He said you were set up." After he cleared his throat, he added, "I thought you might be interested." Then he turned on his heel and left.

I wasn't sure what to make of that. The man suspected

me of murder but plainly said I had been railroaded out of my job at home.

Like I didn't fucking know. Dickwad.

Why had he really come? Could it be Brannon had left another body lying around? At the same time he sent the zombie?

<<<>>>

Tori

My usual nightmares, in my case daymares, mingled with a new one. The last few evenings, I woke crying from intense emotions raging inside my body. After each time, only a cold shower helped me reclaim some semblance of sanity. The memories caused my skin to tingle. I woke with a racing heart and a groin pulsating, that was disturbing and erotic at the same time.

During death sleep, I'd been told we cannot dream, but in the moments between death sleep and waking we could experience what we did as a human. I felt the recurring dream take over my mind and body, and tonight was no different. Though I subconsciously fought it, the dream always started with images of soft hazel eyes and artist hands. Ronan. He stood in the doorway of my private chamber.

Without a word, he stripped off the dark clothes he favored and slowly walked to my bed. My gaze followed him, devouring how each muscle and tendon flowed with a gracefulness of a predator stalking prey. My inspection dropped and I gasped. His cock stretched and hardened as he came nearer. Reincarnation magnified and defined the perfection of the human body. Ronan was no exception. He was vampire magnificence.

I slowly pulled my admiration to his face. Why had he returned?

A gentle wind from nowhere lifted the ends of his hair, pushing the strands away from his handsome face. The corners of his mouth lifted until his smile was nothing but decadent, while beckoning me to taste his lips. Desire flooded my body, craving his masculine mouth to cover mine. I wanted his tongue on my neck, breasts, pussy, between my fingers, over my palm, anywhere I had skin.

He knelt on my bed and lifted my hand to his mouth, and his smile widened until I could see his canines long and deadly. My pulse quickened, wanting him to take everything I could offer. His eyes burned bright with an inner golden glow, showing his raging desire and tightly reined control. He turned my hand over and licked the palm, nipping at the end of my ring finger. A jolt of heat pulsated between my legs all the way to my heart. I wanted him so desperately. He gripped my waist and held me tight to his body. Whimpers emerged from my parted lips as his hardness rubbed and thrust against my willing body.

Sitting up, my nightgown slipped off one shoulder, revealing a full breast, and his hot gaze devoured the sight and then lifted to my eyes. Without looking away, he licked and nibbled his way up my arm, bringing a tingling sensation with each touch of his tongue and teeth. He came closer and closer to my taut nipple. Dazed by his sensual assault I instinctively arched my back, begging him to take the beaded tip between his lips into the moist heat of his mouth.

As if he were reading my mind, his mouth covered a nipple and sucked until the edge of pain. I grasped his head to pull him away, but found the tight ache was pleasure in itself. Releasing my hold, I caressed his broad back, down his spine, over his tight buttocks and hips to grasp his cock, offering him pleasure in turn.

His long and drawn-out moan brought a tightness to my body in reaction, craving more from this man. Each touch of his long fingers I matched with one of my own.

Ronan shifted, slipping down my torso, pulling my gown off to land on the floor. His tongue traced the top of my panties as he rolled them over my hips. He grasped my knees and roughly spread them apart, impatient for a taste of my warmth. Moist heat engulfed me as his mouth lapped and sucked my pulsating flesh.

Another whimper escaped my lips but quickly turned into a scream of release. His fangs sunk into the tender stretch of skin on my thigh. Every tingling nerve ending sizzled, wanting his body sliding against mine.

Mind blank, I was immersed in his touch as he controlled my body. My fingers dove into the long strands of his dark hair. I pulled his face away from his feeding, and brought him nose to nose, staring at those mesmerizing gold eyes. Vampire glowing eyes. Without taking my gaze away, I lifted his hand and licked his wide palm, then pierced his strong wrist for a small taste. Enjoying the attention, he closed his eyes and moaned. He adjusted our bodies with one hand and thrust into my warmth. The explosion was immediate. Then I would wake.

Frustrated and embarrassed by my lack of control, I closed my eyes and a chill blanketed my skin.

I hated waking and finding he was never there. I was alone. No clothes on the floor. My gown on. It was a dream. A tightness grew in my chest and throat until I felt grief take over from the disappointment. I screamed and fell face first onto the bed, muffling my pain in the pillow.

I missed his body, his beautiful eyes, his attention. I had

never loved someone as much as I loved him and I was scared.

Love at first sight had always seemed to be no more than a fantasy concocted by raging hormonal teenagers. Though I tried to convince myself that being a vampire heightened my emotions and it wasn't anything more than that. As it had been pointed out to me many times, female vampires had problems dealing with their emotions as they were magnified by the dark gift. But I knew deep down inside, it was something more, something good and pure.

Rubbing my forehead, I squeezed my eyes shut for a few seconds to regain my composure. Time for me to get out of bed and end this. Find Brannon and kill him and move on. Forget Ronan. Get some distance. Take Connor with me and find another servant or two. Time would tell and that was one thing I had a lot of. An eternity of time.

<<<>>>

Ronan

I woke aching.

Dreams are extensions of a person's fears. I had heard that somewhere. The fear of coffins and the dark I understood. Losing my dad to such a disease and becoming a vampire were traumatic events in anyone's life.

My dreams of the past few days wouldn't fall into what I would consider the realm of my fear. They were highly sensual and erotic, and Tori was at the center.

The things she did to my body were what men dreamed about, and I ached to experience each position and act with her once again. At one time, they'd been real.

Yet each time I saw her, the old anger returned full

force. Then when she was out of sight, I understood I had acted unreasonably, my temper overblown.

A timer clicked the lamp on beside my bed.

It was rather funny, though I didn't feel like laughing. A vampire scared of the dark. Well, more than the dark, the pitch-black absence of light. Connor had helped me seal my bedroom. I figured if the hoodlum was going to spy on me for Tori, the least he could do was help sunlight-proof my home.

The first evening I'd awoken to the cave-dark room without Tori at my side, I panicked. It was like waking in a coffin with no air, no light. Now I made sure to always have a light nearby or one set to come on at the normal time my body released me from death sleep.

I shook my head and eased out of bed. A quick shower would clear my mind. Thinking about Tori and trying to understand my behavior wouldn't do me any good. Being a vampire probably had a lot to do with my volatile temper, but I needed to concentrate on tracking Brannon and keeping my cousin out of trouble.

After I had washed up, shaved, and while I pulled on my dark clothes, I lifted my eyes to the ceiling. Who would ever believe one day I would protect the cousin who had threatened to kill me for an unpaid loan? Gino was a tough guy, who knew the importance of family, while always keeping an eye on the almighty buck. Importance of family...ha! Not enough to not fuck my wife. I shook my head. Why even think of that? I'd moved on. To Tori. Yeah, her.

I turned to looked at my faded image in the floor-length mirror.

Bad habit. Though my barely-there reflection bothered

the hell out of me, I still spurned the thought of throwing out the last mirror.

In the drawer next to my bed, I lifted the .38 and shoulder holster, strapping them on before slipping into my black leather jacket. It was rather ironic I wore a gun I never planned to use. What would a vampire need with a gun? I could simply snap a man's neck with my bare hands.

I only wore a gun out of habit and because Gino expected it. Standard bodyguard gear. Just easier to wear it than to explain why it was unnecessary. My cousin was better off not knowing my new skills. Less to explain.

# Chapter 19

## *Ronan*

"Hey, you're lucky I don't fire your ass!" Gino sat behind his desk, smoking one of the fat cigars he loved, believing they made him look higher on the food chain in the organization.

To me, he looked like a caricature of a mob boss.

"I can only hope." In dealing with Gino the past few months, I'd learned to either ignore my cousin's threats or throw them back with a little humor mixed in.

"Hell, that's what happens when you stay out partying through the night and sleep until dark. Ah, to be young and single again."

I grimaced.

Gino was only a year older, but believed his so-called success meant he was wiser. Conveniently forgetting his paternal uncle was the owner of ATR Industries and the only reason he was in control of their new southeast territory.

Gino eyed me. "Are you feeling okay? You're a little pale. It wouldn't hurt to get out in the sunlight on occasion."

Nah, it wouldn't hurt. I wouldn't feel a thing when I combusted.

"I'm fine. What did you want to see me about?"

Taking his time, Gino snubbed out the cigar and stood. "The investment I spoke to you about the other day is now in the negotiation stage. I need you to go over to my lawyers' and make sure everything goes my way."

"So you want me to swing some weight around and encourage them in seeing things your way, huh?" I glared at my cousin. "When I hired on, it was to protect you and your family from any threats. Nothing was said about babysitting your lawyers."

Gino opened a large oak cabinet and pulled out a bottle of Scotch and held it up, offering to pour me a glass.

Shaking my head, my stomach lurched with the need of what I really craved. After presenting his own neck and being turned down, Connor had offered to bring some of Wolfric's blood supply, but my pride wouldn't let me accept either.

Out of necessity, I had gone to a local butcher and made up a story about pig and cow's blood being used in my artwork. The butcher sold me several jugs, but it had cost me dearly in cash and the pride I had guarded so well.

Gino poured several fingers of the reddish-brown liquor, not looking my way. "When you came to me asking for a job, didn't I welcome you with open arms? Your debt is almost paid and I'm not stupid. I know that you had your own agenda."

Standing motionless, I kept my face blank. I waited for Gino to continue. Some time ago, I learned my cousin enjoyed the sound of his own voice.

"Uncle Sal warned a cop's always a cop, but I told him, you're family. That our mothers were sisters. But you know how Sal is, always worrying. Or am I wrong? Should I worry?"

"My life before coming here was already over with." If only Gino knew how true that was. "Now I work for you and I'll go with the vultures and make sure everything's handled fairly." On seeing the look Gino gave me, I stated, "Fair enough to satisfy you."

My assurance obviously did the trick. Gino quickly gave his instructions and finished with an unexpected request.

"I have someone I want you to take with you. Lacy's been needing a bodyguard for when she leaves the grounds at night without me, and I've found the right person. Whenever Lacy's busy at home, the new employee can help you."

"Come in," Gino hollered.

Then in walked Tori.

I opened and closed my eyes several times in disbelief. What game was she playing?

"Ronan, you didn't tell me your friend worked as a bodyguard for several prominent celebrities," Gino said in his snide, whiny voice.

Saucy. That was the type of smile Tori wore, and I couldn't help thinking how I wanted to kiss her until she grew breathless as I wrapped my hands around her neck. That was all she had to do, was to walk into the room and I became hard and pissed off. The dreams I had the last few nights weren't helping any.

Ignoring the woman, I turned to Gino. "Besides the asshole in the hotel lobby, did you have others spying on me?"

My cousin raised his hands, laughed. "Don't get your dander up. When you left Chicago in such a hurry, I had to make sure you weren't trying to skip out on me. The guys that I put on your tail came back with some fascinating reports." Gino walked behind Tori, eyeing her from heel to head, obviously interested in what he was seeing. "I can say that you've got excellent taste."

I'd had enough.

"Listen, cousin, I work for you but my personal business is that, my personal business." A glance toward Tori confirmed what I guessed was happening. She was amused and engrossed in the conversation. "Who you hire to protect Lacy is your business and I really don't give a damn, but you better be sure you know what you're doing."

"Are you telling me that I shouldn't hire Tori because she's not as good as she claims? Or I shouldn't hire her because she dumped you?" Before I could answer, Gino added, "Maybe you're afraid the two women who dumped you will get together, compare notes, and tear you to pieces."

"Like I give a fuck. I'm here to protect you and help you in areas that need a little muscle and nothing more. Hire her. Don't hire her. It doesn't matter." Tired of my cousin's mind-fuck games, I stalked across the room and slammed the door shut behind me.

<<<>>>

Tori

Tickled by Ronan's reaction, I waited for Gino to say if I still had the job or not. When Connor told me about Ronan's cousin looking for another bodyguard, preferably female, I thought it would be the perfect way to keep an eye on Ronan and make sure he stayed safe.

Besides, from the information Connor and my other sources dug up, I knew Gino had previously done business with Brannon and I didn't believe in coincidence.

Gino chuckled. "Well, it appears your boyfriend isn't too happy about me hiring you."

It was obvious Gino liked the image of a playboy with mob connections, giving him a dangerous edge. He was more than that. In my one and only interview, I took advantage of our handshake to read his past. Taking a few extra seconds to read as much as I could, I'd held his hand a little longer than proper. Before I could read more, a wall came down in his mind as if he sensed my gentle probing, nothing like the deep searching I did on Byron.

That had confused me. It proved startling for a human to have enough control to shut it down.

While I was off-balance, he took advantage of my distraction. Of course, in his own egoistic way, he'd thought I was coming onto him and wanted to take it further. I had the pleasure of giving him firsthand knowledge of my expertise.

After I helped him off the floor, he made sure not to touch me again.

What I gleaned from our contact before the wall came down was that he was jealous of Ronan. Apparently over the years, the family had held up Ronan as the prime example of bad genes turned to good.

Athletic and academic achievements in school, topped with graduating from the police academy with highest honors, didn't endear him with Gino. Having Ronan as his employee was the most satisfying experience to Gino so far.

One other tidbit of information I had extracted was he wanted to fuck me. His twisted belief was that it would show Ronan all his women came to Gino for a real man.

Gino was good-looking in a sort of dark Mediterranean sort of way. But a real man? No. Real men didn't treat family like useable commodities, or sleep with their cousin's wives or girlfriends. Though I wasn't actually Ronan's girl-friend. It has been years since I'd even thought of being anyone's love interest.

The past few months had been hard since he left. I missed having Ronan in my bed. His musky, manly smell. The way his body wrapped around mine. His voice that made me melt with need. Hard to believe we'd been together only a couple of weeks when he left. It seemed I was doomed to endure the pain of loss over and over again. Ronan, Byron.... I refused to think of anyone more. I mentally shut out the distracting thoughts from my mind and turned my attention back to Gino.

"Was that the reason you hired me? You thought I was his girlfriend?"

Gino reached out to touch my arm, and I leaned away. He quickly pulled his hand back.

"You two were seen getting down and dirty in the middle of a nightclub. What was it called? Oh, yeah, Blood-sucker's. Maybe I'll get you to take me there sometime."

"I'm sure Lacy would find it a lot of fun." I almost laughed when his face fell as I made the suggestion. From what I'd seen, Lacy wanted high-end nightclubs. Blood-sucker's was a little too strange for his wife.

"Yeah. Well, you better get going or Ronan will go without you."

"Sure thing, boss." I grinned, tapping two fingers to my forehead, and went after Ronan.

# Chapter 20

## *Tori*

I watched Ronan maneuver his black Corvette, with illegal black-tinted windows, through the evening traffic. His large hands handled the steering wheel with ease. Amused by how he continued to ignore my presence in the small space, I decided to enjoy the view. Namely, the titillating Ronan Michaels.

Strands of his almost-black hair hung to his chin and covered his collar in the back. The five-o'clock shadow on his jaw gave a savage look to his profile.

I liked his profile. A manly nose and sensual lips only emphasized the intelligent forehead and firm chin. My gaze drifted to his neck where the skin appeared thick from so many years in the sun. Memories came to me of tasting the salty but smooth texture in my mouth, along my tongue, his blood hot in my mouth.

Now wasn't the time to allow myself to become excited. My advances would not be welcomed. I turned and watched the scenery zoom by until we reached our destination.

Easily accessed through an underground parking deck,

the meeting was held in a lower floor of the large, downtown skyscraper. Windowless, the room was perfect for two vampires to concentrate on the work at hand. Besides, I didn't worry about a trap or unexpected problems creeping up when we met with Gino's lawyers and the lawyers for the research laboratory.

As soon as I walked into the room behind Ronan, he tensed. Someone or something had him bristling with anger.

Looking around the room, I wondered which staid-looking man had Ronan up in arms. One gentleman with curly hair and squinting eyes paled further when I looked at him. That must be the one.

Before anyone made a move, Ronan had the man by the collar. "Hanson, where's Brannon? Where's the bastard?"

Most of the laboratory's lawyers scrambled for the door, and only Gino's lawyers, hands inside suit jackets, stood against the wall. After working several years for ATR Industries and Gino, they understood the importance of being armed no matter the occasion.

I blocked the closed door, stopping the lawyers from exiting the room. One ill-mannered lawyer decided he could move a weaker female out of the way. As his body sailed through the air, his two companions quickly returned to their seats.

"Mr. Michaels, I have many clients and Mr. Brannon only used my services that one time," Hanson explained. "It wasn't easy to get you out of jail on bond that quickly." The man looked as if he was about to cry.

Even across the large room, I smelled his fear. "He's hiding something. Otherwise, he wouldn't be so afraid," I said softly.

Surely, Brannon wasn't so stupid as to tell the lawyer they were vampires.

Hanson wasn't fighting back and he hunched his shoulders, trying to protect his neck. *Yep, he knew the truth.*

The fewer witnesses they had, the better.

"Everyone, out of here! Tell your boss the meeting has been delayed until next week." When the first lawyer ran for the door, before I moved to the side, I stared into his eyes, knowing mine were glowing. "And no one, and I mean no one, repeat what they heard or saw in here. Do you understand?" The man rapidly nodded his head. "I want to hear the words."

"Yes, ma'am," Gino's lawyers said.

After the last one left, I closed the door and leaned against it. I couldn't help but feel excited watching Ronan hold the man off the floor with one hand, while not giving in to his natural instinct to suck him dry. The urge to bathe in the restrained energy flowing off of him had me wishing I was alone with Ronan.

"What business does Brannon have with Gino?" Ronan asked as he stood almost nose-to-nose to Hanson. "How is he connected to the research laboratory?"

"I don't know what you're talking about. I don't know anyone called Gino." If Hanson squirmed further down in his chair, he would be on the floor.

Ronan shook the man, pulling him up by the scruff of his neck. "Didn't they teach you at that fancy lawyer school you went to how to lie better than that?" Frustration deepened his voice with each word. "Gino Renata heads the southeast division of ATR Industries. They're the damn investor you and your friends were trying to set up a contract with."

"Be careful, or you'll snap his neck." Concerned by Ronan's mounting temper, but still strangely drawn, I worked at keeping my tone neutral. I never remembered seeing him so out of control. Well, except for the day he became angry and stormed out of my house for good. Another thought crept to the forefront of my mind, how wild would our lovemaking be if he lost control?

I sighed. So frustrated with my one track mind. Now wasn't the time to think about that. It was difficult to look at Ronan without thinking lustful thoughts, and when his emotions were boiling over, the room felt like electricity bounced off the walls and along my skin.

Watching him intimidate the lawyer should make me leery, but instead sent a thrill through my being. Was there something wrong with my morality? Maybe there was, but I knew he wouldn't really harm the man on purpose. Taking another look at the scene being played out in front of me, it was plain Ronan was careful not to touch the man again. Humans were such frail creatures. Didn't I know that well.

"The paperwork referred to a Salvatore Renata. Nothing was said about Gino. I swear!" Hanson began crying, gulping mindless crying.

"I really don't give a rat's ass about Gino. Tell me where Brannon's at." Ronan stood straight, shoulders back. He was in control again.

I crossed my arms and raised an eyebrow. The man shook in terror as he looked into Ronan's eyes blazing a green glow. Now it was all for show.

"Hanson, I don't believe you know what you're up against. Brannon's a killer. He's trying to rack up the number of bodies like his brother. If you don't know, his brother, half brother actually, was Tim Gordon." Ronan leaned down toward the man's face. "Do you want to be a part of that? Being a lawyer, surely you know how many years you'll spend in the pen for aiding and abetting, for being an accessory to murder?"

Somehow, the man shrank further in the chair, whimpering and mumbling, trying to get away from Ronan. The sound of liquid hitting the carpet along with an acrid smell was the final straw.

"You might as well give up on him. He's having a breakdown," I suggested.

Disgust filled Ronan's voice. "Don't you have any pride, man?" Ronan turned his back and walked toward the door. He stopped in front of me and when I didn't move, he asked, "What?"

"Is it my turn?" I asked and grinned wide.

"For what?" His confusion was obvious even before he opened his mouth.

Men. Couldn't live with them, couldn't live without them.

"I can't believe you've forgotten." I shook my head and glided around him to the huddled mass of humanity and stooped next to the man. Hanson whimpered louder, then pleaded not to hurt him when I carefully placed a hand on his arm. "Shh. It doesn't always hurt and will only take a minute or less."

The only sounds in the room were the sniffling by Hanson and the dripping of urine on the floor.

Shaking my head, I stepped away from the lawyer and left the room. As soon as the door closed behind Ronan, I began laughing uproariously.

"What's so funny?"

I looked at Ronan and began laughing harder. By the time we reached the car, I had my laughter under control.

"Our little lawyer in there was telling the truth. He only worked for Brannon one time, to get you out of jail. He's working for the research facility and believes the laboratory is blowing smoke up Gino's butt about a youth serum."

"None of that sounded very funny. What was the joke?"

Grinning, I couldn't help the giggle that escaped. "When I read someone's past, the information I seek doesn't always sit on top. Especially if they're trying to hide it from me. So I guess you could say, I move things around in their head. And the lawyer has a few personal secrets he's hiding."

"Tell me. Maybe we can use it later."

"Oh, my, aren't we the opportunist?"

"I'm learning from Brannon and his cronies not to leave anything to chance. We need everything at our disposal to fight them, and information is power."

I nodded. The Ronan I first met was so different from the one standing before me. Both were sexy as hell, but the new one was so much more complex. More self-assured and aggressive. I was right. The cloak of vampirism suited him.

"Well, his secret is he enjoys being tied to a bed post and being *misused* by a woman dressed in leather. It appears he liked my outfit tonight." I wore brown leather pants and a cream-colored silk blouse. My brown leather bra showed at the open vee of the blouse and through the thin material.

I caught Ronan's look. He liked what he saw too. Hope swelled in my heart.

<<<>>>

Looking out the window, I watched the passing houses. Most had lights on. What was their life like? Did they know how lovely the night was? Leaning my head on the headrest, I looked into the dark sky through the open sunroof. Stars shone brightly with the fresh scent of a clear summer evening. The Fourth of July was around the corner. Kids would be shooting fireworks, and adults would be making love under the stars during the warm summer nights.

I looked over at Ronan. Had he ever made love under the stars? He was so serious and solemn nowadays I couldn't help but wonder if he'd forgotten how to have fun.

Had the horror of becoming a vampire made his heart become stone? No one knew what other horrors waited around the corner. There was no telling what Brannon really planned and the not knowing worried me.

The car's interior was closing in on me. Needing more air, I lowered the passenger's window and inhaled the fresh evening air.

"Moving stuff in a brain is painful?" His voice was low and thoughtful. "Isn't that what happened to Byron?"

I looked at Ronan from the corner of my eyes. "Who told you about that?" I held out a palm. "No. You don't have to tell me. You and Connor are becoming thick as thieves. He's going to have to remember who it is that he owes his allegiance to."

"He's loyal to you, just a little afraid of your powers."

For some reason, that hurt. Connor hadn't acted leery whenever he shared his blood with me.

The rest of the drive was quiet. We were enjoying the hum of the tires on the road and the crisp air filling the Corvette.

Before we turned off the highway to Gino's mansion, Ronan asked, "Do you want me to drop you off at home?"

"Trying to protect me from Gino's anger, huh?" No matter what was between us, Ronan still was the good guy.

"No need for you to get in the middle of it." He wouldn't look my way, but kept his eyes on the road.

"Take me with you. My Porsche's there anyway."

"Connor can pick it up."

"No." My tone warned him not to press.

He parked beside Gino's six-car garage and we walked in through the unlocked side door into the office.

"I hope you two can give an explanation to what in the hell happened tonight." Gino sat behind his desk with his hands tented in front of his mouth.

"It was my fault." Ronan didn't give me a chance to say anything different.

"Okay. Then explain and make it good." Gino's anger-roughened voice made the hairs on the back of my neck stand up.

"Tori and I had a little trouble a few months ago and one of the lawyers at the meeting was involved in it. This evening, I decided to ask him a few questions. He was very uncooperative at first."

Then he told his cousin a sanitized version of Brannon kidnapping us. Ronan made it sound like Brannon's vendetta against me was the only reason for the whole episode.

Gino nodded his head. What was it about Gino's reaction that said he already knew about it?

Before I could get a chance to warn Ronan, Gino turned to me.

"Lacy wants to go clubbing. She's waiting for you upstairs."

I wanted to argue, but Ronan shook his head. All right. He could have his way for now, but I wanted answers later.

# Chapter 21

## *Tori*

The woman didn't need a bodyguard, she needed a keeper. After clubbing for two nights, I had hoped for a break, instead she decided to go shopping before hitting another club later. Thankfully, at my vampire age, dusk was tolerable with sunglasses, gloves, hat, long sleeves, and pants.

Hell, Ronan owed me big time. No matter he hadn't wanted me to take the job. I needed to stay close by until he got his bearings. Being a fledgling was very traumatic the first year. New powers developing, bloodlust gaining control, testosterone overload.... Who was I kidding? I wanted to be near him and keep him safe from the likes of Brannon.

A blouse slapped my chest. Lacy Michaels Renata had thrown another piece of clothing.

"Here. Hold this until I make up my mind," she commanded.

If I wasn't the type of person to do what I set out to do, I would've told the woman standing in front of me to take a hike days ago. Or broken her neck and stuffed her into a street drain. I was never one of those women who liked to go shopping for shopping sake. Only once a year could my family talk me into shopping for more than an hour in more than one store. The last time I had given in, it had ended horribly.

Anyway, since the invention of the worldwide web and online shopping, I had more of a choice of clothing. Modern age was a wondrous thing.

Byron had done my shopping. That was why I had so much leather. He'd loved leather. He had always said it was natural for an immortal predator like myself to wear animal skin. Besides, the material breathed and lasted forever. I liked the idea of forever, but Byron had made me update my wardrobe every year.

My throat ached as I fought back the tears. The last thing I needed was to break down in front of Lacy. Hard to believe Byron was gone. It hurt too much to think about him. Shaken out of my dreary thoughts by a scream, I looked up, ready to protect my charge, and saw Lacy had found something else to try on.

"Yes. Isn't this yummy?" Lacy held up a black see-through nightie with red feathers sewn on the plunging neckline. Certainly not for cold nights.

When I caught Lacy's intent to throw it at me, I warned, "If you throw another piece of clothing"—I eyed it with distaste—"I'll haul your butt out of here so fast, your head will spin."

"You're no fun." She stamped her foot and pouted as she hung the nightie back on the rack. "When Gino said I was getting female bodyguards, I thought it would be so neat. We could be like girlfriends and such. Shopping together, hanging around, and telling each other secrets."

I had already heard from the day shift guard all about

Lacy's thoughts on what a bodyguard meant. Jennifer wasn't pleased any more than I was by Lacy's misconception. She had tried to get Jennifer to wear one of her new bathing suits without success. Jennifer was six-two and two hundred pounds and the thong bathing suit would have been like wearing dental floss.

Before I could explain to Lacy for the tenth time that being her bodyguard didn't mean I was her playmate, I spotted Gino weaving through the racks of clothes to slip behind Lacy and kiss her neck.

"Oh, Gino, you scared me. I thought some stranger was attacking and my bodyguard wasn't doing anything about it."

"Did you really believe Tori would let some strange man kiss you without breaking his arm?" The look Gino gave me made my skin crawl. "Come on. Put all that stuff down. I've got a surprise for you."

We started walking toward the front of the store. Ronan stood next to the doors, arms crossed, and looking terribly irritated.

"What's this all about?" I whispered as I walked past.

Before he could answer, Gino shouted, "Time's wasting. Everybody, get in."

Once we were seated, the stretch limo sped down the interstate heading to the south side of Birmingham. I didn't have to guess any longer. Gino was ready to check out the wildlife of Bloodsucker's.

Crowded and jumping, the club overflowed into the streets. Every type of Goth, grunge, and pothead lined up to get inside. Weeknights were unpredictable, but with it being Saturday and a concert of hard rock bands playing at the downtown arena, it would be chaotic.

I normally avoided Bloodsucker's on Saturdays,

along with Halloween, for those reasons. Plus, I was more likely to run into more of my kind during those nights.

Bloodsucker's was known to be neutral ground for the creatures that go bump in the night, but things could still get out of hand.

"What kind of place is this, Gino?" Lacy held onto her husband's arm as we exited the limo and walked toward the club's door.

I wondered what she expected to happen. A spiked-hair, twenty-two-year-old Goth to jump out at her?

Gino laughed. "Don't be such a pussy. This place looks like it knows how to party." He thrust out his hips for emphasis.

I glanced at Ronan. His attention never wavered from the crowd standing in front of the club. Following his example, I looked around, trying to see anything that might spell trouble. Like Brannon.

In no time, the crowd swallowed us. I worked hard to block any stray thoughts from the accidental touch of skin against skin with strangers. Unexpectedly, someone shoved me in the back and I fell against Ronan. He caught me around the waist. His heated look almost had me melting in his arms.

"Are you okay?" Shutters dropped over his eyes. Had our unexpected touch affected him so much?

"You caught me," I teased, remaining in his arms.

His confused look quickly changed to a narrowed one of concern. Without delay, I was placed back on my feet and released.

"Vampire," Ronan whispered.

"Where?" I mouthed.

He nodded to the front door. A young man spoke

intensely to a girl in a barely-there skirt and bare midriff top.

"That's one of Wolfric's soldiers." I shook my head, watching the young couple laugh and flirt. "The solider might as well give it up. He's not getting anywhere with her."

"Why do you say that?"

"She's a pixie. They're known to be big cock teasers."

"Pixie? Like a fairy?"

"A pixie is totally different from a fairy. Pixies are mischievous and all-round troublemakers. There'll probably be a fight tonight."

"So you're saying there are such things like pixies, fairies? Of course, there is." He muttered the last.

"Well, it's like this. If there is a story or myth about it, then it's likely true or partially true." On seeing disbelief flash across his face, I added, "How can you not believe? You're a vampire. When you didn't believe in vampires, did it make it less true? Think of what they tell people in the story of Peter Pan. Never-never land is out there somewhere, but adults can't see it because they don't believe. We believe only what we see, and what we're told is true."

"So there are Santa Claus, Easter Bunny, and Cupid."

"No. Santa Claus and Easter Bunny don't exist."

"You said that if there is a story or myth, that it's likely to be true."

"Santa Claus and Easter Bunny are new stories made for commercial reasons. You can probably refer to someone living in Germany during the fifteen-hundreds who gave gifts to children, but they didn't fly and they're dead. Some traditions can be traced back on the Easter Bunny, but the same holds true."

Ronan pursed his lips and nodded. Then he cut his gaze

at me.

"You didn't say the same about Cupid. Don't tell me a little fellow in a diaper goes around shooting people in the butt with an arrow, making them fall in love."

"Not exactly. He's tall, good-looking, self-centered, and delights in making people with opposite personalities fall in love, simply for meanness. He doesn't use an arrow, but some kind of dust. The bastard knows better than to come around me with his crap."

That brought a smile to Ronan's face.

Seeing his smile, I realized we needed to come back to where it all started. I only hoped Brannon wouldn't show up and spoil the lighthearted mood Ronan was in with our talk of mythical creatures. Thank goodness he hadn't asked about werewolves and demons.

"Hey, Tori, what's holding up you and Ronan? Get your butt over here and tell them to let us in." Gino's face was a little flushed.

It appeared the bouncer wasn't impressed with Gino and who he claimed to be, so he wasn't letting him into the crowded club. He must be new. I didn't recognize him.

Sad that our little private moment of fun was over, nevertheless I strolled over to the bouncer, lightly placed my hand on his arm and whispered in his ear. He promptly told them to go right in. To most of the onlookers, they would see me acting flirtatious with my touching and whispering, and never imagine I was blackmailing him. Like I said before, people's worst past acts were at the top of their memory bank.

Inside, it was standing room only and the dance floor, covered with weaving, bobbing people, gave the impression of a live floor of withering bodies. This was why I preferred the weeknights.

Like a good bodyguard, I followed Lacy. She was swinging her hips with the heavy metal music. It was so loud it felt as if my heartbeat matched the pounding bass. I usually enjoyed it, but tending to the Renatas would put a damper on everything.

I spotted Wolfric and Shani at a table near the corner I favored. A couple of tables away two pixies leaned over the back of a booth, flirting with three burly football players wearing college jerseys.

I detested pixies. Freaking troublemakers.

A shrill scream pierced the music. One of the football players had pulled a pixie onto his lap. Yep, there would be a fight tonight.

Without thinking what I was doing, I clutched Ronan's arm. He tensed and it wasn't from my touch. He'd seen Wolfric.

Concerned and determined to stop anything before it started—pixies starting a fight was bad enough—I raised an eyebrow at him.

"Behave. If you fight with Wolfric, your cousin will be introduced to a world you probably don't want to explain. I have a feeling he'd exploit it for all it's worth."

"Give me more credit than that." His eyes narrowed. "But don't expect me to sit back and watch him treat you like a servant."

Where did that come from?

"What?"

"Nothing." Ronan wouldn't look at me again, but kept his eyes on Wolfric.

Worried about the two strong-willed vampires meeting each other again, it was best they staked out their areas on the opposite sides of the club.

There was one problem with that too, windows lined

that side of the club. Everyone knew windows reflected like mirrors at night. The solution was a table near the dance floor and it worked. I could keep an eye on Wolfric, the pixies, and stay out of the windows' reflection. Geez, why hadn't I just stayed at home?

The band began playing a slow, soft love song.

Breaking into my thoughts, Lacy cooed, "Oooh, Ronan, dance with me for old times' sake."

Lacy leaned forward, letting the two men see her well-paid-for breasts and the red bra lifting them so high.

Ugh, I hated being so petty and a little envious of big-breasted women.

I glanced at Gino, worried about his reaction to Lacy's obvious ploy to make him jealous. Instead of telling her to behave, Gino grinned and looked at me.

"How about a swing on the floor?" he asked.

Before I could say *kiss my butt*, Ronan took Lacy's hand and glided her onto the dance floor.

With my mind fuming at the thought of Ronan touching Lacy, Gino had my hand, leading me to the crowd's center. My gaze remained on the couple. Their bodies barely touched, but his hand was low on her waist, almost on the swell of her butt.

Ronan shifted Lacy closer until I doubted a greased butter knife could slip between their bodies. I bet the swaying of her hips gave a pleasurable friction in Ronan's groin area, the bitch.

The room appeared red and it wasn't from the lighting. My restraint barely kept my fangs from dropping. Between Lacy's actions and Gino's hands cupping my butt, I wanted to kill. Instead I grabbed Gino's wrists and then twisted his thumbs.

Gino's simple "ouch" wasn't quite as satisfying as what I

wanted, but if I released my anger I would break his thumbs and possibly pull them off.

"Keep your hands to yourself," I said between gritted teeth and then returned to the table. Furious with letting everyone see my anger, I glared at Ronan. Did he still have feelings for his ex-wife? Lacy had left Ronan, not the other way. So there was a chance Lacy might change her mind again.

"You're pitiful." Gino smiled like he was about to impart good news.

"What?" Confused by his comment, I stood waiting for his explanation.

"Do you have any idea how many women have panted over him through the years? There was more to Lacy leaving him than he probably told you. She told me he had a fling with a female cop and that was why she divorced him. She's a vindictive bitch." His smirk said he thought it was a good thing. "She took him for everything he was worth. That was why he didn't have enough money to pay for his dad's insurance."

I didn't have to touch him to know he was lying. But which part? The female cop? Yeah. Anyway, Gino was the worst liar I'd ever seen. Obviously, if it wasn't for his uncle, he wouldn't be in the high position he was in the organization. Then again, maybe that was why he'd been promoted, if Gino lied, his uncle would know immediately. No need to guess. But that didn't explain why Gino was saying those things. Unless it was plain old simple rivalry.

"Why does it matter to you?"

"I just hate seeing a beautiful woman go to waste over someone like him."

"You do, huh? Then what do you suggest?" The leer he

gave me made my skin crawl. There was something about Gino that sickened me.

"I know how to appreciate a woman like you."

He slid his hand up the sleeve on my right arm. His forehead wrinkled in confusion. I knew he could feel the strange smooth and rough scars on my arm.

Before he asked the question, I said in his ear, "You could always try, but you would be singing soprano the rest of your life."

A squeak escaped his lips when I grabbed his balls and held tight, but not enough to hurt. Too much.

I licked his neck. Bad habit. I froze. It was what I did before biting. The craving had lengthened my canines. Time for me to leave before I screwed up. When I felt his penis harden and lengthen next to my hand, I knew it was time to explain the danger he was in.

"I've made eunuchs out of bigger men than you. If you ever harm Ronan and try something like that with me again, I promise you'll regret the day you set your eyes on me."

Instead of the expected whimper, Gino groaned. The creep was enjoying my mistreatment.

"Asshole," I said with a hiss.

I released him and stepped back. His look said he'd been seconds from coming in my hand if I hadn't stopped. It made my stomach roil. If I could throw up, I would.

Before I could slap the lust-filled look off his face, a crash and shout drew our attention.

Two of the football players charged each other, knocking glasses and beer cans over. Some of their buddies grabbed their arms and held them back, while another jersey shirt buddy tried to talk sense into them.

The two pixies stood to the side giggling, eyes wide, and fascinated by the violence radiating from the two men. Just as it appeared nothing more would happen, one of the pixies shouted something and fists started swinging. All hell broke loose and chairs and bottles began flying through the air.

I looked for Ronan, but he was already escorting Lacy out the front door. Turning to tell Gino to get out, I didn't see him anywhere nearby. Then I noticed him ducking into the back of the limo. Then it drove off as I reached the doors.

"Well, doesn't that beat all," I muttered in disgust.

What had I expected?

Checking the sky, I needed to call for a cab, or I wouldn't make it home before dawn. I wasn't covered up well enough to combat sunshine. Or I could ask Wolfric for a ride, if he hadn't left yet.

"Want a ride?"

I looked to the side. Ronan sat in a cab with the back door open. A part of me wanted to tell him to go to hell, but I wanted to ask for Wolfric's help less.

"Sure. Why not?" I waited for him to move over and then crawled in, slamming the door behind me.

"That's what I like, a woman filled with gratitude," he said, his eyes twinkling with amusement.

"You don't need my gratitude. Besides you owed me." I looked away.

"How do I owe you?"

"Leaving me with Gino the creep."

"What did my cousin do?" he asked, his voice becoming soft and a little menacing.

I still didn't want to look at him, reluctant to let him see the concern and fury on my face. Concerned that Gino was up to no good and fury at Ronan for allowing that woman to rub on him.

"Did you know that Gino enjoyed pain?"

"Yeah."

"Why didn't you warn me?"

"I never guessed you would be interested in him. Otherwise, I would have. But then again, you could take a lot more punishment than most women. I've heard from plenty of his old girlfriends he liked to receive and give pain to get his rocks off."

"You know, you can be real asshole." My exasperation was clear from my words and tone when I turned toward him.

He winked and grinned. "Yeah, but you still want what only I can give you."

"Yeah, right. In your dreams." The cab had stopped. Shaking my head, I squinted at the front of Ronan's condo. "Hey, I need to go to another address."

Before I could tell the driver my address, Ronan covered my mouth.

"You're going with me." He grabbed my arm, and I stumbled from the cab as he pushed me out before him.

I wanted to fight...but did I really? I liked how he was flirting and teasing. He acted happy. What did he have to be happy about? Was it something to do with Lacy? He needed a challenge. A woman who could meet him toe-to-toe and handle the ups and downs of his new life. Lacy wasn't the one.

Damn. I was such a sap. I loved him, and there was nothing he could do to change it. At least, I didn't think there was. So far he hadn't.

"You didn't argue with me," he stated by the time we were standing in the middle of his foyer.

Looking into those sexy, soulful eyes, I wanted to stay and see if we could get our relationship back on track.

"What was there to argue over? You know what I like." I moved forward until we touched from chest to groin. "I've never kept anything from you." On seeing his eyebrow lift, I added, "Since I reincarnated you, that is."

"What were you and Gino discussing while you were caressing his balls?" His hands quickly grabbed my arms before I could move away.

Throwing water in my face wouldn't have cooled me down faster.

"What?"

"You were standing against him like we are now and your hand was between his legs. He appeared to be enjoying it very much. For that matter, you did too. You weren't being very careful in hiding your canines. If he didn't see them, it was more because he was blinded by lust. Isn't that your specialty?"

I saw the glow of anger in those beautiful eyes now. He'd hidden it rather well.

"You tricked me."

"Come in."

"No."

He grabbed the nape of my neck and pulled my face close to his.

"I hate how everything you do and say *controls how I feel*." He bit off the last few words. He must have seen the confusion on my face. "Though I try to keep you at a distance, work hard at keeping you off of my mind, you creep into my thoughts at the most inconvenient times." Releasing my neck, he grabbed my hair and used his body to press mine to the foyer wall. Heavy lids half covered the glowing green eyes I was so fascinated with. "I want you out of my system. When I see you touch another man, I contemplate murder. I want to make you mine only and keep you in my bed and fuck you until I get every ounce of what I feel for you drained from my body. Do you know how much I hate feeling this way? How much I hate wanting you until I wake up screaming your name and needing your mouth on me?"

His mouth attacked mine. Tongues danced and canines clicked in a need so strong I relished it. My clothes disappeared, and he lifted my legs to his waist. My ankles crossed behind his back, holding him tight to me as he thrust into my heated pussy with so much force I was certain my back would go through the sheetrock. His speech of wants had gotten me so turned on, I was about to beg him to take me if he hadn't kissed and stripped me.

My fingers burrowed beneath material and dug into his back. With no hesitation, I popped buttons and jerked open his shirt. I wanted his skin against mine. When my nipples touched his hot chest, I screamed. The climax was too intense. Cool air hit my shoulders. He moved us through the living room into his bedroom, my legs still wrapped around his waist and his cock inside of me.

He pulled me off him and dropped me on the large bed, flipping me on my stomach. Before I could turn over, he covered me with his body and knifed into my wetness like a man starved for what only I provide. From our new position, his erection felt larger and harder.

Then I felt his mouth at my neck a second before he clamped down. I froze. His teeth sank into my flesh, and the sound of him sucking matched the rhythm of his thrusts. The smacking of skin to skin echoed in the room. I stretched out my arms to grasp the headboard and hold on as he used his vampire strength to pound into me.

I screamed in pleasure again.

# Chapter 22

## *Tori*

"Why is it so important to you to find Brannon?" I entered the bedroom and closed the door. With my purse clasped to my abdomen, I feasted on the sight before me, barely containing a need to touch him.

"Damn it, Tori. Don't locked doors mean anything to you?"

Standing next to the bed, nothing on but his boxer briefs, and unzipped black jeans at his knees, Ronan glared at me as he pulled them up.

I'd been gone for two days since that night we made love. That morning, I had left him sleeping a couple of hours before daybreak, even left a note for him, which was totally unlike me. I had wanted to stay longer but had to check on Connor, but then a couple of problems turned up preventing me from returning immediately. As soon as the sun sunk in the sky on the second evening, I'd raced back.

Undisturbed by his unfriendly welcome, I took in the luscious sight he made. Muscles flexed across his stomach and chest. I could barely remember my name, not counting the questions I'd just asked him.

He scooped a shirt off a nearby chair and jerked it on. Though he had efficiently covered up his chest and zipped his pants, I unabashedly watched as his long masculine fingers buttoned his shirt and then my gaze dropped to his groin. What could I say? My curiosity knew no bounds for I wanted to see if my attention had any effect on him.

When he dropped his hands and double-checked his fly, I laughed.

"Do I bother you that much?"

"What do you want?"

With the warning look he shot me, I felt it prudent not to say what went through my mind. Instead I pointed out, "You never answered my question. What's Brannon to you?"

"Chalk it up to a cop's insistence in bringing a bastard to justice. I'm not much on forgetting when someone has beaten the shit out of me."

"So you hold grudges." It was more of a statement than a question.

Ronan had shown himself to be a man of strong emotions before his reincarnation. The lengths he went through for his father proved that. As a vampire, his emotions were magnified and probably terrifying to him at times. How frustrating would it be for a man who had worked so hard to control those emotions?

"So you want it to be you and no one else?"

"Me to be the one to do away with him?" I checked.

He nodded.

"Of course, I want to kill the bastard. It's because of me he did this to you and got you involved in the first place. His self-centered revenge caused me to make you a vampire.

Not that I'm blaming him for all of it, but he certainly doesn't deserve to live."

I blocked the guilt and pain of taking away a normal life from Ronan. Being a vampire had its perks, but I'd asked for it. He hadn't. When would I ever get over it? That was one of the down sides of being a vampire, I had an eternity to regret my decision.

Not necessarily regret. Looking at the stunning man watching me, I could never regret keeping such a man out of the ground.

"Is this the real reason you're working for Gino?" Ronan stalked across the room and stopped a foot away. He unexpectedly brushed a bit of my hair behind an ear. "Are you worried about me? You want to protect me from big, bad Brannon?" he teased in a deep sultry voice.

My lungs began to hurt. I'd been holding my breath without realizing it. I almost leaned my head into his touch. Every nerve ending in my body screamed for his caress.

I wanted to cry from the pain of wanting him every minute of every day—night in our circumstances—but I couldn't afford the distraction. I wanted his answer to my question. If I hadn't known better, I would suspect him of placing a lust spell on me. Never had I craved a man as much as I had him.

Resting my hand on his waist, I leaned toward him. His chin showed a beard ready for a second shave for the night. He looked dangerous, and the new Ronan was all that and more.

Lifting my hand to his face, I lightly brushed his cheek with the back of my fingers. Then I traced his masculine pouting lips with a finger. His mouth parted, and he inhaled sharply. Surely, he felt the same pull I did.

"Don't push me, Tori," he said in a husky whisper.

"If I were pushing you, Ronan, you would be flat on your back by now, and I would be enjoying this." My hand cupped his cock. Satisfaction bloomed from my chest in knowing he was not unaffected by my presence. I rubbed the hard evidence.

He thrust his hips into my palm and closed his eyes, pleasure darkening his features. Before I could react, he pressed me against the wall, his mouth covering, devouring mine.

"Why don't other women smell as good as you do?"

His words both thrilled and worried me.

"Other women?"

He was an artist with his lips and tongue, and what little breath remained in my lungs was used to ask that question. Faces of different women flashed through my mind. The images weren't from reading his mind, instead from my imagination fed by my insecurities. How could I convince this man that I loved him and knew how to make him happy? Why wouldn't I say it? Because I was scared and afraid to admit it. What if he couldn't love me in return? There was a difference between wanting a person because of love or because they turned you on. I wanted it all.

Ronan stopped, resting his forehead against mine. I watched his mouth tighten in concentration, and fought the urge to suck on his lower lip.

"If you're here in a misguided need to protect your fledgling, leave. I don't want you here." He closed his eyes, straightened, then stepped away. After taking a couple of deep breaths, he opened them. They shone the unearthly glow that betrayed every vampire's feelings.

I wasn't sure if his eyes revealed anger or lust. There was no doubt it wasn't love.

"You can't get rid of me so easily." For the first time in a very long time, I felt uncertain of how to get what I wanted. I desired this man with all my heart. Not for just a little while or a tumble in the sheets, it was a need to feel whole as I only could with him.

First, we needed to meet on common ground that had nothing to do with the physical.

"We both want the same goal. We want Brannon dead."

He shot me a glare.

"That's how you see it. I see it differently," he said.

"And how's that?" I asked when he didn't say more. Remembering what he'd said moments earlier, I held up my hand. "Absolutely not. The police can't have him. He's mine."

"You're not God, Tori."

Those words echoed my sentiment of not too long ago, but I couldn't stop myself from saying, "I am well aware of that, but he's like his brother. Haven't you been listening to the news? The disfigured bodies. That's Brannon. He's carrying on his brother's tradition of carving up women."

I couldn't believe what happened next. Tears welled up in my eyes. Horrified, I turned my back to Ronan, and tried to wipe the tears from my face without being too obvious.

"Tori?"

The heat from his body blasting my back alerted me to his closeness before his hands clasped my shoulders. The urge to lean against his chest was tempting, but I wasn't the type of woman to use my body or tears as a weapon. Regaining control, I pulled away and faced Ronan.

"Listen. I thought we might work together on finding Brannon, but considering you want to hand him over to the police and I...let's say, the government could save a lot of money with my method."

My heart felt like it was about to break in two. Was

there nothing we could agree on? We'd been so connected when he was human. Had my personality changed, even basically, when I was reincarnated? No. It had magnified. Why had he changed? A niggling in the back of my brain said his turnabout wasn't normal, even for a vampire. I needed time to think about it.

Looking into his eyes, the flare of fire there revealed he felt something for me. I only wished it was love and not disdain.

"I'll let myself out," I said, suddenly tired. I walked away and reached for the front entrance's doorknob, but the door wouldn't open. I looked up. A masculine hand held the door closed. "What the—"

Before I could react, he twirled me to face him. I dropped my purse as he shoved my shoulder blades against the wood, covering my mouth with his. Before I could wrap my arms around his waist, he grabbed my wrists and held them in one hand above my head.

"I can't let you leave." In a voice heavy with need, he asked, "Have you cast a spell over me?"

No answer was expected. Less than a second later, he tore my blouse off and then my bra. His mouth dipped, and he licked and sucked a trail of fire from one budded nipple to the other. Each time his lips closed over the taut flesh, sucking and pulling, I released a loud moan his neighbors would certainly hear.

With a frantic jerk, he unsnapped my jeans and pushed them to my ankles. Then tossed my torn panties on top of the other destroyed clothing. He cupped me between my legs. Heat and rolling hunger almost made my knees buckle. I never had a lover want me so badly that he tore most of my clothes off. I was ready for him when he thrust two fingers in my pussy. My hips rocked with each movement of his hand. I wanted more.

Unable to fight my natural reaction to his lovemaking, my canines dropped, craving a place to sink into his flesh.

The material of his pants scraped along the tender skin of my inner thigh. I felt his hand move to his pants, then heard a snap and the rasp of his zipper.

Starving for what only his body could provide, I didn't protest when he grabbed my knee, lifted my thigh to his waist, my jeans staying on the floor, and pressed the tip of his cock into my heated center. He plunged in and groaned.

Unable to hold back any longer, I wiggled my wrists free from his hold and grasped his head. Dark, silky hair slipped between my fingers, seduced and beckoned my hands to remain and play. I tugged until his head angled to the side, giving me plenty of room to sink my fangs into his neck.

He roared.

<<<>>>

Ronan

Pleasure was tearing me fucking apart. Would my heart explode soon? Never in my life had I felt such a satisfying sensation from her canines sinking into my flesh. Unlike the first time. I barely remembered the piercing pain from then.

I wanted her to scream for me. I continued to jackhammer into her, knowing I didn't have to worry I'd harm her. With each thrust, the door rattled and shook. The quest for satisfaction made me forget our surroundings.

Time for her to scream my name. Reaching between our bodies, I rubbed her hard little clit. When she lifted her mouth from my neck, I looked into her face. Glowing with lust and glazed from the intensity, her eyes reflected the mixture of emotions I felt.

Her face tilted to the ceiling and a stream of blood slipped out of the corners of her mouth and down her neck. Without thinking, I leaned toward her and slowly licked her neck and chin clean, savoring the taste of my own blood and the feel of her soft skin beneath my tongue.

The sweet blood brought the uncontrollable urge to feed. Savagely, I slammed into her once more as I sank my teeth into the curve of her neck.

"Ronan," she screamed.

Holding back any longer was out of the question, I had met my match. Tremors ripped from my groin and throughout my body. Her scream and answering waves of satisfaction brought a smile to my face.

Drained, weak but sated, I withdrew my canines. Disturbed by the deep wounds I left, I tenderly laved them until they stopped bleeding. It would probably take her a few hours before the punctures and bruising disappeared.

I released her leg. After tucking my cock into my jeans and straightening my clothes, I stepped back. Every time I was around this woman, I fought my baser desires for control. I hated losing control. If I wasn't careful, I would follow her around like a little, lost dog, wanting another fuck. Much like the way I had when I was human.

She touched my cheek and I jerked my head away.

"Your goodbyes are certainly worth experiencing," she said. Her humor sounded brittle.

I looked at her. She battled with her clothes, buttons missing, sleeve torn nearly off her blouse, and her jeans gapped open near the zipper. Torn, wrinkled clothes revealed only a little of the story, her neck and swollen lips told the rest. Had I hurt her? Was she hating me now?

The half-grin on her face said all was…okay at least.

I reached for the edge of my T-shirt and yanked it off, handing it to her.

She took it and brought the material to her nose.

On seeing my frustrated look, she shook her head. "It smells of you. So delicious."

Fuck, my cock was hardening with her words. I couldn't have that.

"Tori, I think it'd be best if you left now," I said, trying my best to ignore her teasing.

Either I was going crazy or something was bad wrong with me. Only while touching Tori could I forget the horror of becoming a vampire. Where my heart should be, a knot of hate and despair remained in my chest, but that knot had eased and disappeared during our fucking. Nothing about it could be called lovemaking. Love had nothing to do with it.

I had fucked her to punish myself and maybe her too. I hated the pull she had over me and my response to her.

I'd tried so hard to understand her decision to reincarnate me as I wasn't sure death would be the bad choice. The last few months, I tried to forget about her, the feel of her soft skin and the husky sound of her voice that made my body hers.

Was it lust for a female vampire or the woman beneath the horror? There was no way for me to find out. She was the only female vampire I knew, and anyway, I needed to concentrate on finding Brannon.

I stared at the floor, hands on hips, in deep thought for a few moments. I looked up and saw her hurt look. Tori had pulled on the shirt, but still stood in from of me.

It was best. Time to move on and get her out of my system. Placing Brannon in prison would help separate her from my life.

Life? What a joke.

"Shouldn't we talk about this? About us?"

Tired of fighting emotions strengthened by my vampire awareness, I braced for an argument. "I guess this is where I say, there's no us."

Her gaze searched my face for a moment. "Okay. Then let's talk about Brannon. Connor's working on a lead and there's a good chance we'll find out soon where Brannon's hiding." She'd obviously concluded I wasn't going to budge on the subject of *us*.

Why was I surprised by her acceptance of my statement? Had I imagined her hurt look earlier? Yet, how could I forget her single-mindedness in killing Brannon and his kind?

"Fine. Tell Connor to call me immediately with the information."

"Knowing how my servant has been showing his *loyalty* to me, he'll probably tell you before he tells me." With that said, she lifted her purse off the floor where she'd dropped it earlier. Once again, she reached for the knob.

That niggling in the back of my brain was back again and telling me not to let her go. To keep her close and protect her.

For fuck's sake, she was a vampire. I had to remember that. Brannon had several tricks up his sleeves, but I doubted the madman would actually kill her. Unless she trapped him in a corner.

"Tori," I said, stopping her from leaving. "Don't try to take him on your own. Promise me that you'll call me. You need back up with this one," I warned.

Her dark eyes betrayed nothing. No flare. No revealing lights. She stood staring at me for several seconds.

"I can't promise that. No matter how much I wish I could. I can't," she admitted.

Then she was out the front door.

# Chapter 23

## *Tori*

I was sick and tired of the emotional roller coaster I constantly rode with Ronan. There had to be an explanation for his cold and hot attitude.

Shifting down to third, I read the green street signs passing on my right. The hills in this section of Birmingham had brought to mind that proverbial roller coaster, up and down with all the unexpected twists and turns in the dark.

On leaving Ronan's, I called someone who I felt would help me solve his mysterious change from an attentive lover to tense opponent.

Shani.

Knowing how rigid Wolfric was with security, and all his trust issues, if he could trust the witch, I could too.

After leaving Ronan, I'd remembered something he said that could be true.

*"Have you cast a lust spell over me?"*

Strange how I hadn't thought of that earlier. I could easily believe the same of him.

Maybe I was being overly cautious, but it wouldn't hurt to check it out.

The house wasn't what I expected a witch to live in. Instead of dark, creepy Victorian, the home was a well-lit Spanish-style with traditional stucco walls and terra cotta roof. It sat low in a large wooden lot. A beautiful lion's head door knocker decorated one side of the double oak door.

I lifted the ring running through the lion's nose and let it fall a couple of times. Only a few seconds passed before the door swung open. A young man with thick, wavy blond hair stood in the doorway.

"Well, hello." His cocky tone showed his youth more than the mature way he examined me.

"Shani's expecting me." Amused by his typical male reaction brought a bright spot to my dreary evening. I grinned.

He stood up straighter and opened the door wider.

"Come in. She gets involved with some of her work and forgets the time, and she has a habit of not telling me when she's expecting a beautiful visitor."

Surely this wasn't Shani's boyfriend. He looked to be several years younger—who was I to talk, considering mine and Ronan's age—and his green eyes looked a lot like Shani's emerald ones. A brother?

I stepped into the foyer that turned out to be a raised area overlooking the living room and office. Shani's back was to the door as she leaned over a large book open on the desk.

The young man shook his head, tossing his blond locks into his eyes.

"Don't tell me your boyfriend's cheating on you and you want Shani to turn him into a toad?" Before I answered, he added, "Or you want a potion to make some stranger fall in love with you? I can't believe you have any trouble finding men."

His sexy little grin said he was accustomed to getting his way with women, and he used anything at his disposal to make certain of it.

"Quit harassing my guest." Shani stood and walked across the room with her hand held out. "Tori, this aggravating brat is my brother, Alex."

I shook her hand, laughing. "A very charming brother."

"Oh, no. Please don't encourage him. His head is large enough. Most of the girls in his high school call or text him all the time. I hear his phone ringing or chiming nonstop."

"I can see why," I couldn't help saying. In a few more years, with a little weight and muscle, he would be a knockout. Some woman would have her hands full.

"Alex, ignore Tori. She's a flirt, and only teasing you." Shani waved me toward the sofa in the living room. "If I remember correctly, you have a show to prepare for tomorrow night," she said to her brother.

"Hey, Tori. Do you like magic? Why don't you come to my show? It's at the Stardome over in Hoover and I'll save you a seat near the stage."

"You do magic, huh?" I liked his innocent look of enthusiasm about his magic act.

"Yeah. I'm not a powerful witch like Shani, but I have some tricks I perform that make me a few bucks."

His attempt to sound blasé was so endearing I had to work at holding back the laughter. He was a doll, but way too young, not counting being a brother to a powerful witch. Besides, there was the little problem of Ronan.

"Maybe some other time. I've got something I need to tend to tomorrow." I hated disappointing him but he appeared to take it well.

"That's okay. I haven't perfected my act yet. Maybe another time."

I nodded and watched him saunter out of the room.

"Alex can be rather trying at times. He means well," his sister said, sitting at her desk with a notepad in her hand.

"I find him to be charming." I turned to the witch. "Were you able to tell anything by the hair samples Connor brought?"

Shani flipped a few pages as if checking notes.

"Actually, at first, I wasn't sure if I read the chemical analysis correctly, but a little while ago I found the matching ingredients in a common spell book. So it appears you're right."

I sighed, thankful my hunched paid off. "Could you tell who did it?"

"No. The spell and the components used are so common in the southeast, I have no idea who it could be. From the different chemical reactions I received from his hair samples, I believe I can prepare a counterspell. It's a potion he'd need to take pretty soon before the spell settles into his DNA and changes him forever." Opening a large book on her desk, the witch scanned several pages and said, "I can't promise that the changes aren't already complete, but it's worth a try."

"Thanks. When can I have the potion?" Tonight wouldn't be soon enough in my way of thinking.

"Come back in an hour and I'll have it ready for you."

I rose from the sofa and headed toward the door when the urge to ask another question came over me. "Do you mind, but I would like to ask you a personal question?"

"Sure. Go ahead," the beautiful witch said.

"I've been told in most of the world, witches and vampires are mortal enemies. How come you and Wolfric get along so well? And you're willing to help me?"

"You don't beat around the bush, do you?"

"Sorry. You don't have to answer."

"I know. But I don't mind telling you. Wolfric was always kind to a lonely, little girl, and for that reason and many others, I wouldn't hurt him, and deep down he knows that. And he wouldn't hurt me or my brother. There have been plenty of times he could've harmed Alex—my brother is most mischievous—instead Wolfric would send Alex back to me unharmed. See, Alex hates Wolfric and all vampires. If he had known you were a vampire, he wouldn't have been so charming tonight."

<<<>>>

Ronan

"What the hell?"

I threw a towel over the smoldering fire on the rug. Twice while I was getting ready, a fire started out of nowhere.

When Connor finally showed up, I had to ask about demons or ghosts that started fires. It was the only explanation I could think of.

On waking up earlier, I'd felt strange. Besides the unusually strong craving for blood, especially Tori's blood, I felt as if my skin was too tight for my body and my eyes ached. They were all symptoms of a cold, but I remembered being told vampires never had colds, the flu, cancer...nothing.

Cancer.

Such a simple little word. Such a simply devastating disease.

After my father was diagnosed with lung cancer, I was certain I was losing my mind. My father, hard-working with little insurance, was never truly sick a day in his life. He hadn't expected to get cancer, not after quitting cigarettes twenty-five years earlier. But he had.

So when the treatments became more expensive and my dad's insurance got slower in paying, I stepped up and helped. My mom had died in an automobile accident when I was twelve, and it was just the two of us against the world.

Being on the police force, money was tight already and paying my dad's medical bills made it worse. My wife, at first, tried to understand why I felt it necessary to help my dad, but after the second house payment was missed, she started looking for someone else to support her.

Looking back, I couldn't blame her. Our marriage had taken a backseat to my job for years. When she'd turned me in to Internal Affairs for receiving a loan from my mobster cousin, Gino, that had been the nail in the coffin for our marriage and my dad. Without money, I couldn't afford the newer and more expensive treatments.

Without a steady income and no way to pay back my cousin, I sold my dad's guns to pay for his body to be cremated. I couldn't afford a regular burial, so I sprinkled his ashes over my mom's grave.

I pulled the curtains back and stared out at the stars. Being a vampire definitely had its advantages. I wouldn't have to worry about cancer or any of the thousands of diseases that existed out there.

What would my dad think of all of this? He always enjoyed a good scary movie but would've thought his only son had lost his mind.

I chuckled then quickly sobered. If my reincarnation had happened before my dad died, would I have changed my dad to keep him in this world?

Hell, yeah.

Was that being selfish?

I had accused Tori of the same thing. Did it clear up Tori's reasoning behind reincarnating me? No, no, no. That was different.

Frustrated with my seesawing feelings toward the female vampire, I dropped the curtain.

Where was she? Had she gone after Brannon alone? It would be just like her to do that.

Another burst of flame caught my attention.

"Fuck. What is going on?" I jerked the curtains down and stomped on them until only ashes and the smell of burnt cotton, polyester, or whatever remained.

The doorbell rang.

Certain it was Connor, I jerked open the door.

"Connor, you son of a bitch, you took long—"

Tori stood in the hallway grinning ear-to-ear with a large bottle of wine clutched in one hand and two tulip glasses in the other.

"I've come to celebrate," she said, lifting them up.

"Celebrate?"

She nudged me to the side and walked into my condo.

"Yeah. Connor's found Brannon's hiding place."

She popped the cork on the bottle, and began pouring the liquor I could smell from across the room. No, not liquor. Blood. Human blood.

"So tell me where he's at," I commanded as the aroma overtook my senses.

Saliva started pooling in my mouth. I swallowed deeply. Drinking her blood the other night was like an alcoholic falling off the wagon. I craved it even more. Maybe the human blood would satisfy the hunger gnawing at me. She turned around and handed me a glass, then raised her glass in salute.

"No. First, we toast with this fine and rich vintage. No.

Don't give me that look. You'll learn there are humans who willingly share their blood to be in our company. They're treated like favorite milk cows. Pampered, fed, and loved, and all their dreams fulfilled for their life-giving blood."

She'd said the last in a way I knew she meant the physical type of love.

"And you believe this is okay?"

I had learned since being turned, the vampire world was harsh and cruel, but I was a realist. The same people who allowed the vampires to milk them are the same ones who followed any charismatic leader into an agonizing death from a poisoned, fruit-flavored drink.

She shrugged her shoulders and took a sip of the liquid. Her lips glistened dark red. I wanted to lick off the delicious delicacy and work my way down her luscious body.

After a shake of my head, I took a sip. At least I'd thought it was only a sip, but before I realized it, the glass was empty and Tori handed me the bottle. I poured another glass full.

The flavor was what I remembered and more. I couldn't stop. Blood drunk and horny as hell, I threw the empty bottle against the wall and grabbed Tori, heading to the bedroom.


<<<>>>

Tori


What could I say? I didn't feel the least bit guilty about waking up in his bed. Thank goodness, I finally solved the mystery about Ronan's personality change. If I had stopped letting my heart do all of the thinking, I would've realized he was under a spell.

The counterspell Shani provided appeared to have

done the trick, and the old Ronan was back. I felt guilty about not telling him beforehand, but how would he react if the potion hadn't worked? Being under a hate spell could have dire results for either party. Thankfully, the antidote didn't affect me. So Ronan and I could share the same dosed blood wine. It rid the spell from him and only caused me to be a little drunk.

I slid my hand over the sheets, craving the feel of his firm body and silky hair. His side of the wide bed was empty. Puzzled, I sat up and looked around. Long legs stretched out in front of him, he lounged in a chair near the bed, staring at me.

Patting the space next to me, I nodded at the bed. "Come, join me." He was shirtless. The view of sexy chest hair caused my heartbeat to pick up. The foot of the bed hid the rest of him from where I reclined against the pillows.

Would I never get enough of him? Goodness, I hoped not.

"What did you put in the blood last night?"

*Oh, oh.* The words were loaded with anger and suspicion.

I was tempted to lie, but I couldn't. This new beginning was too important to our relationship. "It was a few herbs and a little seasoning." I had to ease into the full truth.

"Connor didn't have the information on Brannon." His voice was tight and controlled. "And you want me to believe it was only to flavor my glass of blood?"

Determined that he understood why I misled him, I said, "No. It was part of a counterspell."

"You mean a spell."

"No. Counterspell. You were already under a spell."

"The only brew given to me was the one you and your master had the witch prepare."

"No. I swear. You were under one to hate me."

Chin down, he studied me between the strands of his hair. The room darkened as if someone had dimmed the lights. Was he weighing every word I said, believing I was a liar?

"Hate you? All I can think of is to fuck your brains out." He stood, and I noticed for the first time he was beautifully naked and erect. The man had a magnificent cock.

I sighed.

Drawn by his boldness, I eased out of bed, wanting him to understand, if it was that type of spell, then I was under it too. As I sauntered toward him, his eyes began to glow and a rumbling growl escaped his lips. His predatory grin grew and flashed long canines. My emotions shot skyward as my fangs lengthened in answer.

Naked like him, I continued to walk slowly until I was a mere inch from his erection. Carefully, I reached out and slid my hand along his hard cock, relishing the feel of hot steel beneath velvet.

His breath shook when I grasped him firmly and squeezed in a gratifying rhythm. With my other hand I cupped his balls, then slipped a finger lightly across and up the other side. He groaned and arched toward my caress.

I began to squeeze and slide and pull along the length. Unable to resist, I kneeled and began to lick and suck the darker head.

What a pleasure it was to hear him moan, then gasp as I swirled my tongue around the little hole and gliding my teeth around the glans. He released another long moan, thrusting his hips toward my mouth. Just before he lost control, I stopped.

I stood, waiting for him to open his eyes.

"Do you really think I placed a spell on you, when you...

we both know from the first day we met, we wanted each other."

"I believe you would do anything it takes to get your way."

"What do you mean?"

"Though you killed the man who sliced you, why did you continue to kill?" He didn't wait for an answer. "You decided to punish them, not caring to find out their story."

A cold chill swept across the back of my neck. I returned to the bed, wanting a sheet to cover my nakedness, and stumbled, but caught the bedpost to regain my balance and composure along with pride.

"You don't understand," I said.

"Help me understand." He sounded so harsh. "When are you going to practice what you preach?"

With a yank, I pulled off the flat sheet and wrapped it around my torso. Shoulders back, spine straight, I faced him, glaring with indignation. "Preach! Pray tell, what do I preach?"

"Let's see—the big bullies of the world pick on the weak. But isn't that what you do? Pick on those weaker than you?"

My heart was breaking. I saw what he was doing. He was pushing me away. Had I not broken the spell? Or was it really a spell all along? It was. I was certain. There was something else going on. What was he hiding? What was he up to? Or was it part of my arrogance he was referring to?

"What's going on? Why are you trying to push me away?"

"Maybe I've had enough and am ready to move on. Once again. Without interference from you."

I watched as he pulled on his pants, leaving them unsnapped as he slipped on a shirt.

What did he want me to do? Beg? He knew better. I would never beg any man to stay. No matter how much I loved him.

While he took his time buttoning his shirt, he stared out a window into the dark, ignoring my presence. I gathered my clothes and jerked them on without another word. In less than a minute, I was dressed and headed toward the bedroom door.

"Watch your back," he said softly.

That stopped me.

After such a clash, I hadn't expected him to care. Without turning around, I said, "I always do. Don't let your cousin send you up the river, if you know what I mean." A glance over my shoulder caught his nod though he refused to look at me.

By the time I walked out into the night air, I was numb. There was another downward slope on that damn roller coaster of emotions.

One moment, I was high on the thrill of finding a man who challenged me mentally and physically and the invisible bond we possessed. Then down to the depths of despair when we were separated by our pride and misunderstandings.

"Hey, babe! Need a ride?"

Somehow I had reached the sidewalk. My brain fought with what I wanted and what I knew was best for me, and they weren't the same. I looked over to the Mercedes sedan following slowly beside me. Connor. His huge grin told me he had good news.

"What did you find out?" Instead of making him move over—as I normally did—so I could drive, I opened the front passenger's door and slid in beside him.

"I didn't find Brannon." His frustration was obvious.

Few people could hide so well from Connor's contacts. "But while I was waiting for you to come out of Ronan's loft"—I ignored his accusing stare—"I stopped a visitor from knocking on the door."

"For goodness' sakes, Connor, spit it out."

"It was a hunter."

"Oh, shit! Turn back. We've got to warn, Ronan. Why didn't you tell me sooner? He's not prepared for an attack." Without thinking, I opened the door and started to jump out.

"Wait! He's safe. The hunter was to deliver a message."

I slammed the door and turned back to Connor. "Say what?" There was no way Ronan would betray the vampire colony. Or would he? For the past few months, he'd gone through a lot of changes. So who was I to say what he would or would not do?

"I knocked him out and searched his pockets. Here." He handed over the folded, cream-colored paper.

I spread open the sheet and read the neatly written note.

*Ronan, come to the Legion's laboratory on Highway 31 tonight per our discussion. Usual terms. B*

Why did Brannon want to meet with Ronan? And why were the hunters involved? What had Brannon meant by *our discussion* and *usual terms*?

"You read the note?" I asked.

"Yeah. Brannon's in with the hunters. That would explain why I can't track him down. The sons of bitches are the most closed-mouth assholes on earth. Nothing leaks out of there but what they want you to know." He eased the sedan into the garage and turned off the engine.

We sat in the car, staring out the front windshield at the bare wall in front of us. I was quite aware of what Connor was thinking. We were afraid to voice it. But we needed to bring it out into the open and examine it before it festered.

"You think that Ronan's involved with the hunters."

"Sorry, Tori. But it's too cozy the way he wrote that they would discuss the usual terms." He cleared his throat, then added, "You know if he works with Brannon and the hunters, you might as well stake him yourself. That would be the kindest way to end his life. If Wolfric's men find out, he would die a hundred deaths before Wolfric ended it."

"I know." Dry mouth and nerves tied up in knots, I wasn't feeling up to discussing the ins and outs of vampire punishment. Just the thought of Ronan not existing in my world was too much to contemplate.

"You're not going to Wolfric, are you?"

Connor hoped I wouldn't hand over the problem to my master. Of course not. Brannon had started this, but I would end it.

Never would I expect someone else to clean up what I felt responsible for. It was my mistake in letting Brannon live. I should have killed him before we escaped his house after he'd kidnapped me and Ronan.

"No. I'll take care of it."

Connor opened his mouth to argue, but I shook my head. Without another word, we exited the car.

# Chapter 24

## *Tori*

The front of the building looked like so many of the doctors' offices lining Highway 31 south of Birmingham. A small, tasteful sign read, The Legion Laboratories. How many people passed it every day and had no idea the horrendous cruelties that were performed in the name of science and public safety? In vampire circles, the building was treated like a myth, a story told to fledglings to frighten them.

I stood in front of the three-story, white-washed building, cold shivers racing down my arms.

One tale in particular, repeated in whispers, was no vampire had ever escaped its walls.

I knew what Brannon really wanted and I was willing to give it to him. But first we would bargain.

Inside the brightly lit lobby, the air was extra cool and scented with alcohol and a sick pine scent. My high heels hit the Turkish rug with a dull, thudding rhythm, until I stopped at the Plexiglass-encased front desk. An older woman looked up with a smile that quickly faded.

I smiled big, allowing the sharp points of my canines to

be clearly seen, and certain my eyes probably glowed in anticipated confrontation.

Earlier, I had made sure to dress the part and had pulled on what I liked to call my prowler outfit: black leather pants with a matching sleeveless shirt, all formfitting so as not to get in the way of my fighting. Instead of flat heel boots, I wore my dangerous stiletto boots. A kick from them would pierce most skin.

Under the fluorescent lights, I knew the woman could clearly see the scars running down my right arm. Frightened, she sat still for several seconds staring at me before making a slight movement beneath her desk. The alarms began ringing.

The bitch had pressed the emergency button.

Amused, I remained still and continued to watch her.

Shaking, her face washed of all color, the woman fumbled with a desk drawer and pulled out a large silver cross. She held it out in an attempt to ward me off. Silly woman. Hadn't the hunters told her anything?

By the sound of running feet, I didn't have much longer before Brannon would show up. I reached through the small opening and took the cross out of the woman's hand.

"This is beautiful. I especially like the Celtic knots etched on it." I handed it back. "Family heirloom?"

Terrified, the woman finally decided she needed to leave and darted toward a side door, almost running into the first armed guard entering the lobby. The guard took a shooting stance, gun shaking and sweat beading on his forehead.

"Would you please point that gun elsewhere? You might hurt someone with it." I shook my head. Where did they find these people?

"Put your hands up and turn around!"

Exasperated, I rolled my eyes and looked up at the ceiling for a second.

"I would, but to tell you the truth, I'm worried that you'll shoot me in the back. True, I won't die, but it would hurt like hell, and I don't want you to put a hole in my favorite outfit." After giving a deep sigh, I asked, "Where's Brannon? I'm here to meet with him."

"You're Ronan?" The guard's voice squeaked at the end of his question.

Unable to resist smiling and showing my fangs, I laughed out loud. He looked as if he was about to piss his pants.

From the hallway on the right, I heard more running. This time at least ten armed men dressed in black with helmets and automatics entered the large lobby, fanned out, with weapons drawn.

I turned my back on the first guard, facing the new threat. Raising my hand, they came to an abrupt stop, half fell to one knee, firearms still pointed in my direction.

"I'm here to meet with Edgar Brannon," I said.

"What do you want with him?" One of the armed men stepped forward.

"He sent a messenger to Ronan. Tell him that his message never made it and I've come in Ronan's place."

The man looked over his shoulder to the dark hallway behind him. Brannon walked into the light. He wore a black uniform identical to the others, except for the brass insignia on his collar. The insignia was a deadly cross made with a stake resting across a dagger's handle; drops of blood at the tip of the knife and stake appeared to be small rubies.

Goodness, save me from little men with big egos.

"I didn't want you, Ms. Amherst. You no longer interest me."

"Well, I believe I can change your mind." There was nothing he could say to change my mind.

"I doubt it. But go ahead and try." His smirk infuriated me.

"Can we go somewhere private?"

All the guns surrounding me made it a precarious situation to say the least, and my fangs kept dropping in response. The guards were nervous, and it would only take one to mistakenly pull the trigger to set off the rest.

He looked me up and down as if I had offered something illicit. Was he going to turn me down and order them to fire?

"Okay. Come this way."

He turned on his heel and started back up the long hallway. I followed, keeping an eye on possible escape routes. We came to a door and Brannon nodded at a guard on the other side. A buzzer sounded, and we walked into another hallway.

The smell of the building changed drastically. From alcohol and antiseptics to blood and fear. Vampires had been in the building, but they were gone. Ashes of a vampire had a distinct odor. But other creatures existed in the building, hurting, craving death.

The room he took me to was like so many rooms in hospitals. Sterile and cold. A long metal table occupied the middle and six metal chairs surrounded it.

"What would you like to talk to me about?" Brannon took a seat and waved to another. "I don't have time to waste, so please hurry."

"I know what you want, Brannon. I can give it to you, without a fight."

That got his interest. His cold eyes widened. "Are you sure you know what you're saying?"

I nodded. My stomach churned. Saving Ronan was the most important part.

"Yeah. You want to be a vampire, and I can do that. Ronan is just a fledgling and neither of you would survive the reincarnation. The amount of blood you would require would kill him and you in turn would die."

I was telling him the truth. Whether or not he believed me was yet to be seen.

He leaned forward. The look on his face reminded me of a snake about to strike.

"That explains a lot. We've captured three vampires and, while converting volunteers, each one has died and burst into a mound of dirt. Then after a week of excruciating pain, the volunteers died. We discovered in the autopsy their internal organs had imploded."

He stood and walked around the table, stopping behind my chair.

"Well, I believe I can be convinced to change my mind." He rested his hands on my shoulders, then slid them beneath my hair to encircle my throat. I wrestled with my revulsion. I wanted to scream. His touch reminded me of his brother. The old saying of cold hands, warm heart wasn't true. Did Brannon even have a heart?

I felt his breath brush against my ear as he whispered, "I would be very interested in having you as my guest for a lengthy stay."

# Chapter 25

## *Tori*

No wonder I couldn't find Brannon. His new home was built into a side of a mountain a few miles southeast of Birmingham. The SUV passed between the iron gates and well-guarded brick walls. I spotted several uniformed men walking dogs up and down the perimeter of the jutting front entrance.

When I entered the foyer with Brannon, I was greeted by the sight of a large flag covering one wall. The symbol of the vampire hunters in full glory with the same insignia as on Brannon's uniform, but larger.

"I believe you've got a theme going here." I stopped in the middle of the foyer and stared up at the flag. Out of the corner of my eyes, I noticed two guards nervously adjusting their guns to aim at me.

"The Hunters has welcomed me as one of their own," he proudly said and waved me into a room off the foyer.

My stilettos echoed on the marble floor until I reached the exotic Persian rug. Elegant and tasteful, the large sofas and overstuffed chairs would fit in any wealthy house. I took a seat in one of the chairs near a mammoth aquarium covering one entire wall.

"What are your new friends going to think when you become a vampire? Aren't you worried they'll hunt you down?"

Brannon opened an oversized oak cabinet, then pulled out a bottle of brandy followed by two bowl-size glasses. He poured a small portion into each glass and handed one to me.

Cupped in the palm of my hand, the glass and liquor quickly warmed, but I wasn't interested in tasting it. Even before I had died, I hadn't indulged in liquor. I was more interested in what Brannon's answer would be. Why did he need so much time to reply?

He downed the brandy in one swallow, then stared at me over the glass still pressed to his lips. A second later, he lifted the glass as a salute and threw it against the wall. The two guards jumped but stayed at their post near the door. Clearly, Brannon's eccentricities were commonplace to them.

"You do make a good point. But see, I've decided I like the idea of immortality and even the thought of drinking blood doesn't bother me. It's the restriction of staying indoors during the day that bothers me the most. Too many opportunities lost. Sad to say, but most of the deals of the world are performed between eight and five, and many of those are on a golf course under the sun. No. I can't live like that. So, I've decided to do something different."

That wasn't the answer I had expected. I eased my glass onto a nearby table, freeing my hands. Whatever Brannon planned, I wanted nothing in my way.

"Like what?"

"One of the wonderful things about having money and

the support of an organization with even more money is that combined, we can hire some of the most brilliant scientists of our time." He walked to the aquarium and tapped on the glass. "And these scientists believe they have isolated the microbes that give you incredible healing powers, and so many other marvelous powers associated with vampirism. With a little more work, we'll have a serum for eternal youth."

Ronan had been right to suspect Brannon's involvement in the so-called Fountain of Youth serum that Gino had decided to invest in. Was this a recent maneuvering of Brannon's or was there more to it?

"Have you and Gino been in business together long?" Keeping all emotion off my face, I hoped to be wrong.

Brannon looked over his shoulder at me.

"I have many investors." With his hands behind his back, he took the few steps to stand in front of me. "You shouldn't concern yourself over Gino or Ronan." Before I could move, he pressed a needle into my arm. "You're very careless, but don't worry, this isn't the same compound I gave you before. It will only make you very susceptible to my suggestions."

Before I could fight, the drug immediately held my body in its control.

His fingertip slid down one cheek. That was when I felt the tears streaming down my cheeks.

"A vampire that cries real tears. That's most interesting."

His laughter frightened me. Before the chemicals overpowered all of my senses and he removed his finger, I had a few seconds to read Brannon's mind.

No, no! It was too horrible. He was thinking of a girl waiting for him in another room. She would be the sixth woman to die for his brother's art this year. He'd already killed another we didn't know about and one still alive nearby. I had to fight this.

My face must have betrayed me. Brannon looked down at his finger and back at me.

"So you do read memories by touch. Byron had warned me, but I'd forgotten. I won't again," he said in a voice filled with amazement. "Another talent of yours. You're truly astounding."

He snapped his fingers and the guards stepped up to each side of me.

"Don't touch her skin. She can use your memories against you." He moved and I felt another sting on my arm.

Brannon's face began to waver. I tried to keep my eyes focused but felt like when I drank too much blood.

"Tori, the serum requires a large supply of vampire blood. I need you to convert several of our volunteers. If you're a good girl, we'll let you live. But I'm afraid the accommodations won't be as plush as you're used to." He nodded his head and the guards grabbed my arms, their hands covered by gloves. "Your blood will be a very valuable commodity. I think it's ironic that the hunters will now use their prey as milk cows. Milking you for your blood and making a fortune at the same time."

I wanted to fight them off, but my arms and legs wouldn't cooperate. My body felt like a puppet and Brannon was pulling the strings.

"Take her to the new lab below and get her ready for me."

What did he mean, get me ready for him? It couldn't be good.

<<<>>>

## Ronan

"Fuck! Ronan, wake up!"

Waking to the sight of a black-haired punk with pierced eyebrow and nose wasn't exactly what I had hoped to see first thing in the evening.

With a jerk of my arm, I tossed the sheets to the side and sat up. The bedroom was dark, but I sensed the sun had set only seconds ago. What the hell?

"Connor, you better have a good reason to get me up so early." I twisted around, searching for my clothes, a little groggy from waking up. "Did you find Tori?"

I had left a message with Connor to have Tori call me. No one had seen her and Gino hadn't shrugged when I asked him. The asshole knew something. And this was the first I had seen of Connor. The little bastard. Everyone was pissing me off.

"That's what I'm trying to tell you. I've searched for Tori the last week and she still hasn't checked in. That's not like her. She always calls and lets me know what's happening and where she's holed up at."

"Did she say where she was going?"

Connor stepped back. The big guy rarely acted afraid of me or Tori.

"Connor?" I demanded, getting ready to panic. "You better answer me now or you're dead meat."

It wasn't hard to guess Tori had found out where Brannon was and Connor knew it too.

"Yeah, man. I just wanted a little space in case you forget I'm just human and can't control her."

I didn't bother telling Connor distance wouldn't save him. With my new power, I could set Connor's clothes on fire without a problem. Though I hadn't really gotten the hang of it well enough to control it all the time.

"Tori may have gotten herself into more trouble than she expected. The stubborn woman. She knew better than to take that asshole on her own. Tell me now," I shouted as I jerked on my pants. Habit had me strapping on the shoulder holster and gun, then my leather jacket.

"A hunter brought a message..." By the time Connor finished his tale, I was ready to break his neck.

"You should've told me then. I don't have time to deal with you now, but know I won't forget you fucked up." I came nose to nose with Connor. "I'm not familiar with that part of town, so you're taking me there," I ordered, working to control my temper. He wouldn't argue with me at this point. "They'll probably be expecting us. That means we'll need to be extra careful. From what information I've gathered lately, Brannon's gotten involved in witchcraft. I bet his hunter buddies don't know that."

The Hunters weren't tolerant of witches and their craft.

After taking care of a few arrangements, I was heading to the door when the doorbell rang. Connor looked at me, unsure what to do. I waved him back.

"Go and get my cell phone—I left it on the nightstand—while I handle whoever this is."

I opened the door to the last person I expected.

"Gino. What are you doing here?"

What the hell was my cousin up to now? I fought the frown wanting to show.

"Is that any way to greet family? Not counting I'm your boss." Gino waited until I moved to the side.

"I'm off tonight and I've got to go somewhere." I didn't care how rude it sounded. My cousin wasn't the one I was overly concerned about.

"Sorry to bother you, but Lacy's really worried about Tori. I figured you and her were shacked up together. You know, doing the nasty." He wiggled his bushy eyebrows. "But when you called asking about her, I made the mistake of saying something to the old lady. Now she's harping about it. I thought maybe you heard something lately. I couldn't get you on your cell phone. So I came here." Leaning toward me as if he was about to tell a secret, he whispered, "I really wanted an excuse to get away from her whining. How could you ever stand it?"

Gino's conspiratorial grin irritated the fuck out of me. Lacy could be a bitch, but she didn't deserve a bastard like Gino.

"I'm going after Tori now," I simply said.

"Whoa, what we got here?" Gino nodded toward Connor walking out of my bedroom. "I knew you were getting a little strange, Cousin, but what would the family think about your alternate lifestyle?"

"Gino, don't you have somewhere else you can go?" I suggested, ignoring my cousin's nettling attitude.

"Nope. Why don't I tag along with you boys? Maybe I can help you find Tori."

"I didn't ask for your help." I stared at Gino. Did he know something and wasn't sharing?

"No, you didn't, but I suspect something went wrong. Otherwise, you wouldn't be going after her. She appears to be a very self-sufficient sort of woman."

I wasn't sure what Gino was up to, but I'd better keep him nearby. *Keep friends close, and enemies closer.* An old saying to live by. In this case, it would enable a person to live longer.

"Come on," I said, grabbing my phone from Connor as we headed out.

The drive to the laboratory was a waste of time. Locked up tight, only a security guard with his feet up, a book opened on the front desk. The building revealed none of the activity I expected. In case looks were deceiving, Connor quietly unlocked a side door and snooped around, while I sat in the BMW with Gino. We stared at the lab's front door expecting an alarm to sound any minute. Not a word was exchanged during the whole time.

"Nothing. It's a dead end." Connor slipped into the back seat. "I couldn't get deep inside. There were cameras everywhere. But I overheard a couple of guards say their boss took her to his compound."

"Damn." It had to be Brannon. I wasn't sure where to look next.

"Who do you think got her?" Gino asked.

"A lunatic by the name of Edgar Brannon," I answered, frustration obvious in my tone.

"Edgar Brannon, you say?"

"Why? Have you heard of him?"

"Yep. Back in Chicago I had a few dealings with a company of his. He's small time, but never caused me any trouble."

"Well, he's caused me and Tori a world of hurt and I want to kill the bastard."

"Let me make a couple of calls and I'll see what I can find out."

"Okay. I'd appreciate that." Color me confused.

I studied Gino as he pulled out his phone and started thumbing in a number. Had my cousin a heart of gold I'd never seen before? In all the years growing up together, he'd never been so helpful without expecting an immediate return.

What was he up to? Was he really concerned about Tori? Or was more going on I hadn't figured out yet?

<<<>>>

I couldn't believe it. We were south of Tori's house. The bastard had a massive home built into the side of a mountain, and from what Gino's sources told him, a large laboratory too.

"How are we going to get into that?" Seated in the back seat of the car, Connor leaned between the front seats, resting his elbows near the headrests.

The sight greeting me was formidable indeed. A large brick wall, guards, dogs, and probably numerous security sensors and cameras. I couldn't see us breaking in without an army. Given a little time and help from Wolfric, we could make it in, but Wolfric would be my last resort.

Driving on until I found a side street off the main road and low tree limbs to hide the car from the mansion, I parked and turned on the overhead light.

"What are you planning on doing?"

I ignored Gino's question and reached into the glove compartment for a small note pad. After scribbling a few words on a sheet, I handed it to Connor.

"Take Gino back to his house and then deliver this to the name I wrote on top," I instructed Tori's servant.

"Are you sure?" Connor shook his head. "Ronan, you can't go in there by yourself."

"Yes, I can. That's the only way I can help Tori. He'll kill her."

"Then I'm going with you," Gino said.

"Why?" I couldn't believe my ears. The man was full of surprises. My cousin was never known to put his life at risk.

Whatever he was trying to pull, I wish he would lay it out on the table and tell me.

"Listen. You're not the only one in the family with balls, so get over it," Gino said with raised eyebrows.

I searched his face trying to fathom why he was being so helpful? No clue. So I decided to go with it and handle whatever happened.

"Okay. I need someone to look out for my back." Everyone deserved a chance to prove themselves, right?

After arguing with Connor, convincing the young man that his services were needed elsewhere, I had him drop us off a quarter mile from the front gate.

All we had to do was go in and demand Brannon deliver Tori to me. If he didn't, I would threaten Brannon with an all-out war. I held back the part *with the local vampire colony.* When the time came, I would explain the truth to Gino about vampires.

It was a rather simple plan. At least, so I thought.

<<<>>>

"Hello, Mr. Michaels. I see that you have brought your cousin." Brannon sat behind a huge desk. Maybe he thought it made him look important. Instead he looked like a little bald-headed boy sitting behind his daddy's desk. "Mr. Renata, it took you long enough to get here."

The last words from Brannon confirmed what I had begun to guess. I looked to my cousin and into the barrel of a .44 Magnum.

"Don't look so surprised." Gino walked around the desk, keeping the gun pointed at me. "I couldn't have you screwing up my plans. Besides you've been a thorn in my side all my life." He glanced at Brannon. "Go and make sure that Ronan's sweetheart is ready for him."

Looking nervously my way, Brannon slipped out of the room.

Though I wanted to follow the little bastard, I didn't move. I couldn't take the chance of Gino firing the large caliber at such close range. It could blow my head off. I wasn't sure if even a vampire could recover from such a blast.

"Don't you realize that you're working with a psycho?" I asked, glaring at Gino. "His half brother was one. The apple, in this case, nut didn't drop far from the tree. Brannon's trying to prove to his crazy, dead brother he's just as crazy." I needed for the two men to doubt each other. True, it was an old trick, but a tried and true one. "Has he told you he believes Tori and I are vampires?"

"Yes. I heard it all. But you see, I agree with you. The man's as loony as they come. What you must realize is that his craziness can come in quite handy to cover up how you died. Uncle Sal wouldn't be very happy with me if he learned that I killed you, but for a psycho like Brannon to do you in..." Gino shrugged his shoulders. "I'll be in the clear."

"What if I told you Brannon was right?"

"I would say you're as crazy as he is. You're only trying to save your own skin. Now shut the fuck up and start walking." Gino waved the gun toward the door.

My cousin never failed to be stubborn to the point of being an idiot. Without argument, I headed down the hallway in the direction Gino pointed out with the Magnum. Brannon joined us in the long corridor.

When we walked into the large lab filled with desks, monitors, and all kinds of medical equipment. At the center was an unconscious Tori strapped in a bed with tubes and wires running out of every limb on her body. Her face was pale and drawn in pain. I could only imagine how long they'd been draining her. Her clothes, torn and bloody, were mere rags hanging on her thin body.

"Don't worry. Though Brannon also believes your girl-friend is a vampire and has been draining her system, he's supplying her with more blood intravenously. She's still alive, so it must be working."

"Fuck you, asshole, I know she's a vampire," Brannon snapped.

Ignoring Brannon, I looked at Gino.

"Tell Brannon to let her go. You got me. That's what you wanted."

"No!" Red-faced and angry, Brannon stepped between the men.

"That's true." Gino walked around Brannon and looked down into Tori's face. "It's hard to believe this is the face of a serial killer. Now take Brannon. He looks like a man who would get his rocks off by kidnapping a woman."

I glanced at Brannon. He had the look of a man about to bust a gasket as Gino and I continued to ignore his outbursts.

Gino stepped back. "Many years ago, one of Dad's men discovered the shy Tim Gordon had a bad habit. He liked to carve up women." He leaned against the wall, keeping the gun aimed at me. "Turns out little half brother Edgar here had the same bad habit."

I waited for my cousin to get to the point.

Gino bent over Tori and smoothed her hair from her face with his free hand as he continued his story.

"I knew the information would come in handy one day and decided to wait before using it. It came when Brannon became transfixed on your girlfriend. All it took was convincing him to use you to track her down, and in the meanwhile, make it look like she was killing all those men on the list. With your reputation, I knew it wouldn't take long before you fell into the middle of it, and become the police's number one suspect. You think you're so smart."

"Brannon killed those men?" I asked.

"Actually, I fuck men and kill women." Brannon huffed.

"Stop talking," Gino warned.

Brannon slammed a fist into the wall and grumbled loud enough to hear, "I take my work seriously. It's Gino who gave me the girls."

"Shut up, you little shit," roared Gino.

He pointed his gun at Brannon. The loud retort echoed in the room. A crater appeared in the wall. Gino had missed. Pale and shaken, Brannon ran for the door and Gino fired again. Screaming, Brannon dropped to the floor.

Gino walked over to the prone man and kicked him in the ribs. Nothing. He was dead.

"I was always a lousy shot. Meant to shoot above his head."

He was a liar. He was an excellent shot. As teenagers, we had often gone to the shooting range together. Gino was probably hoping I had forgotten and would try something too. That was why I refused to take a chance on grabbing the gun or finding a way to use my newest unreliable power. Whatever I decided to do would have to be a definite, sure thing.

"Is this still part of your elaborate plan to get me arrested for murder?" I needed to figure out how to grab Tori and escape before Gino killed me.

Gino stared at me with cold eyes filled with hate.

"I have no idea how you're still alive. Brannon was to kill you, but like all things, if I want it done right, I need to do it myself." Gino shook his head. "My entire life I heard how the perfect Ronan had a great future ahead of him. With your connections, you would move up in rank at Chicago PD. You had married the perfect wife. That was a joke indeed. I'd been fucking Lacy for two years before she divorced you. Each time you were up for promotion, I leaked information to make it look like you were helping Uncle Sal's organization. A little suspicion of bribery goes a long way. But never too much information. I didn't want you kicked off the force, just enough suspicion to keep you from getting anywhere. Not until the time was right."

What Gino was saying made sense. I'd suspected Lacy was cheating for months before everything fell apart. We'd fought over it several times. She'd told me that it was my guilty conscience for not getting promoted once again, for working so much overtime, yada, yada, yada.... Though I couldn't provide her with the luxuries she thought she deserved. What Gino said helped everything fall into place.

"You made sure nobody would loan me money. I guess when my father got cancer, it was heaven-sent in your eyes?" I fought to hold onto my temper.

Then it was like a lightbulb clicked on. I could use the unreliable new power to create a diversion, even if it wouldn't stop Gino from firing on me. I moved faster than a normal human. Only, I needed the right time.

"You have no idea. But I must say, Brannon was certainly a special touch. It took only a suggestion from me, and he ran with it. Of course, it didn't hurt that in his damaged mind he believed your girlfriend was a vampire. He sent you to distract Tori from her little campaign of revenge. He didn't want the police to catch her before he could."

Gino took a couple of steps toward me. Years of envy

had warped his mind, and my cousin had worked hard to ruin every aspect of my life.

A blood-drenched apparition rose behind Gino. I controlled my facial expression so as not to give anything away. Fire or not, all I needed was a short distraction to release Tori from all the tubes and wires. The unexpected help would be appreciated.

"You asshole!" Brannon threw a knife at Gino and the blade stuck in Gino's arm. The same arm holding the Magnum. As the gun hit the floor, a loud blast vibrated in the room. The hair trigger made the gun go off on impact.

While Brannon and Gino wrestled, I jerked out the tubes and wires from Tori's body. She screamed and cried, but time was running out. I needed to get her out of there and then I'd be back to get rid of Gino.

With Tori's arm around my shoulder, I almost reached the door before another blast sounded in the room.

"Stop! Put her down!"

I eased Tori to the floor and turned around. Gino swayed on his feet with his left hand supporting his right arm as he aimed the Magnum. Out of the corner of my eye, I saw Brannon's body on the floor once again, but this time the hole in Brannon's chest proved he was dead.

"You really don't expect to get out of here alive?" Gino's manic laughter filled the room.

Chills shot down my spine. Keeping my gaze on Gino, I took a few steps away from Tori. I couldn't take the chance a stray bullet would hit her, not in her weakened state.

"Of course." Gino's face revealed he was certain to triumph over me for a final time. "All I have to do is shoot you and leave. Later, I'll appear all concerned and upset that you went crazy and shot Brannon and Tori, before I could kill you. So simple."

"Not as simple as you think. I'm not letting you out of here." Concentrating on a pile of printouts behind Gino, a small pinpoint of smoke began to rise and twist. Then poof! The paper ignited into a large flame.

Gino jumped and turned to look at the fire. That was all I needed. Growling, I tackled Gino and wrestled for the Magnum. Rolling on the floor we bumped into equipment tables and stools.

I started to squeeze Gino's wrist, trying not to break it. I needed him alive. It was important to get my name cleared from all of his lies.

Finally, Gino dropped it with a scream. I reached for the gun, but he scrambled for it too and knocked it across the floor. It slid under a large metal desk.

"Fuck!" I reached for it.

With almost superhuman strength, Gino balled up a fist and hit me in the nose. Blood streamed down my face and my anger burst free.

"What the hell?" Wide-eyed, Gino stared. He scrambled back and stood up. "What are you?"

With my canines long and ready to taste his blood, I stood, knowing my eyes glowed.

"You should have listened to Brannon. There are things that go bump in the night that have no need to carry a gun. Welcome to hell, bastard!" I grabbed Gino by the shirt and shook him like a rag doll, then threw him. His back slammed into a large cabinet, one door bent in, then he slid down, slumping on the floor, out cold.

Heaving, I bent at the waist with hands on my knees, trying to calm down. Gino didn't move.

Now I needed to find a way to get Tori away without another fight with Brannon's men. I did wonder why they hadn't come running during all of the shooting. Knowing how insane Brannon was, he probably soundproofed the lab.

Kneeling in front of her, I checked her pulse. It was slow but steady. That was a good sign. Did vampires die from loss of blood? I couldn't take the chance. Damn, she couldn't die. I loved her. There was too much for us to do.

Smoothing strands of hair from her face, I worked on bringing Tori around. Patting her hand and rubbing her arms.

"Tori. Wake up, baby. We need to get out of here." How could I save us both against such odds waiting outside the lab? I wasn't sure but it had to be done.

"How sweet." The sarcastic voice was not what I hoped to hear.

Standing, I slowly turned around and faced Gino once again.

"I knew I should've tied your ass up before I checked on Tori."

A large cabinet against the wall with one door hanging off a broken hinge revealed various weapons from times gone by: stakes, crossbows, swords, and daggers. *Fucking thanks, Brannon, you asshole.* Legs braced apart, Gino held a small crossbow loaded with a wicked-looking wooden bolt. It was aimed straight at my heart.

"Maybe Brannon wasn't as crazy as I had thought after all. He kept claiming he'd just discovered a fountain of youth formula and we'd be the richest sons of bitches." With the crossbow pointed at me, Gino wiped the blood streaming into his eyes with a raised shoulder. "That'll explain why he was draining all the blood out of your girlfriend and filling her back up again. Letting her body convert the blood into vampire-created blood."

"If vampire blood is what you want, let her go and you

can have mine. Won't that satisfy the need you have to bring me low? By making me a money cow for blood?"

"How noble you are. That actually sounds like a perfect plan, but there's one problem."

I heard Tori groan behind me. This wasn't a good time for her to regain consciousness. I needed Gino's attention centered on me and Tori forgotten. Maybe even realize a male vampire could produce more blood than a smaller female and I told Gino that.

Blood loss was taking a toll on Gino as I watched him carefully. Gino blinked several times, almost lowering his crossbow. When Gino began to droop a little more, I took a step.

"Stop, asshole. I might just go ahead and kill you and milk the bitch instead."

Another groan came from Tori. She was awake and had crawled out of the line of fire.

I had to keep Gino's attention.

"You know, I remember when you were eighteen and trying so hard to impress Joanie Appleton. You told her you would hit her a home run on the school's baseball team."

"Yeah, I hit that home run too."

"Me and Joanie had a good laugh that night."

"What do you mean?"

"Well, it's like this. I had bet Joanie if you hit a home run, she would have to let me slide into her home base." I watched Gino's face turn red in his fury. "She only agreed to the bet because she knew what a lousy baseball player you were." That did it.

"You bastard." Gino almost growled the words. Leveling the crossbow, Gino pulled the trigger, releasing the bolt.

Before I could duck, a flash of pale skin and black

leather flashed in front of him. Then Tori landed on top of me.

I lifted Tori and looked down at her, ignoring Gino's scramble for another bolt from the cabinet. The bolt had gone through her chest and blood poured from the wound around the shaft.

"Tori, oh my God, why?"

I knew wood through the heart of a vampire was the end. She had told me vampires would disintegrate into dirt and ash. But she hadn't said how long it took for the change.

Feeling her pulse, I felt her slow heartbeat fade away, then she released a long breath and became very still.

My fury coated the room in red. I slowly lifted my head to look around the room for Gino. Paper scattered throughout the room began to ignite into bursts of flame. Gino jumped when a stack near the cabinet exploded into a ball of fire.

"Shit, shit, shit," Gino muttered as he wrestled with the crossbow, trying to load another bolt. He knocked over several swords. They clanged to the floor.

"Gino."

Arms hanging at my side, I stood, back straight, certain death blazed from my eyes.

"You killed her." My voice emerged deeper than I'd ever heard it. "You've taken the only person that mattered to me. She was the only true reason why I was holding back and letting you live."

Gino finally slammed the bolt in place and pulled the trigger back into release position. "You can go to hell," he yelled.

Before Gino could aim the crossbow, I pushed my power toward Gino with all my might.

"You first," I growled.

And the wooden crossbow and bolt burst into flames with every stitch of Gino's clothes. His horrifying screams were satisfying to my ears.

I grabbed Tori's body, heading toward the door before the place came down around our heads. I wanted her dirt or ashes, whatever it became, to be buried somewhere I could remember her.

Then I noticed for the first time a small door opened in the corner of the room. Brannon's body was gone. What the fuck?

Brannon would have an escape hatch in the lab. So the asshole wasn't dead. It was hard to kill roaches.

I was certain it would be faster and safer than the front door with all of the guards.

The exit was a tunnel through the mountain, opening onto a side road with a couple suspicious lumps covered by green cloth. Tire tracks led from one small green lump. Brannon had left in a hidden vehicle.

Beneath the other green cloth was an old beat-up Ford pickup. Probably used to hunt and capture his victims to carve and throw away later. I would track him down and turn him over to the police, but for now I needed to get Tori's body away from there.

Looking at her propped against the passenger's door as I drove down the highway, she appeared to be sleeping. So beautiful and peaceful. Death had come to my family so many times. I had begun to hope being a vampire and being with Tori meant I wouldn't have to give up someone I loved again. She loved me, though she'd never told me to my face.

Maybe it was sick of me to want whatever was left of her. But I needed something to remember that anything was possible, even eternal life on earth.

The drive back to her house took forever. I was so afraid she'd disappear into a pile of ash before I got there.

I had called Connor and gave him the rundown of what happened, but he wasn't home yet, and I was glad. I wanted her to myself. First, I wanted to clean her up. Sounded stupid, but I needed the closure. My heart was breaking, the pain in my chest wouldn't let up. Maybe the senseless labor would help.

Numb and running on autopilot, I stripped the rags from her body. Laid out on her large bed, she looked unearthly pale and drained. The bolt sticking out of her chest was grotesque, and it had to go. I found a bolt cutter in her closet—the woman had everything in there—and cut the tip off and pulled the shaft out.

Some thick blood flowed out and I quickly placed a towel around her body. After washing her soft, pale skin, noting the cuts and bruises all over her, I wiped the blood off her face.

I looked at the long lashes shadowing her cheeks. The vibrant woman I'd fallen in love with was no longer. I lifted her into my arms and began to cry, shudders shaking my body. I didn't want to let her go. I needed her in my life. A life now that would last for eons.

"No, damn you. Why did you have to jump in front of me? Why hadn't you just knocked the fucking bolt away? Where's the superhero now? I need you," I said, my voice cracking on the last word. Tears streamed down my cheeks and dripped on her solemn and unnaturally serious face. "Damn you. I never got a chance to tell you how much I loved you. How much I need you in my life and how much I want to be part of yours."

"Well, you could start by handing me a hand towel so I

can dry my face, then you could tell me the part about how much you love me."

I looked down into the most beautiful brown eyes.


<<<>>>
Tori


I enjoyed seeing the astonishment in Ronan's eyes. I'd been awake for about thirty minutes, but what woman in her right mind would tell a sexy man to stop bathing her. It was rather sensual and very soothing to my bruised and battered body. Plus having a good-looking man touching every inch of my body and acting as if I was made out of spun glass was an experience I couldn't pass up.

But when he began crying and telling me he loved me, it broke my heart.

"Tori?" His disbelief was clear on his manly face.

"Hello, Ronan."

He kissed and squeezed me tight.

"Ouch, be careful, sugar. I don't know about you, but I've got a couple places that are rather tender."

"You survived." He leaned back, holding me at arm's length. "How?"

"It's easy. Gino's a lousy shot with a crossbow. The wooden bolt missed my heart. Close but no cigar." I chuckled and then groaned. "One of these days, you'll learn to listen to me. The wood has to go completely through the heart, and when we die, we begin to disintegrate in seconds, starting from the heart and outward."

"Why didn't you let me know sooner?" Ronan lightly shook me, his eyes glowing in his frustration. "It was killing me to think that you gave your life up for me."

"I can promise if I could've woken up earlier I

would've," I said in a deadly serious voice. "But when I woke up and you were bathing me...whoa. I enjoyed it too much to stop you."

"Why did you risk your life like that?"

"Don't you understand? I love you. I love you more than my own life. If he'd killed you, there would be nothing left of him or me. I've saved you once before, what's one more time? Oh, and to answer your earlier question, really, I'm no ninja. My body is a bigger target and slapping the bolt away, there was no guarantee I wouldn't miss."

I welcomed his mouth on mine, gently pulling his body over me. He was hard and ready for what I wanted from him. Hungry for his blood and wanting him inside of me, I loosened his pants and released his erection.

As soon as he thrust into my body, I tore his shirt off to get at his neck and sunk my teeth into his flesh and muscle. Blood poured into my mouth and his fluid poured into my body at the same time.

"Ah, heaven," he murmured, and I had to agree with my warrior angel of mercy.

# Her Epilogue



I slid to the edge of the bed, gently moving Ronan's arm from my breast. Big titty baby. A grin spread across my face, a foolish one, as I looked down at him lying on the bed. After we spent an evening of making love in every conceivable position, he slept soundly and was unlikely to wake before the death sleep took him. Even vampires became tired from hours of lovemaking. Yep, I said it. Lovemaking, not just fucking. There was a difference.

Often with our vampire appetites and strengths, our lovemaking became a little rough. Certainly too rough for an average human. Time and again, we would wake so hungry for each other nothing else could satisfy us.

But something about this evening had been different. It was like we had turned a new corner in our relationship.

I'd woken an hour before dusk and waited with anticipation for the man beside me to come alive. Once the sun had sunk in the western sky, I'd leaned over and whispered in his ear, "I'm going to taste every hard inch of your body, and make you scream for release before I'm through."

This evening of marathon sex made me think of the first few months after we'd decided living in separate homes wasn't working. Brannon had disappeared, Gino was dead, and Ronan had finally declared his love for me.

It was hard to believe we'd been together in our new home outside of Cullman for ten years. Our excursions to Birmingham, Huntsville, Montgomery, Mobile, Atlanta, and numerous towns in-between to drop off tied-up presents, including evidence, at the various police stations filled our time.

Connor was still with us along with a couple of other servants. Ronan had wanted none, but had quickly realized we couldn't do without blood and a human handling necessary errands and security during the day. Though Ronan wouldn't admit it, he and Connor had become close friends. Very close friends. I grinned and stared at Connor snuggled up to Ronan's back.

To say the least, Ronan had adjusted to his new way of living, and in turn, I had worked at dampening my feelings of guilt and need for revenge. My years with Ronan had taught me I needed to make peace with my past and look forward to a happy future with the man I loved.

I shook my head. Time for me to get moving for the night.

I pulled on jeans and a frilly top—the nineteen-sixties would not let me go. After one last look to make sure he still slept, I exited our bedroom and walked into the basement.

The cool morning breeze tossed my hair around my shoulders. Ronan loved my hair long. I grinned with remembered pleasure of how my dark hair looked blanketing his hips as I proved I could make him scream my name for the sixth time last evening.

I slipped into the sports car nearest the garage doors. Black and sleek, the 1966 Stingray Corvette was a new addition to our garage and an anniversary present from Ronan. Thank goodness, he shared my passion for fine cars.

For a human, driving with the rag-top folded back would have been uncomfortable in the early spring air, but to a vampire, the air was fresh and welcomed. Never again wanting to endure the driving force of revenge and what led me there, I was finally closing the chapter of my existence best forgotten.

Only a few cars passed me on the deserted interstate before I turned onto a small country road northwest of Birmingham, on the edge of the small town of Jasper. Under the scattered security lights, the ghostly shapes of tombstones dotted the land.

After parking the car near the curb, I threaded my way around the stones. Fog floated near the edge of the cemetery where a large pond glistened beneath the lights, casting a chill of white moistness into the air.

The spot I knew so well but hadn't visited in years was centered in a field. Flowers from a newly covered grave gave off the sickly sweet scent that turned my stomach and reminded me of a time I'd rather forget.

My parents' tombstone shone brightly beneath one of the security lights. The dates revealed what I already knew. My father had died within a month of my mother. Both had lived to see ninety, but not much more. It had been hard on them. The last years being all alone.

A few minutes passed before I turned to the other one. This tombstone stood alone though only a couple of feet away from the larger one. The stone read "Beloved Daughter" with the dates of birth and death.

I glanced back to my parents' graves.

"I'm sorry, Mom and Dad. I should have told you that I was still living, but I wasn't sure how I could explain why I was alive and unchanged over the years."

Returning my attention to the smaller grave, I fell to my knees and began crying. Sobs tore through my chest. I covered my face while I wept and at the same time, horrific memories tore me apart. Memories I wanted to forget but continued to haunt me.

"Tori?"

I wasn't sure if I welcomed his presence at this time. After wiping my eyes and cheeks, I stood and turned to face Ronan.

My heart swelled with love and pride. He was a fine-looking, charismatic vampire. A few feet separated us, but waves of energy flowed from him and brought goose bumps of desire scattering across my body. Would time ever dull the effect he had on me?

I hoped to God it wouldn't.

"You shouldn't be here. It'll be daylight soon." I struggled to not run into his arms and beg him to make me forget.

"You're here." His simple answer pleased me. Resisting him was hopeless.

"Well, let's go before the sun catches us." I started to walk by him and he caught my arm.

"Don't you think that you need to explain?" His voice sounded gruff with anger.

"There's nothing to explain." I jerked my arm from his and headed toward the Stingray.

"Tori." The way he said my name gave me pause. I

turned to see what was the matter. "Harold and Martha Amherst were your parents?"

He was staring at the large headstone.

I sighed. I should've known better. It was time. Ronan deserved to know.

"Yeah. My father was the last to die."

"That was the time you disappeared for a couple days."

"I was too late to be there when my mom was buried, but I watched from the limo when they buried my dad. He loved my mom very much. They had only each other."

Ronan took a step toward the smaller headstone.

"Don't," I croaked.

"Elizabeth Deborah Amherst?" Brow wrinkled in confusion, Ronan looked at me. "You never mentioned a sister."

"Yeah." I waited for him to put two and two together.

He glanced at the headstone again before he turned back to me. "She died about the same time you were abducted."

"Ronan..." I wanted to tell him but I realized it hurt too much. Maybe I was a coward after all. Afraid of what Ronan would think about me and how I failed my sister.

"She was with you, wasn't she?"

Tears had begun to stream down my face without me being aware of it at first. His strong arms circled my shoulders and he pulled me next to his body. It felt so good to rest my cheek on his broad, warm shoulder.

"Yes." I was quiet for a minute and then said, "I loved my sister. We were friends, even long before we became adults. She was four minutes younger." He probably hadn't realized she was my twin. "Some people say twins are usually close to each other and we were, but I can promise you, we were like a lot of other sisters. We argued and at times refused to talk with each other, but we always looked out for each other."

"Were you identical?"

I grinned. Most men asked that question. Liz and I figured it was a male fantasy thing.

"Yeah. It drove our parents crazy when we got older. We played the usual tricks, answering to each other's names, switching classes and, one time, switching boyfriends." I chuckled. "I don't think they ever guessed what we had done."

"Did she become a vampire too?"

"No."

He kissed the top of my head and hugged me tight. "What happened?"

My words started slow and began to spill out. Afraid if I stopped, I wouldn't finish.

"Our favorite time of the year was between Thanksgiving and Christmas. The decorating, the hustle and bustle of the season, but especially the day after Thanksgiving, Black Friday, when we went shopping together. Of the two of us, I guess I was the leader. She was easygoing and wouldn't have gotten in half the trouble that we did, if it hadn't been for me.

"That day, the day after Thanksgiving, we argued over what to buy Mom." My tears started again. "It was such a stupid argument. Over the color of a sweater. Stupid." I closed my eyes for a few seconds to gather my thoughts and regain a little composure before starting again. "We rode together, but we were in the mall so long we had forgotten where we parked. Such a little thing, but after a few minutes of searching, she spotted our car a few rows away. We walked through the parking lot and I figured I'd get the keys out before we reached the car. I looked down for only a second and when I looked up, she was gone. I remember thinking how strange it was. Like she dropped off the face of the earth. I can close my eyes after all these years and still see the parking lot, filled with cars and me expecting her to be in the car, laughing her ass off. The van was so ugly, but I never imagined what was waiting inside for us. *He* pulled me in the van. Made me drop my bags. I don't remember anything else until I opened my eyes in that basement."

"Shh." Ronan began to rock me from side to side, but I wanted him to understand why I had lived for revenge for so long.

My words sounded so far away. Like someone else was saying them. "He worked on her first. Slicing, cutting— mercy, the horrible smell. You've been a cop and know under intense pain the body will release—well, you know." I didn't have to tell him when someone was so afraid or died, their body fluids discharged. "She died on the table next to me. The muzzle he used on her kept her from screaming, but her eyes..."

My voice had changed, it was flat, like I was reciting something told over and over again. "I swore no one would ever suffer like we did."

"Tori, you couldn't help her. You were only human. Brannon's brother was sick."

"Don't you think I know that?" I looked into Ronan's face. "Sorry. I've tried to tell myself everything. That I was only human. That she's in a better place. That it was fate. No matter how many of the psychos out there I killed or scared into turning themselves in, I still feel guilty for being alive." I chuckled, the sound close to hysteria. "Alive. What a joke. Technically, we're alive. But we die every morning. Never to walk under the midday sun. Living off blood."

Ronan grabbed my arms and held me away from him.

"Dammit! Don't start feeling sorry for yourself. What if you had died the same time as your sister? Just think of the lives you helped and saved."

He was right. That was why I had decided to visit my parents' and sister's graves. I had forgiven myself. I was happy. The man in front of me had shown me I had a purpose in this world. The words I'd spoken to him moments ago were really from years of beating myself up. Time to move on and show this beautiful man what wonderful things vampires were capable of.

He added, "Besides, what would've become of me if you hadn't been there. I love you. So get over it."

"So delicately put," I said teasingly and then added, "Okay." I smiled.

"Okay?" The shocked expression on his face tickled me. "No argument?"

"Yeah."

"You're one crazy vampire." He brought his hand to my face and caressed my wet cheek with his long poet fingers.

I closed my eyes for a second, enjoying his touch.

"Ronan?"

"Yes, sweets."

I stared into his bewitching hazel eyes. The depths revealed his beautiful soul.

"Let's go home," I said.

"Lead the way."

I laughed then teased, "That's the way I like it. Now add 'my mistress.'"

He laughed and slapped my butt as I walked by, making me laugh harder.

# His Epilogue

Ronan

"Why?" Tori asked, head tilted, looking so cute in her work uniform.

That was what I called her leather pussy suit. Cat suit, get it? So delicious and fascinating as it hugged her body. Fun to peel off her after a long night of hunting.

"Why? Because it's your birthday and I have a present for you." I grinned and bent down, giving her a peck on the cheek. "You're terribly hard to buy for."

"You're such a charmer," she smirked. "Where are we going?"

"You don't recognize the neighborhood?"

She gazed out the passenger window, studying the houses as we drove by.

"Yes." She became unearthly still. "Again, why? Going to that house is not what I dream about to celebrate my birthday."

"Patience, sweets."

Connor waited in the open front door. He had the sense not to smile or greet us. Head bowed, he kept his eyes on the ground.

As we stepped out of the car and walked up the steps, I glanced at Tori. Connor would be explaining his reasons for talking to me instead of her. But I know she wouldn't kill him. He was special to both of us, but he might be wishing he thought it through before the evening was over.

"You need to tell me for what purpose you brought me back to this hell house. It better be good." Her cold voice even sent chills down my spine.

It would appear Connor and I, both, were in trouble.

"Patience, my love."

She gave me the stink eye.

No one could call me a coward. I placed my hand at the small of her back and guided her down into the basement. Connor had said Edgar had bought the place and kept it clean and in good repair. From what I could see, his intel was correct.

There was one bare bulb, and it was on.

Edgar Brannon lay naked and tied to a gurney beneath the circle of light. A huge scar near his heart the evidence of when he'd been shot and I thought he'd died.

Tori stopped on the stairs and looked back at me.

"Thank you," she said in voice hoarse with so much emotion. "Thank you."

"Anything for you, babe. I would give you the world if I could." I had finally decided the world could do without Edgar Brannon. He'd started his *artwork* again. The man deserved to die and save the government from another expensive trial.

She stepped up and kissed me, deeply, and moved away to gaze into my eyes.

"You're my world," she said. "Now run along and let me unwrap my present, piece by piece."

# About the Author

Carla Swafford loves romance novels, action/adventure movies, and men, and her books reflect that. And on top of it all, she's crazy about hockey, and thankfully, no one has made her turn in her Southern Belle card.

So, it's no surprise she writes spicy romantic suspense filled with mercenaries, motorcycle one-percenters, and southern criminals. And in the last few years, she's included sexy hockey players in books without suspense, except for the kind that asks, how will they ever find their happily ever after?

Married to her high school sweetheart, she lives in the Southeast U.S. To find out more about Carla, be sure to visit her Facebook, Instagram, and TikTok pages along with her website at carlaswafford.com and sign up for her newsletter.

# Also by Carla Swafford

## The Circle Organization

Circle of Desire

Circle of Danger

Circle of Deception

Circle of Dishonor (Novella)

Circle of Defiance (Novella

Kidnapped For A Day (Short Story)

## A Southern Crime Family Novels

Jake

Sen (coming soon)

Ethan (coming soon)

## Brothers of Mayhem Novels

Hidden Heat

Full Heat

Naked Heat

## Atlanta Edge Hockey Romance

Crossing The Line

Fake Play

# Love In A Small Town Novels

Loving The Small-Town Preacher's Son
Loving The Small-Town Hero

# Vampire Novel

Savage Champion

www.ingramcontent.com/pod-product-compliance
Lightning Source LLC
Chambersburg PA
CBHW060739190726
48285CB00001B/278